I0524866

COMMISSIONED

Book 3
of the

Paradigm Shift Trilogy

By

Raven H. Price

Cover Design
http://www.selfpubbookcovers.co
m/mad-moth

Dedication

This book is dedicated to my family. I wouldn't have been able to write if it wasn't for my husband, Ralph W. Price, III, my daughter, Derica S. Hansen and my granddaughter, Thea Hansen.

I would also like to issue special thanks to Shannon Baker who edited my books and kept me on track.

Disclaimer/Copyright

Commissioned

Print history

First edition published January 2017

ISBN-13:978-0692827475
ISBN-10:0692827471
ASIN

Library of Congress Cataloguing-in-Publication Data

Reviews

"The mystery is, God is love, and He is the Alpha and Omega. Before time began, He made a vow to Creation and He will never break the covenant spoken for her and her creations, including mankind. They are entitled to pure, unconditional love where they can become Sons and Daughters of God."

I just finished *The Commissioned* by Raven E. Price, and I must say that this book moved me in the extreme! Instead of writing about characters and settings, I wish to focus on substantial thoughts. This is the third and last book in Price's Paradigm Shift Trilogy, and make no mistake, this book is the best yet! The prototype of good versus evil in this novel is woven in such a manner that you, the reader, will be struck with total wonder and amazement. Floods, hardships, etc aside, this novel isn't like others in a similar vein, and I highly recommend Price's 'polished diamond' book; no matter which realm you are in at any given moment. Five stars all the way. ~ S. Jackson/M. Schmidt, Author, When Angels Fly

Table of Contents

Prologue

While Jesus and Abba were with Gina, Whisperer noticed heaven was celebrating, and shouts of victory were being sung. Gina had humiliated Satan and opened the door for Father God to fulfill a declaration concerning the 3rd and 4th generational paradigm shift, where people changed their minds and welcomed God's Word as truth. All it had taken was one lost soul, (a young woman who had never been taught anything about religion or its meaning) to accept the fact the God Himself, really did care for her and was willing to convince her, once and for all time, that the purest love existed. Soon a harvest of souls would fill God's kingdom and mankind could begin to reclaim what was rightfully theirs, but first, Jesus had to free who Satan had made a slave.

All Jesus wanted was for mankind to nestle under His wings like baby chicks with He and God. He didn't want them worrying about their lives ever again. But, everywhere they looked, Satan had Creation squatting over the area. Her hands and feet tightly bound and her head covered by a tight glistening helmet that kept her mouth and ears shut. He had made sure his influence contaminated her mind, will and emotions to where any energy she created destroyed her body as well as God's resources and His precious people. In the beginning, God loved and had blessed all creation and had called her good. Now she was no better than a harlot, moved only by what she saw and felt.

Heaven and Earth belonged to God, not Satan. Everything about her was spoken into existence and was the works of His heart and hands. Because He loved this world He sent His son to redeem her. But every three or four generations, Satan attacks, bewitching people with laws and causing mankind to trust nothing but money. This forces Jesus to declare war to set things right, and punish Satan, his followers and the sin that was forced into man's mind.

This paradigm shift allows God's love in the atmosphere and its effect stops brother from turning against brother, or sister against sister and His calming kingdom is ruled by love never excluding anyone again.

With a new zeal in His heart, Whisperer focused harder on Jesus and heard Him make His declaration that starts the wheels turning. He said to people in the small community He was visiting, "Awake! Your time has come! We have chosen you to partake in the paradigm shift! You are complete in me! Together, we will infiltrate the planet!"

Jesus proved again He never was angry at people, He was only heartbroken over Creation's entrapment, what she and Satan had done. As Satan's slave, she couldn't bless because her heart and mind were full of rage. So, it didn't surprise Whisperer when He heard Jesus also declare to Satan, "Loose your harlot, for I have redeemed her!"

The spiritual commands released orders on Earth for the first harvesters, Mamie, Hope, Brent, and Gina to change course, focusing only on love, allowing their angels to restore balance. With God's assistance, and His Creation freed, love for everything in the world will start to work its magic.

The mystery is, God is love, and He is the Alpha and Omega. Before time began, He made a vow to Creation and He will never break the covenant spoken for her and her creations, including mankind. They are entitled to pure, unconditional love where they can become Sons and Daughters of God.

Resuming Communications

The moment Gina met Wade, and Satan was under her feet, my mission in heaven was over. But I took a few moments to celebrate before I left. The time had come to be reconnected with Jesus and the Father and reside with them in the spirit realm alongside Earth's reality. So, I, the Holy Spirit, the One referred to as "Whisperer," joined them to begin the paradigm shift that seems to happen according to biblical history, every five hundred years or third and fourth generations.

After touching down next to them, I excitedly spoke up, "Lord, our time has arrived once again! The three of us will usher in a new age!

Turning to face me, Jesus replied, "Yes! Satan is under our feet for a time. He'll uproar soon in the spirit realm once he is through sulking. In the meantime, Father wants to watch over these brothers and sisters. He desires to guide them and help them find the true meaning of 'relationship' as soon as possible. I need for you to go back to Gina. She needs you after what just occurred. Let her know your comforting voice hasn't left her side. Tell her, she is not alone because of the three of us, along with the angels, are with her now."

Jumping the gun, I asked Jesus about future events, "what about Pastor Reed?"

"It is too soon to work on the Pastor. Complacency must grow deep inside of his heart. I want him to get mentally fat thinking his sheep are happy and content. Eventually, you will get to enlighten him and show him what is under-minding everything and you'll get to do whatever it takes to show him the truth behind the façade.

Remember when you started using a thought of grace with Mamie forty-eight years ago? It has taken years for people to accept a different outlook concerning race issues. With the actual spirit of grace in charge, and not just an intellect notion of it, not only will Pastor Reed need to regroup, the people will need time to adjust their thoughts about the truth."

"You want me to encourage him to stop talking about grace's victory over sin?" I asked puzzled.

"No, not entirely. You know I still give favor when people don't understand. Like Gina, the people need to be convinced that I am grace so they can receive proof of God's agape love for them. Once we show Pastor Reed God's true desire, then he will see for himself how God felt when lies separated him from the loved ones." Jesus replied.

"Will I have free reign to show him what true separation is? Can I use severe methods if necessary?" I asked curiously.

"I know you love a touch of drama to get your points across so do whatever it takes as long as my family is protected," Jesus replied with a wide grin on His face.

Happy to see He understood me so well, I asked, "What has to take place before I can start?"

Still smiling, Jesus lovingly informed, "Weddings! Reports of babies! Signs of physical growth within a church which is every Pastor's dream!"

Then, revelation dawned on me and I inquired further, "He'll think six weddings plus a few pregnancies are signs from the Word that you blessed him with the promised increase. This will be the fattening you want for him. His guard will be down and a false sense of peace and pride enters his soul."

"Yes!" Jesus replied.

"I'm going to be very busy," I said.

"Yes, you are. That is why God wants to be on board. He wants to babysit and take your place as comforter and standby while you and I get this new age started. I suggest you get back to Gina now.

I want to move slowly but not at a snail's pace," Jesus said jokingly.

———————————⊰⊱◇⊰⊱———————————

To make sure I was on time for Gina' sake, I arrived back into Earth's reality a few minutes before Gina's expression glaze over when Wade introduced himself. It was a good thing I did because her mental faculties began to malfunction, disconnect and dizziness overtook her.

Gina restated her question to Wade with a slurred voice and then her body began to slightly stumble, "you said your name is Wade?"

Wade answered, "Yes. Are you all right?"

Gina took a step and collapsed. But just before she landed on the ground, Wade was there managing to scoop her up in his arms.

Mamie had also been watching Gina. From where she sat at the picnic table where Gina left her, she knew Gina was distraught over something. So, when Gina collapsed Mamie engaged me immediately.

"Lord! Is Gina hurt?" She asked me in prayer.

I promptly answered, "No, she's dazed. She just had an encounter with Jesus and the Father. Wade was an unexpected surprise and his presence was far more than her body or nerves could handle. Go to her! Make sure she gets private time with me, I am all she needs. She'll explain everything to you in time."

Mamie rushed to Gina's aid and then began instructing Wade, "Take Gina in the house, she needs to lie down. She hasn't been long out of a leg cast. The silly girl went walking too far without her crutch." Mamie explained.

Wade carried Gina inside the house but Hope was lying on the couch so he asked, "Mamie, where do we take her?"

13

Mamie quickly responded, "Take her down the hall, first door to the right there are twin beds. We'll use one of those."

Once Wade lay Gina down on the bed, Mamie shushed him out of the room. "I'll handle Gina. You go outside and enjoy the party." Mamie demanded.

"I can help." Wade countered. "I'm a doctor, Mamie."

Mamie spurted emphatically with her deep southern drawl, "No you can't! She needs some quiet time. I know what she needs and it's not some man hovering over her. Now off with you."

I watched Wade walk out of the house reluctantly. I knew what he was thinking; he'd just found the woman of his dreams. It was natural that he wanted to help. To ease Wade's anxiety, I had to do something quick so I engaged Brent's mind with a request. "Brent, go to Wade. Comfort your friend. He is confused."

Brent replied, "Where is Wade, Lord? I didn't know He was here."

"Go to the main house. He just carried Gina inside after she fainted." I answered.

Alarmed, Brent asked, "Is Gina okay?"

"Yes! Mamie, Father God and I are with her." I shared.

After relaxing, Brent said, "Okay, I'm headed that way."

After I made sure that Wade and Brent were together, I went back inside where Mamie and Abba had Gina. The sight I experienced warmed my heart. Abba had Gina's head on His lap and was stroking her hair while Mamie was quickly looking and praying over Gina's leg.

To a naked human eye, Gina was lying on a pillow where Mamie didn't know of Abba's presence. I gently spoke, "Mamie, I need to be alone with Gina. She and I have much to discuss. She is perfectly fine so stop praying for her leg. We'll clue you in on what happened shortly."

Mamie answered, "Yes, Lord. I'll leave her in your good hands. Just please don't let me fret over her long. I don't like being kept in the dark when one of my babies is hurting."

When Mamie opened the door to leave I had another issue to deal with before I could talk with Gina. Hope was standing outside of the door, just about to knock so she too could check on Gina. I engaged her mind quickly before she and Mamie started to talk.

"Hope, I have this! All is well. Ask Mamie for something to ease your stomach. I'll meet with you soon."

She obliged and her request helped to take Mamie's mind off Gina for a bit.

Now with my crew occupied, Abba and I could interact with Gina. I was ready. Three days had been too long without communication with her. I knew she would have many questions. I faced her lying on the bed but before I entered her subconscious, I asked Abba to keep soothing her and to keep her body still and rested.

While He stroked her hair and gently sang to her, I entered her mind and assured her of my presence, "Gina! I'm here! It's Whisperer. Wake up now. I've missed you."

Gina's spirit connected with me instantly. Excitedly, she asked, "It is really you? Where are you?"

"Open your mind's eye, Gina. I'm standing here with you. You are able to walk and talk with me like you once did with Adrian." I told her.

I watched joyfully, as her mind opened allowing her to glide out of her physical boundaries so she could launch her "spiritual self" at me. Her arms were around me so quickly it almost surprised me. Gina was certainly full of confident zeal. Her very essence was ablaze with love.

When she pushed back away from me, to take a better look, she blurted out, "Whisperer! I'm so happy to see you. I have so much to tell you."

15

"I know all about it, Gina. I watched everything and I was never far away. I just wasn't allowed to speak with you during my time of prayer. I had to make sure you could go through the process with just your promises inside your heart. With Ox alongside you, our prayers worked! Look! You made it!" I comforted her.

I listened to Gina babble rapidly, "Whisperer, God came to me! He blessed me! I thought He couldn't see me unless I was in you and Jesus! But He came to me directly when I felt like I was dying! My heart was shattered into a million pieces and I wanted to drown myself in the lake! Instead, I found Jesus and God! They were there for me and we bonded! Satan was screaming at me so loud and all I wanted was to be with Jesus. I didn't have to die. He showed me the truth. When I saw Satan for who he really is, it made me so mad I burst into flames! Who knew that rage was part of my gift!"

"Slow down, Gina! Don't you see? You finally realized God loves you! When you were convinced of His love, then the love you have for us manifested into the blaze you saw. Satan's verbal abuse is what brought it out. It wasn't his threats against your circumstances any longer that caused your anger, for at that moment you thought all your dreams were gone. It was his threats against God's love for you. Seeing the Father there with Jesus proved not even heartbreak could come between you and God. Nothing could come against that fact. At that moment of realization, Satan's words fell flat, useless and of no effect, you were set free and the more he screamed at you saying 'where is your God?' the more it made your rage grow hotter with righteous anger. Yes, rage brings out a bright orange flame from you when armed against evil but you'll see when it's burning and out in the open in order to win souls for Jesus, it will be a vibrant pure blue." I enlightened her.

"Whisperer, I was also mad at what Satan did to Ox. Ox almost died trying to protect me. He was beaten up so badly," Gina cried.

I stopped her tears and said, "Ox only represented the sacrificial nature of Jesus. He was willing to offer himself for you, Gina." Then, I pointed to the right of her and said, "look to your right, look at your new and improved Ox, he has been fully restored and he is raring to continue in the quest. But, first things first, you have to know something even more important."

"What?" Gina asked.

"God hasn't left you. He is here with us now. Completely turn around and look back at your body lying on the bed," I said.

I watched Gina slowly turn around. It was as if she were afraid to see herself. When she saw Father God sitting at the head of the bed with her head in His lap watching us talk, she couldn't control her tears any longer and burst out crying. I gently wrapped my arms around her and spoke softly in her ear. "Gina, He loves you. Go to Him. He has waited your whole life to speak with you directly."

She timidly asked, "If I go back in my body will He still be there? Will I be able to see Him? If I can't see Him, I don't want to go. I want to stay as I am so I can fix my eyes on Him, see Him loving me like He is now. I want that picture to stay in my mind for a long time.

Abba spoke up then and said, "Gina, my Child, nothing can ever separate us. Come back inside yourself. I want to talk with you while I engulf your spirit, soul, and body with love."

Faster than she left her body, Gina was back inside herself and in God's embrace while continuing to weep. The beauty of that moment melted my heart. Gina was a prize. The love she had for us was amazing. I'm so happy that Jesus chose her for our mission. I stood there gaping, but God wanted private time with Gina and asked me to go to Hope and Mamie. Apparently, I had to get busy soothing down the feathers of two curious and concerned women.

I found both Hope and Mamie closed-off in the laundry room, away from the crowd, frantically praying in the spirit. Insight and

Healer were standing guard cooing and trying to console their humans the best they could but with no prevail.

"Hello, ladies!" I said, getting their attention. "Gina is doing well, she only fainted. You didn't need to fret so much. Both of you know how this plays out. You've each been through your own wilderness experience where everything appeared hopeless. Gina had hers this morning. She is with Abba now, getting re-acquainted with Him. Let her find peace in the Father's arms for a few more minutes. When she comes out of the bedroom she'll be eager to go. In a few days, she'll want to tell you all about her pacific journey.

Hope, your prayers were very helpful today. Thank you for interceding, even though your own body was throwing fits of hormonal rebellion, you held steady and prayed Gina through. Mamie, after Gina passed her test, your healing voice was there to soothe. You've both done wonders with and for Gina. She is in the final stages of her preparation. When she emerges, she will be officially equipped for our mission. It was because of your faithfulness and help that she could stand with angels today. Jesus, the Father and I are very grateful."

Hope asked, "Is there something else we need to do?"

"No, why don't you go outside and join Brent. Celebrate his victory and enjoy yourself." I answered.

Hope replied, "I do feel better. Mamie laid hands on me a few minutes ago and prayed. I really want to be with Brent."

Then Mamie sternly remarked, "I want to stay and find out what that child went through! I'll stay put here in the house and wait on her to come out of the bedroom. Not knowing what that innocent child has endured is bothering me. I was there for Hope after she encountered sufferings. Good thing too, because it took several weeks to see her through. Knowing Gina was already in a weakened state makes me wonder if she will take longer to heal."

I couldn't help but laugh at our sweet healer, "Mamie, Gina is receiving her healing now. The Father's love is all she needs. When she comes out of the bedroom she won't be interested in you, much less want to stop and talk with you. She has a promise from us waiting for her outside. Why don't you go get some food and then go back to your picnic table and enjoy this day? Fellowship with others and learn to relax a bit. It is time for you to be happy for a change."

Mamie didn't know how to answer me. She just grunted and stomped out of the house trying to obey. I came to realize she didn't have a clue what relaxing really was. Most of her life has been spent watching and waiting on others. It was time for her to see the big plans God had just for her.

Before I returned to Gina's bedroom door, though, I quickly checked on Brent and Wade to make sure all was well, then I stationed myself outside and I waited for Abba to call me inside.

When I heard His call, I walked into the room and He motioned for me to have a seat. I sat down on the bed opposite theirs and prepared myself to listen to what He had to say. Abba started by saying, "Spirit, I've told Gina that she is my little girl; one of my prized possessions. I have also told her that I want her and Wade to have a speedy courtship because I don't want to prolong their burning passion. I explained that she is to remain pure until holy matrimony. I have also let her know why. It is now up to you to expound on that reason. You two talk because I want to enjoy the party."

In the blink of an eye, Abba was gone, and I was left there with a very curious and inquisitive Gina. Her first question to me was, "Father said Wade was a horrible womanizer; are you going to tell me what to expect?"

My answer was, "Yes and no. Wade was bad. He has been reigning himself in lately because Ox and I had to teach him a lesson. It is now up to you to show him how to treat women with respect. Abba wants you to have a speedy courtship. Use this short period wisely. Help your mate find true intimacy. Make him desire the real you not just want your body. Gina, you need to listen to me, before your courtship begins, that the old Wade would be able to make Marshall Dunlap's horrible actions look like an amateur's in comparison."

She visibly gasped with horror. The thought caused her to swallow hard before she could proceed to inquire why. She asked, "He's been with many women then and didn't treat them kindly."

"Yes, Gina that is what I am saying. Wade used women primarily for sex. So, it is imperative that he not know you in that manner until after marriage. It is because of his good looks that women were drawn to him. His face is also what kept you hoping, remember? He used his looks to charm women into submission for his pleasure. He has never wanted commitment until lately. Heaven had to intervene. He has promised to leave women alone for a while and wait for the woman we showed him to arrive. That woman is you. Now that he knows you are real, he will be mad with desire. He knows nothing else. We want you to patiently show him how to care for and respect you while he woos you. You'll know how, use the same methods you used with Marshall the other night. Just help Wade find the real you that we know and love so dearly. He needs kind but firm rejection first from a woman he truly wants. Ox and I will be with you. You can do it you already know the courtship will be short. Make a game of this, make Wade beg. We have no doubt you can do this job right for his sexual health and for your mental guarantee of love." I explained.

"You're joking? I almost went mad recently. All I could think about was my own needy desire. I'm not a virgin! I tend to run hot myself. Now that I have Wade's attention, I may need Ox more than ever to keep my mind from being lured into temptation by his gorgeous face. If he hadn't been there while Wayne was tending my leg the other day I would have made a fool of myself." Gina exclaimed.

I smiled at her and said, "That's Ox's job. Call on him! He'll die over and over to protect and help you if you need him."

Again, I had the pleasure of watching Gina's facial expression change. She truly was my little bulldog. She locked her jaw and then gritted her teeth together before blurting out at me, "I don't ever want to see or hear Ox go through torture again! Never ever! If I must wear a chastity belt and pack heat, Ox will not suffer because of my sexual urges!"

Then she did a one-eighty turn. She calmed herself down and then asked, "You said you showed me to Wade? Where? When? How long has he been searching for me?

I couldn't help myself, I laughed so hard. Then I answered, "Wade hasn't been looking, he was too afraid. We had to present you to him. Ox and I had a 'come to Jesus meeting' with him before he came home from Iraq. It was at that time, I ordered him to stop using women. He promised not to be with another after I showed him who he could be with. Like you, I gave him a specific time and told him to look for a specific woman. He knew he'd stumbled upon you at Brent's campaign center the night your dad had the heart issue. Since then, he's been completely consumed in his search for you. You fit my parable to a tee. He saw for himself that there was a woman I promised waiting for him, she would be working with Justice and wearing a leg cast.

Gina argued, "But I didn't see him at Brent's campaign. I only saw Wayne."

"I know, but Wade saw you. He saw you leaving, so it fueled his desire. Your mind was focused elsewhere; on your Dad. You were headed to the hospital to be with him." I explained.

"Explain the 'come to Jesus meeting' to me please," Gina asked.

"Okay. I'll briefly explain. But, I think Wade needs to tell his story to you. Make that a priority. It will help you communicate.

First, I need to make something clear. Wade does not have a personal relationship with Jesus, and he doesn't know me very well either. Religious tradition has stood in his way. The church he attends with his mother doesn't speak much about me." I explained.

"Since you were going to be a critical part of our plan I had to talk to Wade about his behavior. During his internship on board a Navy Carrier, he went crazy using women to pacify his sexual urges. Abba did not approve. So, he sent me to Wade. Ox was with me and he scared Wade while he was on a rescue mission. When he saw Ox's shadow on the ground he had another interpretation of who Ox was. When I confronted Wade about his behavior towards women, he thought since Ox has horns and a long tail that he was the devil and our meeting was a warning for him to fly right or go to hell. His religious tradition has blinded him and wasn't allowing our loving side to filter in so we could gently correct. So, out of fear, he vowed to act right and stop abusing women, but instead of dating, he completely avoided female contact altogether unless necessary. His mindset hasn't changed, though. He is still the sex hungry guy he was before; his libido is intact. We must teach him how to behave differently, so he can engage your mind and not hunger just for your body. All we want for Wade is a genuinely loving relationship. Help him find me, and then you can show him Ox's true nature." I urged.

"Wade hasn't had your baptism? Lord, help him, then!" Gina begged.

"I will! I showed you the future Wade. Remember the flaming helmet? He will truly be your soul mate, Gina. He too will live in passion's loving flame, so you don't have to worry." I assured her.

"How long must I drag this out before saying anything? Do I need to demand anything? Or can I ease into things?" Gina inquired.

"You'll know when and how. Trust yourself and be determined to get to know the man behind the face," I suggested.

"Can I go to him now?" Gina asked sheepishly.

"Yes! Go find your man." I encouraged. "He is very troubled."

Mamie's Reward!

I went outside to watch over my loved ones and was blessed with an awesome sight. Brent and Hope had provided live music for the campaign's victory party and the band was in high gear; playing loudly. What blessed me was watching Abba dance around. He was 'busting a move', as the young people say. He was enjoying the party.

When our minds connected, I heard Him giggling. He said, "Spirit, are you having problems with my mingling among your bunch? I told you I came to enjoy myself. I'm still watching over everyone, so you need to relax a bit. There is a time for play and a time for war. At this moment, I am insisting you relax and allow Jesus to watch over things. Have some fun, I certainly am."

Without hesitation, I replied, "Yes, Sir!"

When I turned around to find a place where I could sit and watch, I noticed Mamie sitting off from the crowd. She was in the watchman mode. *Why?* I thought. I engaged her mind and asked, "Mamie, why aren't you having fun? Why are you fretting so much? This is not like you."

"Lord, something is not right. I feel evil stewing and I'm staying on the lookout. Every nerve in my body says I'll be needed soon. Tell me, are my babies at risk?" She outright demanded.

I sidled up next to her and said as gently as I could, "No more than Goshen was when chaos was covering Egypt during their escape."

I watched her visibly shudder. Then I saw her eyes go wide and very bright with curiosity. "Lord, I knew something was happening! I felt it in my bones. Can you enlighten me?" Mamie asked.

"Why do you want to know future events? Enjoy this day!" I suggested.

"I want to be of service! I'm always at your beckoned call!" Mamie stated.

I was about to assure her when Abba sauntered over to our table carrying a large piece of cake with ice cream on top. He sat down next to me and said, "Spirit, I have this. It is time I had a long talk with Mamie. You can stay if you wish or go check on Jesus. He may need your help. I hear He is about to release His angelic army."

Mamie's mind was still engaged with mine, so she heard everything Abba said to me. I felt her begin to shake. Her body was overwhelmed with this knowledge. She started to kneel! I stopped her quickly, "Mamie! Stop! You don't have to bow down, Abba is not here to punish or correct you. He is here to fellowship with you and loves you like I do."

Tears filled Mamie's eyes and the liquid pools were about to brim over onto her cheeks. She was stunned, but managed to ask, "God wants to visit me?"

"Yes, Mamie, I do!" Abba said to her. "I want you to sit here and enjoy cake and ice cream with me."

"Sir, I don't have any cake." Mamie politely told Him.

I stayed quiet and watched Abba's loving nature take over. He reached out and touched Mamie's temple and asked, "My Child, look at me. Look down at the table and see the sweets I brought us to share. There is more than enough. I even brought two spoons and napkins."

Mamie nodded and tearfully replied, "Yes, Lord! I see you! You're grand!"

Then Abba addressed me, "Spirit, leave us for a few minutes. Check on Jesus like I said earlier. It is time Mamie understands what is about to happen and I want to be the one who lets her know. Take her angel, Healer, with you. He needs to focus on what Jesus is doing as well."

25

Healer and I went obediently, but I kept my mind engaged with them. I wanted to hear Mamie's reactions to what we have in store for her. Abba was about to inform her of her retirement.

Abba said, "Mamie, my sweet Mamie! Do I have a surprise for you! In a few months, you'll be breaking in your replacement."

"Replacement!" Mamie choked out. "Father, you're calling me home? I'm I going to die?"

"Heaven forbid! No! I'm going to reward you! It is time you had a life filled with love and laughter. It is time for a new generation to emerge, so eat some cake and let's celebrate!" Abba expressed.

Mamie didn't want cake as she wanted to throw-up! "Lord, since I was a girl, all I've wanted was to serve you. I don't know anything else. I don't want anything else." Mamie shared.

"Now, Mamie. You and I both know that isn't the truth. You purposefully denied yourself happiness. You refused love at every turn. It is time you and I deal with this fear," Abba stated.

"Lord, but!" Mamie started to argue.

"No buts, Mamie. I'm Almighty God. I know the end from the beginning and everything in between. I know your heart. Since you've declared that all you've wanted was to be of service, let me take you down memory lane. Sit there and let me tell you what I know as fact," Abba said sternly.

I may have been on my way to meet Jesus, but Mamie and I both listened tentatively to what Abba lovingly recalled of Mamie's history. He took us back forty-nine years into the past when Mamie was eleven then He finished with today's issues. "Mamie, I orchestrated a mindset change when you were very young. I placed an Afro-American pastor in position then. His name was Martin Luther King Jr., don't you remember? His proclamations are happening today. It's time for another traditional values shake-up. I'm preparing another pastor and I've already established someone to start a new order in this society. That is why we are partying today. Change must occur.

When you were young, the world was hard on people of color. I chose you as someone that would change events for your race and prove grace loves all races. You went through some very harsh and judgmental times but look at you now. You are a spiritual force to be reckoned with. You've blessed me so much by your loyalty. You've healed so many and loved them for me using your nursing profession and faith. Think back with me, and remember how it felt being one of the first black children to enter a white school? You made it work. Among all those white faces you found a friend that first day. Then you found another friend in her brother; Andrew and Amelia Jones and they have never failed you. Amelia was your closest friend and confidant until the day she and her husband died in a car crash, and then you helped Andrew raise her baby boy. Craig Reed has grown up to be a fine man and a wonderful pastor establishing a wonderful little family of his own."

Next, I heard Abba lovingly say, "Mamie, Andrew is lonely. He has never married because his heart belongs to you. He basically raised Craig alone because you couldn't commit. You and I both know Andrew's love for you is not a love for a sister either. You love him too; admit it. It is time the two of you come to terms and deal with the racial divide that frightens you. It doesn't frighten Andrew; he wants you to be his wife. He has for many years."

Shyly, Mamie confessed, "Father, I truly love Andrew. I just thought since we were two different races you wouldn't approve of us being married."

"What made you think that?" Abba asked her.

"Our parents didn't like our associations, and they said the Bible clearly states not to mix. So, I assumed you didn't approve. I didn't want to cause strife so I dedicated my heart to your son.

I don't want to break my vow to Him." Mamie stated.

"Mamie, Jesus agrees with me. It is aggravating us that you've denied yourself a family for so long. Plus, we don't see color! We see the love between you two and want your happiness. Your parents are no longer with you. It's time you lived fully." Abba expressed.

"I'm too old to have children. I'm almost sixty years old." Mamie persisted.

"Child! Look around! Everyone here thinks of you as a mother figure. I have more family from your loving heart than most bear, from their bodies." Abba corrected her.

"Father, then why do I have to retire if I marry?" Mamie asked.

"Trust me, Mamie. By that time, you'll want to retire," Abba replied.

"Why?" Mamie persisted further.

Abba sighed, things area about to get topsy-turvy in a few weeks and I'll need you and Andrew working in another capacity. A younger generation will be released to carry out what you've done for so long."

"Will my angel stay with me?" Mamie asked.

"Yes, he will never leave your side unless directed by me, Jesus, or Spirit. The two of you have bonded." Abba shared.

Mamie shyly asked another question, "Father, will I get a sign letting me know when to start looking for my replacement?"

"Look for tranquility and unity in the Earth together." He informed.

Mamie couldn't respond to Abba's statement. She was still very confused. I heard her thoughts, '*What is He talking about? Tranquility and unity have never resided together in my lifetime.*'

Abba was stuffing His mouth with cake while Mamie stewed, and He was enjoying every bit of her confusion. He knew the riddle would plague her until it presented itself as a truth. That was just like Him. He loved to joke around. He loves happy drama as much as I do. The three of us feed on joking around with parables so people would have to think for themselves.

<hr />

When Healer and I reached Jesus, He had everything under control. He asked me, "Did Father send you?"

"Yes! He's having fun. I love seeing Him this way and enjoying people." I replied.

Jesus stated, "I'm glad! He was tired of being called 'the man upstairs'. He wants everyone to know He is available all the time and not just there when they have needs."

Then, Jesus said, "Abba wanted time alone with Mamie. You don't have to stay here with me to kill time. I know you'd much rather be on land."

"I'm doing what I'm told," I replied.

"Well, I'm telling you to go back. Kill some time and stay out of Abba's way. Watch Him have fun. Talk with Mamie while Abba focuses on Hope. She'll need your help to gather courage." Jesus ordered.

Once I arrived back on the scene, I could tell Mamie was still pondering and wading through all Abba had said. She was in a mental daze of sorts, frozen in her own thoughts. She hadn't even noticed that Abba was no longer at the table. He'd excused Himself to enjoy the day's attractions while filling in Hope and Brent on future events.

I saddled myself alongside Mamie so I could snap her out of the mental trap. I said to her, "Mamie, what Abba is suggesting is simple. Don't waste another second, go call Andrew. Let him know you've had a heart-to-heart conversation with God. You and Andrew have never kept secrets from each other. It's time you told him you've been released from your vow of chastity and service to Jesus. He'll be overjoyed."

Mamie was giddy now with excitement. She was getting married! Heavenly Father approved of their marriage! She was finally going to know marital bliss. After forty years of hem and hawing around Andrew's courtship and her denying the truth, she was finally going to get to experience physical love. She could hardly use her cell phone correctly her hands were shaking so badly from excitement.

When Doc answered his cell, Mamie didn't have a clue what to say. She stuttered for a few minutes until her confidence arose. Then, she blurted, "Andrew, let's get hitched! I'm ready!"

Enlightenment

I had Mamie and Doc talking and Gina and Wade getting acquainted now I was determined to enjoy the party and let Abba work for a change. Jesus said I could watch from the sidelines, so I found a comfortable spot and watched. Watching Abba was pure joy within itself. He danced, and He ate, sang, and loved on people at every turn. Some of the people physically noticed a presence but others ignored Him, the snubs didn't matter to Abba, though, He was a like kid set free in a candy store.

Hope and Brent were sitting at their specified picnic table next to the barn. It was an isolated spot where Brent could rehearse his acceptance speech in front of Hope. Abba was slowly heading their way. I could hardly wait to see Hope's reaction to Him being outside of her prayer closet. She was going to be shocked.

I turned my ears towards their conversation. Brent asked Hope, "What do you think of my speech? Is it corny?"

"No. It is a little stiff for family and friends, though," Hope replied.

About that time, Abba cleared His throat and suggested, "Brent, why don't you be yourself. Speak from the heart instead of trying to be someone you are not."

The two lovebirds heard Abba's voice at the same time. Brent went dumbstruck and Hope turned around to face Abba with extremely wild and wide eyes.

"Father!" Hope squeaked.

"Surprise!" He exclaimed.

Hope was trying to gain her wits and began sputtering, "Why are you here? Is there something wrong?"

Abba replied, "No, Child. I'm just tired of being cooped up in a prayer room or prayer closet. I want to experience life with you outside in the real world. Spirit has had all the fun. From now on, He and I both will work closely with our beloved ones."

"What about Jesus? Will He be with us also?" Hope asked.

"He is going to be extremely busy for a while," Abba answered.

When Brent calmed his breathing, he managed to ask, "Lord, are you here to guide me on this new journey?"

"I've always been here to guide you both, but neither of you have addressed me directly outside of the church's prayer room or your home closet. I was in Spirit's mind everywhere He went and every time either of you communed with Him." Abba corrected.

Brent questioned, "Were we wrong for not knowing? I thought we were supposed to talk to you in private, through Jesus' spirit?"

"Either way!" Abba countered. "We just don't like a show of prayers. Don't fret. I hear everything! Just remember I'm here, and out in the open for both of you. I don't want to be trapped in a box or considered the man upstairs any longer. Is that understood?"

"Yes, Sir!" They replied in unison.

"Brent, while Hope and I talk for a few minutes why don't you review Romans Chapter 13. I specifically like how it is written in the Message Bible. I think you'll find it is precisely what you want to say to your friends and family." Abba suggested.

Brent excused himself and went off to read what Abba suggested while He filled Hope in on why Jesus was going to be busy.

———◆◇◆———

Hope Dear, you are remembering your dreams and are staying bound in fear. At a blink of an eye, you suit yourself in Jesus' armor. Times are changing, and you will not have to battle any longer. From now on just wear your robe and rest. Keep praying the Lord Jesus into victories." Abba expressed.

As soon as Abba said victories, Hope's midsection began seizing with pain and her stomach rolled violently. The pain and nausea were so severe Hope pleaded with Abba for help. "Father, help my baby!"

I wanted to rush to her side, but I knew Abba would respond with the utmost swiftness. He immediately placed His large hand over Hopes abdomen and spoke calmly, "Quiet down, Shiloh. Mama is not the one fighting in a flesh and blood battle. Mama will be praying your Lord Jesus and into victory. Everything is well, my Sweet. Abba loves you too. I will not allow anything to happen to you or your Mama and Daddy."

The baby calmed down and relaxed and Hope's pain and sickness subsided where she could ask Him about the baby's name. "Shiloh? Did you call my baby Shiloh? Why?

"Well, that's her name. She will be something special, a child of the shift, born from chaos into tranquility." Abba explained.

I could tell Hope wanted to know more details about her baby, but Abba had pressing matters to discuss with her. He explained, "Hope, in a very short time Jesus and His angelic army will be fighting a spiritual battle over this area. He, and all the angels will be calling out demonic forces. A battle between our kingdom of light and Satan's kingdom of darkness will wreak havoc on this community and surrounding areas. People will think nothing of it at first until the media blows everything out of proportion. Chaos ensues from bad weather, and people are frantically quarreling and denying the truth. That is why I'm here. My presence will ruin Satan's plan. For too long, people have blamed me for every bad thing that happens, but that is about to change drastically. I'm here to extend pure love when all around us creation rages in a fierce war alongside angelic forces. It is during this time, intercessors start to pray for my pastor. The message of grace and total inclusion of all mankind must be preached and religious bigotry and condemnation stopped. Once again, Satan has bewitched my followers into thinking they must cast out sinners when that isn't their job. Jesus defeated sin and opened the door for me to come in and fellowship with my people."

"How are my prayers going to help with this venture, Father?" Hope asked.

He went on to explain the plan. "You will understand shortly when the Holy Spirit comes and takes you on another journey with Insight. All things will be revealed to you in the spirit realm. Brent will be giving his speech soon. Go and support your husband. While he is speaking with friends and family, your spiritual self will be traveling."

"Will my spirit become separated from the baby?" Hope asked.

"Of course, not! She gets to go with you." He elaborated.

To ease Hope's mind, Abba showed her a beautiful sash. Then He said, "I am going to place this sash around your waist, up through your legs and then have it attached in the back. You and Shiloh will be completely covered and no devil on the Earth, under the Earth or in the atmosphere, will try to touch either of you."

Hope was sincerely moved, and said, "Thank you so much, Father!"

"My pleasure, Child." He said lovingly. Then He touched her abdomen with the sash and the girdle of truth, and now protection was in place.

"Lord, why do you want me to see what Jesus is doing? Wouldn't it be enough just to know He will win?" Hope asked.

Abba answered gently, "Hope, we want you to get familiar with moving around in the spirit realm. You need to be aware of how we see things. Trust us, we trust you. When you have doubts, you'll remember what you've seen and can get in agreement with the plan during your prayers."

Then Abba urged, "It time to get started. Brent will be here soon to rehearse his speech again. Listen to him. Spirit and Insight will meet with you shortly. Oh, and by the way. Time, while you're away with Jesus, doesn't stand still down here, so remember when you re-enter your body be prepared to run for cover. A storm is on the way with forceful wind and lightning. It will be a sign the war is raging and disturbing the atmosphere. It will be fierce."

Hope asked, "Where will you be?"

"Around! Never far away." He promised.

———————

Abba slowly moved away from Hope and reinserted Himself back into the party. Seeing Him play and mingle was something I could watch forever, but my thoughts had to be on Hope. Just like Mamie, she was sitting alone and mentally stewing over what Abba had just said to her instead of focusing on Brent's needs.

I couldn't let her stay trapped in her thoughts, so I moved over to her and said, "Relax! Rejoice with your husband!"

"Lord, I'm trying to enter this rest Abba mentioned, and I know Brent needs me, but I've been through so much and it's hard not to worry. Will you help me focus so I can be the supportive wife Brent must have as well the faithful servant that you need?" She shared.

"Of course," I said. I hugged her close and commanded her body to receive peace. Moments later Brent walked back to their table and I noticed she had physically relaxed and was able to give Brent her full attention.

———————

Brent excitedly said, "Hope this chapter of Romans the Lord referred to me, is exactly what I need to say. I'd never read it out of The Message Bible before so I looked up the passages using the Bible application on my phone."

"Will you be able to use it in your own words and not as if you are reading scripture?" Hope asked.

He replied, "I think so. Check this out! 'I want to thank everyone here for coming out and celebrating with me and my family. As most of you know, it has been my desire for many years to govern this community with love and order, the way God would want. After all, aren't all governments under His authority? Peace and order are God's methods of existence. I sincerely feel that living as a responsible citizen is our duty out of love for the creator. In this job as a constituted authority figure, I will not be a threat to anyone who tries to live decently. I will only move in judgment when people are acting irresponsibly and hurting others. The way I see it, when people refuse to act in a decent manner they are not only offending you they are offending my God, who loves all of us. This January, I will be sharing my plans with the community. All of you know that I am a firm believer in Almighty God, and with His help I'll do my best to bring order and respect to our community. Thank you for believing in me and voting for me.'"

Hope was in awe and clapped her hands. She expounded, "It was wonderful! Bravo, Honey, Bravo!"

With Brent's speech approved, it was time for Hope and I to give Jesus our attention. She and I ushered Brent towards the platform so he could deliver his speech. After he took the microphone in his hand, I gently helped Hope's spirit leave her body, standing alongside Brent, until we returned.

The Power of Agreement

Insight moved closer alongside Hope and me. In the physical realm, the crowd was gathering around to hear Brent's victory speech. The speech signified that the day's party was winding down. With Brent fully occupied, Hope was content enough to face me and Insight. That's when we heard the direct order from Jesus, "Come up here!"

Instantly, Hope's armor came over her naked and girded body! I didn't have the heart to tell her the fighting clothes were not needed. She was lovely standing there pregnant, stomach slightly protruding with the brilliant sash shining so grand it even made my eyes hurt. It was truly God-given and really all she needed to wear. Even the beautiful robe I'd given her wasn't as grand.

When she was mentally prepared, Insight bowed down low and caused Hope to look at me puzzled. "What is Insight doing?" She asked me.

"He wants you to climb onto his back. You'll be flying atop of him."

"What?" Hope gasped.

"This time you'll be riding your angel into the battlefield where we will be joining Jesus in the air." I clarified.

"I just climb onto his back and pretend he is a horse?" She questioned.

"Yes! He will not let you fall." I assured.

She scrambled on top of Insight's back and found the small padded saddle and halter attached to his torso just for her. As soon as she nestled herself onto the saddle between Insight's wings and grabbed hold of the harness, and the three of us were off.

Hope's expression said it all. She was truly in her element. I've been with hundreds of God's chosen watchers, but none were as committed as Hope. She was a delight! Her leadership will be truly spectacular.

When she saw Jesus, her face softened, her eyes grew bright and her smile grew wide. The love she has for my Master is undeniable. Her excitement to reach Him made her forget that she wasn't on a horse, and she nudged Insight to move faster. The love coming through Hope propelled the angel faster to her goal.

My Lord and Hope acted as if they'd been apart for eons, but because He was on His white horse and her on Insight they could not fully embrace and had to be satisfied just holding hands.

I greeted Jesus and asked if He needed me to stay. He replied, "You are more than welcome to watch the show with us. I think you'll enjoy seeing how Hope responds to what I'm about to show her. When I'm finished, hurry back and help the Earth bound angels with the situations coming."

"Won't Abba be there?" I asked.

"Yes, but He wants nothing to do with this war. He is there to give out unconditional love. Ox will be guarding Gina fiercely and won't rest until she is safely inside the building. His ruckus will upset Justice and Healer causing everyone to be alarmed. Once the sky turns dark, Hope will return to her body. Before then, I want you on the Earth's surface giving orders and smoothing feathers." He explained.

"Then are you starting it now?" I inquired.

He countered, "I most definitely am!"

Hope didn't like that we were leaving her out of the conversation. She asked, "What are you starting? Father said you were going to war. Is that it?"

"Come with me Hope, use your spiritual sight and focus on what has gotten me so angry," Jesus said.

They flew higher into the sky where the clouds exposed a clearing. There, Jesus told Hope to remember how things appeared in another realm. He refreshed her memory by asking what she remembered about Cindy when she saw her in the mall. Hope thought back, *Cindy was a dead person walking around trying to mask over her problems with material things. She also remembered what I told her that Cindy's life would even corrode gold without the love of God.*

Hope expressed, "Everything about her was lifeless."

"Precisely!" Jesus agreed.

"When I looked over this community I see the same thing; a masked-over group of people trying to cover themselves with dead leaves. They are truly naked without me. There is an extremely large spiritual harlot hovering over people and her thinking is warped. I'm about to remedy this error. Satan and his followers have used my natural resources and material things for too long and have forced her to horde the blessings away from my people. Look and see!" He urged her, pointing down.

Hope looked down to where Jesus was pointing and said, "Lord, I only see trees, houses, businesses, cars, and other forms of transportation. I'm not seeing the harlot you mentioned."

"You're looking with your natural eyes. Look deeper, past the pretense with your spiritual sight." He urged.

Hope narrowed her vision, and her expression was priceless when the truth manifested itself. Her eyes grew extremely wide and then her mouth flew open in astonishment. She was too stunned to speak and it took her a few minutes before she could gather her thoughts with the right questions. When she obtained her composure, she spat out, "Lord, our whole community is nothing but dry sticks and rubble! Nothing is green! It even stinks like death! Why haven't I noticed this before? Everything appeared to be flourishing, why was I duped?"

"Everyone is duped, Hope! Satan dolled-up the harlot and forced her to squat over everything instead of creating, so he could blind people and make them lose faith in me. What you see is the truth under a mask of profiteering through abuse and greed. Satan's lair, his kingdom of darkness, has been smothering life. Life and love have been dying and I'm tired of it. I want everything, including the harlot under me and not ruled by him!"

"Have those I love been under this facade?" Hope asked Him.

"No, look down to your right." Jesus urged.

Hope and I both turned our gazes to the right before looking down, so we could focus on what Jesus wanted. Below we saw a beautiful sight of the Boys' Home, and the connecting church properties. They were alive, prosperous, and beaming with health and vitality.

Hope asked, "This is wonderful, but why just these places?"

"Grace is abounding where it is believed, Hope! Life and clear thinking began in this area when your pastor's message glorified forgiveness. Visions into the chaos had to start somewhere, and the movement began when you were shown the role as intercessor. Remember the days at the mall and again when I had you wear my armor? That was the first day I cleaned house. Not only were the spirits of pride and greed removed from your church they were severely wounded in your community. What I did for and against the Reynolds' family, I'm also doing on a much larger scale around the world. The giants controlling territories will be demolished. With Abba out in the open extending His arms, there isn't much time left for the giants to exist. In a short time, people will understand the true meaning of a loving parent." Jesus informed.

"Masses?" Hope inquired.

"Yes! Masses!" Jesus said. "People will be running to Abba, but for this to happen a very stressful time occurs. Hopelessness, panic and suicidal thoughts will be rampant. People will have no other option but to run to Him which is a very good thing. Enough about the future. Look around and tell me what else you see."

To Hope's amazement, millions of angels were waiting for a trumpet to sound. It was as if they were drooling and biting at the bit for this heavenly victory! Hope gasped again, just like I knew she would then said, "It's true then! Kingdoms are ready for war and mankind is stuck in the middle of it all?"

Jesus answered, "Yes, Hope, Father's wrath was never intended for mankind. Man was not the reason His kingdom experienced death. It was Satan and his evil influence that tempted man. Now, the war against him and those who work for him must take place. Our time has come! Many battles will happen before we are satisfied."

"Our time?" Hope curiously asked with an eyebrow raised.

"Yes! God's and mankind. Join hands with me Hope. This will signify that heaven and Earth are in an agreement and angels will get into position. Then repeat what I say." Jesus exclaimed.

I only watched in amazement as commanding angels joined forces between realms. The atmosphere was electric with excitement. Jesus' beautiful white horse was snorting and rearing and Hope's Earthbound guardian angel, Insight was also vibrating with anticipation. He shared privately with me, that the sight reminded Him of the locust, gnats and biting flies that were released in Egypt during Moses' time.

Jesus spoke a command into the combined realms, "Spirit of Idolatry, come out of hiding! Satan will not protect you and your works have been revealed!" Hope was urged to repeat the same phrase using her own words to make the kingdom of darkness on Earth shake. Fear forced the old spirit of Idolatry into view with his hands raised refusing to fight. Showing the agreement between heaven and Earth, Jesus lifted His and Hope's joined hands then He ordered, "Loose the harlot!"

Idolatry removed the golden helmet he'd placed over the obese harlot's head, uncovering her mind, freeing her ears so she could hear and allowing her head to move from side to side. The first thing she witnessed seeing and hearing were legions of demons screaming and scattering. Without warning, while we were watching the harlot, Idolatry shot a bolt of hot blistering steam toward heaven's army knocking them back a pace or two. Retaliating, the King of kings released thousands of catlike and eagle looking angels into the Earthly realm telling them to have fun, kill and devour.

While the angels scrambled, Jesus urged Hope to look over the area again and to use her inner light to illuminate the ground and atmosphere where the angels could see clearer. She didn't understand Him and said, "I've never used an inner light before."

Jesus said, "Use your love force, Hope! Focus its power on those you love allowing it to build inside your heart until it shines from your eyes onto the community below. Love is a powerful beacon of light and the only force able to force darkness away exposing Satan's hordes. It also will illuminate people's nakedness to show them what Satan has forced them to do without. God, never desired mankind to be without anything on their bodies or in their hands, so when your love force connects with mine, the power of agreement strengthens angels to take back what doesn't belong to Satan without confusion or hesitation."

Riding the airwaves alongside them, I was privileged to watch and feel Hope build her inner strength. She had closed her eyes and began remembering how Johnson and Virginia Reynolds acted haughty and prideful for so long. I watched as she mentally revisited the newspaper and media's reviews on how much stealing and embezzling Johnson Reynolds had managed from the greed that had him bound. After that, she remembered Virginia's confidence failing and her nakedness exposed. She didn't want her loved ones naked in any shape, form or fashion, so she centered her thoughts of love on Brent, Greg, and her new baby, and how she'd react if they were duped and scammed, forcing them into a slavery without basic needs. Love changed into righteous anger and she opened her eyes wide so they could be used as flashlights to push out the darkness. When Jesus saw Hope's light, He joined the light of their eyes together, lighting up everything. Then with an expletive scream, Hope shouted, "Damn you Satan! Your kind will never steal from our family! Not as long as I am living!"

Like a trumpet blast, Hope's shout, shook the kingdom of darkness down into hell, where hell's fire lives, releasing the planned sequence of events. Darkness was indeed moving and was in the form of menacing clouds and dreadful sounds that were penetrating Earth's realm. Down on Earth, Ox snorted and pawed the ground, which was our cue to leave Jesus' side. Jesus squeezed Hope's hand and told us to go quickly.

We were going back as quickly as we could, while we watched Justice pace frantically around Hope's body. All around the area, people tried to remain focused on Brent, but they were starting to look worried making Healer work harder to calm nerves. The situation clearly indicated we wouldn't have but a few moments before the conditions were too bad to remain outside once Hope's spirit re-entered her body.

Angelic Dramas

The closer we got, we could hear Ox's bellows growing more frantic and Justice's roars were piercing. Healer was steadily giving orders to Adrian and Trulan, and urged people closer towards the main house. Abba was front and center watching the show and snickering at all the drama. My angelic army was acting emotionally because I wasn't with them and the drama was taking over their thinking making them overestimate and over exaggerate.

I had to confess to myself that my angels know me inside and out plus they know the love I have for humanity will usually cause me to fret inwardly. I hate seeing them caught up in evil thinking, but this event wasn't evil. It was a blessing activated towards my people. With this in mind, I pondered, *"Why were they being obsessive and acting weird?"* In a flash, I saw what all the fuss was over. Satan was standing front and center and was very confused and perturbed. Apparently, Hope's shout had forced him out of hiding.

I was standing beside Ox and he had turned blood red with hate, stomping, snorting preparing to pounce, when the noise forced Satan to look our way. Cursing, he left the scene. There was no telling where he went, he couldn't go back to his hiding place where angels were turning over every obstacle looking for evil. It was my estimate that we'd be looking at weeks or months before the war was over and disasters following it were to stop so clean-up could begin.

I calmed Ox down and told him to go back to Gina. I moved over to Justice to calm him down because his back was bristled and he was also eager to pounce. His concern was well-founded. Until Hope had re-entered her body she was fair game for Satan. He knew Brent would have been devastated if he'd allowed something to happen to her.

Healer was next and I had to see who had his attention and why he was so upset. He told me, Greg and two other small boys had wondered off and were on the other side of the lake, unattended when Satan appeared again. Mamie was no help to him, as she was fantasizing about getting married. Gina and Wade were romancing each other as well. Hope was gone and Brent was occupied. No adults were watching the little scoundrels. We had one option; to frighten the little guys back home. I summoned Adrian and told him to make a loud clap of thunder followed by a streak of lightning over the boys' heads. That would make them dash back home on fast little feet.

With all my Earth bound angels calmed down, I sat on the bench next to Abba so I could rest a bit before another drama started. I looked over at Him and He laughed. Then He said, "don't look at me. I wasn't the one who gave Satan so much clout. This could only be attributed to "Religion", until a small girl, brought up without religious traditions finally realized his weakness. It is time for the rest of my family to have the revelation, don't you think?"

Speaking of Gina, I turned to look for our latest prodigy to see if she and Wade were safely inside the house. They weren't! Ox was frantic again and looking at me intensely because Gina hadn't heeded his warnings. I got up from my seat next to Abba and shouted at the angel, "Ox, Gina is not familiar with your bellowing. She is used to hearing your hassles and barks! She'll move if you revert to dog mode again!"

Ox immediately changed tactics and began barking, growling, and going berserk. Gina was immediately on her feet, with her eyes wide and head turning in all directions. She'd burst into spiritual flames again; a normal reaction due to her prior circumstances. Wade was clueless. He couldn't see Gina engulfed in fire but he knew she was acting strangely. Her countenance was strange so he asked, "What's wrong?"

Gina's face changed from rage to fright indicating to me she had the full understanding of why Ox was barking. She pointed upward towards the sky before answering Wade, "The sky is black, the wind is blustering, and we need to run for cover!" Without hesitation, Wade quickly threw Gina over his shoulder and ran swiftly towards the main house.

Ox began barking and then bellowing louder and when he did Adrian clapped out another thunderous sound followed by lightning. The two angels laughed to themselves, now they had big people's feet scampering towards safety.

Hope didn't waste any time once she returned to her body, being alerted ahead of time, she grabbed Brent's hand and urged him to throw down the microphone and run with her. Abba and I remained at our picnic bench, enjoying the sight. People all around us were running for cover; one of God's covers. Some got into their cars and headed home but most wanted to wait out the storm. Either way, these people were reacting properly to the alarms where calm was under God's loving protection.

When the rain began to fall, Abba stood with His face pointed towards heaven and stated, "The tears of my angels are so sweet to me. In this instance, their joy will bring greater victory for my son."

I had a feeling Abba was harboring a personal secret so I held my tongue and didn't bother to ask what His statement implied. I later found out that He was listening to Satan's thoughts. The old goat still thought he could undermine things to make the community think all this was God's wrath. Abba wasn't emotionally moved in any way, in fact, He ignored Satan's insults because He knew the outcome. When He and I moved into the building to be with the people, He was full of joy and radiating pure love. All He wanted to do was to be a good father.

Caylee was the first-person Abba wanted to approach. He whispered in her ear reminding her of the storm Satan threw at her a few months back. He was using her to say something good about the weather so it would keep the people calm. The thought flooded her heart with good memories about Russ so she stood on a chair and clapped her hands together to get everybody's attention then shared, "Hey, everyone. I'm not one who usually talks in front of a group of people but I need to say something. We don't need to be afraid of this storm. Storms are not all bad. I know from experience. It was a storm that brought Russ and me together. I have a feeling this storm is ushering in good things for our community. Instead of worrying, why don't we continue to celebrate Brent's victory? A godly man in city government is something to shout about!"

Everyone cheered! Russ helped Caylee down from the chair, hugged her tightly to his chest and swung her around in front of everyone. Then he took the chair and said, "Everybody, I have something to ask Caylee and I want to do it in front of her loved ones. I can't think of a better time since she brought up how we met." He, stepped off the chair, faced Caylee and bowed down on one knee, "Caylee Marie Sellers, will you please honor me by becoming my wife?"

Caylee was speechless! Russ' proposal had knocked the wind out of her sails. Everyone in the room was staring and holding their breath waiting for her to say something. Tears started to flow from her eyes. She was dumbstruck so I reach over, patted her head and said, "Caylee, the cat doesn't have your tongue. Tell him yes! It's what you've been praying for!"

Caylee began to sputter, like a car backfiring, "Russ, I want nothing more than to be Mrs. Russ Jackson!"

Her answer made the whole room sigh with relief. All her friends rushed over to them and filled the room with congratulations and joy as the hellacious storm raged outside. Abba only grinned.

Future Tidbits

Being a spiritual being has its advantages. It allows us to be in places unseen by the human eye so we can watch things of interest. While the ruckus roared outside, Abba and I were able to relax and it was during this time I asked Abba what was expected of me in future days while Jesus was tackling issues in our spirit realm.

Before saying anything, Abba laughed, "Spirit, outside of these walls there are more problems than most people can imagine. Only a few have some peace, not complete peace, but more than most. You deserve a Sabbath rest for a time so you can enjoy the fruits of your labor."

"How is that possible?" I asked Him.

"You've gathered the main team together. It only took a few before someone was convinced I really existed and loved them. When Gina proved herself, things changed for others around them. Once the commission goes forth that we do not tolerate division and stress loving everyone, a great offense will begin. Religion as we know it will shift and people will turn on one another, but during this time, those who have been shunned for so long will begin to feel my acceptance. Let me show you what I mean, while we wait out this storm. We'll take the people you choose who are involved within the group and discuss what their issues will be like, this way you'll be able to understand what I mean. We'll consider them our second string of love enforcers." Then, He urged me to pick someone.

I looked over the crowd and my focus fell on Frank Addison, "What about Frank? What's your plan for him?"

"I have Frank strategically placed inside a government office to do two things for us. In a time of financial strain and underhanded practices, he'll show compassion while firmly instructing business owners not to abuse the law. He'll open doors for us to invade government" Abba explained.

"Frank will be good in both areas. How are we going to help Frank do that? The government hasn't allowed you behind their doors in years." I said.

"Here is where you come in, Spirit. You'll get to work closely with him during that time. Use Frank's compassionate nature to help people see their vicious cycle. Show him how to teach the way we do things. Employers need to appreciate their workers not abuse them. You'll also have to help him enforce the law without being rude or abrasive. It will be during those times, he'll need you the most. It is hard for Frank to become something completely out of character, he's used to being soft hearted and being stern doesn't work within his nature. It's a good thing he knows how to lean on you for help." Abba shared.

"What about Cindy Grover, Frank's girlfriend?"

Abba answered swiftly, "We'll have them married before the real issues begin. They'll have a happy honeymoon and a few peaceful weeks before their marital foundation gets tested. Here again, you'll be needed, this time in their home life. Cindy will become stressed in her job, and because she is a new convert, and not spiritually strong, the work will force her to place fears and worries on Frank's shoulders. As we know, Frank is not designed to completely carry her burdens. Days from being an enforcer for the government will make him too tired to take on someone else's stressful situations or have any desire to assist. You'll have to help him be the husband she needs so he'll do what it takes to quiet away her drama. Counsel them, and help them find comfort the right way by encouraging them to seek me. I want to be included in this mess so I can be their stronghold."

Next, I asked about the Boys' Home, "Will there be a shake-up over here at the home?"

Abba sighed, "Here is where sadness enters into the picture. The Boys' Home will struggle, but it will not go under and close its doors. The Elders and Arnolds have done a wonderful job teaching the boys how to live off the land. They know how to run a house and do odd jobs to earn some spending money. Living off the land will be important and they know how to fish, hunt and grow vegetables in order not to go hungry. When finances dwindle, they'll need to be encouraged to depend more on me for their greater needs."

"Can you elaborate why they will have issues," I asked.

"Something on the horizon will cause the Elders to move away. This decision will affect everyone. Opening the door for me to prove my love further and show all involved that I keep my promise to never forsake them," He shared.

I said, "even though times for these kids may be tough, you'll love seeing them through. It's what you are all about."

"Yes, but having someone forced to come to me is not my desire," Abba explained.

"I'm very glad that the whole Arnold family is committed to the home. They will be a huge influence when these times get tough." I remarked.

"I can't let Joe's dream fail," Abba stated.

"You've got something else planned, don't you, and it's with Greta?" I asked.

"You know me so well!" Abba remarked. "My plan is to have Carl and Greta both oversee the home when the Elders leave."

"Please explain your plans! I know this will be great," I pleaded.

"Governmental procedures and red tape concerning child welfare will force Greta to make her move but not until a coaching position opens up for Carl at the University. Once they have more finances, plus a home rent free to live in, they can care for the boys. Carl will also be able to give martial arts lessons in the barn after hours which will allow him to help watch the kids and keep them entertained after school. This way the legacy will continue, Joe and the Elders' dream will survive and Carl and Greta will make it a wonderful and exciting place for young kids." He explained.

Amber Simmons, was next on my list. She is Hope's friend and Frank's co-worker, so I was wondering what her part in Abba's plan was since government practices were changing.

He read my thoughts, smiled then said, "I have something special planned for Amber. Working in government was never her thing. I didn't design her to be a law enforcer. She is artistic and business-minded and loves being around kids. Since she has reacquainted with her daughter, I made her wonder why there isn't a little girls' group home in the vicinity. Events will line up for her to get a girls' home in motion. With the help of her mother, Hope, and Greta, Amber will be the manager."

"How will it be funded? Who will run it if she has to work?" I inquired.

"Amber is very smart under all her pretense. She has an accounting degree. We'll help her set up her own office inside the large home I strategically arranged, it is the perfect place. We'll encourage people to use her services and at the same time give her mother a job, and other job opportunities for someone unemployed. Teamed up with Greta Arnold, they will be able to watch over all the small kids during the day. Of course, when school is out, they'll have other people from the church helping them. Eventually, the church will suggest they make both homes one business called, 'Abba's House for Orphaned Children'." He shared.

"That's wonderful, Abba! It makes a very loud statement that you love little girls and little boys the same without prejudice." I excitedly said.

The church crossed my mind, so I asked, "Abba? You haven't mentioned other churches. Will they also be commissioned to enforce love and acceptance like this one?"

"I can't lie. This war's aftermath is going to scare many people. Then Satan is going to confuse my people into thinking they can run into a building for shelter instead of coming to me. Some of the older, strictly religious churches will not be so welcoming to the 'rift raft, drunks, drug users, homeless or homosexuals' who will be seeking help during this time. Loving them unconditionally would be out of the question. This grieves me deeply. I'll be forced into watching scared and hurting people turned away and mistreated. Even some who went to church, but will be facing lack and homeless situations will be shunned while pompous people that don't think they need me will be allowed inside. Churches that say they are my house, will be businesses minded instead of love thy neighbor minded. It's all about finances when times are hard and if someone doesn't have deep financial pockets, or don't fit a certain mold of conduct they will not be tolerated. I hate this!

There will be a few churches that will thrive. They will have pastors, who teach unconditional love and what I am about. These congregations will have their arms opened wide, and ready for all that come running. But those determined to hold onto old traditions, rules, and judgmental attitudes will not be able to grow. I'm going to make sure they don't. I will not allow any place where people claim to know me and who continually accuse and abuse my children an ability to prosper without first facing the fact everyone has faults. My desire it to help my family overcome their issues, not throw them to the wolves. I am not about fashion shows, backbiting, accusations and fault finding. I am fed-up with hard-hearted judgmental pastors and teachers who demand that people clean up their acts before coming to me. I am the cleaner! People can't get clean without me. Therefore, if they don't heed my commission to love each other as they wish to be loved, I can't allow growth." Abba passionately declared.

I replied, "This church family is thriving. I loved being involved here."

Abba looked at me sourly and said, "Yes, but look at Craig Reed. He thinks he's landed in the perfect scenario; young followers, growing congregation and money flowing into the ministry."

Remembering what Jesus said about Pastor Craig Reed, I already knew what Abba was thinking. Craig Reed would be gloating and happy about the growing church body. Yep, I focused on the man, he was leaning against the large kitchen counter, looking out over the group while thinking to himself, *'three weddings and a baby. Growth! I must be doing things right'*.

Reading my thoughts, Abba said, "Disgusting, isn't it? You and your Earth bound angels did all the work, he didn't. He'll straighten up, though. At this moment, what hurts my heart is that he can't see that someone he cares about is worrying themselves sick. He has no clue Mamie needs him at a critical moment in her life. She is the very one who helped Doc raise him, and she could use his loving arms around her right about now. Instead, he can't get his own arms from around himself."

Abba's mention of Mamie made me look around for her. She was extremely worried and had her face pressed to a window looking out at the storm. Seeing her agitated made me compassionate, so I entered her mind and saw what Abba meant. She was worried about Andrew and wanted him to be with her. She was completely disconnected from the group, the first time in many, many years, and only had eyes for one person other than Jesus. Being separated from Andrew was greatly distressing her.

Seeing Mamie's condition, I asked Abba, "Should I intervene and do something so Craig can see her plight?"

"No. Not with Craig. I think it is time you made sure things were calming down outside so these people can go home. Gina is physically worn out, Wade is flirting too much and Hope is about to burst to be alone with Brent so she can tell him what she witnessed with Jesus. There is one thing you can do, tell Hope about Greg. Have Insight show her what he saw Greg doing while they were flying. If it hadn't been for Insight informing Healer of Greg's whereabouts, the child may have gotten himself and the other two boys in serious trouble. He definitely needs an attitude adjustment. He has developed a sense of superiority because he is an Arnold." Abba recommended.

I couldn't believe that Abba had dumped this large load on me all at once. I didn't know which end was up! Did I need to focus on Gina, Hope or did I need to spank Greg? I had one option, and I combined everything into one issue and used my seven-fold vision's ability to see everything from all directions.

I was glad we had warned Gina about Wade, she was getting weary from his sexual advances. Ox was also annoyed as he was continually snorting and barking to keep Gina on high alert. Something had to be done soon. Wade was using every trick in the book to tempt Gina into letting him go home with her. Probing her mind, I understood the problem. She unthinkingly told him she wanted to soak in a hot bubble bath to ease her aching leg and to Wade the implication meant she wanted sex. So, he kept asking if he could join her in the bathing.

Brent was entertaining several people as they waited out the storm while Hope tried to be a good wife. People needed questions answered so she waited for her turn to have Brent's attention. Biting her nails, all she was thinking about was getting him home alone with the Lord where they could tell him about her journey, plus she was hoping Brent would have a journey of his own.

Yes, I agreed with Abba, it was time for the community visit to end so the real party could start. With this in mind, I instantly had my ground troop of angels work to push back the wind and redirect the overhead battles so the storm would move away. I also ordered more of them to unknowingly escort my children home so demonic forces wouldn't prevent safe travels. Abba joined me outside, and added extra forces to mine, standing close were two of His Archangels; Gabriel and Michael.

Communicating with Everyone

With people trying to go in different directions I was grateful once again that I wasn't human. By being a spirit, I could infiltrate anything, hear, and see everything all at once when the time arose. If I had too, could be in thousands of places at the same time and still have a one-on-one interaction with only one person. Granted, I didn't like stretching myself so thin, but many times it was necessary and today was going to be one of those times. For just a moment, I thought there would be a few hours without working so hard. How could I have ever thought things may slow down?

Abba, the creator, all knowing, all seeing, and all hearing, entered my thinking and said, "Rest assured my friend, not being needed, will never be an issue for you. Even in a loving and prosperous environment, people will need something. It's not feeling wanted that may plague you from time-time, but don't get being needed and wanted confused. You may have to deal with some not wanting you, and they tend to forget you when their needs are met. I know from experience."

"Yes, sir." I agreed.

Then Abba said, "I'll herd the people home while you focus on our main crew. Make sure Gina leaves Wade behind then get Mamie home. Hope and Brent will gather Greg and head home shortly. Since they hosted this event, they need to stay until everyone is gone."

I allowed my mind to drift over to Gina's car, where Wade was relentlessly flirting with her. Thanks to Ox, she was holding on. I whispered in her ear, suggesting she leave Wade her cell number. Then I waited patiently for the exchange to take place before I did something drastic. Once Wade had Gina's number on a piece of paper and placed in his pocket, I asked Adrian to shine a beam of sunlight onto Ox. His shadow produced the desired effect, making Wade humbly back off from tormenting Gina.

Now that I had the two of them going their separate ways, I focused on their thoughts. While riding his bike home, Wade's complained to Jesus, *"Lord, didn't you show Gina to me? If you did, why is the devil still hounding me? Why shouldn't we connect? I'm a man! I haven't been with a woman for a long time. Help me here!"* His confusion made me laugh.

At the same time, Gina cried out to me while she was driving home, "Whisperer! That was close! I'm only human and his eyes mesmerize me! I don't know how long I can hold him off. Keep Ox close to me, please! If he gets loud and bold with me I won't break down under Wade's pressure."

"Gina, you did great! Ox and I will help you find common ground with Wade. You two are meant to be together, he will come to his senses soon. Let him know plainly that seductive flirting is not for you and you feel it is demeaning. If you are up front with him, he'll have more respect for you, see you differently and treat you better. After that, we can convince him to commit to you permanently." I answered.

"Stay close, this is hard! I want to have sex with him as much as he appears to want it with me," she exclaimed.

"I know, Gina. I know. Hold your passion in check. You both need to find love for each other first instead of lust. I don't see the sexual tension lasting more than six weeks. You can do this!"

Gina projected her thoughts loudly, "Six weeks! I thought Father God said our courtship would be short. If I must wait for six-weeks, then I'm in trouble."

"No, you're not in trouble. Trust me, and find common ground!" I urged.

While Gina was thinking things through, it opened a door for me to connect quickly with Mamie. Craig may not be concerned about her, but I knew she needed comforting and patience. I wasn't going to allow Mamie to wreck her car or get a speeding ticket trying to get home. She was seriously focused on getting home to Andrew. What she had unleashed on him had opened thirty years of frustration in a few loving words. She had told Andrew to meet her at her place as soon as he could and she was stressing, big time, because after saying she loved him, her cell phone had died. Three hours had passed since they spoke, and she was on a mission because she didn't want Andrew wondering if she meant what she'd said.

I let her know I was present and then spoke gently to her, "Mamie, you need to slow down, debris is on the road. Take your time and watch out for your safety. Andrew is a very patient man and he knows the storm is what has held things up between you two."

"Lord, I've been an idiot! It's a wonder Andrew still wants me! Will you show me how to be a good wife?" She pleaded.

"Sweet Mamie, you already know how to be his wife. Give him your life as well has your love. All he has ever wanted was to take care of you. Let him love you for Jesus. Spend the rest of your days loving each other because of him." I said.

"I'll do that! I can't wait! Thank you, Lord!" She exclaimed.

I helped Mamie drive calmly around fallen trees and other types of debris on the road so she could get to her home without an incident. When she pulled in the drive, Andrew was there waiting. Outside, in Mamie's neighborhood, several other people were taking advantage of the calmer weather to pick up limbs and to examine their homes for possible damage. Mamie's neighborhood was mostly black people who knew Mamie and her family well and most of them were the very people she feared would judge her for having a white male friend. But this time, Mamie didn't care who was looking, or who may be judging. When she finally made it to Andrew's side, she threw her arms around him and planted a wet kiss on his lips and proudly, shouted for the whole group to hear, "Everyone, we're getting married!" Andrew shouted in agreement, "It's about time too!"

I wanted to dance! Their lives were finally coming together.

It was time to reconnect with Hope and Brent. When I arrived, they were taking a few minutes to pick up things that had flown around their property during the storm. Hope was rushing about which added to her stress and she began to feel nauseated again. She had to calm down, the stress wasn't good for her or the baby. "Hope, stop lifting things! Brent will get things in order and the two of you can have time with Jesus. All this unnecessary stressing is not good for you."

"I want Brent to know things are about to get really bad!" Hope expressed.

"I know, but not instantly. Calm your nerves, as you're putting stress on Shiloh." I informed.

"What?" Hope asked.

"Fretting is not good for your baby. Go inside and lie down. Brent will come find you when he and Greg are finished getting the patio table and chairs put away. Go inside and talk with Abba while I assist with things out here." I suggested.

"Father is inside?" She asked.

"Yes, and he wants to talk with you about Greg." I shared.

After seeing Hope stressed, I took the chance and flopped the Greg issue into Abba's lap. He could talk with Hope while I had the opportunity to discuss Hope's health with Brent. As I waited for Brent to finish his chore, I kept watch on Hope. Her demeanor kept my curiosity piqued to the point I wanted to keep a conscious connection with her.

The first thing Hope asked Abba when she went into the house was if there was something wrong with Greg. He immediately replied, "Nothing is wrong with Greg. You just need to know about his recent adventures. Our little fellow is acting a wee bit haughty. He thinks since he is an Arnold, he has rights the other kids do not and he is trying to prove this by teaching some of the smaller boys bad things. Insight needs a gold star for saving the little fellow's bacon this afternoon."

Gasping, Hope asked, "Why? What did Greg do?"

Abba called Insight over to them to answer her question. "Hope, look into Insight's eyes and allow him show you what he saw while the two of you were flying. By seeing the truth, you can rationally address the issue with Greg."

I wasn't surprised to see Hope get livid with her little man, but at the same time I was very grateful for Insight's mental connection with Healer. Between the two angels, they'd kept Greg and his band of followers out of trouble. Through Insight's eyes, she saw everything. Angry now, to the point of exploding, her thoughts were determined. Greg was haughty! The evil influence over her son was short lived. While in Abba's presence, she calls out the demon and told Insight to finish him so Greg's attitude and wondering off without approval could stop!

Brent was now two paces in front of me when I decided to disconnect from Hope and gently insert myself into his thinking. The day has been busy and stressful so I didn't want to upset him with an abrupt and over excited announcement. I had to interject myself cheerfully and calmly, even though what I had to say wouldn't be very cheerful.

"Hello again, Brent! Aren't you glad the party is over?" I nonchalantly asked.

"Hello to you, too! I'm very glad I have the party behind me. Now I'll be able to focus on making this community something the three of you can be proud of."

"I plan on showing you how to read people and judge fairly." I shared.

"So soon!" He inquired.

Answering, I said, "If I don't, Hope will blow a fuse. She's been waiting for hours to let you in on her experience with Jesus this afternoon."

Brent stopped in mid-stride and asked, "Hope had another experience with the Lord?"

"The most drastic one yet," I shared. "That's why we need to hurry."

Fright crossed Brent's face and he asked, "Why? Is something wrong?"

There was no way around Hope's issue, I had to give the information to him quickly, like someone ripping a bandage off a scab. "Hope's body is under a lot of stress and with her history of abuse, she needs a lot of bed rest. She will be fine if she takes life slow and easy. Make sure she has regular check-ups, but be prepared for an early delivery."

"I've been a dope! I should have suspected that she may have issues." Brent rambled.

"Worrying will not help Hope. Nothing is going to happen to her or the baby. She's just not capable of carrying the baby full term." I informed.

"How am I going to make Hope rest? She's not one to remain still for any length of time." Brent asked.

"For the next two months, while prepping for your new position, stay with her and make sure she doesn't overdo anything. Sit on her if you must, and don't get distracted, it is very important! By mid-April, you will be a daddy." I warned him.

"April! She's only two and a half months along, this means the baby will come sometime during her seventh month of the pregnancy. I'll need to get busy! The baby's room isn't ready! Brent complained.

"Go inside the house, Abba and Hope are talking when they finish their discussion we'll show you things and discuss life around your new position," I suggested.

"Sure thing!" Brent said.

I watched him enter the house calm as a cucumber, not realizing the struggle he was about to face. The second he entered their living room, it struck him, Hope wasn't resting at all even with Abba in the room. She was a powerful force in a small frame, pacing frantically while scolding Greg. She was screaming something about her little guy enjoying acts of superiority. It was obvious that two guys were humbled at the same time. I moved quickly over to Abba, hoping we would drop a sense of peace into their atmosphere, but all He wanted us to do was sit, watch, and listen to how the situation played out. We had front row seats to Hope's full blown fit of rage, Greg's cowering, and Brent's cluelessness.

Abba elbowed me and said, "Isn't parenting grand!"

"Surely, you want me to interrupt this!" I inquired.

"Not at all! I gave Hope an internal warning mechanism. Watch and see what happens," He replied.

Abba was relaxed, which meant He had everything under control. It wasn't long before His mechanism worked. While Hope was filling Brent in on Greg's arrogance and disobedience, her belly cramped, doubling her over and stopping her from being irate. The pain was severe and caused her to cry out to Father.

"Told you!" Abba said with a grin.

Brent picked up Hope and laid her gently on the sofa next to Abba, and he and I stood by as Abba rubbed her stomach and spoke soothing words to Shiloh telling the baby not to fear. His loving care relaxed Hope and stopped the pain. Then she began saying, "Shiloh, sweetie, mama isn't at war. She was correcting your brother. All is well, all is well."

Brent had sat on the floor in front of Hope, stunned from what had just occurred. Too much was happening all at once, but his reaction to Hope speaking to their baby was priceless. He placed his large hand over her belly and asked, "Is Shiloh, a baby girl?"

She nodded replying, "Yes, we will have a little girl. Apparently, our daughter has problems with stressful situations. To calm her down, Father places His hand on me and speaks directly to her. I had an episode earlier this afternoon and that's when He told me the baby's sex and that He'd named her Shiloh."

Greg had been silent until this, and he came over and placed his little hand over Brent's and asked, "Am I getting a sissy?"

Hope's anger towards Greg was deflated. She reached out and hugged her guys. Then she replied, to the little one, "You'll have a little sister this summer, which is another reason your haughty actions have to stop. You will be a big brother soon, and I will not have one child feeling they are better than the other. If it sounds like I'm fussing at you, it is because I want peace and harmony in our household. Do you understand?"

Greg nodded and said, "Yes, ma'am."

Then Brent interrupted the conversation and told Greg it was time he got ready for bed. He knew Hope wanted to talk, but until they could be alone that wasn't happening, because Hope didn't talk spiritual things in front of Greg. So, he grabbed Greg by the hand and took daddy duty seriously so Hope could rest until he got back to her side.

Explaining the Circle

Hope could not rest so she scurried around in the kitchen preparing a snack while asking us questions. "It's been six hours since the journey and I want to get things right. How am I going to explain to him what I went through? Will you tell me what to say?"

Abba looked at me and said, "She's all yours."

Taking my cue, I replied to her, "You don't have to do anything, Hope. Brent believes in the supernatural so tell him what you and Jesus did and leave the rest to me. I'll be taking Brent on his own journey so he can understand from his own perspective."

She quickly asked, "I thought he needed my help to see things in the spirit realm? What's changed?"

"Nothing, and everything!" I answered.

"Huh? Don't keep me in suspense, she exclaimed, tell me, please!"

I suggested that we move the conversation into their dining room and asked if we could wait for Brent to return so they could both hear what had to be said.

It didn't take long for Brent to have Greg settled. Once he was certain Greg was finally asleep, he hurried back to the living room but found it empty. This confused him because he'd wanted Hope to rest. Calling her name, she beckoned for him to come into the dining room so he rushed in expecting to hear about her wonderful journey. Thinking they'd be alone, he was surprised to see three of us sitting around the table waiting on him so we could have a heavenly board meeting.

Not only were the three of us seated at the table and Brent standing in the doorway with his mouth agape, four very large angels were present and they were very happy.

Brent asked, "What's going on?"

"Sit down sweetie." Hope urged.

"Why are we in the dining room? Can't we go to the bedroom and shut the door like we do from time-to-time?" He asked.

"Times have changed, it's not necessary to be so secret. Come in and sit down. Hope needs to tell you her story and then Spirit will be taking you to meet Jesus while I stay here with your family." Abba said.

"Yes, Sir!" Brent stammered.

For the next few minutes, Hope shared every detail about her day. Without missing a beat, Brent said he was very eager to have his own turn. That's when Abba asked Brent a question, "Do you know what it means to have my presence here in a tangible way? It means something wonderful has happened in the spirit realm. We are here tonight to let you and Hope in on the turn of events."

"Why us, Father? What have Hope and I done to be blessed with this honor?" Brent asked.

"I'm glad you asked. Your generation is the last one to experience old beliefs and ways of thinking. It's what we call a paradigm shift or end of an age. The shift in thinking began with your parents. Many years ago, before either of them married things got very hard and through the pressure, your parents never deflected, they toughed it out and flourished. They were faithful to me and my son all their lives and when they married and had children their mission passed down to you. Now, your selfless act has begun to bear fruit and for that, we are very grateful." Abba shared.

Brent said, "Father I think we need a history lesson. What did our parents do that caused this turn of events?"

"Think! You have a brilliant mind, use it! What lies between the ink and page of every Bible? It is my Word followed by events. A reaping! After a community's seed-time there must be a harvest, and this also happens every third or fourth generation. This cycle is just a wheel within several other wheels which are all turning at the same time. Your grandparents were the first generation to question religious beliefs, then your parent's. Now it's your turn. At the beginning of every cycle, spiritual children get their beliefs grounded through a relationship with Jesus. Their beliefs create the seed which forms the new generation's behaviors. Jesus re-sets and corrects lifestyles ruined by Satan. The two of you, with Mamie, have confronted the enemy alongside my son and without even knowing it, spiritual children were born.

When you and Hope married, you vowed to help others plow through issues so they wouldn't have to suffer like you did? It blessed me greatly and from that very day, you started creating spiritual, not flesh-obsessed children!" Abba joyfully shared.

"Are you talking about Greg and our baby?" Brent inquired.

"No, boy! I'm talking about spiritual kids. Two very special young women were spiritually created through your Young Adult's Group. Now they've become gifted and are willing to help gather souls into this new way of thinking." Abba declared.

"Who are you talking about, Father? Brent asked.

"Why, it is Caylee and Gina of course." Abba enlightened.

Hope chimed in by asking, "I don't understand. I knew we were grooming Gina, but Caylee? How? Mamie was her mentor, and I only thought she was assisting us. When did she become one of the team?"

Abba laughed, long, and hard before replying to Hope's question, "Mamie brought her to church and helped mold her morality, but she slipped into your special team quietly without being noticed, simply with child-like faith. She took after her spiritual dad, here. Brent taught her well and by example, he showed her a simple easy way to understand how to lean on the Lord. If it weren't for Caylee explaining her faith to Gina, Gina would still be lost."

Hope probed deeper, "Does she have a gift and an angel like us?"

"Sure, she does! Her gift is maintaining joy, showing grace, and having compassion that few people can understand. Some would say she is over zealous and she opens herself up for hurt, that she attracts people who are starving for pure love but will eventually abuse her kindness and run away from her. Truth is, they fear what that type of exuberant joy has on someone.

Her angel is Ox's twin brother and he stays close to Jesus. He doesn't have to follow Caylee around because Jesus will be continually on the lookout for her. Resting by Jesus' side is where he can watch Caylee and it keeps him from having a warrior mindset. Even though he is beast-like in appearance, his whole demeanor is like Caylee's, exuberant and fun-loving." Abba informed.

"Huh! That explains everything. We were always trying to reign her in because she was too gung-ho. Thinking back, Caylee was always around, willing, and available whenever we needed her even when things got hairy." Hope shared.

"She's a treasure!" Abba said.

Brent asked, "What do we do now? Nurture more young adults?

"No! It's time the two of you retired from the Young Adult Group. Let someone younger take on the responsibility." Abba answered.

"What is in store for Gina?" Hope asked.

"Gina is one hundred percent convinced that I exist so she and Ox will be focused on changing people's thoughts about me and bringing in the lost while Satan's strongholds are being exposed." He answered.

"I'm confused," Brent said.

Abba said, "Your patience is a virtue, Brent. I can tell you are eagerly desiring your own turn with Jesus and seeing what He uncovered, but you need to be informed first."

It was my turn to enlighten Brent, "Darkness has been removed, exposing how Satan blinded people from the truth about a loving God and then manipulated them into believing He was a wrathful and punishing Father. Now, you'll be able to see people are greedy and exploiting each other. Jesus can't stand by and allow this to continue, that is why we follow the cycle we mentioned earlier. One day there will be a last and final generation, but only God knows when that will materialize.

Just prior to the new age, churches won't even be able to change things because they would have reverted to preaching the law all over again. When the law is preached, judgment begins and fingers begin to point, causing alienation of people who are already hurt, making them avoid church, and blatantly rebel against everything resembling religion. Instead of love and acceptance, condemnation is preached with a threat of hell if the rules aren't kept and the people God loves so much will turn away from Him and become addicted to pleasures, obsessed with greed and envy.

Someone had to set a boundary so Jesus pressed the reset button, once we selected this group to help with the task. Keep in mind these people were Satan's targets and his influence has twisted their thinking and they will do anything to keep their beliefs. They are graceless loudmouths full of hot air, and very dangerous just like their master; Satan.

You will be dealing with these predators, just remember their mindsets are warped, and their souls are lost. Save some if you can without using religious references. We will be there to guide you and show you who can change as well those who must be locked away. Abba wants nothing more than children seeking Him so they can live a clean and healthy life without convictions brought on by religion and evil influences. The District Attorney's position helps open doors in God's kingdom, and will turn the community around for the greater good. You'll get to use the brain we gave you correctly."

"When will this process start?" Brent asked.

"The process starts when Jesus shows you what He and Hope uncovered," I answered.

"Can I go to Him now?" Brent asked.

"Sure. It's time! Abba will stay here and babysit."

Soothing the Advocate's Emotions

Brent was so eager to be on the spiritual journey I didn't have to suggest that he remove his spirit from his physical body. He focused and within seconds, spiritual Brent was standing with me poised and ready to fly.

I hated to burst Brent's bubble, but he wasn't going to fly on Justice's back the way Hope did on Insight's. Brent would have to run alongside his cat. Brent had strong spiritual muscles, as well as physical ones, and they suited him for this very purpose. He was well developed to handle the exertion, where Hope's delicate condition required her to be seated and fly on Insight's back.

"Gird up your loins, Brent. Justice isn't waiting on you, he smells fresh kill and needs to eat, so it's time you run." I declared.

Brent's facial expression was comical. He was shocked, but he didn't hesitate and took off running with his cat. With ease, I caught up and ran alongside the two of them and heard Brent shout, "This is exhilarating! Free to run without bindings!"

He was beaming and totally in his element flexing every muscle to the limit. His thoughts were fun and carefree, *"This is wonderful! I can run faster than a race car and I'm not even winded. Things are clear and vibrant! I can even see bugs on the plants as I pass."*

"What is driving you forward, Brent?" I shouted.

"The smell of cleansing blood." He answered back.

"Bravo! You smell Jesus! He can't get away from the glorious fragrance and it is magnified, when something evil had been killed. In his honor, the spirit realm releases the smell from the Lord's bloody sacrifice to re-establish his forgiveness all over the Earth. Let the aroma guide you, seek Him out!" I urged.

The smell was like fresh flowing wine, not coagulated blood that smelled stagnant and putrid. When we arrived by Jesus' side, we found Him standing over an ugly beast that had been killed by an angel. The spiritual place was replacing death's smell with the smell of life and the beast's flesh provided food for Justice.

Jesus was very happy to see Brent and me, and happy Justice was cleaning up a bloody mess. He even leaned down, greeted the cat, and gave him a loving ear rub while he ate. Then He said, "Gentlemen, I've been waiting for your arrival."

Brent bowed, "Lord this is an honor. I'm very excited to see things from your viewpoint so I can serve you better in my new position back home."

"I'm very glad you feel that way, Brent. Your actions have proven to us that you are very wise. Since you were a small boy you have needed to know the truth and sought and dug for answers. That curiosity is what made you become our attorney." Jesus replied.

Brent agreed with what Jesus said, but remembered it wasn't until he'd ran back to the Lord during college, that he could figure things out more clearly.

"Lord, you gave me the ability to see things more clearly. You never failed me when I asked for help and understanding." Brent said.

I watched Jesus get serious and look Brent squarely in his eyes. He took a deep breath and sighed before saying what was on His mind, "There was one time you thought I failed you. Be honest with me, and bring your argument to me before we go any further with my plans. The air between us has to be clear so there will never be another doubt in your mind again."

Brent struggled with the issue and his eyes grew cloudy from unshed tears. I knew he was about to come to grips with the issue he hadn't let Jesus help him get over. Day after day, he dwelled on Hope's abuse and his hatred of Sam, her ex-husband. The question Jesus referred to was a sore spot in Brent's mind.

Brent's tight lip made Jesus ask again, "Brent, it is time you take the man out of your pocket and talk to me about him. If we don't settle this now you will be of no use to me, even if you have the knowledge of Solomon."

Brent squared his shoulders and clenched his fists before blurting out, "Why couldn't I ask Sam some questions? Why did Father take the man's life and dismiss my quest for justice? It doesn't make sense! What possesses a man to hurt a helpless woman, my woman! Hope is so sweet! What made Sam so mean? Every day I have wanted to punch something when I think about what he did to my sweet wife. Now, I wonder if Hope will be healthy enough to carry our baby the minimal term for its survival and it all stems from what the monster did to her. I need justice! I want justice!"

Sighing, Jesus said, "Now don't you feel better? Harboring those questions inside your heart had made you sick. Since your thoughts are naked to me, you are on the way to being healed. I can give you justice by dealing with the issue correctly. If Sam had lived, your anger would not have allowed you to give Sam a fair trial."

Brent fell to his knees in utter shame. Jesus was right he wouldn't have been able. He wasn't sure he was able now so he bowed his head to hide his face before saying, "Lord, forgive me, please! I promised Hope I would forgive and forget about Sam, but I haven't been able to do it. Help me! Show me what my heart and mind need to know."

Before saying anything else to Brent, Jesus summoned Sam's spirit from heaven to stand before Brent and with His help the proper questions would be answered. Brent's face went pale when he realized what Jesus had done and an inquisitive longing began growing in his heart as the man he hated most was standing before the three of us to stand trial.

Jesus demanded, "Brent, look at me! I am here so you can interrogate Sam appropriately, ask your questions, Sam wants to answer them."

Brent jumped to attention and went face-to-face with the villain he thought he hated so much. It was then he realized Sam was dressed in a covenant robe, glowing from the inside out because he had been in heaven. All at once, every ounce of bluster vanished. When Brent found his voice, he asked Sam, "Why are you in a covenant robe? Didn't God send you to hell?"

Jesus and I had the pleasure of hearing Sam's answer, "No, I received grace and forgiveness from God as well as from Hope that day. Otherwise, I would have been damned."

Brent asked, "Hope and I thought the Father shot you?"

Sam laughed, "No, He didn't. He only pointed the gun at me to show me how it made Hope feel. I'm the one who pulled the trigger. He gave me the choice to live or die."

"Why?" Brent asked.

"Because, there wasn't anything I wanted more at that moment than to be in His arms forever. When I realized that I was free from Satan and had finally found true love and acceptance, I didn't think twice. I also knew if I stayed on Earth I'd have to pay the piper and the rest of my life would be hell. After shooting that guy and beating Hope, my own mental torture would have slowly killed me." Sam truthfully answered.

Brent's anger rose to the surface again, and he demanded, "Why did you continually hurt her? What did she ever do to you that made you feel you could beat her for it?"

Sam answered, "I was very insecure. I wanted a toy and she wasn't willing to be that for me. Hope was a free spirit and I hated that about her. She couldn't see I wanted her undivided love, lock, stock, and barrel."

"Toy! Did you need a plaything? What possessed that thinking?" Brent demanded.

"My parents! They made me feel unloved, useless and said I was an embarrassment to them. The more I tried to change to make everyone happy, the more I ran for a drink. Drinking made me feel strong and Satan used it to torment me. When I was under the influence of alcohol, he had me. I thought I was powerful and I was determined not to have anything ever insult me again. Little did I realize that everything insulted me, not just Hope. My lifestyle itself was insulting." Sam shared.

Brent relented some after hearing that. The mercy of Jesus was finally seeping into his heart to help him cope before asking another question. "Were you ever in love with Hope? Did you ever want to know the real person?"

Sam said, "No, I loved myself. All I wanted was a pretty woman like her to want me. I don't think I ever took the time to really know Hope. It was seeing how the other guys desired her that made her interesting to me. I didn't care about her needs or wants. When we divorced, I was driven to win her back as a trophy even if she was broken in the process. It wasn't until she'd forgiven me and released me from Satan's grasp that I came to terms with the way I felt and in a split second, God helped me see what I needed. I needed love, not something or someone to possess.

Hope's love for Jesus changed me and opened a door for God to show me the truth through her eyes. I was finally happy and I wanted it to last forever. Man, living with God and Jesus is amazing."

The festered pocket around Brent's heart burst and all the anger spilled out, leaving him compassionate and feeling justified. He'd tried Sam on Jesus' terms and grew wiser from the experience. He was even able to thank Sam for agreeing to the interrogation and Sam said it was the least he could do after Hope forgave him and showed him peace.

Our gentle giant was totally drained, hate was gone and his questions answered. Jesus wrapped His arms around Brent and let him cry. It took a few minutes before Brent could say, "Thank you, Lord. I should have come to you long ago."

Jesus shared, "I knew it was hurting our relationship and I couldn't allow that to continue. Are you ready to walk with me now? I'd like to show you what your amazing bride did for me today."

Brent shook his head, "Take me around your town and show me the correct way to bring your kind of justice and explain to me how my having this position will heal our community?"

"I am planning to help you with every task. Don't worry. You and I are going to be the winepress plucking out parasites. We will know by the way people speak whether they are guilty or innocent." Jesus answered.

"How will this help people find the Father?" Brent inquired.

"Some will listen to simple hints. Others need a strong verdict. I hate that, but jail often opens a door for some to listen to the truth. Father often locks away people to prevent them from hurting and influencing others with evil plans and schemes. It's His loving nature that spares them man's death sentences while keeping the innocent from danger. There is no other way." Jesus exclaimed.

"When will we start?" Brent asked.

Jesus grinned, and then answered, "I want you and Hope to enjoy the holidays first. Relax and enjoy each other while the angels and I finish tearing down these strongholds. You'll get to visit with me often. It is time the two of you got to know Abba better. Find out just how much He really loves you. Don't worry about Hope, she will carry and deliver a healthy Shiloh; just not to full term."

It was time for Brent and me to begin our journey back to where we started. When we arrived, Justice, Brent's big cat, was already at home lazily bathing himself after his large meal. Brent was extremely tired so I gently assisted him back into his body so he could sleep. The next morning, he awakened by a ravaging appetite that was reacting to an aroma coming from his kitchen.

Hope was apparently cooking a feast, so he hurriedly ran downstairs to find Abba wearing an apron, and helping her cook. Brent filled his plate and while he ate, we all I got to listen to him re-enact every detail of his journey. He even had the pleasure of telling Hope that Sam said, "Thanks."

The Face Off

While Brent and his small family rested, Abba recommended that we visit Jesus to see how far things had progressed. When we found Him, He was deep inside what used to be Satan's dark territory and He was finishing off one of the giants who had a stronghold over the financial systems in the area. Jesus' face lit up like the sun when He realized we were there.

He came over to greet us and said, "You're just in time as I'm just finishing! It won't be long now before Satan shows up and sees what we've done. Find a comfortable spot and rest while we clean up our mess. Then you can watch Satan and I play "who's king of the mountain" all over again."

Abba said, "Son, it may be the same game but it never gets old to us. Seeing you put the old serpent back in his place is total satisfaction."

"One day I wish he'd quit trying to turn things upside down. We've taken his authority away from him, why won't he give up? Jesus asked.

"Pride keeps Satan bound and incapable of surrender. Even before I kicked him out of heaven his desire was to be the most beautiful, the most powerful and intelligent angel ever created. He hates me for stripping him of the material glory. That is why he'll use anything he can to take it from my people and then turn them away from believing in me. He will never admit it, but he still wants all my attention and since I won't give it to him, he'll do anything to keep my children from focusing on me. He vowed to hate me for eternity, when in truth, he really wants my love and adoration. You are the only person he couldn't control and because of you, the children can fight his influences. He hates you! You remind him continually of his humiliations and eviction. That's why he doesn't stay away long, he wants to humiliate you by making people deny me and your sacrifice to win them back. He'll roam around in the spirit realm for centuries if necessary until he finds someone on Earth lacking knowledge of our love and acceptance, so he can begin to mess things up again. All it talks is one person to ruin many.

After each shift, my influence over people affects him differently. He then sets out to learn what will make people deny me all over again. Each time there will be a bewitching based on what people fear or don't understand. Slowly fear invades communities as well as churches until more people begin taking things into their own hands and not praying to me for help. Like I said, it only takes one empty soul to turn others into idol worshipers all over again so they use my resources for personal gain instead of helping and sharing with others. Self-induced prideful people will make Satan cocky and we will go around and around again." Abba explained.

Jesus questioned, "What do you want me to do; go easy on him?"

"No!" Abba quickly countered.

"Then what?" Jesus asked puzzled.

"I want you to continue until I'm certain I have more family members than he has followers. When I hear, and see that my Jewish family wants me more than the rituals and religion they've established, I'll be ready to put an end to this nonsense, but not until then. I proclaimed this through the Apostle John.

I still get angry when I remember what Satan did to them. I never meant for my Israel, my firstborn nation, to bow down to a set of commands. All I wanted was for them to understand I was with them and they didn't have to lie, steal, kill or covet anymore. Everyone was equal in my eyes and they shouldn't disrespect each other, or trick each other to have things. I am willing and ready to provide for them when they ask.

The day I presented myself to them on Mt. Sinai, my intentions were to appear all powerful for them; not scary or threatening. I wanted them to see I was their protector and nothing would be bigger or more powerful, but Satan used my declarations of love against me and twisted their thinking. He made them think I was deadly. He took my words and made them sound like commands people had to follow and work through to receive my approval. They didn't realize regular people could not follow a set of spiritual rules. My love for the world is why I sent you to prove him wrong. You can't stop! Satan is a liar and everyone and everything thing must see I am a loving God, not an Ogre, a true Father. Eventually, my firstborn nation will see the truth, and learn they don't have to stay jealous of others.

Keep doing things your way. I know Satan better than anyone and he won't stop twisting my original message. He'll find ways in each generation to keep those rules front and center. So, do what you must do, prove him wrong, thousands of times if necessary. I enjoy seeing your new strategies, and they make this battle you call "a game" very entertaining.

I've explained to Spirit how he was to assist in this mindset change so people could come back to me. He will make sure love and acceptance are preached. Some churches will rebel and continue to condemn and convict. People will bounce around from church-to-church trying to find peace of mind. Eventually, grace will win over causing all to commit to peace, love, and acceptance and the anti-Christ mindset will dry-up and die-out and true Christ followers will emerge." Abba answered.

Jesus nodded in agreement. Then He stated, "I hate seeing Satan infiltrate churches and use leaders to influence people into becoming prideful, and exclusively giving Christianity a bad name. So, I fully understand what you mean.

I have a lot of work ahead of me; communities to restore, houses to clean, and children to influence. So, let the games begin!"

God was happy we were all in agreement, so He made a demand, "Satan, come here now!"

We heard a growl in the distance and we turned our eyes towards it and saw a dusty cloud approaching fast. Satan was on his way and making a mess in his wake. Abba and I found seats safely out of the way so Jesus could have center stage with Satan and Abba jokingly asked me, "This show will take a while. Want some popcorn and a soft drink to wash it down? I've developed a liking for them since Brent's party."

We sat back wondering if we would see the same old game played out again. Satan didn't prove us wrong, and he arrived on the scene like always, mad as a hornet because Jesus and I managed to humiliate him again. He complained about everything, saying we didn't fight fair and used something foolish to trip him. Then he pretended to be upset that Jesus destroyed his strongholds. He even pouted a bit. After this show, he did something strange, straightened his back and called Jesus a coward. He claimed the Lord didn't have the nerve fight him one-on-one and accused Him of tearing down his place while he wasn't looking. He hissed, "At least I bind people's minds before taking their goods but you don't have the nerve to attack me.

We listened to them banter and argue for hours like two roosters and as I watched, it reminded me of paradigm shifts that occurred in the past. In Moses' day, the people moved, but now things were different with Jesus, He made Satan leave or bound him for a season. Today's threats were sounding more like those of Moses, because Jesus was declaring and threatening Satan's authority in a similar fashion. Satan hollered at Jesus saying how he'd made snakes out of wise men and caused the people to trust more in a book than in Him. He even baited Jesus by saying people could quote the book line by line as if they were slaves to the written word instead of believing in God's spoken Word.

Jesus didn't counter.

Satan thought he had the edge and continued to bait the Lord. He said, "It's different from being on Earth in your fleshly body now, isn't it?"

Jesus threw His hand up in Satan's face, indicating the argument was over, and He ordered, "Satan is it time you stop talking! Your threats have no power over me! The Father has shown me the end from the beginning and everything in between. Pack-up your baggage and leave."

Satan had to have the last word, one more threat, "Oh, I'm leaving. I'll be back, but in the meantime, my angels will not relinquish anything to your people, even if you bind and gag me. They've been told to leave nothing standing; including some of your faithful churches. My home in the spirit may be gone, now I'm returning the favor. The harlot belongs to me and I'm going to kill her.

Let's see if your precious people can find any love left after she is dead. Matter can't exist without her and everything that came from her can't reproduce. I've made sure of it! Once the spirit of creation is gone, the world as people know it will cease to exist and my resting place will thrive. Wait and see!"

We watched Satan slither away with his head held high. This was going to be a different battle than the ones before because he'd left too smug. To my amazement, Abba burst into laughter and His joy began to invade us, "Boys, Satan thinks he has us stumped! He will never get that I'm watching and in control. His threats were for me and he divulged his plan. The old idiot always falls into his own trap."

Gina Forced to Tell All

We love weddings. The first holy matrimony we witnessed was between Gina's parents. They had a very sweet ceremony in Pastor Reed's office to be followed by Mamie and Doc's simple church wedding the very next week. When they tied the knot, there wasn't a dry eye in the crowd.

Today was Cindy Grover and Frank Addison's wedding day. Their wedding was no simple affair as it was over the top extravagant. Cindy had to have the most expensive ceremony she could afford. She hasn't learned how to love the simple things yet and Frank didn't want to complain. Overall, the wedding was lovely, honest, and pure.

Most of our team visited the reception but didn't stay long so the married couple could leave quicker. Abba and I had informed Hope the day before Frank's wedding, that Gina would be sharing her secret with them that day. She planned a huge meal, so everyone could relax, arranged for Greg to spend the night with his grandparents, hoping the atmosphere would make it easier for Gina to talk about her gifts and the relationship with Wade.

Brent wasn't surprised when his brother Carl suggested the guys go to the Boys' Home and spar so they could work off the heavy meal. Of course, Brent declined but watched the other men's reactions to Carl's suggestion. Russ hesitated with the notion, but Caylee encouraged him to have fun with the guys. Mamie ran Doc off by convincing him that he needed to rest a few hours before his night shift started at the hospital. Both men had easy carefree relationships with their mates.

Brent hadn't expected Wade's lack of consideration for Gina's feelings. He was rude and didn't ask if she minded that he went, and he even ordered her to take Caylee home so he and Russ could ride together. The realization disturbed him. Wade was being

81

domineering instead of cherishing and it brought to Brent's mind how Hope must have lived with Sam. Seeing Gina's face grimace caused his emotions to snap. To my side, I heard Abba snicker. Apparently, Brent was reacting just the way He wanted him to act about Wade.

In Brent's mind, I could see his thoughts were to give the younger man a tongue lashing. Hope stopped him and whispered softly in his ear, "Let him go, honey. Remember we need you here and focused on Gina. There is more to this than meets the eye."

Brent agreed and stayed with the women so they could hem Gina in a corner forcing and her to talk. Not one for patience, Hope asked the first question. "Gina, something is going on, spill the beans. We know you're keeping secrets from us."

Gina flushed red and then turned her horrified gaze towards Caylee. In her own defense, Caylee threw up her hands and said, "I promise I didn't tell them anything!"

Gina sputtered, "If not you, then who did?"

I wasn't about to sit still, watch or listen to my girls quarrel over something Abba planned, so I entered the conversation and demanded, "Stop it! Gina, don't you know by now that all the people in this room are connected. Secrets are not supposed to be hidden between any of you. It is time for you to tell everyone present what you've really been through and begin acting like you are part of the family you are transplanted into then all your dreams will fall into place."

Embarrassed from her outburst, Gina bowed her head and apologized. Then she asked me where she should begin and I suggested she start at the beginning when she first submitted to the call.

She didn't hesitate because she had wanted to tell them everything for a very long time. She told them it was Caylee's happy demeanor that convinced her to welcome Jesus into her life. They already knew what happened later with Lyle Horne. What they didn't know was how I convinced her to move ahead. This is where she froze, she was afraid they wouldn't believe her, and seeing her fear, then the loss for words, Caylee jumped in to assist, "Gina had an angel show her the future."

Gina sat back and waited for a few seconds to see how Caylee's words affected them and she was happy to see the news didn't affect them negatively which gave her encouragement. Hope put her at ease, "Gina, we've all been on some kind of journey. This isn't something strange to any of us. Please continue your story, we really want to know."

With a greater confidence, Gina proceeded to inform them of how the angel led her to where she would find a true soul mate. She was shown the man proposing, the marriage, and the birth of a baby girl before being harshly awakened from the coma by Satan. She told them how the grief was worse than her physical pain. Then Mamie and Hope came to her aid and Hope helped her find me, the one she calls "Whisperer."

She went on to explain how she and Ox developed a friendship and told them how he kept her from making a fool of herself in front of Wade's brother. Then she carried her story home saying Jesus' face made a difference, but only after Mamie told her Wayne was married. It was Jesus and no one else who rescued her when she wanted to die, because her every emotion was filled with anguish, and screaming from being so hurt and angry.

Then abruptly, her voice changed and she said sweetly, Jesus took away her fears. He convinced her they were one and nothing could break the connection. That realization changed her and helped focus and direct her anger towards Satan. When she did, she forced him under her feet. Then she said, Abba appeared to prove to her that Jesus would keep His promises and after that took place, Wade appeared, confirming that he was her soul mate.

Even after Gina finished telling her story, Hope wasn't satisfied, she wanted to know more, "Gina, what was the power Jesus gave you? I've shown you mine, you've seen Brent's and Mamie's so it's time you told us what you can add to our group. You've even experienced Caylee's power at every turn."

Startled by what Hope said, Caylee blurted, "I have a power? No, I don't!"

Hope growled at Caylee, "Yes you do! You have this overwhelming joy and super exuberance that drives us nuts but seems to draw needy people to you like flies. Can you be quiet for a few minutes, please?"

Hope focused again on Gina, "What is your gift?"

Rather than speak, Gina stood, looked towards me, and burst into a beautiful blue flame. Then she declared, "I have the power to ignite a flame to exude pure love or extreme rage. Its use is unknown to me."

Abba snickered again and it occurred to me that Brent had been quietly listening until that point. Then I noticed that he was fidgeting, which was not a good sign. His advocacy nature was working overtime, causing him to wonder what Gina was really feeling especially towards Wade. The fatherly instinct also came to life and he bluntly asked, "Gina, are you happy?"

His concerned threw Gina over the edge into anger. It made her realize that she was emotionally drained from fighting off Wade's advances and getting nowhere with him on a spiritual or emotional level. Abba snickered again when Brent rushed to Gina's side. No one in the room heard Abba's snicker but me. I knew He was up to something and before I could stop him, Brent had wrapped his huge bear like arms around Gina while she was still in flames of anger. Instantly, there was a power exchange and Gina's body gave Brent her fire's full strength. His eyes grew wide from shock, but he held tight to Gina. His mind and chest began heaving like bellows because they were on fire! He didn't know how to handle the power and struggled between his love for Wade and Gina's rage. The one he chose to side with was the rage against Wade.

Trying to control himself, he spoke as calmly as possible into Gina's ear, "Tell me what's wrong between you two and how we can help."

Gina gently pushed herself from Brent's embrace and admitted to all of them that Wade was nothing like she had imagined. Then, she confessed he was rude at times and other times he was very sweet. She also said Ox was always having fits and snorting flames in Wade's presence. That's when Abba snickered again and it occurred to me, Abba, not only babysat, He was playing around. The women were laughing but Brent was growing angrier by the second and no one knew what he was feeling except Abba and me. He was wrapped in Gina's rage and couldn't break free.

I tried to defuse the pending problem by encouraging Mamie to talk about something else. Instead of talking about something pleasant and happy, she talked about the rocky times she'd had over the years. I nudged Brent to speak about his family, hoping it would calm his emotions and bring happy emotions into the present. He said we had hard times too. Hope chimed in saying she'd been unhappy until she visited their church and heard Pastor Reed preach. After that, they became unnaturally quiet. So, quiet, we could hear air circulating in the room.

Brent managed to stay in control until Gina finished telling them all her secrets, then things took a turn for the worst. His defensive nature overrode his judgment when Gina said Abba asked her to stay pure by abstaining from sex until marriage, but she was having trouble with Wade's inappropriate advances and hurtful comments. Her words let the cat out of the bag, and I mean the big cat! Justice roared loudly! He wasn't dumb, he knew a demon must be controlling Wade actions and he wanted its blood. When Brent heard his angel's angry roar, his ears suddenly caught on fire. Then he became completely engulfed in Gina's supernatural rage and it caused him to burn all over his body, not just in his mind, will and emotions. Abba laughed loudly, alarming Hope. Noticing

Brent's appearance made her curious, she wanted to reach out to him but thought better of it and restrained herself.

Hope tried speaking to Brent but he would not look her way. Nothing she or Gina said made a difference in the way he was thinking. Justice was roaring loudly for vengeance and Brent couldn't hear past that sound. His mind was reeling and being twisted into a raging force about Wade's actions. He was consumed with the thought of Wade acting like another Sam. He was afraid for Gina, so to keep from going insane, he condemned Wade along with Justice's need for blood.

He looked like a crazed animal and I couldn't stop his pacing. Gina cried for Brent not to overreact, but his thoughts were being controlled by Justice's need to hunt. The calm, mild-mannered Brent was gone as he had turned into a beast.

By this time, my cool, and calm emotions were fading. I was worried about Hope. Abba had to keep Hope calm for Shiloh's sake, but He was on the other side of the room grinning like a Cheshire cat. I calmly whispered to Hope that Brent was focusing more on confronting Wade than on not upsetting Gina. I didn't tell her anything else because Abba had taken the responsibility of calming her nerves.

After leaving the house, Brent's mind was in turmoil, he didn't care that Wade was Gina's intended husband. What he cared about was having this intended man apologize to his spiritual daughter, even if he had to beat Wade to a pulp to obtain it. He couldn't idle around and allow him to become like Sam. His spiritual body needed to run but his fleshly feet couldn't run to Wade fast enough. So, he grabbed his car keys, spun out of the driveway in an urgent trek to the Boys' Home in search of Wade.

A Father's Rage

Abba thought it funny that I was confused and without any direction, especially since this was a dramatic situation that had devastating potential. All He was doing was grinning and snickering. It wasn't until Brent left the house that Abba's words finally made sense to me. I remember Him telling Hope that Brent was chosen for a specific mission. There have been many occasions He wanted to face someone and didn't because he didn't want to be feared. Brent was doing the face-to-face confrontation for Him. Plus, it would finally help Brent heal physically as well as emotionally in the end. He deserved an outlet and Wade would survive and come out thinking and acting as he should.

Calming down a bit, I asked Him, "What is going to happen? I didn't see this coming."

"Wade is about to have an attitude adjustment in more ways than one." Abba laughingly confessed.

Hope overheard our conversation and stated, "I'm going to my husband! He is acting crazy!"

I cocked my head and glared at Abba. He was responsible for this event so He needed to sooth everyone's emotions, not me. He walked over to Hope's side and said, "Stay here with me and the girls. You don't want to upset Shiloh. Brent will be home soon, pacified and his thirst for justice quenched. He is not alone, Justice is with him. I've also sent Ox so he can help control Brent's rage. This evening's events were prearranged and nothing will get the better of your husband. We've been frustrated with Wade lately, and Brent was chosen to correct him. Gina's accidental gift exchange was icing on the cake. Because Brent manifested into the beast I want to be at times but promised myself no one would ever see."

I decided to follow Brent and watch the events unfold for myself because things at the Boys' Home were about to get very interesting. I arrived a few minutes before Brent and went inside to hear the men discussing their women. When Brent walked inside, Wade was bragging about the way Gina looked. He finished his sentence saying he could hardly wait to have her between the sheets. The crude tone of Wade's words caused Brent's ears to burn. Then out of the corner of his eye, something else infuriated him. Not only were crude comments being made, they were spoken in the presence of very impressible boys. Justice roared! He knew what was making Brent upset. The Arnold's had spent years developing a respectful attitude into the boys' minds regarding women. Now, in one night, Wade was destroying all their work.

Justice was circling Wade, he and I knew what was causing the problem. An envious demon was attached to Wade's mind, and feeding off his thoughts. In truth, Wade was feeding, awakening a massive yet dormant hunger and no one could see this but me. Pure energy had engulfed Wade. He was being accepted, my men. But a much larger force was there to stop this madness at any cost. To Brent, Wade was crude and lustful and a threat of one day becoming violent towards Gina.

Justice and I locked eyes. He was letting me know he'd seen the envious demon latched onto Wade's mind. At that moment, I called the ugly thing out into the open so Justice could pounce. Ox, on the other hand, was holding rage's reigns loosely, until Brent loudly shouted for Wade to shut up. When the demon presented itself, Justice pounced and began to eat. Wade knew nothing of the spirit realm or what was happening and was offended by Brent's harsh tone, causing him to snap back, "What's got into you, man? Who died and made you the boss of me?"

Ox snorted, Brent saw red and the situation became volatile! I knew the whipping of all whippings was about to take place if something or someone didn't intervene. I prayed, I cried out to Jesus for Him to come and help these two men save their friendship. Brent was beyond controlling and my peace and comfort were not effective at this moment! He needed Jesus quickly, and on the scene; no one else could stop this madness.

I changed tactics while waiting on Jesus. I tried to slow things down by using Carl, encouraging him to diffuse the situation between his best friend and Brent. He said, "Wade, you've gone too far." Brent scowled at his brother and shouted for him to shut up. We both backed away after that, I couldn't risk having another man abused or injured when this was Abba's plan.

The battle was on! Wade was still clueless because he was living a life without me. Therefore, he was acting stupid and kept playfully baiting Brent, "You want a piece of me? Bring it!"

I had to get the younger boys out of the barn and out of ear shot, so I used Carl and Russ to take authority over them and get them into the main house. This fight was something they didn't need to see.

Abba had sent Ox, and this bantering between the two men was making him happy. When I confronted him, he confessed that ever since Wade had come into Gina's life, he wanted to smack him and that was why he was encouraging Brent and feeding the fire. When Brent tore his shirt off rather than unbutton it, I knew it was to intimidate Wade. He wanted the younger man to see what he looked like underneath the clothing. The action didn't lose effect, Wade blinked twice out of shock, but it was too late for him to apologize. Brent had also kicked off his shoes and was pointing to the ring, "I'm getting more than a piece of you, Wade! Pray, I don't rip you apart!"

Every muscle in Brent's body rippled and was ready for action, but Ox held onto his rage and kept him steady. My eyes fell on Justice. He wasn't satisfied with just one kill and was focusing still on Wade. I followed the big cat's gaze and realized there were another evil creatures attached on Wade. Justice didn't blink. He knew how to wait patiently for prey without losing control. Without being tethered, his energy helped fuel Brent's mind and the freedom to move also kept Brent's body loose and limber when he entered the ring.

At this point, I was sympathizing with Wade. Abba planned this match, and it wouldn't be pretty because Brent was assigned to remove what had Wade harnessed and using his mouth. Wade was in shock, mystified and wondered how Brent could be so muscular and toned underneath his suit and tie. He never entered in their playful bouts before and this hulk was very angry and focused on him.

Justice and I heard the little demon bait Wade. He kept saying, "you have two choices, act like a girl begging for mercy or stand up for yourself and fight." The silly demon taunted him to enter the ring rather than lose face. I watched Wade's mind cloud over with emotion. He hesitated, wondering whether to box or use karate and in that second of confusion Justice grabbed the demon and Brent's fist came down lightning fast against Wade's head, so hard it made the younger man stumble and grab his ringing ears.

Then Brent screamed, "That's for Gina!"

Before Wade could get his bearings, Brent lashed out again with a right uppercut to Wade's chin. The force caused Wade to badly bite his tongue. Brent screamed again, "That one is for damaging the little boys' minds and teaching them to disrespect women."

Flat of his face on the ring's mat, Wade spat out blood. The blood showed me Justice had ripped the controlling demon from Wade's mouth and killed the controlling thing. Wade was stunned. He couldn't believe what was happening and blurted out, "Man, you want to tell me what has gotten into you? If I didn't know better, I'd think you hated me."

Brent hollered back, "At this moment I do!"

Justice and Ox were satisfied! When Carl returned from the main house, he jumped into the ring and grab Brent's arms from behind saying, "Whoa, brother! You've made your point! Listen to me, look at me! We were all talking about our women. You just happened to walk in on Wade's comments. He thinks Gina is hot. We all are guilty of influencing the boys. It's all right! We are truly sorry. Let's all try and forget this ever happened! Take a few minutes and cool down, then you can tell Wade why you acted so violently. He doesn't know about Hope."

Brent smelled Wade's blood and it made him realize something evil had been defeated. That is when his mind returned to normal and his body collapsed onto the mat next to Wade. Brent's heart ached, it also dawned on him that he had hurt his friend. Overwhelmed by this fact, he placed his head in his hands and began to silently weep. It was obvious that he was completely deflated. All the pent-up rage stored in his heart against Sam had been released on Wade.

Abba got his way. Brent managed to do two things; spank Wade and release anger. The Sam issue was finally over for Brent, spiritually, physically, and emotionally and he could be who God created him to be. The first thing he did was to apologize to his friend, and seek forgiveness. Afterward, he began telling Wade Hope's story and how he'd felt about Sam.

Abba's ways are always higher than anything else. Brent couldn't function properly before because he wasn't completely whole until now. My job now, is to restore complete peace and trust between these men. Justice was served, blood had been spilled, the big cat ate and Ox was pacified that Wade had some sense knocked into him.

Things were turning around swiftly, and I knew why. The smell of sweet flowing wine was penetrating the air meaning Jesus was in the room with us. He had come because of my prayers and was assisting in forgiveness between everyone present. Our next step

91

would be easy. The atmosphere was ripe to usher Wade and Russ into my baptism. It was time these two men were equipped to serve alongside their chosen mates. This way, Brent could stop worrying, calm down, and be who he was designed to be rather than Abba's punisher.

The Big Reveal

Wade and Russ attentively listened to everything Brent had to say, even when he got to the part where he had to explain why he was angry. Jesus' presence helped him so he didn't hold back. He bluntly stated Gina was unhappy with Wade's inappropriate advances. This news upset Wade, because, until that moment, he thought all women liked sexual advances. Remembering back, he saw where his mother loved his dad's advances and she even reciprocated by flirting back. That was how Wade learned the art of seduction.

Wade commented, "Brent, I'm sorry, I never dreamed I was ruining her life. I thought I was paying her the ultimate compliment. I can tell you for a fact that Gina is meant for me, but I'm only human and I get over excited. I promise not to be as pushy the next time I get near her."

Brent questioned, "Why be pushy at all? If you know Gina is the woman for you why won't you commit and ask her to marry you? It doesn't matter if it has only been a few weeks. When you know, you know! She claims you are meant for her, so what's keeping the two of you from making it legal?"

Wade didn't answer Brent's direct question about marriage, he was more interested in the fact that Gina had claimed him. He asked, "She feels the same?"

"Yes, stupid, she does!" Brent countered.

"What did she say?" Wade asked.

"Do you really want to know, or are you just trying to find a way to get in her pants?" Brent demanded.

"I truly want to know Brent. I think if I heard what she told you and Hope about me then I'd understand what may be holding us back." Wade replied.

Brent changed tactics then asked another question, "Do you know the Holy Spirit?"

Wade replied, "Why, yeah! I was baptized when I was twelve."

"That's not what I asked. I asked if you had a personal relationship with the Lord Jesus." Brent questioned.

"I think so." Wade stammered.

Then Brent looked Russ in the face and asked, "How about you Russ, do you know Jesus?"

Russ answered, "Apparently, not the way you do, or you wouldn't be so serious about our answers."

I was getting ready for my entrance. Brent wasn't holding anything back. He was determined to have Jesus and me on board with Wade and Russ before he began telling them what Gina said in their group.

Brent enlightened, "Fellows, your two women have a better relationship with Jesus and His Holy Spirit than the three of us do with each other. They talk with them daily, one on one, and heed their counsel. So, before I tell you anything further I want to know if you would like to have the same relationship with them as you do with your two women. If you do, then I'd like to introduce you personally to Jesus and His Holy Spirit. They are watching and want you both as friends and brothers. How about it? Do you want to meet them?"

Wade's mouth was agape and Russ' eyes were very wide with amazement, but both nodded a yes in agreement to Brent's questions.

Brent said, "Great! Huddle up so I can invite them into your lives."

Brent's prayer was very sincere. He asked Jesus and me plainly in the hearing of these two men, to come and be a part of their lives. Then, he asked for us to prove ourselves and make ourselves known so there never would be any doubt we existed again. In Brent's very direct and blunt style, he asked with confidence, "If we would speak to Wade and Russ as well as show ourselves as their living and breathing God."

What happened next proved Jesus was real. His love enveloped the two men and surrounded them with His covenant blessing. When the water bubble appeared around them, even though it frightened them badly, the emotion fled and the fear of dying vanished after a few minutes. That is when I entered their hearts and minds with my eternal flame, showing them the process of baptism was finished and they were more than dead men walking on Earth.

To solidify the process of Brent's prayer, we materialized in front of all of them. The real proof of our existence did a miraculous thing, as it allowed us to wrap our arms around each other and welcome these two newborn believers into God's kingdom without any barriers between.

With us in their presence, Brent would be able to explain everything they needed to hear in a believable manner. The men sat quietly and listened to everything including the part about the angels. Afterward, I wanted to open a door where Wade could come clean about things in his past, so I said, "Allow me to start the interrogations, Brent."

He stepped aside and allowed me to speak, "Wade, please tell everyone why you hunger for acceptance from men."

Wade looked dumb-founded at me and then frankly replied, "I don't think that is any of their business."

Brent calmly urged, "It's time you began trusting in the Lord's guidance my friend. There must be a reason He wants us to hear or He wouldn't have asked you to explain yourself."

A few minutes passed. The Lord and I knew Wade was coming to terms with his heart and mind. With the two controlling demons gone, he wouldn't feel entrapped or ashamed any longer and would want to uncover a hidden secret. When he took a few deep breaths, stood, and popped his knuckles, we knew he was ready. All at once with a huge deep breath forcing out his words, he blurted, "Dad never loved me. He always favored Wayne."

Carl and Brent looked at each other puzzled. They'd grown up with Wade and Wayne and never sensed a rivalry or saw favoritism in their house. Brent couldn't wait for further details so he asked, "What made you think that?"

"Wayne got everything from Dad! I had to work for everything! Even when we were little Wayne had Dad's attention. I didn't know why. We were the same in every way, not just in our looks. We loved sports and medicine, but to Dad, Wayne's dreams were the only ones that mattered." Wade replied.

I relinquished the questioning, and Brent's inquisitive nature had been whetted and he dug deeper for answers, "What does that have to do with why you need acceptance from other men?"

Wade cried out in frustration, "Because Dad is dead, okay! He died before I could prove I was just as good as Wayne. I'll never get his approval! Having other men listen to me, even if they are younger gives me confidence and a sense of being respected."

"How do you usually find peace of mind when there aren't any men around for you to baffle and brag with?" Brent asked.

Wade was calmer now and wanted to be truthful, "I found release in the arms of women, and the more I had, the more I felt desired, and secure with myself."

"Ah! The truth comes forth!" Brent proclaims.

Wade responded to Brent's condescension by saying, "There is more to this than people know, and Mom is the only person who seemed to care about my hopes and dreams. She recommended that I join the service like her father had. Dad never mentioned sending me to college. I watched him dote on Wayne as if his own personal life depended on Wayne's success. Wayne went to college. I, on the other hand, scraped my way through night school while in the armed service and I finished medical school after re-enlisting by doing an internship on board a naval aircraft carrier. I graduated a few weeks prior to Dad's dying. I'd hoped to shove my papers in his face to prove I was the better man, but that dream died with him. I moved home to be with Mom and now I have a wonderful job working at the VA."

"What of the women? What changed for you? You stated they were how you found release. Are you still seeking them?" Brent asked.

I looked at Wade and lovingly gave him some encouragement. Jesus did also and he was able to answer truthfully again, "I slept with any girl that gave me the time of day before settling back home. I'd use one girl, and then move on to another. They were like changing clothes. Service men have one track minds, sex, sex, and more sex. We didn't care if they were pretty or ugly. The women gave us something in common. I got high fives from the guys and the sex was a bonus, a way of escaping parental failure. I thought to myself, '*Why not?*' I needed love as much as Wayne. If I couldn't get the kind of love and respect I needed from Dad, then I'd find it anywhere and anyhow I could. I was good at wooing women until I had a "come-to-my senses" meeting in Iraq."

The last comment piqued Brent's interest and he said, "Explain!"

"I came to my senses while I was helping with a retrieval mission in the desert. We were to locate a few injured men and then copter them back on board the carrier. I got separated from the guys and had to hunker down for a few minutes until they located me. It was during that time, the devil showed himself to me, horns, and all. I was stupefied! Then he spoke, declaring if I didn't stop using women as toys I'd wind up losing myself. He terrified me! I certainly didn't want to go to hell for having sex. I vowed to him I'd wait until I found someone I could love. Before he left, a cool breeze came over me and I had a vision of a lovely redheaded woman and a softer voice say, 'You'll find her working for justice and she will be wearing a cast on her leg.' I assumed Jesus came to rescue me because of my vow. It wasn't long after the incident that I received word about Dad's death. I returned home, found my job at the VA and reconnected with my good buddies. The rest is history!" He shared.

Brent suspected it was Ox who had met Wade in the desert and not the devil so he was having a hard time listening and not laughing in the man's face. When he found his composure, he asked, "So, you think the Lord showed you a picture of Gina in the desert, but it was the devil that scared you?"

Wade declared, "The dude had horns and a tail! Who else could it be?"

Brent was struggling not to laugh so I took over the conversation. "It was me, Wade. I'm the voice you heard that day on both occasions; the one you thought was Satan's and the other you assumed was Jesus. The large beast with horns is an angel. He had accompanied me. We wanted you to understand if you didn't stop seeking sex for relief you'd never find true love. By that time, Father God had already chosen Gina as your mate, but if you insisted on having your own way you'd never find her. We were very pleased you came to yourself that day. That is why we gave you some encouragement and showed you a glimpse of your future. We also gave Gina a glimpse of your life together so you would have a common bond. Grow from there, and learn your likes and dislikes. She loves being involved with medicine and she helps the mentally handicapped find peace and love. Work together as a team all through life."

Wade was amazed and asked me, "What angel has horns? I thought they all looked like men."

The look on Wade's face was comical and none of us could keep from laughing. I said, "Most do look like men but thousands more have animal like features. The angel you saw that day is Gina's guardian angel and he is very special. Ox lays down his life continually for those he loves. He represents Jesus' sacrificial nature and assists his human with faith issues. Without him, your lovely mate would be lost and in limbo thinking, Wayne had betrayed her. Satan's plan was to deceive her, and keep her from believing in Father. You see, Gina is your special gift. Treat her special because Father loves her dearly. If you do, you too will also be guarded and cared for by Ox."

Wade asked, "Can I see this angel? I want to thank him for finding me."

I granted Wade's request and said, "Ox, old friend, it's time for you to make yourself known to Gina's true soul mate. He won't think you are the devil any longer."

Ox materialized, Wade quickly backed away and Russ couldn't move. His size alone would intimidate anyone. When Ox bowed low in front of Jesus and me, Wade's composure softened and Russ moved behind Wade.

Once Russ found his tongue, he asked, "Does Caylee have an Ox?"

I replied, "Sure, would you like to meet him?"

Russ nodded.

"Cherub, would you please come visit us?" I called out.

Instantly, Cherub appeared and I made the introduction, "Russ, meet Cherub."

All this time, Brent was sitting patiently to one side of the group. When he saw how well the two guys were acclimating to the supernatural, he decided to ask Jesus to help the men understand their duty, "Lord Jesus, would you please explain to these two men why they are so important to you. You're the only one who can show them. You helped me to love Hope in a way I never knew possible."

"I'd love too," Jesus said. "Gather around me fellows, there is someone else you need to meet before I get started. Then after that, I'll explain your roles and what you need to know."

Wade and Russ scrambled to find a place to sit close to Jesus. When they were comfortable, Jesus spoke from His heart and asked them, "What is my priority?"

Both men shook their heads in bewilderment because they truthfully didn't know how to answer the question. Seeing their confusion, Jesus said, "Family! In order for everything to come together, you must accept the most important One in the trinity."

Then Jesus turned and faced Wade. Then He said, "Wade, you will never have to fear losing a Father's love ever again. My Father loves you no matter what and wants to be who you need."

Then Jesus faced Russ and declared, "Russ, you have a wonderful father, but he wasn't there to guide you through life. Abba wants to be your guide, your friend, and your confidant."

Afterward, Jesus looked skyward and said, "Father, I know you're listening to this conversation. Would you come join us so Wade and Russ can meet you?"

I looked over at Brent and as expected, he was excited that Wade, Russ, and Carl would be seeing Abba face-to-face and not any of them left out of this supernatural experience. All of them would be taught by the masters and become the men God designed.

Abba didn't make a grand entrance, He chose to fill the room with soft, moist fragrant air; He loved riding clouds. The men were dazzled and in awe when He slowly materialized in a human form. He was magnificent; tall, and well-built with beautiful white hair and beard.

Abba said, "Hello children! You have made me very happy, having you as part of my family makes me extremely happy. There is no greater joy for me. I am always listening, and please call on me anytime now that you know I exist. Now, I will let my son explain why you are here."

The three men were in awe. Determined to obey God, they focused on Jesus with spirits hungry for the truth. Jesus said, "Carl, you already have a family, but I still need you to listen to what I will tell the others. It is important all of you fully understand why family is important to me."

Carl nodded and agreed to listen. He didn't know that Jesus also wanted him to develop a greater love for Greta after hearing what He had to say. "Gentlemen, when I find women who care for me deeply, I fall in love. Greta and I are in love. Now, Gina and Caylee have both pledged their love to me. Their devotion to me allows me to provide for them. So, they can be provided for correctly, I've chosen you to be my vessels. You become extensions of me. Through you, I have arms, legs, and a voice on Earth. You are my entire body. Without your help, I'd never know physical love. I'd never have human children. In other words, I need you as much as you need me. So, I'm asking you to please share my life and love so we can provide for our women."

The men were very moved and overwhelmed they were deemed worthy enough to live and love for Jesus. It wasn't until that moment they really understood why they mattered. It was because Jesus continues to live through them as the son of God, and they had to love their women for Him. The impact of this mattered more than any sexual encounter or making a living, it meant bringing a holy family into existence.

After Jesus finished, all three men were overcome with a sense of guilt. They had been talking very degradingly about their women. They didn't know Jesus felt their shame and all three were shocked when He stood and said, "There is no guilt here! I've already forgiven your foul mouths and evil thoughts. You must forgive yourselves! You can do this by showing love toward our women. Star over if you must."

Abba shouted, "Amen! Remember you're talking about my girls. I don't like it when they're disrespected."

Finding Traction

Abba, Jesus, and I waited for questions where we could see if all three men understood. They asked a few questions but nothing to indicate they wouldn't accept Jesus' offer. In time, their new perspective of their women would develop and they would experience our wonderful lifestyles as a family unit. Their spiritual transformations made it easy for Abba and Jesus to bid a goodbye. I, on the other hand, had to stay on the sidelines with them where I could help direct their moves.

I enjoyed sharing the new brotherly love and being connected to these guys. It was going to be a delight watching as promises that were spoken before time began to seek them out. Brent had experienced some of the blessings already and he would be a great asset once the others began wanting more out of life. I was extremely happy. Renewing mindsets was my favorite job and I could hardly wait for their new assignments to kick into gear forcing them to ask me questions and relying on me for guidance.

It didn't take long before the men began to crave their mate's presence. Russ didn't know he could love Caylee any more than he did already. He saw her differently now as someone extremely precious and Jesus' treasure. The fact she had chosen him made his heart full. All he wanted was to love and take care of her for Jesus.

Wade, on the other hand, realized he hadn't seen past Gina's physical beauty until that night. He wanted to see the side of this woman who had a passion as strong as his for helping the broken. He couldn't wait to uncover other things she may love, mysteries inside this woman that God wanted him to find and nurture. He pictured unpeeling layer after layer to find out what made her tick as he enjoyed the process. This new challenge intrigued him and uncovering her heart meant more to him than having her body.

Gina was the first woman he ever had a desire to really know inside as well as outside. This revelation drove him to ask, "Who wants to give me a ride back to Brent's? If I don't see Gina tonight, I fear I may wake up tomorrow thinking this was just a dream."

Brent suggested, "Call my house first. She may already be gone, you did throw the keys at her, remember."

"You call!" Wade asked.

"I can't. I didn't bring my cell phone. Come to think of it, I don't even have my wallet, so if you want a ride you have to drive." Brent answered.

"Fine then! I'll drive you home and if she isn't there you can take me to my home. I have to see her, but I won't rush things." Wade agreed.

Russ said, "I've already called Caylee and she's still at your house talking with Hope and Mamie about our wedding. I asked her if Gina was still there so Wade could come by and she said Gina went home with a headache."

"Great! I've made her sick. Pray, I can get through to her somehow. If I don't apologize for my actions I won't be able to rest." Wade said.

Brent laughed, "Stop worrying and take me home, I know the ultimate prayer warrior."

———————

The plan was for me to stay with the guys, but Abba informed me Gina was confused and didn't need to be left alone. When He volunteered to be with the men again, I knew it was my cue to find Gina.

One whisper from me was all she needed and she confessed to being sad. She told me she needed a place to think, somewhere she felt secure and loved and decided to go to her mother's house after she left Hope's. It was a sweet gesture because she wanted to return to the place where she and I first got to know each other and had some of our most intimate moments.

She knew her parents were on their honeymoon and used a key to let herself inside. I found her in the kitchen weeping. I read her thoughts before saying anything else. She needed answers. Nothing was as she pictured. She and Wade were already past their fourth week together and no closer than when they met. She was also concerned for Hope and Brent. She had really upset Brent and talking about a Caylee's wedding was too depressing. Seeking my advice was all she wanted, so she faked a headache.

I knew Gina needed confirmation of Wade's transformation, so, I encouraged Brent to suggest they drive by the Grimes' home while He and Wade were en-route to his house. This way they would see Gina's car. Prophecy has a way of unfolding and as soon as Wade was home I convinced him to ride his motorcycle over to Gina's parent's home. Gina would be very grateful for this visit. The ride over to the Grimes' home gave Wade and me a chance to talk. He was a man bent on repairing a breach he'd created. To make the message clear to Gina, I gave him a gift that would signify he had nothing but pure love on his mind.

I made sure Gina was in the kitchen and properly aligned looking out the door so she would be ready to receive the final proof she needed that Wade was her true mate. Abba was also honing His hearing into the Grimes' home so He could also enjoy their meeting. Once I had her in place, I whispered, "Do you remember a vision we gave you of Wade from this kitchen door?"

She replied, "Yes Lord. Why?"

I said, "Turn out the lights and look out the kitchen door window. Trust me, I do not lie."

Ox couldn't stand it any longer, and he propelled himself into the kitchen. He had been flying over Wade's head and needed to be with Gina. He also wanted to see this beautiful promise manifest.

He and I watched her face light up when she saw Wade coming with his helmet on fire. She pressed her face to the window and focused her eyes on the vision which was the same we'd given her months before. She wasn't crippled this time! She could open the door and rush to the man outside because it meant the promise was kept and she had her soul mate. Her fears vanished. We owned their hearts. Now, it was time to develop their stories outside of the promise given.

Wade's face was just as radiant when he saw Gina watching him from the kitchen door. Time seemed to stand still for a few minutes as they adjusted to their new revelations. We didn't have to say anything because their love was having its own say. Gina opened the door only after Wade removed his helmet and when their eyes locked, they ran to each other and kissed intensely.

When Wade broke their kiss, he said, "Sweetheart, can you forgive me? I've been such a jerk! I don't know how to love you properly. Please teach or show me what I'm missing! I need you! Just remember, I am a male and will probably get sidetracked into lustful actions. Don't get me wrong when I say this, but I love the package your spirit lives in. You are gorgeous! If I do get too demanding, knock me upside the head. It'll remind me who is looking after you."

"Stop it!" She laughingly begged. "I forgive you! Whisperer promised me you'd come around. He said, if I waited, you'd come to me full of love for Him and acting like you should and I wouldn't have to worry if it appeared you just wanted my body. I will confess, though, I almost gave up and was about to admit defeat, and declare I was finished."

Wade asked, "What changed your mind?"

Breaking free from his arms, Gina walked over to Wade's bike, picked up his helmet, and looked at it closely before turning to face him. Then she answered, "Seeing this helmet actually on fire as you rode into the driveway changed my mind."

He was stumped by her statement and wondered, 'How would the flame painted on my helmet make a difference?' Clueless, he asked, "Why?"

Gina squinted her eyes and decided to make sure he knew what I'd told her. "Wade, do you believe in God-given signs or that some people may have particular spiritual gifts?

Wade knew she was baiting him, so he said, "I've accepted the complete Godhead. I have the Holy Spirit inside me and I've seen Ox. What else should I know?"

"Did Whisperer tell you about my gift?" Gina probed.

"Who is Whisperer?" Wade asked.

Gina said, "It's the nickname I gave the Holy Spirit."

"No! He told me you were very special to Him. Please don't hide anything from me, let's be honest with each other. After tonight, I'm ready to accept the weird with the amazing." Wade encouraged.

With a sweet smile on her face, Gina walked over to Wade while still carrying his helmet in her hands and said, "Months ago, Whisperer showed me a vision of you riding your bike. You were coming to me here, to Mom and Dad's house. That night I asked Him if you had the baptism and His answer was yes. Do you want to know why I asked Him that question?"

"Sure!" Wade replied.

"I asked because your helmet was on fire that night. Not like this picture painted on it, your head was on fire and fire is my gift. I can burst into two kinds of flame depending on my emotions. If I'm glowing blue it means I'm happy and content, but if I'm glowing bright orange, watch out. Orange means I'm mad, confused or I sense something has come against the authority Jesus has over me. This bright orange flame indicates an emotional rage brewing on the inside of me plus it also affects Ox and I don't know what to expect from him." She explained.

Wade asked, "What does this fire have to do with me?"

"I learned to live in the Holy Spirit's fire after receiving Him in my life so I wanted to make sure you lived in Him also and had the same gift given to me," Gina replied.

Wade asked, "May I see your flame?"

At last, Wade wanted to see past Gina's physical body into what made her special. Not only did his request make her happy it delighted Ox and me. Ox was hassling loudly and I watched in glee as Gina ignited into her gift and glowed a lovely blue.

Wade stood in awe. "Gina, you are beautiful!"

Then Wade heard a weird noise in the garage with them and it caused him to shout, "Who's there?"

Gina happily stated, "It's Ox! He was just letting me know that he approves of what we are doing. He wants you to ignite. Try it! Focus on the face of Jesus and allow love to flow through you."

Wade didn't like being watched and he had trouble focusing. To help him, Abba and I both materialized in the room to give him strength. Proving our love and support to Wade was all the young man needed and once he was convinced of this love, he too slowly caught fire. When he had the flame firmly established, he reached out for Gina to take his hand. When their fingers touched and their flames joined, the fire changed colors from blue to a shockingly bright white. The color white indicated to us that purity had entered and intense love and holiness would force all of evil's darkness away. Even in the darkest of hours, purity was a beacon for anyone or anything in times of need.

Abba jumped up and down shouting, "Awesome! Excellent! You've got my interpretation of love down pat!"

Surprised by Abba's exuberance, they released their hold on each other which extinguished the light and they asked in unison, "We have what down pat?"

"With my passionate love, of course! With me by your side, the two of you can force evil's dark powers away. Darkness will be afraid of you and Satan's strong influence can be turned away with love." Abba revealed.

Gina didn't hesitate to ask, "Father, I'm still confused. How will our love for each other force Satan away? I need you to explain this in detail. Please!"

"Later, child, everything will be revealed in time! Be happy, and begin learning each other's likes and dislikes. Start by asking things like what is your favorite color, favorite foods, or hobbies. Grow! You'll be surprised to find you have more than loving us in common. Try to stay pure, and Wade, keep your mind out of the gutter. Uncover your lady's heart, do things my way and you'll have no regrets." Abba shared, before turning into a vapor and vanishing.

After Abba left their presence, the two of them faced me. "What?" I asked.

"Could we please have some privacy? It feels like our parents are watching our every move. I want to get to know this woman without a chaperone." Wade said.

I didn't take offense at Wade's comment but politely exited saying, "you'll learn that you're never alone. Rest assured, if Abba and I aren't watching over you, Ox will be intently guarding Gina. Get used to this, you can no longer hide, and listen for Ox's growls." Call me nosey or overprotective, but I had to get the last word before taking my physical form away from them.

Wade asked Gina, "What did He mean by Ox's growl?"

Gina answered, "It's a long story and I'm not sure you want to know all the details?"

"Beats asking what color you like best, so tell me everything," Wade answered.

For the next two hours, Ox and I listened to their discussions. We were very pleased Wade wanted to know all about Gina's angel. In fact, I was so inspired that I decided it was time for Wade and Russ to have guardians, too. It only took a moment for Jesus and me to assign them two angels. Two from Ox's and Cherub's clan who would assist and help promote brotherly love once they adjusted to Earthly living.

Heart Cries

Carl was the first to call out for help. He'd taken Jesus' advice to heart. Greta was fast asleep after a very satisfying session of love making, and he lay next to her unable to rest. He had a great sense of guilt. He replayed everything he'd witnessed earlier that evening over and over again in his mind. Carl thought he was a follower of Jesus, but realized he wasn't. It took more than reading the Bible, and he had to live the life Jesus portrayed. In the past, he prayed, and he just didn't listen to our replies. Now, he was struggling with unanswered questions about his lifestyle. He slowly crawled out of bed so he wouldn't disturb Greta and moved into the living room where he sat in the dark space. The questions tormented his soul: *What was he doing with his life? Why hadn't he lived better? He went to church, he prayed, and he lived a moral existence, so why was he feeling like he'd wasted most of his twenty-eight years?*

When he said, "Lord I need answers!" It opened a door for me, so I whispered softly (as not to startle him), "Carl, stop wondering and begin asking your Heavenly Father to help you understand. We want you to know the truth. He is always here for you and wants nothing more than to relieve your stress. Reach out to Him before this tormenting spirit destroys your confidence in us and guilt ruins your rest."

My words were like a slap that forced him into sobriety. He quickly turned on a light and began looking for the Bible he'd left on a lamp table. I watched as he quickly turned to the concordance and found what he needed. There before him were the words I'd just spoken. Like a little child, he knelt next to the couch, placed his face in his palms and said, "Father God, I'm sorry. I should have been different. I see now that I've lived my Christian life through my natural father's methods, never taking your lifestyle for my own. Help me! I've seen and heard you tonight, so I'm convinced that you truly exist. It took the Holy Spirit's voice to guide me to you and when His statements rang true and I found them on paper, they were as if I'd heard the clues for the first time. I do not want any evil to steal my peace. I want you as my Father, Jesus as my example and the Holy Spirit voice as a loving reminder to seek you first. Please help me be who you want me to be. Make me a better mate for Greta and show me how to become a better father for our own two boys. I love and respect my Earthly parents and my brother, and I've strived to be like them, but they were only a road map to you. Now it is time I learn how to be independent and more like you."

Abba was thrilled! He loved having someone's complete attention so He materialized and placed His hand on Carl's shoulder, "Stand-up Carl, don't grovel, I won't bite."

Carl slowly rose to his feet and cautiously looked into the face of God, "I thought the Bible said we couldn't look at you and live?"

"Nonsense! Son, don't you know anything? I'm not looking at you in the physical sense, as I see you dressed in the covenant robe Jesus gave you. Through his grace, Jesus made sure my children were covered so you can communicate with me."

Carl said, "Huh?"

"Carl, you are covered by Jesus' blood. Wear it proudly! Life is in His blood and I love seeing Him live through you." Abba explained.

Watching and listening to the two of them talk the night away was precious to me. Abba helped Carl through many issues that were holding him back. Even though Carl was twenty-eight years old he already had two children with Greta. He realized he hadn't taken life very seriously or wanted to be a grown man until that evening. When Abba explained why He followed Joe Arnold's profession, Carl took the news proudly. Through Him, he and

Jesus would be taking love and acceptance into the school system so it could end critical and condescending behaviors. Carl's mission was to love the students unconditionally without regard to race, religious beliefs, physical abilities, or sexual orientation, encouraging the men to become leaders. Equality was important and all should be allowed to participate in sports without partiality.

Like I've stated before, being God has advantages. We can be everywhere, at the same time, because time and space don't apply to us. So, it didn't surprise me that Russ would have questions the same time Abba was talking with Carl. When he had Caylee home safely, he began having questions. Something Jesus had said about his dad worried him. He loves his dad and because of him, Russ went to church and learned about the holy trinity. Living with one parent was something he and Caylee had in common. Both had grown up without a mother figure in their lives but had fathers who wanted them to have a religious upbringing.

Caylee had changed him for the better, but after hearing how Wade had been warned and chastised about his lifestyle, a feeling of shame came over him and he began to worry, '*Why hadn't the Holy Spirit confronted him about his actions? He used women sexually before he found Caylee. He was drawn to seductive, pretty women who were willing to have fun without commitments or strings attached. What was different between him and Wade? Could it be that he didn't have a mother and Wade did or was it a matter of having a father who loved him?*'

His plaguing questions hurt my heart and just as I did for Carl I whispered in Russ' ear, "Why don't you ask your Heavenly Father if you need counseling? He's able to meet your needs and He would like nothing better than to heal your heart. Seek Him and stop wondering. He can be anything you need; a mother, father or friend and will give you a hug in you want."

Russ asked, "Why won't you answer my questions? You're here and the Father isn't."

"It is time you believed and trusted in your creator. I'm talking to your head and He lives within your heart. Allow Him this opportunity, and He's waited a long time for the two of you to know each other. I'll still be present, you're not alone. Just open your heart and ask Him to come. Try it, and He already knows you need Him."

Russ humbled himself and took my suggestion, but he just didn't know how to pray. From a young age, he'd been taught mechanics and told the Bible was to be used like a truck's manual straight from the manufacturer. So, he pulled his truck off the road in a lighted parking lot read a few scriptures and then asked, "Father God, help me. I feel broken and I'm ashamed of myself. Can you repair me?"

Abba met Russ where he was at because He'd been moved with compassion. In the truck, He hugged the large man and said, "Son, you're only heartbroken. Losing your mother at such a young age created a void only I can fill. For a few minutes, I want you to close your eyes and visualize her arms around you."

In Russ' heart and mind, Abba had transformed to become the one he longed for the most. Russ' mother was holding him tightly and she was young and pretty as he remembered. Then Abba whispered breaking the vision, "drink in this experience, Russ. Always remember I am all things and will be what you really need. There is no force greater than my love."

Russ asked, "Why didn't you make me confess my sexual issues this evening in front of the guys? I'm just as guilty as Wade."

"You and Wade are exact opposites. He loved the game of seduction; it made him feel strong and powerful over women. You love being the seduced because you never liked the romancing game. Both of you need to learn patience." Abba answered.

"I haven't slept with Caylee yet!" Russ said defensively.

"I know, son. I was trying to tell you something. Caylee is very gullible and it wouldn't take much to persuade her to lay with you. She and I have had to deal with that issue a few times after her heart was broken and she felt cheap. I got tired of watching men abuse her sweet spirit.

Caylee has many other good qualities as well as being alluring that's why you fell in love with her. Honesty and frankness were the seductions she used on you. Trust me, there is nothing phony about her. In so many ways Russ, Caylee is like your mother. She is smart, trustworthy, lovely, and lovable and will be a woman you'll be proud to have by your side. She'll nurture you and give you a sense of peace while respecting you as her husband. If you let her, she will treat you like a big baby in private. It's something you'll need, but don't worry, as she'll be the vixen in bed you crave when the time is right."

Russ confessed, "Father, it is weird talking with you about my sex life. I've always had the impression you thought sex was evil."

Abba softly laughed, "Russ, I invented the sexual act when I told mankind to prosper and multiply! I wanted the method of procreation to be enjoyable as well as fruitful so life would continue. Satan is the one who has twisted people's minds into thinking sex is dirty and inappropriate. He didn't want my loved ones to multiply because there is strength in numbers and he would lose everything."

"I want a big family. I didn't have any siblings. I hope Caylee will too." Russ stated.

Abba shared, "She does. Her heart's desire is to take care of many children."

Abba urged Russ to go home and get some sleep because there would be something special waiting for him in the morning. When

Russ asked what, it was, Abba said, "Remember the angels? Jesus has chosen one for you."

"Will he be like Caylee's? Russ inquired

"Yes! Jesus' has chosen one of Ox's and Cherub's brothers. Romper can't wait to meet and work alongside you, Caylee and his brother, Cherub. He has the same spirit as Cherub and is perfect for you. He's playful and will want to play and run free, but when it's necessary he'll be a powerful adversary." Abba shared.

"Will I be able to see him?" Russ asked.

"We'll let the two of you get acquainted. Then he'll stay out of sight most of the time. You still need to trust me before leaning too much on your angel. Angels were created to assist, protect, and demolish evil. They are here to prevent tragedy; not give you hope for a future. They are programmed to follow my Word and heed your requests when they are formed through by my Word." Abba explained.

Russ said, "Sounds like tomorrow will be very exciting."

"When Romper arrives, we'll be around to help you keep him in line. Try to sleep because tomorrow will bring challenges." Abba shared.

I liked sitting in the background, relaxing and enjoying the future as it played itself out for Wade and Gina. I was also allowing Ox to chaperone so I could listen. I took this respite, knowing Satan wasn't hiding somewhere trying to control every issue, helping Ox take this job seriously.

It was an hour and a half before midnight and even I knew Gina was exhausted and Wade would have a special day ahead of him. Ox found his chance to interrupt when Wade tried to embrace Gina for another kiss. He began growling deeply and the noise forced

Wade to back away quickly. Startled, he asked, "What did I do wrong? I had no intentions of groping you."

Gina giggled, "I think it's time we both went home. Ox knows I'm tired. We don't have to figure each other out in one evening. We can plan to see each other tomorrow afternoon after church. When you have your mother back home and settled, give me a call. Maybe we can go bike riding, I'll even prepare for a late afternoon picnic."

"Sounds great! I'm tired myself. Can I at least get a hug before I walk you to your car?" Wade inquired.

"Yeah, I think Ox will permit one," Gina said.

Wade made sure Gina was in her car and driving home before he veered away toward his mother's house. During the ride, his thoughts were traveling a thousand miles an hour. I knew he needed rest before he met his angel. To meet an angel like Thrasher, a human needed a strong mind as well as an able body during their introduction. Wade had both when he wasn't exhausted. Abba and I trusted Jesus' judgment when He explained why He assigned Thrasher to Wade. He convinced us they were suited for each other and the two of them would work well with Gina and Ox. I had one concern. The only difference between the two angels was their training in mercy. Ox spent years on Earth walking with me learning mankind's weaknesses, whereas Thrasher hadn't learned human nature. He was trained by other angels who had strict and firm beliefs that if words or actions didn't line-up with Abba's desires, they were to destroy the conflict. In Wade's current mental turmoil, he wouldn't be able to take charge of his angel, and Thrasher would act too harshly. Seeing how he reacted to Ox's growl, he'd be terrified by Thrasher's look.

Before intervening, I had a thought. *"Maybe Thrasher had been assigned to Wade to provide a sense of security. It was something his father never provided. Thrasher's attribute wasn't fun-loving, carefree or a joker like Wade, his was being extremely large and ferocious.*"

Wade's mind reached out to me while I had the thought. His had mixed feelings just like the other men's feelings had been. What hurt my heart was his lack of faith in our love. He asked, "Will you always be here for me? I am always making dumb moves. Will they cause you to give up on me?"

"Never doubt our love, we will always be there for you even if you do unthinkable things," I answered.

"Are you going to help me figure out my issues?" Wade probed.

"Yes, but not tonight, you need rest. It is imperative you sleep." I answered.

"I've gone days without sleep, I'll be fine, right now I need help," Wade begged.

I urged gently, "Wade, we know what you need. Tomorrow is a special day for you and we want you ready to meet your angel. Take something to help you sleep! Rest is that important! You only have a few hours and if your mind is slow and your body tired from lack of rest, Thrasher will not understand your weakness and won't answer to your authority."

"His name is Thrasher? Why will he be judgmental of me?" Wade asked.

I firmly stated, "His name is Thrasher for a reason! His job is to tread through harsh territory. Weakness in leaders is not something he respects. He is not like Ox. You do not want your first impression to be jaded by your physical condition. If fact, it will place you in jeopardy. Do you understand?

Wade sighed and said, "Drugs make me dopey. Do you have another suggestion?"

"I'm glad you asked! Call Abba and let Him give you rest." I joyfully exclaimed.

Wade's mind shifted and he didn't hesitate, "Father God, help me! I'm new at all of this. I need you!"

117

Deep inside Wade's heart, Abba answered, "I'm here, son. As soon as you park your bike go straight to your room, get into bed, and close your eyes. I will be there waiting. You must let dead things lie and stay buried so you can have a rested body. Delusions have kept you coiled like a spring for too long."

Abba meant well, but from my viewpoint, I could see what He said scared Wade. Wade may be strong, but he'd been exposed to so many supernatural experiences for one night. I knew Abba wouldn't mind if I interrupted their conversation, so I said, "Don't be afraid. We love you and want to make you feel better."

Wade muttered a response, "Why will I have to face dead things?"

Abba giggled which helped to diffuse Wade's tension, "Son, it doesn't matter. They are dead and can't harm you. It's time you realized this and open parts of your heart that have been closed and allow me to work."

Angels

As soon as Wade pulled in view of his family home, a reality faced him. Everything Abba said left his mind and reminders of his dad rushed into his memory. His dad's car was still in the garage. When he opened the back door, the house smelled of his dad's cigars. There was no getting around that fact that this place was his dad's home even though the man was dead.

Wade struggled with the same hurts even though he knew the house itself wasn't causing the grief. What I saw in the house was disturbing. Demons and imps were everywhere, but I took pleasure knowing their fate. To make things worse, I noticed Wade's mother was being tormented by these creatures too. They were hurting her and used her to hurt and insult Wade. The man needed relief.

Doing exactly what Abba recommended, Wade tore his mind away from the verbal jabs, bid her a quick goodnight and bound upstairs where he could meet a loving Father. As quickly as he could, he stripped down to his underwear, slid into his bed, and closed his eyes and prayed, "I'm ready Lord. Please put me under. I feel like I'm in a haunted house."

Abba touched Wade's body and instantly he fell into a slumber where deep and steady breathing took over his body. We beckoned his spirit to awaken and without hesitation Wade opened his heart and he stood before us as naked as the day he was born.

"Good evening!" Abba greeted.

Wade responded, "Hello sirs. I'm ready to face the inevitable."

Abba handed Wade his covenant robe and said, "What makes you think I'll be taking you through hell? I don't want to make you suffer! That's the furthest thing from my mind. What I plan to do is to show hell who you are. We're going to make it tremble.

You'll never have to set foot in another dark and oppressive place ever again."

Wade's expression changed and his energy and emotions were lining up with ours after a few minutes. His heart was healing and he was experiencing his first taste of peace. This meant he was ready for a helper. This new attitude came right on cue, the new day was upon us and all three of us heard a rip in the atmosphere meaning Thrasher had torn a hole into Earth's realm. The angel would be joining us shortly.

Wade was still in his peaceful state asking questions about stories in scripture and was amazed to learn they were all true. Abba explained some examples would be recurring throughout history for all mankind and not just for Israel because Jesus didn't divide, He included everyone.

Wade confessed, "I learned your Word as a child and was brought up under strict religious guidelines. I was forced to memorize scripture. I didn't fight it. I wasn't like most of the kids in my Sunday school class, I enjoyed memorizing. Studying appealed to me and I'd find myself seeking comfort from the words I read."

"Why did you stop?" Abba asked.

Wade thought for a moment. Then he said, "I was in my late teens when I got angry. It all started when I felt Dad rejecting me and seeing him favor Wayne. Hate filled my heart and I didn't want rules or scripture anymore."

"Good answer," Abba states.

"Why does this resonate with me now?" Wade asked.

Abba laughed, "You've accepted my gift and allowed the Holy Spirit to enter your head and guide you back to me. He is the one drawing out the scriptures you learned as a child. With your heart opened to me, you are free from hate and I can live in the words you learned through Jesus. Your willingness to learn the words and actions of Christ is why we chose you for this mission. You are still willing to learn and follow."

"I know Jesus is the Word and He was made flesh. Now you're saying I can be the same." Wade inquired.

"Yes! We live in you! I can be anything you need, all you have to do is ask and then believe from your heart, where love reigns. Don't ask your head questions, as that's where knowledge is, always rely on your gut and trust in me. Jesus did, and saw what He faced, and went through. He used the words I spoke into existence and lived in the blessing they created, making Him the Word and interpretation of who I am!" Abba informed.

Wade continued to inquire, "When you said we'd make hell tremble did you mean we'd make all dead things fear us? Will that include all the demons? I remember something about this from the book of Exodus."

"Yes!" Abba urged.

Then, Wade quoted the scripture, "'I will send my terror before you and will throw into confusion all the people to whom you shall come, and I will make all your foes turn from you in flight.'"

"You remembered that verse exactly. Who's your Daddy now, Wade?" Abba shouted.

"You are, but you are a loving and merciful Father. Why does this verse make you appear wrathful?" Wade asked confused.

"I love mankind, Wade and I want the best for them, but sometimes people are mean and need correction and I must use other people or my angels to do the dirty work. Angels see the culprits behind people's motives. Think of policemen, they are authorized to enforce peace. Angels are like them and follow my instructions to the letter and sometimes their actions will appear very wrathful in the natural realm. Flesh is weak and must be trained. Sometimes it takes a heavy hand to make it do right, and that is where other people come into play. Many times, I have had to use police or other law enforcers to corral them to keep them from harming others. My intentions are never to kill. Remember this when directing your angel and keeping him on course. Angels see the culprits behind people's motives." Abba instructed.

"Why?" Wade asked.

"You can memorize my words and keep them in your heart. Use them, but only in a loving manner. Never use any word or thing to divide, destroy or harm anyone. Thrasher, will be guided by the things I've said or will say. My words set him loose and on a route of destruction but at the same time, they can rein him in. When in doubt, allow the Holy Spirit to guide your thinking then you can speak from your heart. Your strong will controls your voice, but your mind and heart must work together so your voice will sound like mine. Angels act when your mind, spirit, and body are in harmony." Abba shared.

"Cool!" Wade said.

"Are you ready to meet your angel?" Abba asked.

"I think so," Wade answered.

"One last thing. Rely on your military training, Thrasher is a warrior and responds best to firm directives. You'll do well." Abba said.

"Am I portraying weakness?" Wade asked.

"Not any longer. Your heart is open again, it resonated with the pure love and you overcame the old person by welcoming me. You started believing in me again." Abba said proudly.

"Will I be able to see him anytime I want?" Wade asked.

"Yes, but he will need to work in the shadows. He'll be another Ox and you'll have to communicate most of the time without speaking. He can't communicate with you verbally, but you'll be able to read each other's thoughts." Abba explained.

"Will he make any sound? Ox barks and growls." Wade said.

This amused us and Abba said, "He'll snort and blow, for sure."

"You already know him. Think! He's described in a scripture verse you learned as a child." Abba directed.

My job was to help Wade recall so this task wouldn't be hard. War and creatures of war always fascinated him, so finding the appropriate verse that described Thrasher was easy for me. It was the descriptive words given to prophet Micah, which said, "Arise and thresh, O Daughter of Zion! For I will make your horn iron and I will make your hoofs bronze; you shall beat in pieces many peoples, and I will devote their gain to the Lord and their treasure to the Lord of all the Earth."

When I had, the verse re-established in Wade's memory, I urged him to speak it out the way he understood, but he had to ask me a question before he acted, "That scripture refers to a daughter of Zion. Is my angel female?"

"No! Everything, including angels, are from God's Word. Thrasher will respond to you as if your own body is rising to the challenge. Now speak! The words will call him! Make him rise up and take on his duty." I ordered.

It took a few moments before Wade could properly say the verse in his own way, but when he spoke his version of the verse, it came out strong and in a commanding manner. I was very proud of Wade, he understood the necessity of having a firm understanding of God's Word and I knew Thrasher would hear his new master and he would take up the banner proclaimed. Together, these two would beat evil into pieces and take back what Satan had stolen so their gain could go back to God. Instantly, we heard heavy hoof beats approaching and I urged Wade to brace himself. Then out of a mist, Thrasher appeared as an enormous beast, took his position, and stood at attention, like a warrior before Wade.

Wade was in awe, Thrasher was just as the scripture described. He stood ten foot tall, had horns of iron and hoofs of bronze. He had a face that was ferocious, with brows deeply furrowed, and eyes a flaming red. Even his teeth were impressive. They were not straight and blunt like most oxen's, but dagger-like, very sharp and set in a mouth that continually scowled. Wade loved the beast

123

right away. Our boy was very impressed. In his mind, Thrasher was even fiercer than any devil he'd imagined.

To the side, Abba was snickering under His breath, and I knew why. We may have met a need in Wade by giving him Thrasher, but Wade wasn't in for a joyride. He would soon find out that his memory of scripture was sparse and he would have no choice but to call on us regularly. He would have to be spoon fed the words he needed when he realizes that a Bible is another man's interpretations of what God said in the past. It is a history book of sorts that has been rewritten and re-worded over-and-over throughout history. Thrasher would need fresh and vibrant words from the source like was given moments ago, or he would become unhinged, or refuse to act at all choosing to stand like a statue. In time, all will work out, both man and angel were young and had to be broken like wild stallions so they could obey and retain the understanding and knowledge of God with me.

———————◇———————

The hole, Thrasher tore in the atmosphere, also set Romper loose and he was playfully finding his way towards Russ. Like Thrasher, he would need a firm directive and steady disposition to guide him and until this evening, Russ had dodged the responsibilities of fully maturing. Mr. Jackson had done everything for him and Russ never learned responsibility and suffered from the Peter Pan syndrome. Because Romper needed a leader, it would force the man to could out of a child's mentality.

We were fully aware that Mr. Jackson played two roles in Russ' life, and we knew why he raised Russ the way he had. A fear of being alone and not wanting his son to grow up, and want to leave the nest enabled Russ. Everything he did made life easy for Russ, but it kept him from taking responsibility. Russ lacked nothing.

He had a worry-free life and anything his heart desired. It was time that way of living and thinking changed.

A loud crash alerted Abba and me of Romper's arrival. It was time we urged Wade back into his body so he could get more sleep. It would be dawn soon and he and Thrasher had to work out their issues. We quickly rushed to Russ after leaving Wade and found him sawing logs. Sound asleep, in his father's house.

Abba nudged Russ and whispered, "Wake up, son. I have someone I want you to meet."

Russ didn't have a problem obeying Abba's command, and his naked spirit man slowly slipped out of his body and excitedly looked around in anticipation. Abba quickly dressed him in a covenant robe before he had a chance to speculate why he was naked. Then He took Russ' hand and guided him towards the angel. "Russ, meet Romper."

Russ looked dumbstruck at the angel, then back to Abba and me. We knew what he was thinking. He was disappointed. He was anticipating a large and very powerful creature and his hopes were let-down. Romper was very young, with a large and muscular body, but he was noticeably unintelligent to the point of looking retarded.

Russ questioned us, "What's wrong with him? He looks nothing like Cherub or Ox."

Abba countered, "He lacks wisdom, Russ. You've been assigned to train and guide his way. He will become strong and confident like Cherub in time."

"How will I do this?" Russ demanded.

"I think that's obvious, Son. It's time for you to grow up and take responsibility. One day you'll be required to take your Father's place and he hasn't shown you how. That's why we are here." Abba answered.

Russ argued, "Dad is great! He made sure I never had a want for anything. He has men capable of running the company."

"Do you want other men to babysit you and oversee everything you do after your Father dies?" Abba asked roughly.

Russ answered with another question, "What's going on? Is Dad ill?

"Your Father is fine, but you are not. Like Romper, you also lack wisdom and you are spiritually retarded. This must be corrected and the only way you will learn is from me. Inheritance is important and when you grasp the meaning, you'll receive mine as well as your father's." Abba declared.

The statement made Russ say, "What?"

Abba says, "Answer these questions. Did you learn anything in church or were you there to play and socialize? Have you asked your Father to explain his business to you or are you satisfied driving one of his company trucks? Did you ever consider what legacy you'd leave your kids one day? What are you going to say to Caylee or the kids when you have to ask for some allowance? Are you planning on being a husband and parent or were you expecting Caylee to make all the decisions? To keep Caylee's respect, she must feel financially secure as well as loved and to be a good father, you need a strong mind and willingness to lead. Are you ready for this challenge?"

"I see what you mean and I agree, it's time I grew-up. How are you going to teach me?" Russ asked.

"With a will, there is a way. We will teach you and while we train you, you will be teaching Romper. He is a lot like you, playful minded, undisciplined and without knowledge of operations in this sphere. He has listened to my words and followed my ways since the first day of his creation. He'll need these from you. At the moment, he's a little intimidated, but don't let his appearance fool you. He looks dumbfounded because he is unaccustomed to Earth's ways. There is too much negative energy and he is very confused.

This will change once curiosity is peaked. He becomes intrigued with humans the same way you are curious about us. You both need to be reminded not to react hastily and as we direct you, you'll need to direct Romper. This won't be easy and you'll want to run away screaming and so will Romper. You both will grow by helping each other cope. The only way to stop Romper from hollering and crying, or from running off playing, is to pay attention to him and figure out why he is complaining or unfocused. He's a big baby. Help him mature by growing up yourself and don't be afraid.

He was created to run, play, corral and steer people, but he has never lived in a place where my peace and love didn't reign. If you are brave, then Romper becomes brave. Take charge! Bend to a different tune and the two of you will become very special." Abba said proudly.

"When do we start?" Russ asked.

"Start by listening to me. It is good to go to church, but I want you to know me personally instead of relying on what a preacher or teachers tell you about me. Learn to commune with the Holy Spirit, and move as He guides your thinking. Soon you'll be trained to see what I see and speak what you've heard me say." Abba dictates.

"You want me to stop going to church?" Russ asked.

"No! Get more active in the church. Spirit will help you find your niche and Romper will be there to help you." Abba answered.

I knew where this was leading. Someday in the future, Russ would find out that he liked working with the youth, especially with younger men. He would be great with them and with Romper by his side their playful and competitive natures would draw attention like a pied piper.

"When do we start?" Russ inquired again.

"Today! Open your heart and focus. Life around you will give you clues and cues where you'll need my advice. When I instruct, act on my instruction and if I speak don't hold in the words. Romper understands mental or verbal communications so use whatever is appropriate for the situation. Romper responds to the understanding you have about what I say and it takes your agreement with me for him to function and assist you properly.

When you've mastered communication with me, the two of you benefit, and so will your friends and family. A relationship is the key to my way of living." Abba encouraged.

"You've answered two of my questions the same way. I'm to stay glued to you and the Holy Spirit, but what about Dad? How do I interact with him? Do you want me to ask him for a position in the office where I have to wear a suit and tie to work?"

"No, not yet. Start learning the business on your own. Form bonds with the employees. Gather knowledge and work upwards as we guide you. The entire business is yours, there isn't another heir. Learn it from the ground up like your Father. Just don't become prideful or arrogant. Remain yourself, remember the bonds you form and take over the reins when the time comes. As of now, the employees do not have a clue you are the owner's son. They think you are just a relative or you'd be working in the office alongside your Dad." Abba shared.

Russ confesses, "I want to see the countryside. I have no desire to stay cooped up in an office, that's why drive a truck."

"You can still have your cake and eat it too after you take responsibility for the whole operation. Think of this venture as an uncover operation. Find areas that can be improved upon not only for your family but also to help improve the standard of living for your employees. It happens when you begin to live a life for Jesus, you become my heir and your life improves as well as those around you." Abba urged.

Russ was overwhelmed with emotions at the thought of being Abba's heir! Daylight was fast approaching and it was time our new converts faced the day, their new duties and learned how to live covenant lives.   We ushered Russ back into his body and told him to call on us anytime.

House Cleaning

As Thrasher and Romper entered the Earthly realm, Jesus, and His angel armies were clearing away evil and fighting huge battles. While we were with the men in their homes, rain gushed outside, lightning popped and thunder roared causing problems all over the area. We later learned Satan even joined in the battle, huffing, puffing, destroying property, and toying with people's fears. He knew Abba and I were up to something, which usually meant more oxen were being unleashed to try and ruin his reign over the area.

It was a good thing that Wade's alarm clock was a battery back-up because the buzzer alerted him that it was time to arise and shine and face his challenge. When he noticed there was no power in the house, he looked out the window and saw it was still extremely dark for a morning. His heart sank when he thought about the plans he and Gina had made for the afternoon. Riding a bike in the rainy weather was out of the question.

An evil imp, who was living in the house, leaned over and whispered in Wade's ear. It was a tormenting thought about his Dad's old car that made Wade say to himself, "I'd hate driving that old car, it makes me feel foolish! Plus, it smells like Dad's cigars. As soon as possible I'm getting rid of that thing and get a cool car like Gina's to drive on rainy days."

Instantly, I knew the situation was dire! Wade had spoken negatively. Because of the fierce battles going on outside, and the evil imp's presence inside, Thrasher went berserk, because he'd taken Wade's words as a command. Before I could say anything to guide Wade's thoughts back to being gracious and appreciating everything, Thrasher had taken the situation into his own hands and suddenly, there was a crash that rocked the entire house.

Thrasher had seen the imp making Wade angry. So, he focused on it and began carrying out his orders, so he thought. The imp had fled outside and was sitting in a tree so Thrasher's first action was to rid Wade of his tormentor. In the process, he started a domino effect by killing the imp, which destroyed the tree, which fell on the garage damaging the house and totaling the old car.

Wade watched in horror and started screaming that the garage was gone. I had to be honest with him, so as calmly as I could manage, I said, "Your thoughts made Thrasher go berserk. Not only did he damage the house, he flattened your Dad's car in the process."

"Why? I thought he was sent to help me, not make more problems." Wade asked.

"Remember the saying, evil communications corrupt good manners? Plus, cast down evil imaginations and not allow them a place in your mind? Thrasher is young and doesn't know you well yet. He heard your thoughts after an evil imp whispered a tormenting suggestion in your ear. He thought he was honoring a command by killing the wicked creature that made you hate your circumstances. In the process, the house and car got caught in the skirmish. Don't fret! Abba has already made a way for the house to be repaired and another car to enter the picture." I informed.

"What do you mean?" Wade demanded.

I countered quickly to ease his mind. "Insurance! Remember the verse you quoted last night? 'You will take back what the enemy stole.' Well, insurance is a tool Satan uses to lure men into false securities. Now it will bow and work for you. A grand reversal to give you and your Mother guaranteed favor."

Wade's countenance changed and he said cheerfully, "I need to check on Mom and her nurse before setting this plan in motion. It looks like going to Mom's church is out of the plan for today."

To affirm suspicions, I asked him why he said there would be no church today, and he honestly said "I hate going to church there. The messages are boring and condemning. I'd rather go to Gina's church. Pastor Reed makes you feel welcomed and you leave encouraged."

It was like I suspected, the old ways were still being preached. No wonder the family had issues. So, while Wade dressed, I suggested he keep his mind glued to positive issues and to stay grateful for all things. I reminded him of what Abba said when we introduced him to Thrasher and said if he didn't use positive energy, there could be worse things happen than repairs to the house or getting an old car removed. I explained that Thrasher's ears were sensitive and even a harsh thought, even it was about his mother's church, could set him off on a rampage.

We were down only a few stairs when Wade's emotions changed, and he acted if I hadn't warned him at all about staying positive. All it took was hearing his Mother's complaint about a very bad headache and begging the nurse to call Wayne, for Wade's heart to fill with envy. I immediately saw the culprit behind the attack on Wade's feelings. It was not his mother, but an evil spirit using her mind and tongue to torture Wade. Thrasher was snorting loudly, and he saw the creature as well and was confused by Wade's emotions. I knew if I didn't speak quickly to get him warrior minded and re-focused, Thrasher would kill the creature and damage Wade's mother.

I screamed inside Wade's mind, "Wade, wake up! You are wallowing in self-pity! You must get a hold on your feelings! Thrasher is enraged by the way you feel! There is a demon using your mother and if you don't say something quick he won't be efficient. Say something now to change his course!"

My words of alarm forced Wade to beg Abba for clarity and with his request answered, he saw for himself what Thrasher was about to do. Like a soldier, he regained his composure and took control of the matter. With pleasure, I watched him use knowledge about God and begin to mutter "Peace! Be still!" to Thrasher. Then he said, "Father, forgive her because she is not herself and doesn't know what she is saying."

The words addressed to Abba, froze Thrasher's sword of judgment against Wade's mother, but they didn't stop him from using it to kill their tormentor. We watched Wade's face turn extremely white and his knees buckle as he witnessed Thrasher's weapon slice through his mother's skull. He thought he'd witnessed his mother's death until he saw a creature impaled on Thrasher's sword and his mother living. Apparently, forgiveness had opened a window for Thrasher to see the demon clearly and it also provided access for him to remove the demon embedded in her head.

Wade's mother had felt a jolt but wasn't harmed. She was grabbing her head because she felt relief instead of more pain and was crying with glee! While on his knees, Wade wept with joy because God had used him to heal his Mother by stepping out of self-pity and controlling the issue where He and Thrasher could work together.

Then he heard something wonderful, Mrs. Polk said, "Wade? Honey, when did you get home from Iraq? I've missed you so much. I've been so sick worrying about you."

Instantly, the energy around Wade changed and he snapped out of his slump so he could crawl over to his mother. As he hugged her, all he could do was praise us, "Thank you! Thank you! You've healed both of us!"

The gratitude was welcomed, but he and Thrasher weren't finished. I quickly urged Wade not to stop giving Thrasher orders, but to tell him to clean house where nothing like this could happen again. Wade obeyed and mentally gave Thrasher an order demanding evil creatures and weapons designed to attack him or the family to be destroyed. Little did he know, but he'd rephrased a scripture verse out of Isaiah that made Thrasher eagerly begin sweeping the house and making sure nothing resembling evil lived.

While Thrasher worked, Wade made sure his mother was more comfortable. After eating a hardy breakfast together, and making sure his mother was settled, he went outside in the rain and began surveying the damages done to the house so he could call the insurance company.

At the Jackson home, an extremely upset angel woke Russ. Romper was moaning and crying so loudly that Russ shot straight up in bed. Trying hard to gather his wits, Russ rubbed his eyes with both fists so he could see why the beast was crying. As soon as his vision cleared, his heart melted. Romper was sitting on the floor, with his large head between his knees pulling his floppy ears down over his eyes and moaning as if he were in pain.

Russ prayed, "Lord, what's wrong with the guy? How do I help him?"

"What do you hear, Russ?" I asked.

"Nothing!" Russ said.

I exclaimed, "Try harder!"

Russ tilted his head and strained to hear and I noticed when his realization came. He heard two things; bad weather and a television. Instantly, he relaxed because it wasn't something to fear. Rushing wind and hard rain weren't scary and the voices were from the TV show his father watched every morning in the kitchen downstairs.

Russ asked, "Why would rain and television make Romper cry?"

"Rain isn't bothering Romper, it's the news broadcast. Every word on the program is being spoken in a negative tone. It's drawing attention to what Satan did to the community overnight. Romper is crying because no notoriety is given to Jesus for stopping evil bent on destroying the whole town. He doesn't like the words, they are breaking his heart. He comes from a place where everything was done and said was for the good of mankind giving Jesus all the praise. These words are terrifying to him and he thinks the newsman is proclaiming doom and gloom." I explained.

"It's all noise to me. I've never taken the news seriously before." Russ said.

"Precisely! You never had too. Your Dad did, though. He feeds on the drama and he makes vital decisions based on the situations. When you begin learning the business, we want you to entently listen the way Romper does. If the news media doesn't give good reports, then you seek the truth behind the "why." Most times, it's because Satan and his bunch are trying to confuse people's thinking and causing chaos with mass negativity. Remember, emotions stir up whatever energy they create whether good or bad." I explained.

"Okay, but how do I stop Romper's crying jag?" Russ asked.

I said, "Get his attention! Turn on your television, and find a church service being broadcasted. Then wave your hands, stomp your feet, clap your hands until Romper looks at you. Show him you can change the atmosphere around him. You have the power!"

"Good grief! This is like babysitting!" Russ exclaimed.

"Get used to it!" I replied.

Russ placed Romper in front of Pastor Reed's television broadcast and told him to stay put until he finished his shower. I had to laugh because most parents used television to entertain children so they could complete a task. This time, the child was angelic and a huge baby to handle. When Russ exited his bathroom, he found Romper acting completely different. He was bright-eyed and very happy and no longer looked retarded. Nothing about his appearance drooped any longer which made Russ take pride in his angel's appearance. Soon Russ would understand his gifting and start embracing his fatherhood and leadership abilities and enjoying them.

After Russ dressed, Romper followed him downstairs where Mr. Jackson was eating breakfast. When he asked his dad how he was, negative words starting flowing from Mr. Jackson's mouth which made Romper whimper. Instead of lingering for breakfast, Russ made up a story so he could get Romper to church before he had another meltdown. Even in the heavy rain, as we rode, I enjoyed watching Russ and Romper try and communicate. Only this time, it was Russ who got a little unhinged and overcome by what he saw.

What we saw was devastating. Trees and houses were destroyed from the night's battle. I watched Russ closely and noticed he used his truck radio for comfort by turning it up full blast. Apparently, Christian music was his way of getting some peace making him no different from Romper. Only he wasn't relieved from his torment like the angel was. Russ was concerned for his neighbors, but Romper was happy. To Russ, the angel should be crying and screaming, but instead, he was looping the truck, riding the breeze, and turning cartwheels in the air while he flew alongside the truck. Romper wasn't in the least bit fazed by the destruction.

For most the ride, Russ hadn't engaged Abba or me in conversation so when Romper's actions worried him he finally asked, "What's with this angel? Shouldn't he be bellowing? Doesn't he see how much suffering there is around here? Neighbors may be hurt and most will be cleaning up this mess for a while. He's not even affected by this tragedy. I don't understand him at all!"

Abba answered him right away, "I'm happy too! Jesus and His angels raged a mighty war for you last night. Few people were hurt, it was mostly property damage. Trust me, if people were severely hurt or presumed dead, Romper wouldn't be acting playful. He'd have his nose stuck in the mess seeking out their life. He's better than any rescue dog for that. You'll see."

What Abba said stunned Russ, and he couldn't believe Jesus had waged a war for him. To soothe his mind, I said, "Russ, Jesus loves you dearly but you weren't the only person He fought for last night. He has great plans for you as well as this whole community. He wasn't the one that hurt the people or destroyed this property, Satan did! Can't you see Satan wants people to focus on this mess? He does it so they'll focus more on themselves and worry about their losses. Then when people can't or won't help each other they begin to point fingers and start the blame game. Satan's favorite tool against Abba is having people to accuse each other and say God will not defend them. God is not wrathful, but He will use what His enemy meant for harm to bless those who trust in Him. Property can be restored. People are not the issue. Don't fall into this trap of thinking all this happened because God was angry. No! This happened because it is time for believers to realize just how merciful and compassionate He really is."

"We've been taught that our sinful actions make God mad at us." Russ declared.

"Actions are not who you are. He doesn't judge people by their fleshly deeds. God looks at the hearts of people and determines their motives by gauging their personal knowledge. Wrong mindsets contribute to bad attitudes. Bad attitudes start rash acts. All people need is an attitude adjustment, proper teaching and a guide to help them live a better life." I answered.

Russ states, "I definitely have a lot to learn. I'm all mixed up because I can't be happy about this storm damage."

"Don't lose your compassion, Russ. In fact, develop more of it and let it guide you through. We will be here to unscrew your thinking and help you know the truth. Satan's lies are what you are used to hearing. He has a way of twisting the meaning of scripture so you'll feel guilt, shame, or disgust instead of compassion. Untruths hurt the soul and until you adjust your attitude to face the challenge of seeking the truth, you'll stay bitter and won't be surprised by my answers.

Here's food for thought. Not all storms are bad. Some are good, even if the outcome has some damaging effects. Just remember what you found in a storm not long ago, and when Caylee comes to mind, then you'll be able to smile and not frown." I interjected.

Routines Change

Due to Hope's role in the intercession team, she established a Sunday morning routine. She'd have Greg fed and ready for church before she left him in Brent's care. Usually, she left home an hour before Sunday school started but this morning she left even earlier.

As she entered the church she began asking us for one thing. She wanted to experience the power we gave Gina, so she could stop relying heavily on her past experiences. She knew she'd grown in her spiritual quest, but after seeing how Brent reacted last evening, she understood she'd relied more on physical abilities than she should. After praying, she waited a few moments and began looking for Gina. She knew in her heart they were meant to meet this morning.

She searched the sanctuary, looked in the ladies' restrooms, she even went into the fellowship hall hoping to find her friend. When every place turned up empty, Hope went outdoors into the pouring rain to search the parking lot for Gina's car and it wasn't there.

Exasperated, she asked, "Lord, where is Gina? I just knew we were supposed to meet this morning. Could I have misunderstood this nudge I have in my spirit?"

I answered her question, "Hope, if you feel like Father expects you to see Gina, then rest assured, you will. Take into consideration the bad weather that happened last night. There are many factors that may be keeping her away. If you want to speak to her before church, stop worrying and give her a call."

Hope babbled, "Your right! I know she'll be here. I was hoping it would be before intercession. I'm fretting over nothing."

Hope didn't know I'd asked Gina to meet us before church. I walked alongside Hope and tried to keep her busy. We even prayed quietly in the spirit while pacing in the sanctuary hallways. With fifteen minutes left before intercession, I could see Hope was about to give up on Gina arriving beforehand. As always, Hope visits the ladies' room before the group starts so she can step inside the Lord's armor. Since her first day in the prayer group, she has never entered prayer without it on. This time the struggle to change the habit she'd formed out of fear and act in faith was great. Faith won over, and when she threw open the stall door to go to group, Gina was standing in the room.

Hope flung her arms around Gina and squeezed her hard in hopes of receiving Gina's gift. Only the hug didn't give her anything. Hope's hug surprised Gina causing her to ask, "Hope, are you okay? Have you been sick again? Whisperer told me to rush to your side and I've been waiting for you. I got worried and decided to look for you in here."

Hope says, "I'm not sick, I've been searching this whole church for you. I even went outside to look for your car, so where have you been waiting?"

"I've been in the prayer room waiting for you for about twenty minutes. Plus, I had to park out back because there is a tree limb blocking the main entrance." Gina replied.

Hope took Gina's hand in hers and said, "There is no need for a debate. We should hurry. I needed to partake of the gift God gave you. That's why I hugged you so hard. Will you share it with me now, please? I don't have but a few moments before prayer."

The thought of Hope wanting something from her, caused love's bright blue flame to jump outside of Gina. The sight was beautiful! But before she touched Hope, Gina exclaimed, "Hope, I want you to know I love you! You've made me very happy. I want to share this pure love's glory with you. With it, I'm sure you'll be able to pray better so take all you need from me."

The two women embraced again, and Gina's powerful gift penetrated Hope's heart and engulfed her body. Instead of a shield around her body, Hope was now fully ignited in God's love. The effect didn't take Hope by surprise she was prepared for it and knew it would affect her deeply. So, when the jolt of electrical power released inside of her, she staggered, and almost fell to her knees. Gina held Hope tightly to keep her from falling until she regained strength in her limbs. When she was ready, there wasn't any time left for them to talk. So, on the way out of the ladies' room, Hope quickly thanked her friend and said she'd see her during Sunday school.

Before prayer began, Hope realized she was vibrating and full of energy. Her heart, mind, and body were burning with love so strong it made her feel invincible. The sensations were making it very hard to keep her mind on track, so she opened her spiritual eyes and ears and braced herself for a fight. When the group joined hands, she let me have control of her mouth and while we prayed together, Abba showed her what love accomplishes during intercessory prayer. Instead of hearing happy sounds around nurseries, or the threats coming from emotion suckers, Hope heard terrifying screams, moans, and groans coming from low-lying areas and inside walls. Her heart raced until she realized the sounds were coming from demons and imps instead of humans. Then Abba showed her why. Angels had invaded the church and were hunting down the evil creatures. Some were even pleading for mercy.

Suddenly, Hope glimpsed a bright light and a heard a clash of metal. She quickly blinked her eyes and adjusted her spiritual vision to see angels standing over dozens of demons. The prayer room was a bloody mess. Everything happened so fast! She stared intently at the other intercessors around her and not one of them seemed to be affected by what had happened around them. In fact, all of them were oblivious to the attacks and they were spared. Peace filled every space but inside Hope's head and even though she still prayed with me, her mind was seriously asking me questions.

"Lord, why am I the only one opened to what just occurred? Why am I different from the others in here? They're not affected at all. Seeing our attackers has made me want to take up arms and do something myself. Shouldn't we be praying more forcibly at least, instead of softly?"

Abba answered her instead of me. He said, "Hope, there is no need for you to fight any longer. As for these faithful ones, it is time they had peace as their reward. They faced evil for Jesus many times in their lives, just in a different manner than you. It's time they rested."

"Lord, why haven't we been fighting evil before? We always had an agenda that required us to pray for the sick or certain functions going on within the church instead of praying directly against this evil. Why haven't they noticed that our church was infested?" Hope asked.

Abba countered quickly, "It's not for you to know why they do things differently. Jesus knows what is going on, that is all that matters. Don't ever think otherwise!"

"Yes, Sir. Please forgive me." Hope repented.

"Be happy this is happening in your generation. Think of Shiloh! Don't you want her to live and be free from evil's influence?" Abba asked gently.

The other intercessors tightly held Hope's hands, but I noticed her mentally touch her belly after Abba's remark. Shiloh was growing inside her and the thought of her having to deal with evil the way she had didn't sit well in her heart. Even while praying with the group, Hope reached out for help and said, "Father, I need an attitude adjustment so I can have peace. Why am I so high strung and focused on evil all the time?"

Abba answered softly, "Your heart has been severely scarred far worse that the scars you bear on your wrists and belly. It takes more time to heal and my love is the only thing able to wipe away the memories you and Greg have suffered. These people sitting around you don't understand the way you do. They've never been abused or threatened by someone under evil's control. You've faced that kind of evil too many times and your heart withdrew from intimacy. It was only natural for it to find comfort when you hide it in my son's suit of armor. That is why I urged you to seek me and depend more on Insight's abilities so your heart doesn't have to fear. I am here with you. Insight has been appointed to guard you and your loved ones. It is time your heart finds rest and trust in me. Look around, doesn't this victory convince you? It was Insight who called in heaven's army and while your hands were bound, you had the privilege of seeing their battle. I don't want you fighting anymore, not through your mind or with your body. Focus on prayers of love and if you want to wear Jesus' armor you can. I want you happy."

Hope mentally rattled out a response, "I can pray that others have peace. I hate all forms of abuse and since I'm sensitive to the effects of it I'll know when to pray. I'm beginning to understand."

"For the next few moments, use this time to rest your mind. Watch Insight work. Trust me and open your heart. Let go of anything weighing you down and when you are able, allow yourself to freefall without fear, into my peaceful place." Abba said lovingly.

Tears flooded my eyes as I watched Hope's heart open. Abba's love washed over the scars and removed the terrifying memories living inside it so it was free and able to soar like a bird. When the prayer time ended, Hope was flushed with love and so embarrassed by her red face that she couldn't look anyone in the eyes. She wanted that experience all for herself and left quickly before someone asked her if she felt okay. Even I didn't want her to share this experience with the prayer team. It was something she had to savor until she could talk privately with Brent and Gina.

Clues

After Hope left Gina to go to intercessory, I encouraged Gina to go outside and sit in her car because I didn't want her to feel threatened once the ruckus started inside the church. On the way out, Ox began to snort and growl making Gina very uncomfortable. Safely inside her car, she asked, "What is up with Ox? Is Satan nearby?"

"You're not far from the truth. Ox is protecting you while the intercessors pray. Other angels are taking care of an infestation in the church." I answered.

"He spooked me! I don't want him to get hurt again because of me." Gina exclaimed.

To calm her down, I said, "Gina, Ox will die for you if necessary. Let him do his job. He honors Jesus this way. If the two of you communicate, you'll be fine. Losing faith in us and succumbing to doubt will cause him to shut down. Being cautious when Ox is noisy is to your advantage. You don't have to fear when he is on guard. This way, if you have to act you'll be ready for the occasion and not taken off guard."

Gina's love blue flame appeared, and she said, "I promise to honor Jesus and let Ox do his job. I really appreciate the love you have for me."

"Good!" I replied.

The two of us watched several men clean up the mess made by the night's storm and the teamwork they portrayed, gave me an idea. I asked, "Gina, do you see how these men work together? Each has taken a task and flow together. This is how we want you and Wade to be."

"I don't follow." She answered.

"You and I help people every day. You allow my words to flow through you and they affect the thoughts and actions of other people. It's time you and I showed Wade the true definition of teamwork." I shared.

"I still don't understand," Gina said.

"Where does Wade work?" I countered.

She said, "The VA hospital."

"Where do we work together?" I asked.

Gina softly said, "The Mental Health Center."

"Correct! Don't you want to show Wade a different side of yourself? You can if you allow him to show you around the VA. There are a few veterans we can help there if you are up for this challenge. The three of us could work together as a team and it will help him see the real you." I said.

"That is a great idea! He loves the patients there. When can we start?" She jovially asked.

"Today!" I replied.

Instantly, her cell phone vibrated and she told me it was Wade.

Perfect timing! He'd called to ask if they could do something in the afternoon that didn't require riding his bike since more rain was expected. Gina, eager to prove to him that she was more than a pretty face said, "Why don't you show me around your VA clinic? I think that would be fun! You talk about your patients a lot. If it is okay, I'll pick you up around three this afternoon."

Wade agreed and our date was set.

<hr />

When Russ arrived early at the church, he noticed some men working diligently cleaning the parking lot of fallen trees. Rather than sit and watch he offered his help. The manual labor was good, but the negative thoughts running through his mind were poison even if some of them were true. Russ was certainly a spoiled, rich kid that didn't know how to run a business or a home. Worry and fear were taking root in his brain and their influence made him doubt his self-worth because he didn't know what it was like to be self-sufficient.

When Caylee arrived, the negative thoughts made him realize what he'd done. He'd asked her to marry him and he didn't even have a place for them to live. How could he take her to his Father's house? It wouldn't be fair to her. She deserved a place she could call her own not somewhere with two men to take care of. He had to think of something fast. His first thought was to run to her and confess his stupidity, but he didn't want to appear unmanly and stupid. Then truth hit like a kick in the teeth. He was acting like Romper. He was a dopey acting man-child without a clue.

His thoughts made me sad. They had to stop immediately. I said scornfully, "Stop this self-abusive thinking this instant! You know better! Yes, you are a man-child, but you are not stupid. You have an awesome brain, so use it! You've made mistakes, so what? I'm here to encourage you and help you make things right for yourself, Caylee, and Father. It is time you manned-up and do what Jesus did."

"What is that exactly?" Russ asked.

"Jesus fell in love with humanity. He loved mankind so much that He stepped out of heaven and became one of you." I said frankly.

"So, I'm supposed to turn my back on my identity and live in poverty?" Russ asked.

"No, son! You'll never be able to lose your identity. You're still entitled to all your Father owns as well as what your heavenly Father owns. If you need another example, read about Moses in the Bible. He was born a Hebrew slave but he became a powerful son of an Egyptian King. When he grew up, Moses refused the privileges of the Egyptian lifestyle. He chose a hard life with God's people rather than an easy, opportunistic life of sin with the oppressors." I referenced.

Russ stammered, "I'm pathetic! I've done nothing but live an easy life."

"You are not pathetic. You have a willing heart. You don't run from hard work. That is evident right this minute. You didn't have to assist with this clean-up. You did it out of compassion. All I'm asking is that you take time and mature. Start by finding a modest place to live for a while, and then you can ask Caylee to share it with you once you've married. Try and make ends meet on your own salary. Find out how most of your brothers and sisters live by sharing the workload at your Father's business. Get to know how they live. Find out what it is like to budget and plan while relying on your Heavenly Father to provide when times get tough. Caylee will show you how she accomplishes this, and so will Romper. Now, stop with the pity party. Go tell Caylee what you want to do this afternoon, and get her excited about sharing the space with you soon." I encouraged.

Russ surprised Caylee with his plan to apartment hunt that afternoon. Then he relaxed and enjoyed Pastor Reed's message and seeing how Caylee and Romper relied on the Word of God. They were transfixed and their state of being spoke volumes to Russ. He finally understood how Caylee survived. She was a spiritual sponge drinking in life, energy, and wisdom directly from God's spoken Word. He wanted their peace, so I whispered a soft word in his ear, "it's yours. Keep seeking after love."

He answered me through thought, "If having this peace means I have to study the Bible to know more about God, I can't wait to read it for myself. You'll help me understand what I'm reading won't you?"

"You can count on it, Russ. I'll even read to you while you let your eyes move along the page. If I narrate you'll understand and you'll be able to reason with Abba when you have questions. Discuss your new study interest with Caylee. She is a good example for you to follow. She sits at our feet every morning." I said.

"I think I want to study alone at first. I'll make it a habit to include her after we are married. I really need the one-on-one for now; if that's all right?" Russ said.

"We'd love it! Let's make a date for this evening after you take Caylee home." I answered.

Secrets

After speaking with Gina, Wade went back to the den to be with his mother instead of dealing with the insurance company. She was adjusting to drastic changes, and she didn't want him to leave her side. Her mind was clearing and she suddenly became very curious. I encouraged Wade to be patient and listen to her. She would rest better if he answered her questions. Plus, he would find out he thought wrong about her condition. She'd had a problem for a long time, it was something she and Wade's father had planned for in advance, but everything fell through.

Mrs. Polk asked Wade, "Son, how long have you been here?"

"Mama, I have been back in town about six months. I moved into the house with you after your stroke so I could make sure things were taken care of properly." Wade answered her.

Mrs. Polk started crying. She was still having problems understanding. Then she blurted, "It happened! What we feared happened! I just didn't die!"

"What are you talking about Mama?" Wade questioned.

"Dad and I knew I had a clot on the brain. I've had it for years, but it was inoperable. I wasn't supposed to out-live your Father. The doctors told us that if the blood clot burst and I lived, I'd either be in a vegetative state or need assistance for the rest of my life. We kept this secret from you boys. We didn't want your lives to change because you feared something happening to me. Then your Father died without warning and left me carrying the burden alone. My mind was so confused back then. I was dealing with so much grief and I couldn't make vital decisions. I never meant this to happen to you. I didn't want you to give up your military career because of me. I should have moved way before now," she sobbed.

"Mom! I didn't leave my career! The reason I was in the service was to be a doctor. I'm working at the VA hospital. Don't cry, I'm still working for the military I'm just not in active service. Wayne and I are fine. We've made sure you had a nurse to manage your physical needs. I just moved in to oversee everything else. We haven't sacrificed anything." Wade said to soothe her.

She looked into Wade's eyes with a fixed expression on her face and said very sternly, "Wade, you mean well but you and Wayne didn't follow through. Our wishes weren't considered. Provisions for me have already been made. Everything was properly documented so find your Father's Will and have it probated. Go through his desk and find a key to unlock the safe."

"Okay, Mom! I will. Do you want Wayne to come over?" Wade asked her.

"No! Call him later. Just find your Father's papers so I can rest. I need to know I'm not imagining things. I think he wrote each of you a personal letter. Don't waste any more time, you should know everything. I'm blessed to still be around but I may not have tomorrow and I want you to have some blessings now. Wade, your Father was a good man, he loved us. You, more than anyone else must know this. Now, go find his papers!" She insisted.

Wade obeyed his mother and went in search of the safe key. While in the office, he planned to search for the insurance information on the house. Thrasher was waiting for him in the room. He'd been busy. Dead demonic corpses were piled up on the floor. The sight would have flabbergasted most people, but Wade felt relief and said, "Thanks! I can search without any surprises. They're all gone, aren't they?"

Thrasher answered, "All gone. House is clean."

Wade sat in his Dad's office chair and addressed Abba directly, "Heavenly Father, I don't know if I'm ready for this, but Mom is insistent that I find Dad's legal papers and some letters. Will you stand by me?"

"I'm right here Wade. There is nothing to fear. It is time you know the truth so you can move on with your life and be happy." Abba answered him.

"Happy? What will I find that's going to make me happier than I already am?" Wade asked.

"Truth!" Abba states.

Wade opened the desk and found the safe's key. Then he removed a picture off the wall that kept the safe hidden. Inside the safe, he found all the information he needed to call the insurance companies, along with a box that was stored in the back. With shaking hands, he removed the box and took it back to his father's desk and looked inside. The box had four envelopes inside. The first one was labeled 'Last Will and Testament of Ronald James Polk,' underneath that envelope, were two more, one addressed to him and the other to Wayne. The last envelope held two deeds, one for the Polk home and another for an apartment in an assisted living complex.

Wade didn't know where to start. One part of him wanted to read the Will and the other wanted to read the letter addressed to him, so he addressed Abba again, "Lord, where do I start? This isn't easy for me, I'm emotionally torn."

"Wade, both documents will give you a better understanding of your Father, but I feel he would rather you read your letter first before reading his Will. Before reading his letter, focus on how his voice sounded, then allow it to sink into your soul the same way my voice is right now. Trust me, I understand being a father. Sometimes it is hard for us to adequately express what we feel. Your dad didn't express his true feelings to you personally, but this letter will make up for his imperfection and he'll make himself clear," Abba shared.

He opened the envelope with his name written on it, fearing the same old jibes he'd heard many times before. 'Wayne needs the classes, Wayne has to be coached, Wayne this or Wayne that;

always Wayne.' But what he read shocked him. The letter said, *"My dearest son, Wade: Son, you are so much like me. From the day, you turned four years old, I knew deep in my heart that you would be a success. We share the same spirit and drive, and we're both very independent. As you grew, I had no fears where you were concerned, and I knew you would succeed in life.*

It may have seemed that I didn't care for you, but in truth, I cared a lot. I would watch you when you weren't looking and was proud of my studious and very athletic son. Nothing could stop you, but when I watched your brother, I didn't feel the same. I feared he would never be successful, and he was easily distracted and would not focus. Unlike you, he hated studying and wanted to hang with the wrong crowd. I had to push him. If I wasn't around cheering him on, he'd give up and blame the dog for not doing his homework. He was fair in sports, but for him to be on top of his game, I had to coach him. You didn't need my help. You were a natural. I'd look at you and knew you had everything under control.

When it came time for the two of you to go to college, I lost the ability to communicate with you altogether. You shut me out and when I tried to talk with you, you became defensive and hateful. Then before I knew it, you had joined the Service. Your Mom said it was her idea for you to enlist. I can't say I was happy about your decision, but I was proud of you. From the time you and Wayne were little boys, I would brag that I would have two boys going to the University of Georgia. It just didn't work out the way I wanted. Instead, you found your own way without my help. I guess you had to prove you didn't need me.

It was very ironic to find out you and Wayne both wanted to follow me and become doctors. I couldn't imagine Wayne applying himself to the rigors of advanced study, but I had no doubt in my mind that you could. You even managed to study while working for our country. That is something I could not have done. I can honestly say, 'you are a better man than me.' I salute you!

My health is poor, so I retired to rest and take care of your mother, but I am leaving my orthopedic practice to you and Wayne. I established Wayne in his position, and we are waiting on you. I only hired Dr. Elliot Carter to substitute until you decide if you want to work with Wayne or sell him your share of the practice. If you decide to take the offer and Dr. Carter suits the two of you, you may want to keep him employed. I have payroll services, investment bankers and lawyers running the day-to-day business ensuring the employees are paid, expenses, and inventory are managed properly. If I die before we discuss this, the two of you cannot change these arrangements until my Will is probated. Make sure you do that quickly before the state overrides my decisions. It is my deepest wish that the two of you find peace and happiness, working together or not. Make the Polk name proud, do this for me.

Along with my 'Last Will and Testament,' there are two deeds. The apartment is for your mother. She is very sick and will soon need long-term care. If something has happened to me, this deed provides for her care in an assisted living and medical facility. The medical services and amenities at the facility are outstanding, I've done extensive research and I'm confident they will give her wonderful care. We want our boys to be free from financial burdens concerning our healthcare, and don't want to place any other stresses on you. If for some reason, she passes before me, I will move into this facility myself (I think I'd enjoy being pampered). All we want is your love and peace of mind.

Wayne has already found a lovely wife and I pray you will too someday. He already has a home furnished by our family's estate, so your mother and I want to leave you the deed to our house. It has served us well and it would be a nice place for another large

153

family someday. If you don't want it, you are free to do whatever you desire.

I love you son. Dad."

Wade's emotions were off the Richter scale. He was grieving, but at the same time very happy. Abba and I both were glad he finally knew the truth. The stresses of the day came together causing Wade's head to ache and he was struggling not to cry. To keep from upsetting Thrasher, he decided to get busy, placing calls to insurance companies. He finished making the arrangements then went to be with his mother. He showed her the papers and then sent Wayne and urgent text message. He didn't know how Wayne was going to react to all the secrets his parents had kept from them, but it was time he also knew everything.

Duo of Fire

After showing the papers to his mother, and telling her that Wayne had been called, she asked if she could take a nap before the family meeting. Wade didn't argue and asked the nurse to help Mrs. Polk to her room. If the issue were moving fast for him, he knew his mother was overwhelmed.

To pass time, Wade and Thrasher walked around the house looking at everything. Wade was looking at things differently and the knowledge that the house belonged to him was still weighing heavy on his mind. The place had been recently remodeled and the space was nice, but he was thinking that it lacked his personal touch.

Since Abba and I had been watching them, I noticed when the air around me changed. Abba was up to something because He was wearing His happy, mischievous expression. Before I could ask what He was up to, He stepped around me and whispered in Wade's ear, "give it a new queen and fill it with babies! Put your eager libido to good use with a good wife! Make your Dad and me proud papas."

Wade flushed red, and then he went pale in a matter of seconds. Abba had embarrassed him and frightened him in the same instance. Wade stammered, "Marriage? Isn't it too soon?"

Abba countered with questions of His own, "Are you doubting me? Wasn't Gina my idea, or do you want to stay celibate a long time?"

"No, sir. I mean yes, Gina was your idea and no I don't think I can stay celibate much longer. But marriage is between two, is she ready?" Wade asked.

"Keep the date you planned for this afternoon. Let her prove to you that she is your equal and your completion. Then do something about it." Abba said.

Wade questioned, "What about Wayne and Mom? We have a lot to settle."

"Boy, it has already settled! Once Wayne reads his letter and the three of you look over your Dad's Will there is nothing else to discuss. You can't probate until tomorrow and when the insurance agent calls, he'll suggest seeing you tomorrow as well. Don't put things off! Call your woman after the family meeting. It shouldn't last longer than two hours at the most." Abba firmly replied.

Wade's cell phone rang interrupting their conversation indicating it was Wayne. He answered, "Thanks for calling me back. Mom's had a breakthrough. She's remembering things so you need to come over."

Wayne's response was, "Can't it wait? We are about to go into the church."

Wade replied, "It's concerning Dad's Will, Mom's well-being and our future. It's important enough I think you should miss the service."

"If you insist. I'll buy sandwiches for all of us before we come." Wayne volunteered.

"That'd be great! Get me some fries too. Mom needs a grilled something and her nurse also needs a meal." Wade suggested.

Frustrated by Wade's demands, Wayne said, "You can't be choosy. I know what Mom needs or have you forgotten that I'm a doctor too? Plus, I planned on bringing extra food for the nurse."

Like Abba said, the Polk meeting was short. The two boys agreed to honor their parent's wishes and made the arrangements to have the Will probated the next day. Neither of them wanted to discuss working together, even though they had a new perspective on their careers. Abba and I understood they needed time to get reacquainted and mend their broken relationship. Prayers would be made on their behalf.

After Wayne and Amy left, Wade could hardly wait to see Gina. He wanted to know just how she was going to prove to him that she was ready for marriage. The thought intrigued him greatly. While he paced the time away waiting for her to arrive, I took the opportunity to remind him of a statement she had made to him earlier that morning. "Hadn't she said she wanted you to show her your VA clinic?"

Wade shouted back at me, "She wants to know more about what?

"She wants to know what makes you tick. Know your dreams, and what they entail. She wants all of you not just what she sees. It's important to her that she loves what you love and wants you to love what she loves. True commitment is a partnership of giving and take. It is caring about each other's passions as well as the person, not everything is about physical attraction. Gina wants to respect you as a man." I informed him.

Wade answered back, "I wanted to know more about her last night, but Ox ran me off. If he wasn't guarding her so closely I'd still be digging through her brain."

"No, you'd still be trying to gratify your hormones. You had a one-track mind until recently. Ox knew what he was doing. Plans were for you to meet Thrasher and deal with family issues. We knew when you would be ready to dig into her likes and dislikes. Becoming spiritually attuned will allow you to know the real Gina and how she feels." I explained.

After our brief conversation, Gina arrived and Wade developed a smugness I almost didn't like. He was too cocky and had a wicked grin most women would think was charming. Gina noticed the attitude. Having been around a lot of men like Wade, she boldly asked, "What's with the sly smile? Just what are you thinking Mr. Polk?"

"Oh, nothing special." He lied.

Upon hearing his lying words, Ox snorted and Thrasher pounded his fist on the car window next to Wade's ear making him jump in the seat.

Gina sang, "Liar, liar pants on fire!" Come on, even I know a fib when I hear one. Be honest with me. We can't lie to each other anymore. We have a witness, remember."

"We have two! Didn't you hear the thump on the window next to my head? That's my angel letting me know he didn't appreciate the fib." Wade shared.

"I heard the noise but I thought it was Ox hitting the glass," Gina replied.

"I've been blessed with another Ox, only he is nothing like your angel. Thrasher is ridged, has no sense of humor, and won't bend any rules. He's the reason I have insurance issues today." Wade confessed.

"Good!" Gina giggled, "It's time you learned life isn't all fun and games."

Wade came back, "Honey, I know that well enough. Being a jokester usually helps me cope, but now I should be serious-minded. Thrasher is very literal and responds to all my thoughts and words as if they are my actual wishes. It's unnerving."

Gina made a sweet gesture by reaching over across the car seat and taking Wade's hand in hers before responding. "Wade, trust Whisperer. When I saw Ox for the first time, I was very confused and frightened. Now, I wouldn't trade him for anything. I'm sure you and Thrasher will become just as close as Ox and I are."

Before Wade and Gina entered the VA hospital, demons began wailing. Their screams were very loud, as if in protest. Abba and I were thrilled to know they were frightened. To torment them further, Abba sharpened their cries so Wade, Ox, and Thrasher could hear them clearly. We knew Wade would jump into action and Ox's alarms would warn Gina that something evil was present.

The VA's lobby appeared to be empty to Wade and Gina, but as soon as the hospital doors opened demonic wails pierced Wade's ears. Their painful cries and verbal threats were so loud Wade could hardly stand the noise. With both hands, he covered his ears and looked around to see if Gina was hearing the same thing, but she was engulfed in flames of red. She was an awesome vision to behold when she was in battle mode. The sight of her raging fire prompted him to also beckon Thrasher.

The thought of his workplace being invaded by demons brought our warrior to life. Wade also burst into flame and began loudly shouting, focusing his words towards the demons. "This is a place of refuge and it is under my authority! Leave this instance or be destroyed!"

Then Wade commanded, "Thrasher, clean the hospital of everything evil!"

Gina gave Ox permission to assist Thrasher and once the two angels began their duties she said to Wade. "Apparently, we have a job to do for Jesus or we wouldn't be under attack. Let's make sure we don't let Him down!"

I whispered into Gina's ear to stop fretting and cool her jets, hoping Wade would follow suit. Then I suggested they carry on with their original plan and let the angels do their job. After calming down their emotions, Wade introduced Gina to some of his favorite people and showed her the facility he loved. We urged them to use their powers to spread joy and happiness instead of fear. Abba and I knew if they focused on loving others the outcome would solidify their love for each other as well.

While they ambled along in the hallway, Wade complimented Gina. He confessed she looked fearless and gloriously beautiful covered in her flames and seeing her that way changed his whole perspective about their protection with God. Then he admitted it was nice to know they had Him on their side.

Gina replied, "Trusting in God is a good feeling, isn't it? Whisperer said, 'Who or what can come against the love of God.'" Since then, I totally rely on my raging flame if I have doubt or fear of anything. It was God's gift to me, so I hide in it. Trust me, I'm not a fighting warrior, I'm really cowering inside of it where I feel safe there. I was hiding in my flame, but I was also standing behind you and spoke because you did. I wanted to follow your lead."

Abba nudged me in my ribs, "She's making him feel like a man. Look at him blush! Our true love story in the making!

Shyly, Wade changes the subject, "I want to introduce you to one of my favorite patients, Adam Granger. He has been here a very long time and we can't figure out why he can't move his legs. He sits in his wheelchair all day and visits people. He is one of the friendliest people you'll ever meet."

While Wade rambled on about his patient, I whispered to Gina, "Here's our chance. You know what to do, let's show Wade the truth."

She agreed silently with me and said to Wade, "I love encouraging people. I try to do that every day where I work."

Wade tapped on Adam's door, and he and Gina entered the room when they heard Adam say they could come in. The first thing Wade did was introduce Gina. "Adam, I'd like you to meet my girlfriend, Gina Grimes. Remember me telling you that she was lovely?"

With a broad smile on his face, Adam said, "I'm pleased to meet you, Ms. Grimes. I was hoping to meet you. Please forgive me for not rising. I'm bound to this chair."

Gina walked over to Adam and extended her hand. In that moment, Wade saw she was in the blue flame and was giving God's love to his friend, Adam. Every word out of her mouth was gracious and caring as she expressed that she didn't see an invalid but a very strong person who used a wheelchair.

Adam told Gina he appreciated her compliments, but he was damaged goods because he killed people. He was trying to prove to God he was a good person and that he accepted the punishment since He hadn't sent him to hell before he could make amends.

Gina replied, "I assure you, Adam, Jesus doesn't punish people. You are already forgiven of all your transgressions and He is very proud of you and what you did for this country. You protected us and it is His deepest desire for you to walk again."

Adam said, "I want to believe you. I would love to walk and dance again, especially after seeing how lovely you are."

Here was our chance! I told Gina to repeat after me, "Adam, did you know that being crippled is ninety-nine percent in our heads? I know from experience because I was damaged not long ago. I couldn't move about freely, but I still danced. You and I can dance now if you let me tell you how."

Adam nodded in amazement. Then Gina said, "Close your eyes, and picture yourself dancing with me, sway to the music you hear and allow Jesus to move you."

Before Adam closed his eyes, Gina searched inside her handbag for an iPod. With loving blue flamed hands, she placed one ear bud into one of Adam's ears, and the other one inside hers. When Adam closed his eyes, I eased into their atmosphere meshed with Gina's flame so when their hands clasped, it was as if we were all holding hands. With a free hand, Gina spun the wheelchair around and from side-to-side until Adam's body began swaying to the beat of the music. That's when Wade noticed Adam could move his body to the rhythm.

I urged Wade to take a closer look. When he saw Adam's mouth moving, I told him he was praying and asking for a miracle. Then I showed him who else was in the group of dancers. Not only had I joined Gina, Abba was dancing with us as well.

Joy invaded Wade when he saw his loving Father dancing with two of his favorite people. Then suddenly, he noticed a twitching in Adam's legs and he stopped the dance to say, "Adam, your legs are moving!"

When Wade touched Adam's legs he noticed his hands were also extending God's loving blue flame. The warmth they gave Adam caused him to flinch and express, "I felt something!"

"Don't move! Let me massage your legs to get the blood flowing." Wade ordered.

While moving his flaming hands over Adam's legs, Wade telepathically asked Thrasher if he saw something blocking Adam's movements."

Thrasher answered, "Yes. The devil is hiding in the backbone and it is being very quiet."

"Kill it without disturbing Adam's excitement?" Wade ordered.

Thrasher drew his sword and swung it swiftly and cleanly through Adam's torso all the way down his spine until he impaled the tormenting demon. When Thrasher showed Wade the dead demon, it signaled to him to take Adam's hands, and tell Gina to hold Adam and ease the wheelchair away as he attempted to help Adam stand. Adam looked scared but his heart showed us he was excited. Then Wade encouraged him, "Use your arms and pull yourself up, we have you. You can do it! Prove to us you want to dance." It was delightful to see him want to try with his whole heart.

As Adam stared into Wade's eyes, he drew in a deep breath and used all the strength. Once he stood, Gina slowly pulled the chair back where she could stand behind him. Then she whispered in his ear, "Told you Jesus wanted you healed."

Tears flowed down Adam's cheeks and he began praising God loudly, "The Lord hasn't forgotten me! Thank you, Lord! Thank you, Lord!"

Wade interrupted him, "Let's not rush things. I want you to build muscle slowly by steady physical therapy. We'll have you walking in no time, but for now, I want you to get around using your wheelchair. Move as much as possible while seated, your back and legs are weak and I don't want you to injure yourself."

The Unlovable

The news of Adam's miracle spread like wildfire throughout the orthopedic ward, and each time he was asked what happened he gave God credit.   Gina and I stood on the sideline enjoying Adam's happiness. While Wade was making notes about Adam in the doctor's transcription room, Abba was about to bring another patient to his attention. I already knew who Abba wanted Wade to introduce to Gina. It was the person specifically designed to reap the most from this mission.

Abba suggested, "Why don't you introduce Gina to Paul Hastings? Don't you think he needs encouraging as much as Adam?"

A startled Wade quickly replied, "Officer Hastings wouldn't be friendly to Gina. He's bitter and hateful ever since I had him transferred here for treatment. He would spoil our afternoon."

Abba convinced Wade, "Paul is the person I really want Gina to meet today. I know it is always easier to be with people you like, and who are likable, but I also need someone willing to go to the unlovable.   Paul is trapped inside his own mind. He feels abandoned, thrown away by the very people he loved and was willing to die for. He feels no one wants him anymore because of his condition. I think it is time we proved that is not the case. Don't you? Explain to Gina that you need to check on another patient and then tell her why. She'll be fine in our care until you come back to her. You and Thrasher have issues to take care of in Paul's room before you introduce Gina."

"Hastings has a demon giving him a bad attitude, doesn't he?" Wade asked.

"Son, Paul has a legion of them tormenting him with pain as well as sucking the very life out of him. This man is being eaten alive by the creatures. Brace yourself before entering his room, the sight is very unpleasant. You'll know what to do." Abba shared.

Wade walked over to Gina and asked her to follow him to his office. When inside, he told her about another patient, who they needed to see after he and Thrasher visited him first. Gina knew what Wade meant so she agreed to wait.

When Wade was out of earshot, Gina asked me to tell her more about Officer Hastings. I replied, "During Wade's last tour in Iraq, Officer Hastings is one of the men he rescued. He was severely injured and not expected to live when they found him. Wade and several doctors did all they could to save the man's life, but unfortunately, he was left with only one eye, one arm and one leg. Officer Hastings's whole purpose in life, prior to this injury, was leading men and teaching them how to survive during combat. With no close family to speak of, he gave his heart and soul into developing marines. The Marine Core was his family and since the accident, he fears the Corp will abandon him. He is being tormented into thinking he is worthless because his body has failed him. Because of these evil influences, he wants to die and has been very harsh with anyone wanting to help him.

Wade highly respects this man but because he wouldn't listen to reason and was hard to work with, he had him moved from Maryland's VA hospital into this facility. Even though Wade works with patients needing orthopedic assistance, Office Hastings resists his care. With new prosthetics, Officer Hastings could function as a whole man again and could work on a military base again just not in a combat theater."

Gina wanted to know, "Are demons causing him to be mean spirited?"

"Yes, Gina! There is something you need to know, Officer Paul Hasting is the human version of Ox. He willingly gave his life to helping his fellow Marines and to fight for this country's freedom. He bled and was willing to die if necessary. Abba and I appreciate his bravery, but he doesn't know we care. He has lost hope because he doesn't have anyone to lay him at Jesus' feet like you did for Ox. He feels betrayed by his fellow Marines and his own body. We arranged for him to be brought to Wade so the two of you can give him what he needs most.

Don't you remember hearing Satan screaming at you once you found out Wayne was married? He was tormenting you so bad you wanted to die. This is where Officer Hastings is, but he doesn't know how to reach out to Jesus. He knows about Jesus, but he depended on his own strengths and now he doesn't have them anymore. Here is where you fit into this picture, and he needs to know his dreams have not been shattered." I explained.

"Me? How?" Gina asks.

I spoke directly to her tenacious bulldog nature, "When Wade calls you in to meet Officer Hastings, I want you to remember how you felt when you saw Ox beaten and broken. Talk to him like you would to Ox. Encourage him but don't show him pity. Look deeply into his good eye with those thoughts fresh in your mind. I'll direct your words and when we have the man's attention, we'll order him to continue fighting. Think of how you would feel if you saw Ox giving up on his life, and dying before your eyes. Officer Hastings doesn't want people's pity, but he needs to feel appreciated and loved. Warriors hate pity but they will respond to compassion. Compassion will open the door for us to touch his soul after Wade and Thrasher have the demonic activity under control. Officer Hastings needs a new mindset and then a goal before Wade can give him new and improved limbs. The goal in life will encourage him to walk and eventually run again showing the Marine Corp that good men are hard to take down."

By expressing in the manner Gina could understand and act upon, her armor changed into a raging red flame. Her eyes glowed red as she remembered how Satan abused Ox. She blurted, "I can fully sympathize! Take me to this man!"

Laughing I said, "It's obvious that you do! Cool your jets! Wade and Thrasher will notify us when they've cleared the area. Just remember the man needs compassion, not a biblical lesson. There will be a time and place for that later when he's ready. This is another rescue mission. Only we are rescuing his soul. Relax while we wait on Wade. This battle has already been won. One day Officer Hastings will want to know more about us and he'll ask. Then someone will explain it all to him."

On the way to Officer Hastings' room, Wade asked Abba, "Father, why haven't you destroyed the evil that's tormenting the men here?"

Abba said, "We want you to do it. When I raised Jesus from the dead, He gave man His Earthly authority. He didn't hand it back to me. You can face evil, destroy, or banish it from your presence. It's up to you to decide. You've been given all my resources on Earth and every heavenly blessing to see that your desires are met."

"You said I'll know what to do once I enter this room, but how is that possible?" Wade inquired.

"That's easy! Remember who is lying in that bed. He took you under his wing. Don't you recall how he made you feel at boot camp? You were very rebellious when you first arrived and the treatment he gave you wasn't pleasant, but it made you feel worthy. Learning true discipline changes a man. It's what you saw your own father giving Wayne and what you were craving from him. Turn the tables on Officer Hastings. You be in command and don't cower under his harsh words. He'll respect you for it.

The demons are Thrasher's problem. Just give him mental commands and he'll do what you say so you can focus on the discipline training of Paul Hastings." Abba recommended.

Wade braced himself for a wicked sight and a verbal onslaught when he entered the room. What he got instead was a horrible smell of unwashed flesh and sounds of demonic activity. Anger filled Wade's heart and mind. This man, he had come to respect, was bound by Satan's lies and his emotions were the main source of food for the evil vultures. And the sounds of their demonic beaks clicking and bone gnawing were deafening.

Wade's first order of command was for Thrasher to turn the tides and send heaven's eagles to feed on the vultures. Then he ordered him to destroy every evil creature he found in the hospital ward, whether it was a spiritual demon or Earthly parasite Satin had sent to attack the recovering patients.

Abba clapped His hands in joy after He heard Wade take charge. Thrasher bellowed for angelic eagles to join him and when they appeared, he told them to feast on death's vultures. Then he bellowed out to Adrian and Trulan to send angels under their authority to help him search the ward for imps and parasites. Within moments, the VA was a spiritual battleground again.

Wade strode over to the room's closed, shaded window and drew open the blinds giving the room light. When the room filled with light, it woke Officer Hastings from a tortured sleep and caused him to begin a profane onslaught.

Wade became angry when Hastings cursed God and the effect made him burst into an angry red flame. Abba mentally intervened so He could redirect Wade's anger, "Wade, remember this is the man you respect. This is not him using my name in vain. Don't entertain the demon, he's testing you."

Abba's warning reminded Wade of a scripture saying that even the angels refused to vindicate God. So, he calmed to allow Abba to fight His own battle. His calm nature would prove to the demonic giant that he depended fully on his savior and was in the room operating in love. Wade's passion for God changed his flame back to blue and the room became clean. It was true a puppeteer spirit could not exist in a loving environment. Love was Abba's own kind of vindication. Now that the room was clean of evil, Wade had to rid the room of its foul stench. Hastings smelled awful, it was no telling how long it had been since he washed or brushed his teeth, plus he was in much need of a shave.

Officer Hastings demanded, "Why are you here? I don't want to be bothered."

"I don't care what you want. I'm going to help you wash and then introduce you to my girlfriend." Wade said.

"Why?" Hastings asked stunned.

"Because I respect you as my Commanding Officer and want her to know the man who made me what I am today," Wade stated.

Hastings coldly replied, "I'm some officer, I'm half a man."

"That's because you won't let me help you," Wade stated bluntly.

"Bah!" Hastings jibed.

Wade took charge and firmly reprimanded, "I'll have you know this hospital has the best prosthetic team in America and soldiers have the first shot at getting the best equipment available. You'd be a bionic man and with my coaching, you could be running again in no time. Only you want to wallow in pity and act all wimpy!"

"Who do you think you are ordering me around like some kid?" Hastings demanded.

"I'm your doctor, Officer! Now, I'm the one giving the orders, so wake up and see how you're acting. Wimpy kid!" Wade bluntly replied.

Wade's words were forcing Paul Hastings into a fighting mode, which was good. Anger was an emotion Wade could use to help him recover.

Hastings bellows, "I'm not a kid and I'm certainly not a wimp."

"Then prove it to me by allowing someone to help you be the man you really are!" Wade bellowed back.

"How?" Hastings asked.

"Let an orderly clean your body until you can do it yourself! Like I said, I want to introduce my girlfriend to my Commanding Officer." Wade answered.

"Why?" Hastings softly asks.

"We want to show you some honor. You deserve it and she wants to show her gratitude and give her support to the men in my ward." Wade answered.

Wade's statement deeply moved Officer Hastings. He bowed his head so he wouldn't appear to be a wimp before replying in a choked voice, "Have an orderly help me bathe. I'm not shaving, though. I like the beard."

"You can keep the beard just brush your teeth. Your breath smells like a sewer! We'll be back in to see you in about thirty minutes. Try finding some manners while I'm gone." Wade happily answered.

Wade gave orders to the staff to help quickly bathe Officer Hastings, and have him dressed before he returned with Gina. Then he went to the lounge area and purchased two cups of coffee before going back into his office. On his way to the office, he commented to Abba. "That was fun! I wish I'd treated him like a wimpy kid earlier. I would have had him walking way before now and we wouldn't have wasted so much time."

"It's not over yet. You're about to witness another miracle. Allow Gina to speak her mind and don't hold her back." Abba shared.

Wade questioned, "I thought you just wanted her to meet him?"

"No one just meets our Gina. They get to experience her beauty and her forceful zeal. You of all people should know this first hand," Abba remarked

"No, they certainly don't! Her beauty is like a punch in the gut and her zeal for living is amazing. She definitely will be like a breath of fresh air for Officer Hastings." Wade agreed.

Reasons for Praise

Wade and Gina met with Officer Hastings and Gina didn't disappoint us. She proved to Wade that she was the woman he couldn't live without. The way she treated Paul Hastings was something for the storybooks. Wade watched as the heart of stone of the gruff old warrior melted like wax with Gina. He was putty in her hands and what she said to him restored him back to the Commanding Officer he really was.

Wade was amazed that Gina understood what the old warrior was going through. No one at the hospital could break through his depression and critical attitude until Gina appeared on the scene. Listening to how she lovingly explained to Hastings the way she felt about his sacrifice, and then watching her use effective emotions to influence Hastings made Wade very proud of her. She convinced him he still had a vital role in the military and she challenged him to improve himself physically. Then she begged him to accept Wade's expertise and use the prosthetics provided so he could walk and prove to everyone that bombs could not destroy who he really was on the inside.

Officer Hastings agreed to be Wade's guinea pig and the good news spread through the ward like wildfire causing soldiers and sailors to praise God. Hastings wasn't praising us yet, but the patients in other rooms were asking questions about Abba. Today was a very good day for my sweet Abba.

While eating their hamburgers and French fries, Wade and Gina talked about their feelings for each other and their passionate love for life. It was the revelation that Gina was his soul mate in many ways that convinced Wade it was time to take Abba's advice and ask Gina to marry him. The place wasn't right. He wanted to make the proposal during a very intimate and lovely dinner with music and dancing afterward.

Wade said to Gina, "I've got a plan! Since you and I love dancing, why don't we go on our first fancy dinner date tomorrow night at Reo's? Monday evening should be slow and we would have the whole dance floor to ourselves. You can show me some of the moves you told Adam about earlier."

Gina's heart clenched and she wanted to cry. She knew what a dinner date at Reo's meant. Trying to act normal, she said, "You've got a date. I'll prove to you that I'm a very good dancer. What time to you want to go out?"

"I've heard Reo's is a formal restaurant so dress up and be ready by seven," Wade replied.

"Then you and me better go home and get some rest. Tomorrow night, I'm going to make you dance a lot." Gina joked, not wanting him to know why she was so happy.

After dropping Wade off at his house, Gina started rambling, "Whisperer, everything Adrian showed me is about to come true! Wade is taking me to Reo's tomorrow night! I thought my life was moving so slow, now everything is moving too fast! Do you have any suggestions?"

"Don't be phony. Wade is aware you know more about the future than he does. My only other suggestion is that you wait and tell him your secret after the wedding. By then, the two of you won't care who knew what or when. You'll be focused on other things." I told her frankly.

"Good point, details leading up to our marriage won't matter," Gina replied.

"Why not enjoy the rest of your evening talking with Caylee. She knows everything already and is the perfect person for you to talk with. You can plan weddings together." I urged.

———⬥———

Abba and I enjoyed listening to Caylee and Gina talk. They talked for hours on their phones planning weddings. The memory of where her wedding took place, took Gina off guard. It disturbed her so much she needed to talk with me.

After politely making excuses to end their conversation, Gina instantly addressed me, "Whisperer, I remember every detail of my wedding and something has me very confused. The place we get married is not at my church. I love my church and Pastor Reed, why would I get married somewhere else?"

"You won't. Ask Caylee to show you the small wedding chapel at your church. It's the perfect place for a small, intimate wedding. You'll love it. Pastor Reed will be the minister. You just didn't take the time to look at him while on your journey, because you were staring into Wade's eyes." I explained.

Gina let out a deep breath and said, "That's a relief. I felt disconnected for a minute and you're right, I don't want a fussy large wedding. I only want a few friends and our families to attend so a small chapel will be perfect."

Gina quickly called Caylee back and asked if there was a small chapel at their church. Caylee exclaimed, "Yes! I'll show you on Wednesday before service. You'll love it! It's so pretty. The room is small but it has beautiful stained glass windows just like our large sanctuary. Plus, they keep it staged with candelabras and beautiful plants so there wouldn't be much need to decorate."

"Then it's the perfect place for Wade and me." Gina commented.

Caylee inquired, "Do you remember what day you were married?"

"No, but Whisperer keeps saying it won't be a long wait," Gina said.

"Why don't you and Wade get married on Christmas Eve? That would be an awesome time to seal your vows." Caylee recommended.

Gina replied, "I like it. Only if you help me arrange it, plus I want you to be my maid of honor?"

At the Polk home, Wade talked with the only person he wanted to share his good news with. He tapped on his mother's bedroom door and waited for her to answer. When she bid him inside, he noticed how much she looked like her old self. The sight made his heart melt.

"Mom, do you mind if I talk with you for a few minutes. I've got some good news and you are the first person I want to share it with." Wade asked.

Mrs. Polk said, "I could use some good news."

"I'm asking Gina Grimes to marry me tomorrow night," Wade told her.

For a minute, Wade thought his mother didn't remember Gina because she'd closed her eyes and bowed her head. Then she said, "Wade, my mind is still foggy but I do remember a lovely young lady going to church with us. Is she your Gina?"

"Yes, ma'am. She's the love of my life and I can't wait to make her my bride." Wade told her.

"Then move me out of this house quickly so the two of you can have your own private place. It does my heart good to know that you are happy. Promise you'll give me some grandchildren before I die," she said firmly.

"I will do my best," Wade replied with a smile.

Mrs. Polk remembered something and said, "Wade! Bring me my jewelry box. I have a ring for you. It's one of your grandmothers. Look at it and see if it is something you would like to give your bride. You may want it to be her engagement ring."

"Shouldn't you ask Wayne first if he wants to give it to Amy?" Wade inquired.

"No, I've given him one already. This one is my favorite, and I saved it for you," she said.

In the jewelry case was another tiny box that held a beautiful sapphire and diamond ring. Seeing it in his mother's fingers, made Wade eyes filled with tears. He remembered his favorite grandmother wearing it and it brought sweet memories to his mind. That ring was very precious and the perfect way to express his love to Gina tomorrow night.

Overall, Abba and I say this day ended very well and the people we loved were content and giving us praise.

Taking Care of Business

Christmas Eve, two weeks after Wade's proposal passed extremely fast. Many things were accomplished, and Wade and Wayne moved their mother into her new apartment. Russ agreed to take over Gina's apartment lease and Pam Grimes and Mamie took care of all the wedding and reception details

Because neither Gina nor Wade wanted a fancy wedding or reception, Pam, and Mamie enlisted help from some of the ladies in their Women's Group instead of hiring caterers. The church Fellowship Hall was reserved instead of having to travel to a fancy club for the reception. Gina was very appreciative for all the help. She didn't have to lift a finger other than finding herself and Caylee a dress for the occasion.

I stood off to the side and listened to Gina and Abba talk while she got ready for her ceremony, I heard her ask Him, "Father, are you proud of me? I made it. I kept my promise."

Abba sweetly replied, "Gina, even if you hadn't kept your promise I'd still love you. Nothing is ever going to change how I feel. I asked you to stay pure for your benefit, not mine. I wanted you to respect and feel good about yourself?"

"Yes sir, I do." She interjected proudly.

Gina asked, "Would it be too crude for me to say, I can hardly wait? I know Wade will be a fantastic lover?"

Abba laughed, "Sex was my idea. I'm the one who made it pleasurable so when you are being honest about your feelings is refreshing to me. It shows me you don't embarrass easily, even in front of me."

"Can I be honest again?" Gina asks.

"Yes. I already know what you're thinking anyway." Abba informed her.

"I want to rip his clothes off the moment we say I do! My panties have been on fire for too long." Gina said frankly.

"Well then do it! Bring him back in this dressing room and lock the door. It's my house and I don't care if you find a corner somewhere after your vows. Just make sure the two of you are discreet and don't leave any signs. I'm in full agreement that the two of you need to take care of business quickly so you can relax and enjoy your reception party. You both are like two volcanoes ready to erupt." Abba expounded.

Gina questioned, "Are you serious?"

Abba countered, "You have my permission to procreate. Conceive your promise as soon as you can."

"What if we get caught? Would that embarrass you?" Gina asks.

"Not in the least. It could embarrass you, though, so take the necessary precautions for privacy. Enlist help from someone you can trust and who understands to stand as 'look-out.'" Abba recommended.

Once Gina had Abba's permission, He and I stood back and enjoyed watching her make the arrangements for the fun she and Wade would have after their vows. She laid out wet wipes, took the sofa pillows off the couch, and then proceeded to take off her pantyhose and to our amazement she removed her lacy new thong underwear and looped it through the blue garter surrounding her leg.

As soon as Gina finished prepping, Mamie knocked on the dressing room saying, "Showtime, you ready?"

Gina replied, "Mamie I thought this day would never come. I'm more than ready. Do me a favor and follow us out of the church once we walk down the aisle together."

"Sure child! Why?" Mamie asked.

"I'll explain after the service," Gina offered.

The ceremony was very sweet and it had many guests weeping from the heartfelt vows. After their kiss ended and they were announced husband and wife, Gina practically towed Wade down the aisle. It was a comical sight because she wasn't wasting any time.

On their way out of the chapel, Gina caught Mamie's eye and motioned for her to follow. In the lobby, Gina said, "Wade and I are going to slip off for a few minutes, please make excuses for us. We'll see everyone in the fellowship hall shortly."

Mamie stuttered, "Tell me, you ain't gonna to do the deed here in the church?"

With Wade in tow and just as dumbfounded as Mamie, Gina replied, "Call it what you want, but it's gonna happen! Just make sure the guests are entertained and out of our way until we get back."

Mamie wanted to argue, but Abba quickly intervened and said to her, "She has my permission. Don't you interfere or judge, just help them Mamie. You were in her shoes not long ago; remember."

"Ok Lord, but what do I tell their guests," Mamie asks Him.

"It won't take them long so tell the truth. Say the love birds wanted to be alone for a few minutes and to start enjoying the food." Abba suggested.

—◆—

Nothing can be hidden from our eyes or ears so we were fully aware of what was about to take place. We loved seeing our plans come together and prosper. Gina took Wade aside once they were in the locked ladies dressing room, focused her wild beautiful blue eyes on him, and then fumbled under her wedding gown before bluntly saying, "You are mine and it's time you know I'm not a prude."

Wade asked, "Shouldn't we wait?"

"Nope!" Gina wickedly replied.

Before Wade could utter another word, Gina handed him the thong she had looped in her garter. Then she said while wrapping her arms around his neck and nuzzling his ear, "if you help me lift my skirt, you can have your way with me on the couch."

The man didn't need coaxing. He swiftly complied, and in a few minutes, the deed was done. Satisfied and refreshed, they exited the room to meet Mamie waiting for them in the hallway.

Mamie ordered, "Stop! Wait just a second. Let me make sure the two of you aren't showing evidence of 'hanky panky' before you go in there. We don't want anyone wagging their tongues."

"Thanks, Mamie," They said in unison.

No one but Mamie was any wiser to what they'd done in Abba's house. All three of them entered the Fellowship Hall as if nothing had happened, looking tidy, calm and collected. When their guest had finished eating, and enjoying the festivities, the married couple left on their three-day honeymoon and began enjoying each other more thoroughly.

Wade was a very satisfied man knowing he not only had a soul mate, but he had sexual wildcat for a wife who could fulfill all his needs. Gina, on the other hand, wasn't disappointed either. Wade was every bit the good lover she dreamed he would be and she was deeply gratified knowing something was growing in her womb.

Confession Time

The night of Gina's and Wade's wedding Russ made the decision to be truly open with Caylee. He needed to confess that he had an angel, and why he rented Gina's apartment. Having to babysit Romper had taught him a very valuable lesson. Abba and I suggested he be truthful about who he was and honest about his current finances which led him to rent Gina's small furnished apartment.

During dinner, Russ said to Caylee, "Sweetie, I need to tell you a few things."

"Shoot! I'm all ears." Caylee said.

Russ shyly stated, "I know about the angels."

Caylee took a huge drink of cola, and then she said, "How? We've never discussed him."

"I didn't say him, I said angels." Russ gently corrected her.

"Okay, if you aren't talking about my angel, then what are you saying?" Caylee asks.

"Let me start over," Russ suggested.

"I met your angel several weeks ago, after Frank's wedding. Brent introduced me and Wade to God at the Boys' Home. That night I searched my heart and asked several questions and was granted an out-of-body experience with Father God and the Holy Spirit. They introduced me to my angel. He isn't grand like yours, he is a big baby and cries at the drop of a hat." Russ informed.

"Why do you think he's so immature and sensitive?" Caylee asked.

"The Holy Spirit told me to ask you. He said your angel is strong because of the way you live and believe. If I train Romper the way you did Cherub, he could cope and adjust. Tell me your secret!" Russ begged.

179

Caylee replied, "First off, I didn't know I had an angel until recently. I can't see into the spirit realm like Gina, Hope, or Brent, but I've always known that I had someone looking out for me. I knew it in my heart and felt it in my bones. What I think the Holy Spirit wants you to know is how I learned to rest and wait. If I worry about my life, I don't function well. I take all my issues to the Lord and I search through my Bible for clues or references. I follow the teachings of Jesus. I trust the Holy Spirit to guide me correctly and I apply the Word made flesh to my life issues. Then I wait. Some people say I'm weird. Others have called me creepy, but I don't care. I've learned to sit at my savior's feet and listen with my heart. Sometimes I've had to wait a long time. Then there are occasions where I didn't have to wait but a few minutes. I use all my faith in Jesus and His works so I don't get confused. When I asked the Lord for a soul mate, I waited a long time. I got lonely but I didn't stop praying or enjoying my other friends. That's why I involved myself with Hope's and Brent's young adult's group. The fellowship helped me cope while I passed the time away doing fun things."

"I still don't understand how that strengthened your angel," Russ remarked.

Caylee explains, "Don't you see! God's Word is what strengthens my angel not me. By resting at Jesus' feet Cherub must have done the same thing. Serving us and fulfilling God's plan for us the way God ordered in scripture is an angel's purpose for living. A purpose for living makes anything stronger."

"So, by seeking the Holy Spirit and following the words and deeds of Jesus, Romper will know what to do. That shouldn't be hard." Russ acknowledged.

Russ continued, "I have something else to tell you. I was given a direct order from Father God to live on my own for a while, so can we plan on having a spring wedding?"

"Why?" Caylee asked.

"I was told to learn how to live on what I made." Russ confided. Caylee looked at him puzzled. Then she confessed, "I may live with my Dad, but I trust God to provide what I need. I fully believe in giving for Him and receiving from Him. What I make at a job is not the final say for me. It's easier for me to trust in sowing and reaping than in a paycheck. It's like farming; seed, time, and then harvests. Life placed hard issues my way at times, but I learned to be patient. Things have a way of working out."

"I get it! That's just not what I'm trying to say. I guess I need to come clean and tell you the whole truth." Russ admits.

"You have me worried and I don't like worrying," Caylee said.

"Don't worry! It's not a critical issue and it won't affect us. I hope." Russ stated.

"Out with it!" Caylee demanded.

Russ took a deep breath, then asked, "Caylee do you know who I am?"

"You're joking, right?" She said.

"Do you know who my father is?" Russ asks her instead.

"Yes! He is Albert Jackson." She answered.

Russ says, "My dad is the founder and owner of Jackson and Jackson."

Alarmed, Caylee choked out a question, "Your dad, is the owner of the largest manufacturing plant in this state, and you drive a tractor trailer for a living?"

"Yeah! I drive a large truck but not for a living. I drive it because I'm crazy about trucks and I like to see the countryside. Driving it is fun. I'm the other Jackson of 'Jackson and Jackson'," Russ confessed honestly.

"Why have you kept this a secret from me? Did you think I'd be after your money?" Caylee asked tearfully.

Russ took Caylee's hand and assured, "Honey, look at me. The thought of you wanting me because I was rich never crossed my mind. I truly didn't mean to keep this a secret from you. My relationship with Father God showed me how irresponsible I was living. I was playing not working. I wasn't becoming my own man, and I still live with my Dad. I didn't have any responsibilities or a purpose until now. If I wanted something that cost more than I had in my checking account, I usually tapped Dad's account and purchased what I wanted. He never questioned me. I've never had to live from paycheck to paycheck. That's why we are having this discussion. It was Father God who ordered me to start learning how to manage on my own, and live off my income. He wants me to learn Dad's company from the ground floor up so I can operate it correctly someday. He wants me to know how most people live so I can properly understand their way of life. By the time we marry, I want to be able to support you without leaning on Dad. You are my life and I want you happy."

With bright eyes from unshed tears, Caylee replied, "I'm already happy. I don't need much. I knew you lived with your dad so when you suggested apartment hunting, it didn't faze me. Most young married couples don't want to live with their parents. Since I've never been invited to your place, I assumed it was like most bachelor pads and you were embarrassed. I never dreamed you lived in a mansion; with servants!"

"Honey, I didn't invite you over because it wouldn't have been appropriate. Dad is gone most nights because of business meetings, and I didn't want people to think we were shacking up. You're my lady and I refused to have people talking trash about you. We don't have live in servants anymore. We usually eat take out. Neither one of us cooks, so when Dad joined us for dinner it was because we wanted you to have a good meal and relax. He's crazy about you by the way. I haven't told him I'm moving out. I'm sure he is going to throw a fit when I do." Russ consoled.

"Why haven't you told him," Caylee sniffled out.

"He would insist I bring you under his roof. I want you to have your own place. One day I want to build you a mansion like Dad built for Mom." Russ replies.

"I like your house," Caylee said honestly.

"Then, if you want it when Dad's gone we'll move into it. All I want is your happiness." Russ said.

"Like I said, I'm already happy," Caylee exclaimed.

Oh, Holy Night of Reconciliation

On Christmas Eve, I watched Brent and Hope play Santa Claus for Greg. The little guy was very blessed with love and gifts. After they finished laying out Greg's presents, Brent suggested a snack before going to bed in hopes it would help them fall asleep. It was while they were eating that I decided to surprise them.

I materialized in front of them and said, "Hi guys. Merry Christmas!"

Hope choked on her apple but managed to squeak out, "We're not used to you making personal appearances. Usually, you just speak. Is something wrong?"

"Far from it Hope. I'm here as a special messenger for Jesus, inviting the two of you to a wonderful event. Call it His Christmas present to both of you." I answered.

Brent asked me, "Are we going somewhere in the natural or will we travel spiritually?"

"Spiritually of course. That way you don't have to find a babysitter for Greg. Hurry and eat your snacks. You are going to need the energy. When you finish, we need to go to your bedroom." I told them.

They took my advice and ate quickly anticipating a long journey. Watching them scarf down sandwiches and fruit was comical, especially Hope. She usually didn't eat much at night, but since she stopped having morning sickness, she had a healthy appetite. The few noticeable pounds she'd gained looked lovely on her and were a good sign that Shiloh was growing nicely.

When we went to their bedroom, I told them to get comfortable in their bed so I could place them in deep slumber. Eager for their journey, they crawled into bed, held hands, and closed their eyes. It was only a few seconds before they passed into a deep sleep.

Leaving their sleeping bodies, Jesus was waiting for the three of us in the spirit realm. He said, "Greetings! I'm very happy you are here to share in our special occasion. We don't get to watch Abba reconcile with His bride very often. The two of you will learn to love and forgive from the master."

Hope said, "I thought you were the master."

Jesus countered quickly, "My sweet and lovely Hope, you and Brent have been invited to watch my Father in action as He woos back His long-lost bride."

Hope confessed, "I'm confused. Who are you talking about?"

"Hope, do you remember the harlot you and I encountered last month? The old harlot is the spirit of the world and she is why God sent me into the Earthly system. In the natural realm, mankind only knows her as dirt; of what the Earth is made. Abba created the world for His pleasure and once she awakened to His declaration of 'Light Be' she acknowledged His presence. It was then He gave her the spiritual name Zion. She is the mother of all creation because everything living comes out of her." Jesus answered.

Hope exclaimed, "She wasn't lovely to me! She was gross darkness and I thought you said she was evil assisting Satan with destruction. How can she be creation?"

Jesus sighed before correcting Hope. "From Abba's hands, everything was formed from the dirt of Earth to become a garden. Her soul is a spiritual garden and isn't evil, but just like humans, her mind can get dark and weary after seeing what Satan does against God's children. Her ears and mouth were bound so she couldn't hear any form of praise or worship for Abba. What she saw were the actions of mankind and her energy grew dark and chaotic. Over time, her negative energy influenced everything. That is why we ordered her to move. It was the only way we could force positive energy back into the atmosphere. You see, Hope, Zion's mind must rely on what she hears, and she was denied the

185

luxury of sound, and her faith couldn't incorporate with Abba's Word. After many, many years of watching people being tormented by Satan, she tried to cover mankind's sin when she should have allowed me to cover them.

This cycle is forever being repeated, she suffers a lot as God's kingdom. But every third or fourth generation of mankind, she is freed and allowed to hear and see the truth. All over the Earth, not just in your area, a change will occur when she unites with Abba again.

The Holy Spirit and I began helping Abba redeem her after we convinced Gina that He was real. Now, Zion knows she has daughters willing to acknowledge God's presence within their being. You and Gina accomplished this by joining with her in spirit, soul, and body. She witnessed the two of you overtake Satan using your minds and overtaking him with your soul's. She couldn't hear or assist you because he had her bound. On the afternoon that Gina faced Satan, I demanded that she be unleashed and freed from her bindings. Our voices gave her the strength to move when we screamed. She hadn't been acting evil as she was brooding, sad and lonely. Everything created was being used against mankind and Satan has beaten and tormented her by pointing fingers at God's children. She felt abandoned and like a failure, and had no choice but to stew in negative thoughts.

Instead of punishing her, Abba wants to restore her to her rightful mind and position. He takes much pleasure in making her feel special. You see, Abba sent life into the world the day He said 'Light Be!" When we used our lights and voices to free her a new cycle began. There's nothing new on Earth. Everything has come in cycles from heaven to Earth since the beginning of time nothing escapes this fact. This celebration is a renewal of God's intention for the Earth.

You and Brent will be taught how Zion's thoughts are renewed. While Abba woos her, I will deal with Satan and his hordes.

Unlike Zion, he has no soul and he stays trapped inside of a cycle of revolving time. He forgets the embarrassment we put him through and then he begins waging war all over again. Mysteries will be revealed to you tonight, so pay close attention to every detail. Everything you recall after tonight will help you change others around you. As Zion's mind gets renewed so will man's."

We followed Jesus to our front row seats and patiently waited. When the ceremony began, two huge golden doors to our right opened wide allowing the archangels Gabriel and Michael, to enter. Once they were in place, golden ram's horns were raised to their lips. The horns blast was extremely loud. Instantly, everyone fell to their knees except for Jesus and me, we just lowered our heads. As the room became quiet, Abba walked in. His magnificence had everyone gasping. He radiated power and authority because He was wearing the most glorious clothes and accessories found throughout all His creations.

Taking His place, center stage, we watched Him sit in the largest of three chairs that were arranged on the royal platform leaving one to His left and right empty. That's when Hope couldn't contain herself and had to ask Jesus a question, whispering just loud enough for Him to hear, "Why aren't you up there with Him?"

"Wait and see. It will all make sense to you soon." He answered.

Abba ordered everyone to rise, and then He ordered Michael and Gabriel to bring in His bride. Within moments, we heard very heavy footsteps, along with the sound of something dragging approaching the group. Zion, dressed as an overindulgent harlot slowly entered the room assisted by God's two angels. Her body was enormous and so heavy laden with gold and silver jewelry, and she could hardly move. Even her clothes were gaudy and made with layers of furs, silks, and linens and the sight of her exuded greed and lust.

Before Abba could approach her the dark energy that followed her had to be removed. In front of all the witnesses, Abba rebuked every influence Satan had fed to her even some religious training he had warped. Then with one touch to her face, Abba approved of her and proved to everyone watching that there wasn't anything able to keep them separated. Then He took her chin, tilted it up so he could look in her eyes then He said, "Welcome home."

With a soft voice, she replied, "Hello Sire. It is very good to be back."

"That old Dragon did it to you again, didn't he?" Abba said jokingly while He stroked her cheek.

"Yes love, he did and I'd given up hope and this weight is almost unbearable. I'm so ashamed!" she confessed.

At her confession, Abba stood and addressed the crowd, "I want everyone here to take note. Zion is innocent! I will not allow anything to hold evil thoughts against her. She was a slave to Satan and my Son has freed her again. It is time we all welcomed her home and stop turning our backs on her existence. She must be able to see my family and know that you have forgiven her."

Zion thanked God then she turned and faced us and bowed her head. I watched Brent and Hope both squirm. I knew they didn't understand so I reminded Hope about her coronation day with Jesus and I asked Brent to remember his feelings when a madman kidnapped Hope. The memories helped them understand Abba's feelings and then they relaxed.

Uncovering the Prize

Abba turned Zion around to face Him and asked, "Are you ready?" "Please," she begged.

He held out His scepter and then rammed it hard on the floor then He commanded the care giving angels to, "Undress her! Let everyone see the truth!"

The angels worked so fast they were a blur and the air whirled around Zion as sounds of tearing cloth and scattering jewels filled our ears. When the sounds stopped, we knew the task was complete and standing before us was a beautiful, well per-portioned and naked lady who was still bound hands and feet with chains. The chains looked miles long. It was evident to everyone that the chains were what made the dragging sound upon her arrival.

Again, Abba slammed His scepter on the floor told the angels to take care of Zion. They were to feed her and make sure she was comfortable. While she was preoccupied, and out of earshot to Abba's voice, He began addressing the crowd. "I'm the one who bound her. The chains you saw connect her DNA with all creation. Don't look concerned! Through them, she can connect with anyone, anywhere and anytime. I ordered her to watch over my creations this way. She had no choice. It was decreed long ago so I'll take the blame for Satan using the chains against her. They are why she can hardly move. Through them, her spirit has a purpose. It was my will that she be a nurturer and work with my children to prosper the planet and everything I blessed. Satan has always attacked her and used her emotions to cause chaos. That is why I free her from time to time so I can show her love, and pour calm into her negativity. Jesus is the only one I trust to vindicate her. So, I declared a failsafe. Zion's mind can't be freed from Satan unless Jesus gives a direct order for her to move. When the Word made flesh speaks and is understood, she will respond allowing her mind, soul, and body to work as a team. Everyone must understand that 'anything made of dust falls under this same rule of authority'. That is why Jesus is now at war. Satan has blinded and deafened mankind for too long so Jesus will set my world system right.

The way Zion looked when she entered my presence tonight is not how she is supposed to dress. Her spirit was not created to carry man-made items. She was tricked into accepting the trinkets as offerings in a man-made place, and her submission, due to a heavy heart, fueled Satan's greedy plan. I'm tired of watching him abuse my family and making them think there is no choice but to hoard and save to survive. And I am sick of him causing divisions. I am no respecter of persons, no one is better than the next. Everyone is entitled to dress in fancy attire with real jewels if they desire. But to do it to with a haughty attitude of superiority is nauseating to me.

He also forced my people into thinking they had to sacrifice their earnings for my love and this caused bitterness towards me. I never demanded anything from mankind but a relationship. Fear was causing them to think they'd go to the place I designed for Satan if they didn't adhere to a method. Tithes were created so people would never have to be without. It was just a method, not a rule, to show them if everyone participated in sowing and reaping, give and take they could survive."

Zion walked back into the throne room. She was beautiful and all aglow and we could tell she wanted to talk. Then Abba declared, "Let her shed light on her feelings. I love hearing her glorify my Son the way I want mankind to do."

The first thing she did was fix her eyes on Jesus before speaking. Then she said, "Before you came for me, I was insane with worry. I do apologize to you. My mind was shamefully warped and the emotions Satan created in me caused all forms of famine, parasites, and diseases to enter Earth's realm. I knew it was wrong. Shame only made life worse. I am forever grateful to you for repeatedly coming to my rescue and I'm happy you will be rescuing the children from the chaos I created as well as from Satan's evil."

Then she spoke to the rest of us. "Even though these chains hold me tight to a mission, my mind can't run free unless I have my ears open to hear. One voice can pierce the cage my own thoughts trap me in. After I heard Jesus' voice I heard the voice of a woman's signifying to me one of my daughters didn't hold me accountable for their mixed-up life. I held onto their voices and their light with all the mental strength I had. I had a glimmer of hope that began to break through my depression.

When the rains came, I watched Satan viciously take pleasure in destroying the kingdom he'd made in the spirit realm from my resources and my negative energy. His fake and lying storehouses with their safety measures crumbled before me and it even shook some of the churches in the natural realm as if a major Earthquake had happened.

He knew torturing me was over so he went viciously against mankind. The kingdom on Earth would soon suffer violence but the violent will take back what Satan tried to steal. People must start over, but they won't be able to do it the right way. I am so grateful that the Son of God purified me with His blood when He died on the cross that caused God's plan for me to be set in motion Now, I'm asking for your forgiveness and as soon as I can, I promise to recognize the sons and daughters of man and work properly with them."

The crowd roared "We forgive! We forgive!"

We watched as she sagged from exhaustion into Abba's arms and He carried her to the throne with three chairs. Then He beckoned for Jesus to join them. Jesus ran to them and took Zion from Abba's arms, and Abba banged His scepter again and exclaimed, "It's time my bride took her rightful place alongside me after I dress her like the queen she really is. "

Jesus sat her in the chair to Abba's left. Then Abba lovingly began to adorn her with sunbeams of gold. The crown He designed was made with jewels from stars and He shod her feet with the light of the moon. She was the most beautiful thing ever created but Abba wasn't finished. He gave her the ability to change anytime she desired. Color was no option. If she wanted to change hair, eye, or skin tone, He left that up to her. She was truly the common denominator for all humanity. A racial division had no place.

Zion Given Authority

After a few moments of recovery, Zion could speak again. She addressed Jesus, "I would love to meet your brides. Would you please ask them to come and introduce themselves?"

Jesus replied, "My Queen, I only summoned one of them along with Earthly her mate to your coronation. The other one is on her honeymoon."

Zion said, "It is very important that I speak to the two women who have recently been victorious over Satan. Have the honeymooners brought here. They can resume their time together again in a few hours."

Deep in the shadows of the room, we heard a shout, "Sacrilege! She's a whore! Why is she giving orders?" We all knew instantly the reason Zion was so adamant to talk with Hope and Gina. An uninvited guest was present and he was now demanding Zion to remain silent. Satan was extremely angry and taking chances making an appearance.

Abba stood and the angels prepared for something ugly, but it was Zion who spoke first, "Enough! Let him in. I have something to say to him after my prodigies are here alongside me."

During the commotion, I quickly spoke to Brent. "Take note! Open your mind and listen intently to everything said and then watch what happens. Keep what you hear and see firmly planted in your spirit so you can assist Hope when the time comes. Be prepared to answer questions thrown at you   Truthful answers only. Tonight will prepare you for actions needed in a few months. After Hope gives birth, a new order will begin. Shiloh's entrance into the world will proclaim peace.   Hope will be made intercessory leader of your church and a new team will emerge to replace the older prayer warriors. She will need you on the team and your powers of agreement are important to her."

Brent said back, "Being truthful won't be a problem. I know what to say if attacked by Satan but I'm confused about some other issues. I thought I was supposed to focus only on my new job duties."

"Hope's assurance of you is all that matters at this moment. Learn to take each moment as it comes and don't be afraid to ask us for clarification if you need some. Right now, get ready for Satan's accusations." I swiftly replied.

While Brent and I discussed vital issues, Michael and Gabriel returned with Gina and Wade and Zion beckoned for the two women to approach her. Then Zion faced the shadowy corner where Satan hid and addressed him again, "So you think it's a sacrilege for me to speak. Why don't you show your face and confront me instead of screaming at us from the shadows?"

Satan slithered into the great hall and pointed his finger at Zion. "You have no right! I have not given you permission. You are mine, so get back to your position on Earth this instant!"

Zion laughed loudly. Then she stepped down from the platform, walked up to Satan and looked him directly in the eye. "I have you know, I've never been nor will I ever be yours. My mind and body may have betrayed heaven and Earth, but my soul never will. The things you formed with my flesh and negative energy even belong to God. What you released through my depression will be used for good from now on. The people I thought had abandoned God will see the truth shortly and you won't stand a chance."

"But you accepted everything they offered you. You even swallowed the mental food I fed you. You cannot tell me you didn't enjoy it, nor can you say you didn't like looking good." Satan huffed out.

Zion blurted out, "Do you see any of the trash on me now? Who has it? Tell me! All the gifts you gave, the money and evil thoughts you shoved in my head are gone. If you want them back you'll have to ask the rightful owner for them."

"What do you mean I can't have them back? Who has my goods?" Satan demanded.

Zion pointed to Jesus and said, "Your stuff is with its rightful owner. It's lying at His feet to do with as He pleases."

We all turned then and looked in Jesus' direction and sure enough, all the gold, silver, jewels, furs and other clothes were piled neatly at His feet.

Then Zion did something disgusting, she vomited all over Satan before saying why she did it. She wiped her mouth and said, "There's the food you gave me! I held on to everything you showed me and I kept it in my stomach instead of my brain. The taste of it kept me sick for a very long time but I refused to use any energy from it. The longer I waited for things to change the sicker I got. Now you use this undigested food any way you want since I refused to digest any."

Satan forgot where he was and reached out and grabbed Zion by the throat. When he did, Abba went nuts. Love incarnate pinned Satan to a wall instead of instantly killing him. Abba shouted, "You dared touch her in my presence and expect me to do nothing? You'll not do that ever again!"

Gabriel and Michael came in and took Satan out of Abba's grip. While they held him, Abba growled out, "Listen to everything she has to say. Remember accusations will get you hurled back to Earth."

We stood waiting for Zion to continue her speech. Rubbing her neck and walking closer to Satan she said, "Your touch always loathed me. I hated every second of it!"

"There is something I want to show you. It's what your efforts really produced in me." She shared.

"What?" Satan hissed.

Grinning broadly, Zion began to shake violently. She bent over and let out a loud scream of pain before her chest ripped open and exposed her core. Inside her chest was a big heart engulfed in a blue flame. She reached inside her heart and pulled something out of the flame. Then she shoved her opened hand in Satan's face. "Take a good look at what I keep harbored in my heart. It is the broken and bloody body of death. Jesus gave it to me. I've held onto this to anchor His love for me. Now that my mind is free from you, it has produced a new desire to spread Jesus' love. You see, His love never fails. Sometimes it hides, but when it is exposed watch out for a renewal. It's time to prove death no longer stings, and it can be a beautiful thing."

Not heeding Abba's warning, Satan bellowed for all to hear, "This still doesn't take away your stains. You're still a whore and so are those two women beside you. They've had men paw on their bodies and they liked it. Make them tell the truth. They can't lie in God's presence. Then make their men tell you how they lusted for them."."

I elbowed Brent, "You'll be up there soon. Get ready for a debate."

Zion replied, "Ask them yourself. They will tell the truth no matter who asks."

"Okay, I'll start with the brunette," Satan replied.

Zion stepped back and Jesus, placed His hand on Hope's back and gently nudged her forward. Then Satan pointed at Hope, but we already knew what he would say. He thought he had proof of guilt and wanted to expose it in front of all of us. With her front and center, Satan began to laugh, then he said, "Everyone, look at her belly! We all know that Jesus didn't place that kid in there. She's been playing around behind His back. Come on, Dearie; tell everyone the truth, whose child is this?"

Hope squared her shoulders and began addressing heaven's witnesses. "This baby has been dedicated to Jesus. She belongs to Him and to us. I admit I've lain with three men in my lifetime, but my body refused to accept two of the men's seed. It wasn't until Brent, that my body responded the way it should because of something Jesus said to me. He asked me to accept one of His brothers as my mate, and then I could produce a family for him. I fell in love with the man He chose for me, but we didn't have sexual intercourse until after we said our marriage vows. This baby has God's approval. I can prove it by showing His holy seal."

"What holy seal? I don't see anything proving this is true." Satan hissed.

Bravely, Hope began to strip. At first, Brent wanted to object to her actions, but I quietly urged him not to say or do anything to let her prove her words. Naked as the day she was born, Hope stood proudly for all of heaven to see. She showed them the only thing she could not remove, and it was the golden belt Abba had placed around her middle. Seeing it wrapped around her waist made heaven's witnesses applaud loudly.

Satan growled and ordered Brent forward. "Tell everyone the truth. Wasn't it your lust that placed that brat in her body?"

Brent didn't hesitate to answer truthfully, "No! We were both inside of Jesus' armor the moment her body accepted my seed. Only naked flesh and a clean spirit are allowed inside the armor. Lust couldn't enter. He was fully aware that His love connected our bodies. It was the best experience of my life and I was happy to share it with Him."

Everyone applauded again and Satan hissed. Then he pointed his finger at Gina demanding her to step forward.

Wade stood very still and kept his mouth shut. He wasn't worried about Gina, and he knew what she was capable of. Satan's first question for Gina was a low blow. He wanted her to tell the crowd how many men she'd slept with. Rather than exposing her guilt the question insulted her enough she burst into a raging fire and she didn't hesitate to strip naked, laying her soul bare before speaking. "I can't count all of them. I will confess after being jilted by my first love, I used men for sex and other pleasures, hoping to find my perfect match. None of them were worthy of my heart. It wasn't until I met the Holy Spirit that I truly fell in love with a good man, and His name is Jesus. I can't live without him. It was His plan that I marry and have children, so I promised God I would not have sex with another man until marriage. I kept that promise. When Wade and I married, we didn't waste time. It was God's suggestion."

Satan snapped, "How do you know this man was right for you and not just another sex fiend or drug user? I know for a fact, he doesn't respect women and used them for sexual pleasures."

Gina's flame grew brighter and she shot Satan questions of her own. "You tell us, in God's presence, is it true when God speaks it becomes fact? Have you ever heard something God say, not come true? I never have!"

Then she addressed the rest of us, "Jesus sent one of His angels to me while I was recovering from a car accident. He showed me what God and Jesus had in store for my future. I wrote down what I saw and kept the paper as a promise from them. Satan tried very hard to prove to me that God was a liar. With my angel's help, Jesus and God appearing to me, I was able to order Satan under my feet."

Shouts of 'Amen' rang out throughout the building making Satan furious. Then he called Wade to the front, "I know you. Women were your drug. Once you had sex with them you weren't interested anymore, am I correct?"

Wade hadn't wasted time worrying. He was reacting the same way Brent had when he'd disrespected Gina at the Boys' Home. Standing there watching Satan accuse Gina of being a whore infuriated him, but when he was accused of using her as a drug of pleasure, rage overtook his mind, will and emotions and his body burst into an inferno. He knew Gina was a gift to him from Jesus, so how could Satan say those words in front of them. All he had on his mind was vindication."

When Satan witnessed Wade's change and saw that Jesus was reacting in the same manner, he held up his hand and submitted to defeat, "I can see you are not the same man. I don't want to hear anything you say. The two of you have made a point. But no one is perfect."

Jesus turned and spoke to Brent and Wade, "Abba warned Satan not to make accusations in this place, but he didn't listen. He caused rage to make an appearance in the house of love. Tell your angels to throw him out of here. He accused you so it's your turn to humiliate him, and show him who the boss really is."

Zion suggested, "Your angels can throw him into some molten lava I have brewing below. Once he is in my grip I will harden it into rock and show him what it feels like to be trapped. Rocks hold grudges for a very long time, but I'm sure he'll find a way to get loose so be prepared for his wrath."

Brent roared like a lion and Wade noshed his teeth, giving Justice and Thrasher the order to grab Satan and hurl him into the lava pit below. Satan screamed, "You can't silence me! I'll torment everything! Nothing is safe from me!"

Abba watched the show and saw Satan land into the pit, and then He said, "Zion, my love, Satan is all yours. Tell your lava rock to hold tight to him until we've fully instructed our Shepherd."

Empowered!

Our four guests stood quietly listening to everything being said after Satan was gone. They were wondering what would happen next. I told them that Zion wanted to speak with Hope before I ushered them back to their bodies so they could enjoy Christmas. Zion motioned for Hope to follow her into another room after hearing about her intercessory position. She wanted to warn and encourage this new mother and intercessor how not to fail as a woman in leadership. She didn't want Hope to suffer her fates and become separated from Brent and Abba. So, out of earshot from all the others, she said, "I want to let you in on one of my deepest secrets. This way you will stay close to your husband, and be able to function better as an intercessor when you take your new position."

All Hope could say was, "Yes ma'am."

Zion asked, "What was the first thing you remember doing as a group in intercessory prayer?"

When the memory came, Hope said, "We joined hands one at a time before agreeing with our leader's prayer."

"Do you remember the words to her prayer?" Zion inquired.

Hope said, "Yes, they were a marriage vow connecting all of us together. With our hands joined it symbolized the ring of God's eternal love and covenant."

"Yes, you really do understand. Now listen carefully to what I have to say. You were trained by a loving spirit who showed you the circle of quiet peace provided by our covenant ring. Within that circle, our loved ones are protected from any evil voice, including their own fears voiced inside their heads. Know for a fact, God will never walk away from His precious people who rely on the covenant whether they are single, married couple, or in an intercessory group. Rest assured that justice will prevail and everyone's heart will be set right if Satan tries to pull you away from this belief. I understand you went through trying times and came through with Jesus' help. Rely on your experiences; draw from your memories, even the one where God broke through to a stony part of your heart a few days earlier to show you He cared as much as Jesus."

Hope was confused by Zion's statements and asked, "I'll be relying on memories through intercession?"

Zion replied, "Yes! When Mrs. Jonesboro steps down from her position, you will be made the leader. It's time the older intercessors retire. Don't get off into fear; it's God's plan for you and Brent to start something new together. Your heavenly Father has not left you two alone He has others who will be willing to join you when the time comes.

Always, always focus on God's love and the covenants written for His people. Study more on the time Jesus walked on Earth as a man, and notice what He said and how He acted. No other man has the absolute truth. Do not focus on the harsh times, and stay in the Lord's presence always, and depend on His grace. You'll know when circumstances change. A spiritual birth will happen inside of me, but before then, times will be hard because of an extreme war for souls on Earth. Direct your prayers in agreement with your pastor's messages. The Heavenly Father's love will set mindsets right, just stay in your secret place of covenant."

Believe that the kingdoms of heaven and Earth are working for the good of God's family. Satan's threats will be loud. If it gets too loud you can silence him. We will always be by your side and the Holy Spirit will guide you. Open your eyes and ears more than you ever have. We love you. Go home now and enjoy your Christmas Day."

Hope asked. "Will we talk again? I enjoyed this very much."

"I'm everywhere, in everything you'll see. Nothing exists unless it came out of me, mankind, birds, trees, fish, everything. That is why Jesus said, 'He is in everything because through my flesh, He came as a man, even though His body was created through Mary'. You will hear wisdom from me through the voices of the older generations and you will feel young and carefree again through the babies. The cycle of life is beautiful and never ending. If you can believe all this mixed with the love God has for you, then you can be very happy and will nurture creation the way heaven wishes." Zion answered.

When Hope returned, Jesus was talking with Brent, Wade, and Gina. He was telling them, "In a few days, I will have your pastor's undivided attention. He will be consumed completely with God's love and preaching a different message. His grace message will change to include one explaining God's love and Jesus' way on Earth. Religious mindsets will be broken and true Jesus followers will emerge. Some people will be offended and leave the church. Do not let this worry you. Everyone will agree with the love message, in time. Stay in agreement with us and pray things through.

Rest in me and listen intently to your pastor's new message. Futures are at stake and all of you will have babies to care for soon. Having the proper mindsets will make a peaceful place for them to live and grow. Hurry back and enjoy your Christmas."

The angels and I put everyone back in their bodies to resume their lives. Then I returned to heaven to resume festivities with Abba, Zion, and Jesus, and where we could watch our new little families from above.

Brent and Hope have had a few journeys with us, so once they returned their nerves weren't frazzled. They began to have a wonderful morning watching Greg open his gifts. Wade's nerves, on the other hand, were frayed and he could not sit still. Gina suggested they take a walk on the beach or relax in their room's hot tub. The latter suggestion got Wade's attention and they began to undress to further enjoy their honeymoon.

When they finished making love, washed, and toweled off they went to bed where they could finish exploring each other in bed. There, Gina leaned into Wade's chest and whispered, "I have a secret. Do you remember what I said while on trial last night?"

Wade said "Yeah. What did you mean?"

She shyly stated, "When I had my first spiritual journey the angel showed me two people in my future. I saw your face and then me giving birth. I'm pregnant! We will have a daughter soon!"

Wade turned white "How do you know this? We've been together less than twenty-four hours!"

"God told me to make it happen on our wedding day. That's why I nearly raped you after our vows. I wanted the whole package; you and our baby. Now, I'm completely whole!" Gina confessed.

"How do you know it a girl?" Wade asked.

"I saw her, and she is beautiful! She has dark hair like yours and blue eyes like mine." Gina explained.

"Do you know her name? Hope said God gave their child a name." Wade inquired.

"No! But I have one picked out." She admitted.

"Let's hear it! I may not like it." Wade said jokingly.

Gina said, "I thought about my heritage and remembered Dad was Russian so I began to search what the meanings of Russian names mean. Oxana means hospitality, unity and self-sufficient. Another name for Oxana is Xena. Remember the program 'Xena, the warrior princess'?" I want our children strong and dependable so I thought the name Oxana would honor Dad and Ox because they were my protectors until you came along."

Wade replied, "I fantasized about Xena when I was a teenager. She was a powerful and beautiful woman, so Oxana will be a great name for our daughter. The name will honor Thrasher also since he is also an ox. Things are moving very fast for me, but I love the thought of being a dad."

"You'll be the best dad! More than that you are our spiritual leader and the best Christmas present I've ever received." Gina lovingly said.

A Shepherd Awakes

Jesus left heaven early that morning to watch Satan and continue overseeing the angels' battle with the demons, while Abba and Zion got reacquainted. Since it was Christmas Day, and a Sunday morning, I felt it was the perfect time to present Pastor Craig Reed with a new attitude and way of thinking. He needed his head pulled out of the sand. Over the last few years, he'd alienated the vital part of his ministry. It was time that changed because he wasn't acting like Abba wanted. He was taking on the ministry by himself and it had formed a rift within his marriage.

A few nights ago, I overheard a conversation with Connie Reed and Jesus. She told Him about her heartbreak and it made me want to find out what happened. I listened intently as she told Him every detail. Apparently, the ministry she and Craig were supposed to share had become his mistress. She was always being placed on the backburner of his life. He never did anything with his children unless it involved the members of the church.

She was living in a deep depression and was always angry with her husband. Every time she tried to tell him she harbored hurt feelings, he pretended to listen, but wouldn't do anything about the issue. He'd promise her this or that, but never dealt with the problem.

On Christmas morning, when I arrived in their house, instead of Craig being with Connie and the children enjoying the birth of Christ and family fellowship, he was locked in their bedroom rehearsing his morning message. Neither he nor Connie knew something more serious was taking place inside of their household. While Craig focused on the church service, Connie seemed to be in her own depressive thoughts cooking breakfast, while their own children were fending for themselves, unprotected without a shepherd or a shepherdess in the house. The kids were playing willy-nilly unsupervised and in danger of being taught and trained by something else. Satan was only bound for a short time, but his demonic forces were still at large and able to enter any negative arena.

Before I knew it, I was enraged! Yes, it was time Craig Reed had a rude awakening! The only thing that saved him from tough love, was Jesus' warning. Before I went to their house, Jesus had assured me that Connie was waiting on us. He'd given her a sign to wait, and have faith in a change. I thought I'd find her in a state of calm and peace. Instead, she was very angry and crying.

Instead of dealing with Pastor Craig Reed, I was scoping the area for demons. This was not my plan. I called out to Jesus and asked if Adrian and Trulan could assist me. After they showed up, I continued with my mission. This Pastor's mind was preoccupied with the Christmas message of 'peace on Earth goodwill towards man,' while evil was invading his house. Connie was having depressive thoughts of being his slave; always cleaning the house, in the kitchen preparing meals, or doing laundry.

I waited for the proper time to make my point known. When it presented itself, I jumped on the opportunity to grab Craig's attention. As soon as he had his pants down around his ankles and sitting on the toilet, I slammed the bathroom door and locked it and shouted, "How do you like your throne? Is it comfortable?

Craig gasped from the shock of my unannounced and angry entrance. He wasn't use to me slamming doors and speaking angrily with him, especially while he was in a humbled position. He softly asked, "Excuse me? Lord, is that you? What's going on?"

I bellowed back, "You have foxes in your henhouse, and they are about to eat your biddies!"

"Pardon! Lord, why are you angry?" Craig asked.

"Idiot! You've abandoned your mate and because of it, her heart is broken, she lives in negative energy and demons will soon eat your children for lunch! Wake up and get your head out of your butt! After God, your love should be towards your family next, not church members." I demanded.

At the warning, Craig quickly tried to rush to Connie's aid but found I had tightly locked the door from the outside. He kicked and shoved at the door only hurting himself in the process. When he'd realized his mistake, he sank to the floor and begged me for help as tears streamed down his face, "Lord, I can't get to them. I'm locked in! Please don't let Satan have my family! Please!"

His cry broke my heart so I firmly said, "Sit back down on the throne you prepared for yourself and let's talk."

Craig picked himself up from the floor, closed the toilet seat, sat down and he prepared his mind before saying, "Okay, you have my attention. I messed up. How did it happen and what will fix the problem?"

"Who made you the repairer of the breach?" I growled out.

Craig swallowed and asked, "Wasn't I made your shepherd? Didn't you grant me power over evil to protect my family? I thought I was supposed to fix things."

I harshly answered, "You are Jesus' sidekick! He is the repairer. You were called to love them, show them how to be more like Him, not to have guardianship, especially at the risk of losing your own family. The church members are His children; not yours, they are your brothers and sisters. Instead, you treat the church like your wife while abandoning your children. With Connie's mind dwelling in darkness, the children have been left to teach themselves about love. What are they seeing at home? You don't talk with them and their mother is mentally unable to help."

Craig quickly objected, "No I haven't! Connie is a good wife. She takes care of all of us, especially the girls."

"So, you are telling me that your wife has agreed to raise your kids alone?" I inquired of him.

"No sir, I'm saying she is with them while I work," he answered.

I expelled a laugh and said, "Truth comes out at last! You're working, it's all about you!"

Objecting to my viewpoint, Craig said, "Sir? I live for the ministry! Helping the people is all I care about!"

"Precisely! Now you know why your wife's heart is broken. Your actions prove you love her less than the ministry. No wonder she feels like an abandoned slave. You listen to anyone else but won't listen to her fears and dreams. She stood alongside you from the very beginning, hoping one day to be a part of everything."

Craig asked, "Why does she feel like I've abandoned her?"

"It all started after she overheard you pray aloud. You were quoting scripture and praying in agreement, but she misunderstood your prayer. She thought she heard you say she was your house servant and not your bride, and that misconception changed her heart and has kept her mentally bound with hurt feelings. She was called to be a shepherdess alongside you. She doesn't want to be your maid. Nor was it her aim to be the stay-at-home-mom. Each day you went to work, she felt you loved a mistress, while she cooked and cleaned everyone's messes."

A sober-minded Craig said, "Lord, I didn't know. I love Connie. She has been with me through all of this."

"Because she has been with you, through the whole process, is the very point I'm trying to make. Listen to me! Remember your beginnings! Wasn't Connie the young woman we gave you? Didn't we tell you from the very start that the two of you were one person? You met Connie at the seminary. Before you met her, her dreams were to have her own ministry one day. When she fell in love with you, she agreed to share one with you. That is when we put the two of you together in holy matrimony.

After you married and had your first child, we gave the two of you a church to shepherd together, but you didn't see the ministry belonging to both of you. From the start of 'your' ministry, you made the declaration money would not control your method of leading the people, and at the same time you prayed over your wife. That is when Connie overheard you pray and misunderstood the meaning. She was in the grips of postpartum depression after having the baby and took some of your words personal, since she wasn't included in the room while you prayed. Demons have tortured her for years now, especially after your last child. They kept telling her she wasn't good enough because she gave you daughters instead of sons.

While Connie digressed, the ministry grew and you became complacent. Not once have you been able to see that your wife had a suffering spirit. She couldn't talk with you about her feelings because you were too tired to listen after doting on everyone else. She had no outlet to relieve her pain, until recently, when she managed to pray to Jesus. That is why I'm here. It is time you told her the truth about your feelings for her and begin sharing your ministry. Let her feel equal to you and you start taking more responsibility for your own children. She will benefit the church and you will also set things right in your home. Jesus is all about love and sharing. He wants to use you, but your message must change. The message of love has to be preached. You can do this! Don't harbor shame for one moment after you leave this bathroom. Connie is waiting for you to hand her a boy child." I enlightened.

"A child?" Craig questioned.

I said happily, "Yes! Share the happiness of Jesus' birth and give Connie a place in His ministry as your Christmas present. The place alongside you will be like a child to her. She will nurture it and share with you the joys of love. Because 'A child is born and there will be peace on Earth and goodwill towards man!' Finish what the two of you started. Connie's heart will heal after you begin again."

When Hearts Collide

Since Craig agreed, I unlocked the bathroom door, but I encouraged him to brush his teeth, comb his hair and splash on cologne before attempting to woo Connie back. If he went to her looking like he'd been frightened by death, she would have freaked.

Connie was standing in the living room looking out the window instead of watching the girls play with their gifts when Craig entered the room. He could tell she had been crying and it gripped his heart, but at that moment she wasn't sad. Apparently, Adrian and Trulan had removed the evil creatures causing her anguish. She was mulling over what she saw at Gina's wedding yesterday afternoon.

Craig wrapped his arms around her and asked, "Honey, are you okay?"

She turned in his arms, took a whiff of his cologne and said, "I am now."

Craig urged, "Come sit with me. I have a confession to make to you."

Alone in the kitchen, Craig bared his heart and apologized for not being a good husband and father. He explained to Connie that he could not live without her and didn't want to think of something happening to the family. Then he went further to reveal my visit to her, down to the humiliating visit which showed him the errors of his ways and explained how he could make appends. Before he allowed her to speak, he said, "I need you by my side in the ministry. It's time you had your own office so you can begin your counseling career the way God wants."

Connie could not control her tears. She wasn't crying because of what Craig had said, she was overjoyed knowing Jesus' promise for her had come true. When Craig asked why she was crying she told him about her visitation with Jesus and what she would see indicating life would change for her. Then said she was thinking about yesterday's wedding when he came downstairs.

Craig took Connie's hand after what she said and commented, "The Holy Spirit said I needed to hear you out. I want you to open your heart to me and tell me every detail.

"So, you want to hear my morbid story?" Connie inquired.

Craig answered, "All of it from start to finish!"

He sat and listened to everything. Then he apologized again for making her so unhappy and told her he wanted to know more about her visit with Jesus and the sign she had waited for. She hesitated for a moment to gather her thoughts and then said, "He gave me a vision of a soldier, standing proudly before you and said he would signify as the first person in my ministry. I saw the soldier last evening."

Craig asked, "You mean Wade Polk was in your vision?"

"Yes! When I saw Wade standing in front of you dressed in his best military clothes, I knew he was the one! I've known the Polk family a long time. Wade has always been a fighter and recently became a part of our church." Connie stated proudly.

"Are you convinced now? I meant what I said. I love you and want to start fresh. Why don't we have Doc and Mamie babysit the girls and take a few days to honeymoon again?" Craig pleaded.

———————————

Craig and Connie rushed the girls through Christmas giving so they could go to church and ask Doc and Mamie if they would babysit until Wednesday afternoon. They found Mamie and Doc in the church nursery, where they liked to volunteer their services. When Mamie saw Craig inside the nursery door with Connie alongside him, she asked, "Are the girls all right?"

211

Craig said, "Sophie and Karen are fine, but they are why we are here. Connie and I need a favor from you and Doc. Would you mind babysitting for a few days? We want to take a short trip alone so we can regroup."

"I knew something was up! I sensed it the moment you came in! Are you two fussing?" Mamie asked.

Doc came over to the door, "Hi, Son."

"Hi, Pop! I was just asking Mamie if the two of you would watch the girls for us so we could go on another honeymoon. Mamie thinks we may be fussing but we are not; thank goodness. We just need time alone as our Christmas present to each other. I know this is short notice, but do you mind?" Craig asked.

Doc said, "I'd love it, but you need to settle it with Mamie."

"You know those girls have my heart. I can't think of a better Christmas present all the way around. We will spoil them rotten." Mamie agreed.

Once the babysitting issues were settled, Connie went with Craig to his office and they kissed for several minutes until he had to stop and prepare for service. They both prayed together, thanking God for a second chance at marriage and for joining them in ministry together.

<hr />

While Jesus and I were away from heaven, another love story continued to unfold. Abba was listening to Zion tell Him about the horrors she'd lived through. Consoling her as much as He could, He knew it would take months, if not years to restore her complete faith in the words and acts of love. Zion knew of God's love and had experienced it many times throughout her existence, but having only her eyes opened to facts for many, many years her faith was thin. After every conflict with Satan, it always took time with

Abba to restore her faith in loving words and touch, instead of only sight. Living with her ears and mouth bound along with her hands and feet affected her deeply. She had a very good reason for not wanting anything to touch her body, especially her ears or mouth. Plus, the extra weight, Satan made her bear only added to her distress making her despise clothing.

Abba didn't mind Zion's nudity - in fact, He preferred it when she was alone with Him. Every chance He got He would lightly brush His fingers along her cheeks, neck, and down her arms to massage her risks. While they were together, He removed the shackles hoping she would want to move freely. But she was not willing to leave His room yet.

She knew her place was alongside Him showing love to all created things, and He wanted her dressed to show her royal and authoritative status when they walked together and enjoyed life, but she had a few panic attacks and couldn't take her position. She wanted to be His queen, His companion in all creation, but all she wanted to do was lie around in their private place talking with each other without interruption.

It was obvious to Abba why she was stalling. She wasn't ready to love unconditionally, but the prophecies were unfolding and she had no choice, the new age would begin in a few hours. Then her labor pains would come and she would have to forget her abuse and become like any good mother, willing to risk life and limb if her children were in danger. Creation's eyes were about to open to the love message. The harvest would begin for souls and Satan's battle to prevent this would increase.

Old But Not Finished

All during the church service, Mamie worried about uprooting the girls from their home on Christmas day. Instead of listening to Pastor Reed's message over the intercom, she fretted having to take the girls away from the toys and the comforts of home while their parents were off frolicking. While she was feeding babies, she formed a plan to tell Craig and Connie how she felt. She wasn't worried about Doc, he would agree with her.

When all the babies were in their parents care after the service, Mamie urged Doc to follow her to Craig's office. While walking with the little family outside, Mamie said, "We're moving into your house! It wouldn't be fair for my sweeties to leave their Christmas presents so the two of you can find yourselves again. Give us an hour and we'll be right over."

Connie objected, "We don't have a king-sized bed like you do. We can bring toys to your house."

"Shush now! We won't take no for an answer. We'll manage," Mamie demanded.

Doc joined in, "She won't take no for an answer. You're wasting your breath."

"If you insist!" Connie replied.

Two hours later the lovebirds were off on another honeymoon and Mamie and Doc were playing house with their grandchildren. Later that afternoon, Gina called them to wish them a Merry Christmas and she took the opportunity to share with Mamie why she had her stand as their designated look out after their wedding. When she told her the baby's name, Mamie asked why they chose a foreign name. Gina's answer shocked Mamie through to her gut. God's prophecy had begun, unity was coming.

After her conversation with Gina, unexpectedly Doc asked, "Ever wonder how our lives would have been if we married young?"

Even though her mind was in a thousand places, after hearing Gina's news, she mumbled, "Sometimes."

As Doc rattled on about not spending enough time with Craig growing up and not making his life special, Mamie was wondering about the other half of the prophecy. If unity was a baby called Oxana, where was peace? Could Hope's baby be peace? She left Doc talking to himself and went to the kitchen where she could call Hope and talk in private. Sure enough, when Hope gave her the meaning of Shiloh, it was peace. It was time for her to think about retiring.

Mamie didn't go back in the living room, instead she sat at the kitchen table and called out to Doc. He was watching the kids as they played, while he verbalized his thoughts about Craig's childhood. As he talked, he hadn't noticed Mamie was gone from the room until she called his name.

"Mamie, what is wrong? Why are you disturbed?" Doc asked.

She said, "I'm going to retire. My nursing career is almost over."

Doc was thrilled! "I think it's time we retired so we can be better grandparents."

Mamie reacted quickly, "God told me I would soon retire, but you'd give up healing? What would you do with yourself? If you didn't work you'd get sick."

He exclaimed, "I want to enjoy life, Mamie! You should too! We've missed so much. We should have raised kids of our own, not my sister's. I know we can't change the past, but I'd love to have time to take Craig fishing and camping. I want to watch his kids play sports or other things. I love my job and I considered it my God-given mission, but Mamie, I'm tired and I want to spend the rest of my days loving you and being with these kids. I want to play and be with children instead of dealing with trauma victims all day. Don't you understand?"

Mamie said, "I can tell this is important to you. We can't quit tomorrow. We need to think this through. I want to make sure I get my full pension."

As they prepared dinner, I decided to make my presence known. Mamie was used to me showing up unexpected, but Doc was not. Doc fell flat on his face when I materialized before them and blurted out, "Greetings! Merry Christmas! It is good to see you've decided to live the good life. Live it to the hilt! From this day forward, I'm making a covenant between us and I'm giving the two of you a very large family."

Mamie had rushed to Doc's side. "You're okay! It's just the Holy Spirit. He won't hurt you!"

Doc was white as a sheet but managed to answer her question, "I'm fine, I think! Why is He here? I've never seen Him in person before, He scared me."

"Get used to it you old coot! The Lord is welcome in our lives anytime He chooses. Stand up! You're embarrassing me." Mamie said softly.

Mamie helped Doc to his feet and then faced me. "We're sorry Lord. Doc is not used to your physical presence. Merry Christmas to you, too!"

I asked them, "Are the two of you happy?"

Doc answered by shaking his head up and down. Mamie exclaimed, "Yes Lord! We enjoy babysitting our grandkids."

I couldn't help but joke with them, "babysitting? I thought Doc wanted to raise children of your own."

My statement quickly sobered Doc, he said, "Excuse me? Mamie is past the childbearing age. It would be strange if she were to get pregnant now! So please don't do that to her; to us!"

Laughing I said, "I'm very aware of Mamie's condition and your ages but that doesn't mean you can't be parents."

Mamie stood dumbfounded while Doc and I talked. I had to snap her out of her wonderings. "Mamie, didn't Abba give you a sign a few months back? He said when peace and unity were together on Earth you should be considering retirement. There is a reason behind His statement.

Times are about to be hard and we have another mission for the two of you. We need you to rescue children. We need you to be foster parents. You know how. The two of you would be great. If not foster parents, consider opening a daycare so the kids can have a place to go and not be trained by the world's system. You both love children. You could save the children from ruin and keep them off the streets. Maybe even stop the formation of gangs."

Mamie said, "You've dropped a bomb! It's a lot to think about! Abba didn't say anything about starting a business. He just said I'd be begging to retire soon. Why are things getting hard if He said we would have peace?"

"Abba was talking about two children, not a peaceful existence. Heaven is in the middle of a spiritual war and people will suffer because of this. We want you focused on young minds instead of healing bodies." I explained.

Doc said, "I'm all for that! You can count me in!"

"Think about what I said. Enjoy your time with the girls. Have a blessed day!" I said.

I left them with a lot to muddle through to resume my eavesdropping. I was confident they would do the right thing. Heaven made a very good choice.

Mamie asked Doc, "Are you interested in a daycare or being foster parents? Both are very consuming."

"A daycare really appeals to me. We can start small. If we like it, we can expand later down the road. I'm sure we can find good help to assist us, especially if it is God ordained. I already have a name. We can call it 'Laughter House,' it will be an Isaac moment for us after all." Doc exclaimed.

217

Mamie sighed and then confirmed what Doc said, "We do love kids. Laughter House fits! Everyone will be laughing at us and think we've lost our minds."

———————

Doc was still mulling over their plans after Mamie and the girls had gone to bed. It was the perfect time for him and me to have a private conversation. Before manifesting this time, I softly spoke, "Doc, we need to talk."

Doc responds, "Yes Lord, I'm here."

"I need for you to lie down. Abba and I want to discuss something with your spirit man." I urged.

"I've heard others talk about spiritual journeys, but I've never been on one. Will I be gone long?" Doc inquired.

"There is nothing to fear. Time does not matter in the spirit realm. We must empower you for service that's all." I told him.

Doc stammered, "Empower how?"

Rather than waste time, I asked, "Has Mamie ever told you about her angel?"

"She's told me about him, why?" Doc asked.

"It is time you met the one we've chosen for you. Don't keep us waiting, lie down and go to sleep." I prompted him.

Doc made a comical sight clearing off the sofa so he could lie down. This jolly man was the perfect match for the angel with the mama bear attitude.

Mamie came down to see what was keeping Doc awake. When she saw, him lying on the sofa she asked, "What's going on? Why don't you come to bed?" Doc exclaimed, "The Holy Spirit and I have a date. Go back to bed, I'll see you soon."

Mamie didn't even respond to his statement, as she was excited for her husband. Doc would be a new man in the morning. So, she padded back upstairs, crawled back in bed, and thanked God for His wonderful Christmas Gift.

Vicious Nature

Before Abba and I called Doc into the spirit realm, we gave him dreams. We forced him to see through two short dreams what a mama grizzly bear does if her cubs are threatened. In the first dream, the bear placed herself between the rival and cubs until the threat was over. In the second dream, the mama bear was crazy with rage. Everywhere she went she left a blood bath until she found her cubs.

When Doc finished seeing the dreams, we called him to be with us in the spirit realm. He was very cautious until he saw me. I motioned for him to join me so I could introduce him to Abba. I said, "Doc, I know this day has been overwhelming to you, but God wants to prove He loves you. Will you be able to handle his presence?"

"I want to try," Doc replied.

"Wonderful!" Abba said behind him.

"Doc, meet your Heavenly Father. I call Him Abba." I introduced.

Doc stared at Abba in amazement. He couldn't speak. Abba calmed his fright by reaching out and wrapping His big loving arms around Doc, and then He kissed his balding head. "Son, I love you! You are still my child, no matter how old you are"

Then with a raspy voice, choked with emotion, Doc said, "I love you, too. I haven't felt a parent's love for a very long time. Thank you for showing me what this feels like again."

Abba asked him, "Son are you up to a journey with me and Spirit?"

Doc's eyes brightened with excitement. "I'll go anywhere with you!"

Abba asked, "Do you remember the dreams we gave you?"

"I remember the dreams, but how does a grizzly bear's rampage apply to me?" Doc curiously asked.

Abba shared, "It's how we are empowering you. Your next phase in life will be to protect, defend and if necessary rampage for the new generation. Mama grizzly bears are notorious for their protective skills and when provoked they are vicious and deadly."

"Will I be fighting evil?" Doc asked surprised.

Abba laughed, "No, not in the natural, but your angel would if you told it too!"

"Spirit said you were giving me an angel, but I don't remember ever reading in the Bible about one like you are describing from my dreams. Do bear angels exist?" Doc asked.

Abba replied, "There are many bear-faced angels in heaven. The prophet Daniel tried to describe them from what he saw. Read chapter seven. Are you willing to be my bear?"

It pleases me to know you are happy and that you are content with occasionally watching your grandchildren, but what if something evil took them away and you didn't know if they were alive and well? How would you feel? Would you stand by and wait for someone to rescue them or would you fight anyone or anything to get them back safely?"

"I see what you mean Father. I'd be riding and walking the streets, buying information even going broke if necessary. If I had too, I would kill to have my precious girls returned safely. So, to answer your question, yes I am ready to take on the responsibility of this calling." Doc proudly stated.

Once Doc had verbalized his desire, I joined in their conversation and asked him, "Would you like to meet Preservation?"

"Yes! Bring her on!" Doc exclaimed.

I watched Doc closely as Preservation made her entrance. I wanted to make sure he could stand up to Preservation's ferocious appearance before leaving them alone together. Preservation, the gigantic bear-like angel appeared, with glowing red eyes and razor

221

sharp teeth, Doc stood straight. He tried to stick his chest out further than his belly to show the large creature respect. Preservation's attitude didn't intimate Doc one bit. I was very proud of the jolly ole soul Abba selected as Preservation's human. Preservation was also impressed with his stance and returned the proud gesture by standing on her two legs like a woman.

I asked Doc, "Are you ready to return back to your body? Preservation will go with you."

Doc turned and stared at me inquisitively, "You mean she goes back with me? I get to keep her?"

"She's not a pet! She's your helper assigned to minister to you and help when needed, when you take your new course in life. Think of her as an extension of yourself." I explained.

"Me? I'm not ferocious and intimidating! People see me as a Jolly St. Nick." Doc exclaimed.

We laughed at his statement. Then I replied, "Your spirit is nothing like your natural appearance. You have a loving disposition but if riled, you'll fight a monster. We are very proud of you and from Preservation's actions, she is also. You two enjoy your camaraderie. If you need me, I'll be around to explain any questions."

"How do I communicate with her?" Doc asked.

"You communicate through thoughts. You'll know when she is speaking to you just like you know when I speak to you. Now, you'll get to work with Mamie and her angel. Work as a team." I explained.

"Will I get to see her when I return to my body?" Doc asked.

"From time to time she will appear to you but most of the time she will be hiding in the shadows. It's time you returned to your body." I said.

Doc said his goodbyes to Abba and me and reluctantly returned to his body. We could tell he didn't want to leave. He was enjoying his first spiritual adventure and didn't want it to end, but he left with a young man's desire for change.

When Mamie woke up, she didn't find Doc in the living room where she'd left him. Curious about his journey, she set out to find her husband. "Doc, where are you?" She called out.

She found him wrapped in blankets outside on the patio, reading the Bible. When she opened the French doors to join him, Doc looked up and said, "Mamie, I feel like a young man again. Laughter House will be a reality as soon as possible. I'm ready for a change. I want to instill good values in people's hearts instead of repairing body injuries. I couldn't stay in the house. I needed fresh air and an open environment after the amazing journey I experienced. I have an angel companion now and an entirely different view on preservation. I'm even ready to change the way I eat, say no to my sweet tooth, and begin getting this body in better shape. I want our grandkids to see a healthier gramps that can walk the talk."

The Shift to Love

Craig and Connie returned home like two newlyweds. They even prepared a church message together with me by their side. My plan for the message was to have Pastor Reed preach God's love and persuade people to drop their differences and begin acting more like Jesus. I knew it would cause mass confusion at first, because for centuries, pastors taught to able to live in God's kingdom they had to shun the less fortunate, the drunkards, gluttons, the sexually active or the people who were of different sexual preferences. Even Pastor Reed taught the message of exclusion until I pointed out to him that Jesus embraces all sinners with love and affection. Jesus taught forgiveness of sins and then He asked God, while dying on the cross, to forgive sinners because they didn't know what they were doing.

For love to work, people had to believe everyone was included, no matter what they believed or did. The plan seemed simple to Pastors Craig and Connie Reed, but they would soon find out where love is preached, around the corner, hate and violence will increase causing more Bible bashing. It would take time for previously taught lessons to be forgotten. Loving the people with negative or critical comments would be a challenge. It will be overwhelming for them without help.

⸺⦿⸺

In heaven, Jesus called another meeting. When His gavel sounded, the atmosphere changed, even on Earth. Abba and Zion rushed in to see what the commotion was about. When the angels saw them at the meeting an uproar of praise sounded. Abba wasn't in the mood for their exaltations and He banged the scepter on the floor and shouted, "Enough! Your interpretation of our presence is skewed. We want to know what happened to make Zion's body quake violently."

At Abba's question, the room silenced. Jesus said, "I plan to start my biggest battle against evil on Earth today. I was about to open another scroll and give out orders. Zion's quaking body could be a result of Satan's violent methods to escape his bonds or they could be from me enforcing love into humanity through reading these scrolls. Do you want me to stop the meeting until Zion recovers?"

Zion screamed, "No! Continue, I'll be fine."

Abba agreed and took Zion back to their room where He could sooth her with music and massage her body. He knew she had conceived, and that was why she quaked. The new age was moments away so He ordered all His assistants to give them privacy. He wanted to be the only one with her throughout the process. The age of love would be their soon.

After His father was gone, Jesus stood and began to profess, "I am the Lion of Judah the one Satan thinks he has conquered. It is time I proved him wrong one more time. God's love will reign! We will leave no stone unturned, or waters unfiltered. Everything must be operating through love or it is not allowed to rest. If any demonic activity is found, terminate it. If Satan's giants claim territory, we will remove them. Assist and defend mankind as they should not have to fight against them. My grace is instantly sufficient for every person that wants to live in the flow of love, and if they don't want to love unconditionally, take pity on them until they conform. Just allow their circumstances to follow their negative flow. Remember, I died for all mankind and someday every knee will bow."

Jesus called His Father's archangels and asked them to come up front. "Beginning today, there will be no more complacency or judgmental influences tolerated. I want peace and unity to reign on Earth like it is here in heaven. Your job is to terminate any demonic giant out of the territory. The rest of the angels know their positions. I will be waiting for my enemy to confront me. I know his plans. He never changes. Are you with me?"

Archangels, Commanding Angels, and our Earthly Angels lowered down on one knee and bowed their heads in agreement. The shouts inside the temple were deafening. Everyone was saying holy, holy, holy is the Lamb.

In Abba's chamber, Zion wept. He asked her why she was crying, and she said she wasn't ready to endure birth pains. She wanted more time alone with Him.

While He rubbed her back, He hummed beautiful music in her ears. Her time was near and in a few moments the pains would increase, and He wanted her relaxed as much as possible until then.

When Brent pulled into the church parking, I whispered to Hope, "It's show time! Open your spiritual eyes and ears. Look at the big picture and tell me what do you see."

Hope closed her eyes, and then opened them again so she could focus on her surroundings. I could tell immediately that she was aware of who she saw. I asked, "Do you see her?"

With her mouth agape and throat dry, Hope replied mentally, "I see Zion's face covering our church. The lights glowing through the windows look like her eyes and the doors opened for us look like her mouth."

"Are you afraid?" I asked her.

"No! The sight is very comforting. I want to run inside dragging Brent and Greg with me." Hope exclaimed.

"Good!" I replied. "Enter in and go to your prayer group. Specifically, pray for your Pastor and his message. Remember, Abba is with you and Zion is all around you, 'the Kingdom of God is at hand'. Afterward, listen intently to Pastor Reed's message. It the birthing of Abba's commission Zion warned you about. Soon, her body will give birth to a new spirit of love "

Hope took Greg to his class and met Brent outside the prayer room. "What's going on? You have that look." He asked her.

Hope whispered, "The change we were warned about has begun. Even the air inside the church is moist with excitement and anticipation. I can hardly wait to hear Pastor's message. Don't you feel it?"

"I'll take your word for it, Hope," Brent answered.

Disappointed in Brent's answer, Hope addressed me, "Lord can I please share my spiritual sight with Brent, again? I need him to see the same thing I do this evening."

"It's your gift Hope. You can give either of them to him anytime you want." I replied.

Hope whipped around to face Brent, "Come closer so I can share my gifts with you before the others get here. I want you and me to experience everything together tonight. It's crucial!"

Hope placed her hands onto Brent's face and laid her forehead on his so she could give both of her gifts to him. Brent didn't shun her gesture, he wanted the abilities again. When they transferred to him, the impact was stronger, because it was critical to her that he was a part of this evening. With the two of them empowered with the same gifts, things would get very interesting in the months ahead, but tonight, the prayer meeting went smooth and without any problems.

In the sanctuary, Hope and Brent met with the team. Out of everyone there, eight were already empowered for the change. The team knew without saying a word about it that their lives would never be the same after the evening's service. They were excited and eager for the new beginning.

When Pastor Reed took the platform, the first thing he did after the praise and worship ended was to tell the members his wife would be joining him in more of the ministry functions. He took a few minutes to explain why and the congregation stood and applauded, bringing Connie to tears. We'd suggested Craig announce it so the members could show her they didn't disregard her feelings, they really loved her.

Next, Pastor Reed bowed his head and asked the Lord to take control of his mind and mouth. With a grateful heart, I swiftly took over the service.

I preached the message we'd prepared the night before. I explained the love was available to everyone, that God Himself was love. I ask them not to frustrate their commission any longer and to stop doubting the love available to them. Living like Jesus did while He walked the Earth was the only way to live. It was His commission for us to love others the way we want to be loved. It is our responsibility to welcome everyone to come to church. In a team effort, we can extend helping hands through gentleness, compassion, and acceptance, while showing Gods' loving power.

You are God's holy temple! His children! God has promised to live inside of us and be our Father. All He wants is for us to love each other unconditionally and leave corruption and compromise behind for good. Judgment and criticisms pollute our way of thinking and cause divisions. God's love has no boundaries, and He loves everyone no matter what they believe or what they've done. He isn't holding our short comings against us. It is time we gathered in the broken, the deceived and abused, and it is time we mind our own business. From this night on, I declare this 'a mind your own business zone.' People need to come in here not hearing gossip or seeing critical stares.

Our loved ones are outside these doors. Go get them! Beat the bushes, walk the streets, go into marketplaces, hospitals, and jails, and bring them home to a Father who wants them happy, healthy and loved. Don't preach to them! Love them! Show them acceptance so they will want to be with you."

Both Hope and Brent heard a loud moan. They looked around but didn't see anyone in distress. Then they felt a slight shake around them and I had to explain to them that the miracle was taking place. A new era had been conceived and love was being birthed; Zion and everything created from were about to react to the unstoppable seed that came from God's unconditional love.

I asked them to look around and listen. What they saw was iridescent robes covering everyone in the sanctuary and a soft weeping coming from the background. Then I explained to them Zion was crying, happy that her labor was over and she and Abba were covering everyone with blessings so their seeds would grow.

Then, without warning, the three of us heard loud screams outside. Satan was hissing and shaking the ground in attempts to free himself from the Earth's grip. Then we heard him give loud orders to kill and torment anything living.

His drama made me laugh. His screams were louder than Zion's moans of labor. If Hope and Brent didn't know better, they would think he was the one giving birth and dying in the process.

Wade and Gina quickly joined us because they could tell by the expressions on Brent's and Hope's faces something supernatural was happening around them. Before any words could be exchanged between them, bolts of lightning lit the sky and a harsh wind started blowing outside. Hope knew from her prior experience what was happening because of the storm. The storm was horrible, but she managed to explain to them Jesus was setting things right and not to be afraid. To her, lightning strikes meant Jesus was in another spiritual battle.

Winter Rains

Abba tried to sooth Zion, but she told Him she couldn't help crying. Since she'd stopped having birth pains, postpartum depression began taking over her emotions and she couldn't think straight. She needed a few moments to regroup. Abba's gentle heart swelled when she told Him that she needed privacy. To Him, the request meant she would be willing to start her destiny with Him soon. While she rested, He mixed the blood of the new age just birthed, with the blood of Christ, and used it to spread total forgiveness over everything in heaven and on Earth. Everything would be marked with its blessing except the demonic hordes and giants infesting the area, to them, it would be pure poison or liquid fire.

Inside the church, Hope watched as people ran out into the rain to get in the vehicles. That was when she noticed the rain wasn't normal. It wasn't clear water but drops of liquid tinged pink. Alarmed, Hope asked me, "Lord, what is this? Is this one of Satan's tricks?"

I answered quickly, "It's the blood of Christ. It is a blessing, not a curse, but I do urge you to get home soon. The water isn't designed to saturate the Earth, but cover the lost souls with forgiveness and torment demonic creatures. You need to get inside your homes before evil thinks they can seek refuge inside them for protection."

Hope told the others, "We need to hurry home! This isn't just a battle, it is a flushing of demonic creatures, ask your angels to guard you and your property."

Gina wanted to offer her gift so nothing could come close. I had to correct her thinking quickly so she wouldn't act in a rage. Whispering in her ears always help her calm down and readjust. The battle belonged to the Lord. It was time they relaxed and watched the show from the sidelines and allow the angels to do their jobs.

Under the angel's protective canopies, I ushered everyone out in the pink-tinged rain to their vehicles. The moon was unusually dark and almost hidden. With their empowered hearing, Brent and Hope heard sizzling noises as the rain touched the ground, trees, and underbrush. That's when they realized the clouds weren't hiding the moon, as it was evil creatures trying to escape from the bloody rain. The harsh wind came from the creatures stirring up the bone-jarring cold air that made trees shake and branches snap like twigs. It certainly was not safe to be outdoors.

Brent enjoyed his new abilities. Being able to see and hear supernaturally eased his mind. Watching what the rain caused proved to him justice was being served. What he didn't like seeing on the drive home, were creatures seeking refuge in homes of unsuspecting people, instead of running to dark and dank places to hide.

He tried to tell Hope, but he didn't want to frighten Greg. He prepared for action when he parked the car. When they got out of the car, he and Hope both overheard several imps whispering among themselves, and hovering around their next-door neighbor's home. Brent roared with anger not caring who heard him and motioned for Hope and Greg to wait. Obeying her husband, Hope stopped and immediately alerted Insight, who appeared and covered her and Greg with his wings. Brent and Justice surveyed their property. When he returned to Hope, he told his cat, "Make sure the demons know they are not welcomed here. Have a feast my friend, but save some food for the bird!"

Before Brent and Hope began to pray, Jesus made a personal visit, "Good evening! I'm here to tell you how to pray. Before I do, you need to understand our plans. The bloody rain was designed to force evil into the open. Abba created this rain from love. It will bless his creation yet kill anything evil. Evil beings can't consume my blood nor can they wear it. Before Abba finishes, anything liquid will have the blood in it, even colas, alcohol, and bottled water. The truth is evil will starve or be burned to death. Pray with a patient attitude and keep your minds free from fear.

Don't come against evil, pray for the people instead. Evil's days are numbered but before they die, they will play havoc on many. They want their last actions remembered. Without any prayer cover, many people are in danger. If you see your friends without angelic protection, ask for them to receive some."

Hope asked, "Does that include the people who don't go to any church?"

"Yes! We are no respecter of persons. We don't judge the way evil has scared people into believing. Pray especially for the people you witnessed changing this evening. Their hearts are tender. I'm sure when rough times occur they will revert into fearful thinking. Relax in your prayers when asking God to send help. Keep your energies positive. Both of you have lived through harsh times and have been assisted. You were told hard times will come. Satan will be focused on hurting or killing weak-minded people." He explained.

Brent asked, "We don't pray against these the disasters?"

Jesus replied, "No. We will be using what Satan means for harm for a good purpose. Many hearts must be changed through severe humbling. But don't think it is a punishment. Sometimes, tough love must be administered. Pray harder over Pastors, the emergency teams; the police, firefighters, EMT's and hospitals, they will have their hands full and get no rest for several months. You will also be very busy and must ask for continued wisdom.

Listen to your angels and stay in the Holy Spirit's presence. Abba and I will be with you always even while we are dealing with these serious issues."

Interventions

Doc and Mamie were bone tired New Year's Eve morning. They hardly had any rest from all the emergencies brought to the hospital over the last few days. Their thoughts and worried discussions reached Insight's ears, but he held his tongue not wanting to alarm Hope too often. When he overheard Wayne complaining of being called into the emergency room to set broken bones, he looked deeper into the situation. People were getting hurt by falling from the ice on walkways or in car wrecks from the ice on roads. His daily practice was suffering as well; to the point he had to beg his brother for help. Insight knew the negative forces surrounding these caregivers had to change so he squawked loudly for Hope to begin praying for positive interventions.

When Hope heard the alarm, she called on me, and I said, "Pray with me Hope. Insight is worried about Mamie, Doc, and the Polk brothers. Their weary bodies have their minds creating negative energies. Negative thoughts create negative actions and like a magnet, they bring more negative conditions. They need rest so we will be praying they get assistance. Abba will answer our prayers."

With a content and happy heart and mind, Hope mixed her words with mine and we prayed. We asked Abba to send them help. Regimes of angels were sent to the hospitals and Healer and Preservation gave some their energy to Doc and Mamie.

Wade was shocked Wayne called him for help, but he didn't reject his brother's plea. He was scheduled to have an extended holiday but was so impressed that his brother needed him; he worked on his day off. Wayne was already at the office when Wade entered his father's practice. Heartwarming emotions flooded his spirit when his dad's note came to mind reminding him this business belonged to both he and his brother. He caught a glimpse of Thrasher in the building and with him were many other healing angels. The time he spent helping his brother sped by fast and they enjoyed working together. At the end of the day, he knew he had a decision to make and wondered if every day with his brother would be the same.

Justice had roamed the streets on New Year's Eve keeping Brent informed on the issues at hand. The streets had been full of partygoers as well as others bent on criminal activity. All Brent was asked to do was pray for the protection of all involved whether they were carefree drunkards, criminals, or the ones the criminals focused upon.

Life was Justice's focus until Abba's plan had more time to work. Most people would consider bad actions boomeranging as karma, but heaven knew negative energies were to blame. Anything designed to threaten life was a negative force whether it was intentional or unintentional and came with its own reward of justice. Drunkards would be sick the next day and criminals would get what they dished out. Most of the time, people would blame the actions on God's wrath, but he never had to do anything to create their pain or discomfort. Everything fell within the law of seed, time, and harvest and, depending on the action, would always determine a warning or result of the same kind.

Shift effects

The love message Pastor Reed preached was changing the hearts of many. Brent's was no different. In his spiritual state, he was magnificent and a perfect representation of Christ. Both he and Jesus were extremely muscular men, fast, and strong-willed, but Brent heart wasn't humble enough for us. His thinking came from years of legal studying as well as enforcing what he'd learned. With his new position beginning the next day, he needed to see the truth.

During his sleep, Jesus beckoned him into the spirit realm where he and Justice could walk with Him and see what the angels had accomplished. They ambled along allowing Justice to lead the way. He took them to places where the stench of death was nauseating. Brent couldn't speak. The carnage was like nothing he'd ever seen and Jesus was forced to begin their communication.

"What has you intrigued, Brent?" Jesus asked.

Brent expounded, "I am confused."

"Why?" Jesus asked.

"I was expecting to see a peacemaker, but I see you carrying a sword, covered in blood, and everything around us smelling like something dead. I thought you didn't believe in violence, but I can see clearly you must. It looks like you won this battle."

"I enjoyed settling accounts against evil immensely. I don't war against flesh." Jesus replied.

"Why am I here, Lord if not to fight?" Brent asked.

Jesus said, "To show you clearly, by these signs, God has declared justice and freedom from Satan and given me full authority. Follow me. I want you to see what is around you."

As they walked, occasionally Jesus would order some of His angels to finish clearing the area by burning the remains. Then He waved His arms into the air and removed the shield surrounding them so Brent could see the insanity on Earth. Justice growled loudly and ran away from them. Brent wanted to object and reign his cat back beside them, but Jesus said, "Didn't the Holy Spirit instruct you to let your cat walk freely?"

"Yes, Sir!" Brent replied.

Snickering, Jesus said, "Let him be. He's searching out the truth for you."

Brent was puzzled. Justice was going in the opposite direction from where he wanted to look. He wanted to investigate a building where people appeared to be breaking the law. Instead of arguing with Jesus, Brent prayed silently to Abba. It didn't take Abba long to straighten him out. Abba quickly touched Brent's mind with agape love and the love exchanged stopped Brent from wanting to protest. Love broke Brent's pride and the supernatural effect helped him to reign in his will only to desire the advice from the One standing by him.

Brent humbly asked Jesus, "There is more to this than I see, even with my opened eyes, isn't there? Will you please show me how you perceive what I am seeing and tell me what you would do? I want your wisdom and methods on how to handle things, Lord."

Jesus smiled, "I'm happy that you've decided to slow down instead of jumping to wrong conclusions. The main reason you are here with me is so I can teach you how to see things differently. Take a few minutes and reflect on the past. Remember when Hope was kidnapped and you were powerless? Didn't you allow Justice to run free then, and didn't the circumstances change for you? Not long ago, after Gina shared her fire with you, you couldn't control your emotions and you judged your friend unfairly. Tell me this, in each case what changed things?"

Brent knew instantly, "It was me praying for you to help."

"That's right, you submitted to me!" Jesus answered. "Now that you've asked me for revelation, I want to tell you what I know. The people you see in that building are not evil. They are homeless and desperately seeking warmth. They were not the ones who broke into the building. Justice is seeking out the culprits responsible for that. Look around at the people sitting in cars and others who are huddled together by a small fire. These people are shunned by society as well as the church, so they refused help for fear of judgment. Think about their plight! What would you do for your family if you had nowhere to go, no money, and the weather was extremely cold? Don't fall for one of Satan's tricks, Brent. He wants you to be critical and suspicious when the truth is simple.

Before tomorrow, I want you to understand what has happened to most of these innocent people. Anytime someone trusts something other than me and God's love, they've been violated by Satan's tricks and are hard to sway, but don't worry we are in the process of repairing the breaches he made, and uprooting those evil seeds to expose the truth and bring wickedness out into the open as you witnessed upon arrival this evening. When we came in to disrupt Satan's endeavors and ended demonic rule, his Antichrist spirit came to life within a lot of people. The same time God's seed of love became alive a few days after Christmas. This Antichrist spirit can only be defeated by love and people believing in God's power through love.

Brent, Abba overtook your mind with unconditional love a few moments ago, He did this so you can be my sword of Justice. Love teaches how to divide bone from marrow and judge fairly. As District Attorney, you had to be anointed by me to be the people's advocate against injustice. Look at your clothes, what do you see?"

Brent said, "Blood."

"Not just any blood," Jesus said. "Demon blood is blood stolen from my people. Life is in the blood and all of it belongs to me. Now, I've shared it with you."

Their conversation ended because Justice appeared and was shoving Brent with his head. There was no denying the cat wanted them to follow him. Behind the building where Brent saw people huddled together in plain sight resting, three men were loading a van with merchandise in the dark. He and Jesus prayed quickly and law enforcement showed up arresting the true criminals, and the victims found in the building were taken to a proper shelter.

It wasn't hard to read Brent's thoughts, the next day. He constantly wondered if all the training he'd received in law school was for nothing. Law school had taught him to be suspicious and think critically, but the Judge of all creation had shown him differently. A loving viewpoint would always cast out darkness.

Rubbing Salt into a Wound

To humiliate Satan, we planned the next meeting very close to where he was bound. When Jesus made His entrance, Satan screamed condescendingly, "What have you done? How dare you shed blood in front of one of your followers! Won't he fear you for the wrong reasons? Why not let me loose so I can have the pleasure of watching him bleed?"

Satan's words struck a nerve. Jesus, being energized from His demonic genocide, was in the mood to tear Satan's tirade down. He strode up, faced his enemy and calmly said, "The judgmental blood you see on me is not human; it is demonic blood I wear and for your information, I've put an end to your business. It's finished! When will you ever learn, everything you or your horde of evil takes belongs to me! Mankind is not my problem. The anger I exhibit is towards your followers and I've dealt them a guilty verdict, punishable by death. No longer will this area be subjected to their disgusting ways or feeding habits."

Satan pulled harder against his bond until the arm and leg that was bound bled. When he couldn't free himself, he screamed, "I may not be able to move around, but my words still have power. Has the whore forgotten how I ransacked or abused her creation? At this very minute, fear is having a jolly good time tormenting the people. Getting my enemies tired and weary is one of my favorite plans or has she forgotten they willed themselves to me?"

Jesus snapped back, "Did you think Abba, or I, would allow your evil words a chance to grow strong? We watched you torture Zion and build your empire all around her!"

"Blah! Blah! Blah! It's not me who will be starving soon. I have a front row seat to all the events, thanks to you, and I'm going to enjoy watching your precious people destroy each other when they have to scrap for money, food, and cover. Then I'll get to watch them die from stress, murder, and suicide. My seed grows just like your prophetic Word." Satan spewed.

Jesus just grinned. "You, stupid beast! Have you forgotten who created you? He is my Father! He made me heir over all creation, not you! You've destroyed your economy, and not mine when you ordered the landscape to be ruined. When you ordered the demons to intervene, I knew you wanted them to get drunk off innocent blood. I had no choice but to intervene! You planted a seed next to me, but we'll see which one gets uprooted by the very people we influence. Your precious Antichrist seed is no match for love. It will be destroyed quickly because our kingdom is on a fast track of restoration. Zion and all her children will be surrounded with love and they will experience joy within a kingdom that does not die."

Satan's eyes grew wild with fury, "You can't make me believe that I don't have the upper hand. I'm going to enjoy seeing the whore's children die and lose hope. Healthcare is under my rule and my mightiest stronghold. I couldn't destroy it. Death still has a sting and I love knowing it! I will always use it to keep your people under pressure and worry."

Jesus looked Satan straight in the eyes and said, "There is only one angel besides Michael that you fear, and you've killed and stolen from her master for too long. I'm looking forward to the bloodbath Preservation will cause soon. She will have revenge on healthcare. In fact, she visits the hospital every day."

After His declaration, Jesus turned His back on Satan and walked away. Satan was so angry, he began calling Jesus every obscene name he could sputter until Abba shouted, "Enough!" and placed a gag in his mouth and taped his free arm behind his back. Gratitude rang down from heaven as angels everywhere praised God for silencing the beast.

Satan moaned, groaned, and kicked with his free foot against the rock that held him captive, and he didn't want to face the maddened bear angel in his humbled state. With the gag in his mouth, he couldn't even summon help. He could not wait until one of his followers found him. Patience was never a virtue for him so he continually tried contorting his body enough where his toes may be able to remove the gag but the effort was without success.

Helping the Shepherd Stay on Course

I was extremely busy keeping Pastor Reed focused on the love message. The more he preached love the opposite would come against the people for a while. Connie had already begun spending a lot of her time answering frantic calls and assisting when she could. People were panicking and leaving the church. They couldn't understand that God's love and grace were for all. This urgent message about Abba's presence had to be preached whether people stayed committed to the church or went elsewhere. Pastor Reed was worried, and he didn't want his members to abandon his ministry. I had to remind him of his vow and kept explaining to him that money would not be the church's salvation. It would be the simple message of God's unconditional love that would cast out fear and doubt, not financial support. In time, others would seek the truth and run back. We had no time to waste so I took him on a spiritual journey through the past and showed him how scripture unfolded. We sat and watched Jesus as He talked with His disciples so Craig could understand fully what had to take place.

I asked Craig to listen to Jesus and everything would become clearer for him. In the spirit, he would get firsthand knowledge instead of another's interpretations. We listened to Jesus explain the vine, the farmer and why limbs had to be pruned. Removing dead wood made the vine stronger so it could bear more fruit. When we finished watching each scene, I asked if he had any questions.

Craig looked up at me with a puzzled expression and asked, "Is the church membership being pruned back so a greater harvest can come?"

"Yes!" I said.

The answer pacified him and he said he wanted to see more. In the next scene, I took him to where Jesus was telling the group to live in Him, to make their home in Him the way He did in Abba. Otherwise, they would not be able to bear fruit. If anyone was separated from either of them, they could not produce anything because they would be considered deadwood and an offense to their process. Unbelief was worth nothing, and believing thoughts kept a bonfire going.

Craig looked at me again, perplexed, "The bonfire He is talking about is not hell. It is hatred, anger, jealousy, gossiping, skepticism and cynical thoughts towards God's grace and all who belong to Him. They trust in themselves and are like candles burning at both ends."

"Yes, negative emotions create more negative energies surrounding them. Living like that is self-destructive." I explained.

Then I pointed his attention back to what the Lord was about to say next. Jesus ordered, "This is my command: Love one another the way I love you. This is your commission. Life is worth living when you place your lives on the line for your friends."

After that scene, we went back to Pastor Reed's home where I could answer more questions. The first thing he asked was, "Can you give me a picture of how you perceive deadwood? I think I know, but I want to make sure I understand."

I looked outside and saw their Christmas tree lying in a ditch behind their house. County garbage management had forgotten to pick up the tree when they came by the house to remove trash. I could use this scene to answer his questions. I asked Pastor Reed to join me at the kitchen window then I said, "Look at the Christmas tree you had in your living room a few weeks ago, and tell me what it says to you?"

"It was very pretty. Why?" He asked.

"Even when it sat in your living room, it may have been beautiful, but it was very dead. When people have, their minds separated from God's love and focused only on themselves they are like that tree. Every part of them is dead because they are no longer connected to a root. Your tree was decorated and placed in a window, but what did it offer mankind? What hope was it giving? None! Did it give love? No! All it said was 'look at me, I'm beautiful, I'm richly decorated, I sparkle and I'm adored'. The same is with people who live self-centered lives. They have no thoughts for anyone else and if you ask them to give to the poor, hug a homeless person, or welcome a drug addict, they balk because they feel they are too good for that. They don't want to share anything.

Now look at the cross you have hanging over your fireplace mantle. It is also a dead tree. It has no limbs, no greenery; nothing. When you look at it what does it tell you?"

Pastor Reed said, "It says the Lord died on me so I could live. He gives me peace by exchanging His life for mine."

"Now, what vision does the Christmas tree give you?" I asked again.

He said, "A dead tree leaves a mess. When we removed the decorations, we threw it out into the trash so the needles wouldn't cause a mess on the floor. Having negative people in the church will only leave a mess with their complaints, evil gossiping and intolerances for others to clean up or get blamed for."

"Precisely! Jesus is always connected to the Father. He lives God's love message and shares love with everyone else. If everyone believed this, it would be a much happier planet. Everything and everyone belongs to Abba, and until they come to this understanding their time and thoughts are useless to our plans. Their words and actions hurt people, cause arguments and cause other people to point fingers in judgment. Jesus used His time, body, and words with His positive energy to help others, and He gave away resources so people could live and enjoy their time on Earth. Everything is made up of energies. He wants your time, words, resources, and even your flesh to be alive with love so it can benefit the people as well as the Earth. When we begin to love this planet the way God commissioned at the beginning of time, we would be taking care of His kingdom and Zion would be happy." I exclaimed.

"This isn't going to be easy to watch, is it?" Craig asked me.

I replied, "No, people become attached to each other and it is obvious that you love all the people in your church. It will be hard to see some leave - especially the ones you thought would stick with you through anything. But a new age has been born so everything will eventually balance out. All you need to do is keep reminding yourself who Jesus hung out with while He walked the Earth. His friends weren't the priests or the scholars, they were the prostitutes, evil businessmen, the sick, and the poor; the group society threw away and blamed for the harsh issues of the day.

Keep encouraging your members to invite and encourage the people society has thrown away and watch what happens. There will be a harvest of souls for Abba, those who felt they didn't belong." I shared.

After all that, I showed Pastor Reed that Abba wanted to protect His family like He did the Israelites in Goshen. He will have nothing to do with the harsh times ahead. He wants to love and bless as many as He can while assisting with the harvesting mission.

Effects of Governmental Woes

Two and a half months into the New Year and the government was facing the worst financial period since the recession of 1939. Businesses were closing and terminating employees on every street and the unemployment lines grew long. Frank Addison's and Amber Simmons' jobs were to enforce the unemployment tax law and he was having a difficult time securing the employer's tax dollars which paid the unemployment benefits.

Because of the state laws placed upon business owners who had employees, and the harsh trading systems they had to endure, their negative attitudes made the job of a tax agent difficult and sometimes dangerous. Employers were worried and stressed to survive and some were forced into breaking the law. Amber refused to make personal visits alone anymore. If her supervisor insisted, she asked Frank or a sheriff officer to go with her.

At the Mental Health Facility, Caylee and Gina faced their own issues. Government funding had been reduced and both women were furloughed. Gina found another job quickly working as a receptionist in the Polk brothers' family business. Caylee, on the other hand, faced the unemployment line. We urged Caylee to draw all her benefits and not to worry about another job. She would be well taken care of and in a few weeks, would be the wife of one of the wealthiest men in the state able to do anything she wished.

The New Year posed another issue for Russ. He must redeem the family business. Jesus and I explained to him what our plans were. I said, "With our help, obscene wealth, cheating, and fraud will be exposed."

Then Jesus declared, "I don't tolerate shady deals, shifty schemes or bullying within a company. I'm fed up with the evil practices going on at Jackson and Jackson, and want to help you begin running the family business fair and honestly."

When our meeting was over, Russ marched into the business office of Jackson and Jackson and spoke privately with Mrs. Wallace, his father's secretary. He told her his plan to study the business and asked for her assistance. He asked that she not inform his father or the Vice-Presidents of his plan but to make it possible for him to work undercover in all the departments.

He witnessed several issues that he did not approve of and took notes along the way. His main complaints were the payroll differences among the various people and the underhanded shipping and receiving conditions. Brokers responsible for the merchandise being shipped weren't truthful and sold freight deals among each other. Every department operated in greed and the ones who suffered unfairly were the immigrants and the uneducated.

When Caylee lost her job, he wanted to make her a place within the company as soon as he could. We had to intervene and convince him she would be well provided for so he wouldn't break his undercover learning. It wasn't time for him to take over the company yet. The real culprits of greed were higher in the chain of command, not only in the few departments he temporarily worked. He hadn't visited those departments yet for fear of running into his father.

Wade decided to work alongside his brother in the family business and work a few hours part-time each week at the VA. Funds for the VA were also being cut back and forcing unemployment, but he wasn't willing to abandon the officer or Adam before he was sure he had them walking again. When he asked us for assistance, we made the way for him to work a few hours every other day.

When he began working with Wayne, Gina was given work with them after losing her job. We were the ones who helped with that situation as well. We knew Wade would love seeing his beautiful pregnant wife at the office every day. He would also be able to watch her nurture the patients and it made it easier for him to be by her side when the delivery date came.

Abba and Zion were assisting the Polk family as well as helping them mend fences and recover from the bad influences that had kept them apart. Zion convinced their mother to change churches and be a part of the ladies group where the boys went. She had Sue Joiner and Olivia Arnold renew their friendships with her which guided her the right way without family tension.

———————◆◆◆◆———————

Brent worked long hard days and he came home to see Hope growing weaker and weaker because of the pregnancy. She had to stay home almost every day, and fear for her safety placed added pressure on his shoulders. When Caylee lost her job, I urged Brent to ask her to sit with Hope while he worked. I also suggested they help her pay for wedding supplies and other needs instead of giving her a paycheck.

Caylee and Russ were thrilled with our plan and Caylee started immediately. At first, it bothered her when Hope offered her money for dresses, shoes, and food for the reception, but when Hope explained how the unemployment system worked she understood why she couldn't receive a paycheck. Our plan wouldn't take away from Caylee; it would benefit her needs without breaking the law. Plus, when Mamie and Doc found out about Caylee's plight, they also agreed to pitch in and help with the wedding arrangements.   Everything was working out as planned.

An Untimely birth

Insight and I had to watch Hope closely. Brent was always called away from home after working hours, and he sometimes forgot to call Caylee to come sit with Hope.

Shiloh had grown as much as she could in Hope's womb and she decided it was time to leave her cramped conditions. Hope was overexerting herself, Greg spilled a drink in his bed and she had to change his sheets. When she leaned over to tuck in the covers, she picked up the mattress and her abdomen twisted violently causing her to grab the bed and sit down quickly before she fell to her knees. She quietly called me. "Lord, I need your help! My body is rebelling!" Then she told Greg to call his father and tell him it was an emergency and to come home quickly.

Abba and Zion appeared when I told them the baby was coming and she begged Abba to comfort her mind so her body would relax, but instead of comfort, another pain violently racked her body. "Please Father, calm me down and help my baby, it is too soon for her to come!"

Zion held Hope's hand and soothed her, "I am here Hope. I understand your pain. Take deep breaths and talk to your child. She is going to make an early arrival. Stop thrashing about, you'll make the labor harder on yourself. Father God, can massage your body, but the contractions have already begun. Try and sing, it will fill your lungs with air and help you get more oxygen in your blood."

Hope tried to take Zion's advice, but her water had broken, the labor pains were increasing, and she was beginning to bleed. Instead of singing, she screamed from the pain. Brent panicked when he heard Greg's crying voice over the phone telling him mama was screaming and in trouble. He told Greg he was on the way home, hung up, and immediately prayed while he punched

911 into his cell phone. After he alerted the ambulance, he called Doc and asked him to go to their house, and check on Hope since they lived a few streets away from them and he could get there before the ambulance.

When Brent got home, he saw Abba and Zion holding Hope's hands, but two angels were steadily pacing in their bedroom waiting for Doc and the ambulance to arrive. When a third angel burst into the room, in a raging mood, fangs showing and claws outstretched, Brent ordered Justice to attack. Justice didn't. Instead of fighting with the bear, he embraced the maddened angel and calmed her down. Microseconds later, Doc pushed his way into their room, flushed and out of breath, and told Preservation to settle down.

A panic-stricken, Brent exclaimed, "That's your beast, Doc?"

Reaching for a place to sit and catch his breath, Doc answered, "Fierce, isn't she!"

"She's a little intense! I'm sorry I ordered Justice to attack her. I didn't know what else to do." Brent expressed.

"I would have done the same, Brent. Her name is Preservation and when she heard me praying about the baby, she went insane with worry. Nothing I said would stop her from charging over here. I shouted at her while I drove, hoping she could hear me talking positively with Abba. I didn't know what I would find in here, so I ran up all your stairs when Greg let me in. I'm not accustomed to the exertion."

Hope whispered, "Guys I need help. The angels can talk amongst themselves or with God and Zion. They know more about what is really happening than we do."

When Doc checked Hope's condition he knew it was serious, and Preservation went to Hope's side and laid her huge head on her belly. Then she stared into Hope's eyes with loving concern. Seeing this sweet gesture, Doc patted the angel's head and said, "There, there now, old girl, you were right. Hope is having issues and you wanted to be with her and God, but we will do all we can to make sure the baby arrives safely so Hope can recover. From now on, ole girl, we must trust each other. I'm sorry I screamed at you."

It didn't take long for the ambulance to arrive and they managed to get Hope to Labor and Delivery on time. Brent, Doc, and Mamie went in the room with her, while Hope's parents and in-laws waited with Greg in the waiting area. When the OB/GYN Doctor examined Hope, her condition demanded she undergo a C-section within the hour, and Shiloh Arnold was born.

The happy father visited everyone in the waiting room while Doc and Mamie stayed with Hope. Baby Shiloh had to have a few small issues addressed and was taken to the NICU. The doctors told Brent when he returned to Hope's side she would recover, but she must take life slow for a few months until her hemoglobin count improved because she'd lost too much blood. Her body was in good condition and Brent figured that was because of all the martial arts she learned.

Mamie could not get enough of baby Shiloh. She visited her tiny bed all through the night and during her waking hours. The baby was a miracle and because she was special to God, Mamie wanted to be a part of her growing up. The Lord knew Mamie wouldn't have a problem retiring when the babies of the girls she loved arrived.

Caylee's Wedding

The Saturday before Easter Sunday, Abba reminded Zion they were invited to a wedding and He wanted to bless Caylee and Russ by attending their ceremony. Even Jesus took time away from the war to celebrate. That afternoon, He took a few minutes to reminisce and realized how much He really loved Caylee Sellers. Out of all the brides He'd obtained from this area, she was very precious to Him. None of the others had taken the time to simply lie at His feet, listen intently, and obey with simple childlike faith. She believed Him with her whole heart and danced her way through life instead of fretting. He was eager for this sweet person to be happy.

Jesus also liked Russ. He was proud of his new attitude. Russ was their gentle giant and the perfect match for Caylee. Jesus wished He could tell Russ what laid ahead for them but that would delay their plans. Russ had to find his footing and become the champion they needed without any props. That was why they had stripped him of riches and forced him live in lack until he was ready to be a leader. He and Romper were already learning at a fast pace. He would soon rise to become a giant among men.

Hope, Gina, and Mamie helped Caylee get ready for her vows. She was lovely in her inexpensive wedding dress and shoes and they assured her that everything was beautiful. Many of the women in the church had joined forces, decorated the small chapel, and made the reception hall pretty, with simple trimmings from the money Mamie and Doc had donated. They also helped buy a beautiful wedding cake to complete the reception. Along with the snacks Caylee managed to buy, she purchased a few flowers and tied them with ribbons for her matrons to carry. She was shocked to see the beautiful bouquet Russ had ordered for her to carry. Everything on the bride's end was ready to go.

In the men's dressing room, an entirely different conversation was taking place. Russ and his dad were almost arguing. Mr. Jackson wanted Russ to take the family jet to Paris and show Caylee a grand time, but Russ refused and was determined to live by our standards and within their means. The only way Russ could make Mr. Jackson stop complaining was to agree to take Caylee to their beach home for a few days. That way he wouldn't have to pay for a hotel room and it would make it easier to take Caylee out for at least one romantic dinner.

The chapel was beautifully lit with a few candles. Hope and Gina took their places on the church platform, along with Brent and Wade waiting for the Pastor's cue. As soon as the wedding march began to play, Pastor Reed motioned for everyone to rise as Caylee and her dad walked down the church aisle. When Caylee walked passed Doc, Mamie started crying. Doc leaned into Mamie's shoulder and she told him, "She is the last one of my girls. My baby is finally getting married. There were days I worried she wouldn't find love, now look at how happy she looks."

Since Satan was trapped very close to this church, we knew everything he thought. He still harbored evil, with intent to kill. He stayed in a violent rage, especially against Zion. He loathed watching the harlot, he once controlled, waltz into the church building with Abba. He was even questioning Abba's judgment. He thought he was weak because the whore had lured Him back into her life. He called Abba a sucker for love.

Satan was very curious so we knew he would be listening to what was happening inside the church. When he heard Jesus', voice overtake the Pastor's during the wedding ceremony, he became enraged. He never heard of Jesus ever performing a wedding ceremony. When he heard Jesus say Caylee Sellers, he shook his chains so hard the gag popped out of his mouth and he began to shout foul words everywhere.

He cursed the demons who allowed her to live. He had finally understood why she was protected. If Jesus was responsible for her protection, then she would be birthing a boy child soon, maybe one who was designed to lead this nation. He had to free himself, even if he had to humble himself to get free. Then we heard him shout for the very ones he'd just cursed to come to his assistance. That is when we knew life around here was about to become interesting.

Satan didn't wait for the demons to free him before he began giving orders to his giants. He didn't care if the water all around them was mixed with blood, he was going to use it to destroy as many churches, business, and homes as he could. His thoughts sickened me. He relished in death and destruction. Nothing was sacred to him. We were going to have our hands full very shortly.

Satan's orders stirred up hot gale force air. The air had to be strong enough to travel miles for the giants to hear his command. To our advantage, Zion took control of the air guiding Satan's command and distorted the words so when they arrived for the giants to hear, all they heard was a mumbled 'break a dam' instead of 'break this town's dam,' so they broke one a hundred miles away from where we were instead.

We knew we didn't have long before the water from that dam would combine with the rivers here. We had three days at least. The media would soon have a field day spreading negative energies along the airwaves. It was time Zion was more involved with our mission

An Ounce of Prevention

We sent a legion of angels along with Cherub and Romper to escort Russ and Caylee safely on their honeymoon. Jesus wanted them to enjoy their time together before coming home and facing new duties. News of the broken dam was quickly spreading. Every few minutes the news media broke into regularly scheduled programming to spread bad news. People everywhere were in a panic and had Pastor Reed in a dilemma. He had to stay focused with the Easter message, but the phones wouldn't stop ringing. Easter was supposed to be pleasant.

At the Arnold house, Insight's continual squawk made Hope edgy. The Courthouse had called an emergency meeting forcing Brent to leave Hope, Greg, and baby Shiloh at home alone. He made Hope promise she would not leave the house and he placed Justice on guard duty.

While Brent was away, Hope kept busy doing a few light household tasks and praying. She couldn't help but remember what happened to the community the last time it flooded. She wanted to be at the Boys' Home, helping them pack and prepare but because of doctor's orders, she wasn't allowed to exert herself.

At the orphanage, the Elders were saying goodbye to their family, who had paid them a visit. Since the flood was coming they thought it best to shoo their son, daughter-in-law, and their two grandchildren home early, so they could begin reinforcing the facility before the floodwaters came. Throughout the night, they worked, Mr. Elder and Joe Arnold, had Carl and Wade busy sandbagging around the main house while they took some of the older boys and began reinforcing the barn and water pumping system. Inside the main house, Mrs. Elder had Olivia and Gina gathering the boys' belongings while Greta drove the younger kids to Doc and Mamie's house, so they wouldn't be underfoot while they worked. They placed as many things as they could in the attic before tackling the pantry and freezers. Before dawn, they had dry goods stored upstairs and coolers of frozen food ready to take to Gordon's Grocery to be stored in their large coolers until after the flood. The remaining boys were divided between Wade and Gina and Carl and Greta, and once everything was secured, the Elders went to Mamie's and Doc's to be with the smaller children.

I was with Pastor Reed when I heard Mamie cry out for help. Shortly after she called us, Pastor Reed's phone rang and at 4:00 a.m., he received the news from Doc asking that he come to their house. The Elders had received news that their son and daughter-in-law had been killed in a car accident. I urged the Pastor on and told him I would join him shortly.

Mamie and her angel, Healer, were a tremendous help. They soothed and stroked the grieving parents. I left them with Pastor Reed and went to prepare Hope and Brent for what was about to take place.

I entered their bedroom and had Insight and Justice by my side. I gently woke them up by filling the room with the positive energy. I was there for two reasons. I had to deliver this very sad news about the Elders and I needed them to pray for protection over their Pastor before they left for church. Everyone was weary and tired from the hard work and worry, and this Pastor had to deliver his finest message.

"Good morning! We need to have a discussion." I said softly. Brent rose from sleep and asked, "Something bad has happened, hasn't it? Justice is pacing and I can feel his sadness."

"Yes son, it has. You will be receiving a phone call soon. The Elders need your support and prayers. Their son and daughter-in-law have transitioned to heaven leaving their two grandchildren

259

orphaned, but that is not the reason Justice is pacing." I gently informed them.

"Oh, no!" Hope said out of concern.

Before they could ask me why, I increased my positive energy and comforted them first by saying, "Both of you know that Jesus personally walked Ray and Alice Elder into heaven so they could continue living in paradise. Ray's parents need our prayers. They are unable to make proper decisions now."

"How did it happen?" Brent asked.

"Car accident; deer ran in front of the car, Ray veered away too quickly and the car slammed into a tree. Their transition was instant, and neither one of them suffered. The children were found a few minutes after it happened by a passerby. They are fine, just in shock from losing their parents."

I went on to say, "The Elders need us to stand in the gap but we also must pray for Pastor Reed. He has been instructed to do whatever it takes to convince the congregation today that Abba is with them. His faith has to be strong enough to strengthen the members instead of frightening them. Time is short! That is why your angels are restless."

Hope said, "I have a lump in my throat! If I'm to pray I need your help. All I want to do is cry over my friends' loss. The thought of the Elders having to deal with this has gripped me with sadness."

Grief had Hope distracted, but I understood. I placed my hand to her throat assisting her so she could pray along with Brent and me. I was determined to have Abba involved so good could come from this nonsense."

After praying together, I explained that the next hour would be critical. The Department of Family and Children Services had been called to rescue the girls, and I said our prayers would help the Elders make the proper decisions. Then I left them and returned to the grieving grandparents.

New Prayer Team

When Brent and Hope arrived at the church, they were asked to go to the Pastor's office, and they were told Mrs. Jonesboro and the elder intercessors had resigned, and voted Hope as the new intercessory leader. Because of the threats and hardships of the community, Connie handed her a stack of prayer requests. Hope wasn't used to leadership and the number of requests appeared to be three times more than normal. After dropping Shiloh off at the nursery and taking Greg to his Faith Builders class, she and Brent went straight to the prayer room. Since it was her first time as leader, I made an appearance because I knew she had questions. She inquired, "Lord, are you going to show me how to lead? I've never seen so many needs. Who will join Brent and me in prayer?"

I assured her I would always be available for prayer and that guiding her would be a pleasure. I also told her, Abba, Jesus, and I were aware of the overload of prayer requests she had, and had recruited some of her closest friends to join her and Brent in the group. As the recruits came in, I instructed her on how to seat them around the table. Doc and Mamie were to sit at her right, Wade and Gina at her left, with Brent at the other end of the table. When they were settled, I told her to stay with the same pattern she learned. She passed around the prayer requests and when everyone finished reading them they were placed in the center of the table. Then I reminded Hope that she could share her gifts with the others if she wanted to when they joined hands.

Hope agreed the others would be better equipped if they could see and hear better. Before the group joined hands, she told them, "The Lord has impressed upon me before we begin to pray that I take time and share my abilities with all of you. We think you would benefit from this."

261

Gina had an issue, "Hope, I don't like seeing demons. I do better listening for Ox's signals. Can I refrain from the vision part?"

"Not this time, Gina. The Holy Spirit has assured me evil will not be present with us. Times have changed. He wants us to be able to determine a person's true nature. The evil influences that are used to control people are hiding. From now on we will be able to see inside a person's heart by what they say and do. Think how you would be without your flame. Wouldn't you feel vulnerable? People without their evil influencers will react instead of reason, they'll follow the traditions of man instead of letting love guide their hearts. We must pray they are enlightened. It is hard for some beliefs to change without prayer asking for wisdom. When I begin to pray, we will join hands one at a time, beginning at my right. Once we make the circle complete, I expect you will have a clearer vision of what will come next." Hope explained.

Connecting the prayer ring was electric for all involved. Then the room filled with a cool pleasantly scented smell. When Hope ended the scripture verse and they opened their eyes, standing before them was the Lord Jesus Himself. Without saying a word, He disrobed and stepped onto the table. Then He lay His loin girded body down over the prayer requests, stretched His legs towards Hope, lay His head down in front of Brent and stretched His arms out towards Mamie and Gina, making the sign of the cross.

The six angels; Insight, Healer, Justice, Ox, Thrasher, and Preservation, joined their wings and covered everyone and slowly walked around everyone counter clockwise while they softly hummed.

Jesus said, "Join your minds with me so we can pray in agreement! With me in the lead, your words will be mingled with mine and our positive energies will affect everything we pray over."

After they finished praying together, Jesus focused His eyes on the ceiling and said, "Father, it is time these people know I have been honored not cursed. Help them understand dying with my heart filled with love and forgiveness, opened heaven's door for you to walk among them again with reconciliation and life eternal on your mind. Just as you granted me power to live again, I want them to know we love them and they will never die.

Show this newly developed prayer team the prayer requests on this table have already been considered, and the issues being corrected. Your name will be honored and revered along with your loving nature. We will give the people who come to me seeking you a blessed life, with their joy full and complete. Thank you for listening Abba. Amen!"

When Jesus finished praying, He sat up but remained seated in the center of the table. Smiling to Himself, He said, "Are there any questions? Did I make myself clear?"

With their hands still grasped together, not a one of them could say a word. They were thoroughly convinced God's love had been commissioned and through His order, they would be safe and happy. Their job was to pray others received the same conviction.

Suggestions

Jesus remained in the room for a few more minutes with His friends. He robed Himself and began to address them individually. He told Hope to lay any issue at His feet. Doc was to pray with his instinct for healing while he used the abilities Hope shared with him. Jesus wanted him to see how people bled on the inside from wounds the naked eyes couldn't see.

Mamie had not met Zion yet, so He explained she needed to use an extra method to heal. With Zion's spirit involved and benefiting creation again, Mamie could speak to flesh and have it respond. The ability will also transfer over to raising children. Her voice would be able to sooth little hearts and encourage them to become strong adults, too, so they could avoid harm or harmful issues.

Turning to Brent, Jesus placed His hands onto Brent's huge shoulders, said he was to remain their balanced one, and to look at both sides of every coin before reacting.

He took both of Gina's hands in His and told her not to ever lose her spunky and free spirit. She was to stay positive and allow love to guide her instead of anger and rage. Then He looked at Wade and told him to be a team player with Gina and Wayne, but never lose his rebelling and determined spirit when praying for others. He was to focus on finding the foundational issues that were broken inside a person's spirit affecting their soul.

Then He addressed the group and said, "It's time we go hear the sermon, but before we do, Mamie and Doc must see who else will accompany us."

A bright light came into the room. The angels moved back and stood around the room's perimeter for Abba and Zion to enter. Mamie was awestruck at Zion's beauty and Doc bowed his head to show respect. When introductions were made, Zion said.

"Father God and I want to show you something; Our way of proving I work along with Him."

She and Abba exchanged looks before she began to strip naked before the group. Then she asked, "Do you remember the serpent Satan used to tempt Eve? He was one of our creations. Innocent, until Satan used him unfairly. People are also innocent victims, but the point I want to make is my flesh relates to every element on Earth; soil, water, air, and fire. Plus, I can change forms when necessary. I can become your double if you wish. Recently, I was bound and could not help with the cycles of life correctly. Now that Jesus has freed me to hear and speak the truth, I vow to assist the sons and daughters of God and make Satan very afraid of us."

Slowly, her body began to change and we all watched her shape turn into the mother of all serpents. Then she hissed, opened her mouth to show sharp fangs before blowing fire. Abba took this opportunity to say, "The serpent is forgiven just like the people. You can work together within the love of Christ. Just like the armor of Christ, the serpent's armor is impenetrable and if she has to, she will protect you within her body."

As an example, Zion's serpent form swallowed Hope and Gina and then she spit them out like the whale in the book of Jonah. They were clean and dry and not one hair out of place. Then Abba said, "I declare by the love I have for this world it will be extended to you through Zion. Everything in heaven and on Earth is in her care because of the blood of Jesus. He not only cleaned heaven with it, He shared it with Earth and made a way for Zion and me to reconnect.

Feel the atmosphere, and if you sense negative energies do whatever you can to reverse it back to positive. What you've just seen will inspire you to reinforce love and help people relax and trust the flow of love."

Light Casts Out Darkness

As everyone left the prayer room, they were met by a very anxious Greta Arnold in the hallway. She had no idea we were with the intercessors. Her stress level was on overload and the only people she wanted to talk with were Hope and Mamie. She rattled off, "We don't have any nursery volunteers or pre-school helpers, and only two Sunday school workers are here today. What should we do? The church is practically empty. I have all the small kids in the nursery playing. Carl has the others in the activity area with him. Do you think we'll have a service? People are saying the floodwaters are very close!"

Mamie realized Greta was drowning in negative energy and said, "Calm yourself down, child! We didn't expect many folks today, but the ones who are here need to hear this message. Take some deep breaths and relax. Bring the young'uns in the sanctuary with us so they can hear the pastor preach."

"So, you think we need to stay?" Greta asked.

"I sure do! There may not be many folks here, but we must carry on. We're the pastor's right-hand team. What we need now more than anything else, is the good Lord. We are being threatened so there is no safer place than by His side." Mamie soothed.

Hope chimed in, "Greta, all of our families will be here today, including yours. Brent talked with everyone earlier. There will be no separation of loved ones so there is nothing to fear. We can get through this like Mamie said, we must stay focused on God's love for us. Call Carl and have him bring the kids into the sanctuary. Mamie and I will help you get the others."

Like Greta said, attendance was slim. There were more angels in the sanctuary than people. The media had people frozen in fear. What had me sad was seeing the separation of some of our faithful couples. Their jobs had forced their hands. Frank Addison was here without Cindy, and Pam Grimes was without Brady.

Amber, and her mom with Lacy in tow, strolled in late followed by Wayne, Amy, and Mrs. Polk. In all, we counted seventy in attendance; very different from the normal five to six hundred that usually attended each service.

While we surveyed the building, Abba went to encourage Pastor Reed. The Pastor was sitting in his office chair and looking out the window when he began to pray. "Lord, I am filled with love for you, but I'm going to need your strength to convince the people you are real and very present."

Abba answered him, "Don't you believe I'm real?"

Pastor Reed spun around and faced the voice behind him. Then he began weeping. "You're here!"

"Yes! Just as the Holy Spirit told you I would be." Abba kindly said.

Pastor replied, "He told me I was chosen to be a leader of a new generation grounded in your love. He didn't mention I wouldn't be afraid."

"Are you afraid now? If I'm with you, fear must leave. Love doesn't tolerate unbelief of any kind." Abba said.

"Then, let's get started convincing everyone else." Pastor Reed expressed.

Pastor Reed addressed the congregation, "I will not keep you long. As you can see, we don't have enough people here to have a regular service. Praise and worship music will be just one song played by Olivia Arnold, on the piano. We are also attempting to record the message to air at a later date on television and radio, but it will be live on the internet."

While everyone was singing, Jesus said to me, "I want you to watch our team closely. As the love message changes the atmosphere in this room, I want to know what they see with their new abilities. Take one person at a time and see if they understand what we want from them. If we have too, we will tweak their abilities."

Pastor prayed, and then began speaking. He went over every line we'd rehearsed the night before. His words were forceful and powerful because of his visit with Abba. He told the people to count on Abba, to ask Him anything and if they felt threatened not to worry. Then he stressed emphatically no one loved them more than God.

The Probing

I watched Doc's face during the sermon and I told him not to be afraid. Then I asked if he could share mentally what he heard and saw. He said, "I hear something like a dog lapping water and I hear whispers coming from the person on my left. When I looked at him, his mouth wasn't moving but he was worshiping and drinking in the message of love."

"You're doing great, Doc. You're hearing the heart and soul of these people and reading them the way we do." I encouraged him.

Mamie was next. I asked, "What do you hear and see?"

She stated her thoughts very bluntly, typical Mamie, "I hear nothing but complaints. The lady in front of me doesn't believe God wants her. She says He keeps her on a diet of tears for breakfast and supper, and Pastor Reed's message wasn't true."

I told her, "Mamie, she has the Antichrist spirit. This dear soul lives in his trap and only repeats what she's been taught."

Mamie asked, "Instead of having a judgmental spirit, how do I look past her complaints? How do I know what's right and wrong?"

I shared, "That's easy. Doubt filled words are an indicator that Satan has planted the last thought in her mind. That is your cue to pray. Empty out your heart for her and ask Abba to prove Satan wrong."

Gina was next. She blasted me with her thoughts. "Many people don't have a bright light inside of them! My own mother's light is flickering. The only reason she is here is because I'm here. She feared being separated from both me and dad. My heart is breaking!"

"Gina, many people know about God but only a few know Him. You were the same not long ago. Your mother is fortunate to have you. Do not feel guilty or worried about her. More seeds of hope

and love will be planted in her heart today. She is a quick study."
I said.

Gina breathed a sigh of relief and asked, "What are my duties?"

"Share your gift. Spread the love around. Hugs go a long way.
Ox will work with you. He will gently nudge you when and who
to share with." I said gently.

Brent told me he saw fog in the room mixed with sighs. I
explained to him they were sighs of relief. People were calling out
to Abba for peace, even if it was a small measure.

Moving next to Wade, he shared with me, "Pastor is speaking
very confidently, and I can tell he has the inside scoop. But when
I look around, some of the people are scrambling through the pages
of their Bibles more than just listening to his words. It is if they
can't believe what he says without verification."

I asked, "How does that make you feel?"

"I'm angry! I want to tell them to put their books down and listen
to their man of God!" Wade screamed with his inner voice.

"Me too! I want to scream the same thing. People want to know
more about Jesus than knowing Him personally. The Bible is
wonderful, but it has been reduced to man's interpretation more
than God's intentions. Love is God's focus, not retribution. Abba
and Jesus want the same thing, a relationship with people willing
to take care of each other." I declared.

As soon as I finished speaking with Wade, Pastor Reed banged
his hands on the pulpit and shouted, "Please put your books and
electronics away. Listen to me! We are in dire straits and God
Himself wants you to know He is here for you. What more do you
need! Trust Him! Count on Him and not something that was
previously written by someone else. Ask around! Some of you
already know the Lord is here. You can feel Him! You've heard
Him speak to your hearts! For the rest of you, I need you to believe
me, please! Seek God for yourself and do it now." The whole
room went silent after Pastor's plea.

I saved Hope for last. She was being bombarded with people's emotions. Everyone had a different story and had escaped abuse one way or another, and their experience was affecting their perception of the love message. It saddened her so I encouraged her to pray often with me.

Our probing was complete. Each of the team were guided and encouraged to depend only on the love of God. I finished just in time because the trial was almost upon them.

The sermon was almost over when Hope flinched. Brent had stood up suddenly and quickly vacated the room. She asked, "Where is Brent going?"

I said, "Brent is in constant contact with the city leaders. His cell phone just vibrated."

"What is happening?" Hope asked.

"The bridge connecting two counties will wash away soon by flood waters and the National Guard is directing people who were ordered to evacuate, to turn back around and find shelter elsewhere. We've encouraged Brent to tell the Guard to have people without anywhere to go, or who are short on money come to the church. In a few minutes, the church and the fellowship hall will be overrun with refugees. We are bringing the needy to you." I answered.

"Me?" Hope gasped.

I laughed, "No silly, to this body of believers. Many of you will stay and take care of these sad and scared people. Others will get to practice hospitality at their own homes."

"You are expecting us to take care of these people?" Hope yelped!

"Why yes! I want you to share, listen and help them any way you can." I giggled.

Out of total confusion, all Hope could say then, was, "But? But?" Zion chimed in and said, "Covenant! Remember God is responsible for everything!"

God Orchestrating People and Places

Pastor Reed was closing the service and giving the final prayer when Abba stood and Zion and I followed him outside. While we stood on the front steps of the church, He said, "Everything is under control inside. We have other situations coming our way. Zion, it is time for you to take control over the waters. Wash everything clean. Flush evil out into the open where I can see it."

She asked, "What if I accidently kill a believer?"

Abba answered, "They will be with us forever. Do not worry, all will be for good."

Zion sighed with relief, and then asked, "Do I have control over the land as well? If I want to shift it around, would that be permissible?"

"What do you have in mind?" Abba inquired.

"I want to confound some who think they are wise. I've listened in on some of Brent's conversations with the city and county leaders and they are more focused on saving governmental properties and places owned by the rich than the properties owned in low-lying areas. The people in the low areas were forced to evacuate and directed to the church. They weren't even allowed to sandbag around their houses." She offered.

Abba said, "Sad, isn't it? I turned my attention towards them the moment the dam broke. I heard their cries, knowing they would be victims as I watched the iron grip of oppressors take over with their filthy threats. Do what you deem necessary."

Before leaving Abba's side, Zion thought to herself, "*I'd love to flood Satan! Drown him in his own plan.*"

"I heard that" Abba said, "but, I'll pretend I didn't. Scare him if it will make you feel better. Just don't drown him as I want him to see everything, as we clean up his messes."

After Zion left, Abba and I watched the action taking place. Brent was explaining to the pastor and some of the men about the bridge and what was about to take place when the National Guard showed. They were to expect trucks and cars carrying refugees who had to be forced to leave their homes and had nowhere else to go.

Abba looked over the crowd showing up said to me, "these refugees are fortunate. They wouldn't have found aid from another church today. Pastor Reed was the only preacher who taught about my love during this threat, most of the other churches closed. In a short time, patrons from other churches who had to find shelter inside will see how I want people to mingle. Even the people who were called unfit for my kingdom will be treated fairly by Pastor Reed's followers.

I've arranged for other pastors to volunteer later in the week. I'm looking forward to hearing what their patrons tell them about Pastor Reed's non-exclusion policy. Satan thought he had the last laugh by causing division. I'm going to take pleasure in seeing his face when the underprivileged and the rich work together. In time, most of the community will work closer together whether they believe the same or not. Loving others is all that matters. Loving Satan is entirely different, I told Jesus not to take any more of his verbal jabs, to stand up to him and tell him what is about to happen to his world."

We enjoyed watching the church group in action. It proved that last Wednesday's message on hospitality and acceptance had also registered with them. They were greeting the scared people with open arms. Some of the people who lived on this side of town took refugees home with them, and those who had to stay, gladly showed the newcomers around and didn't ask what their religion was, whether they were heterosexual, what nationality they were, if they were addicted to alcohol or drugs, or what financial status they had. Among the refugees were a few families who didn't want to mingle, acted snootily and were ungrateful, but most of the people were grateful for the safety.

Pastor and Connie Reed, Carl and Greta Arnold, Joe and Olivia Arnold, the Joiners, and Frank Addison were some of the patrons who were forced to stay at the church. They made the church a stockade. Rooms were arranged for families, other areas were cornered off for singles to stay inside. The church patrons took issues in stride. The teenagers of the church treated other kids kindly and showed them the activity room where they could play basketball, volleyball, or other games. It appeared everyone was getting along.

Greta and Olivia Arnold noticed there wasn't enough food in the Food Bank to feed so many people. Instead of going to the Pastor they went to Connie instead. She took the news to her husband, and they brought the issue to us. Their prayer was simple and so was Abba's answer. He told them to take the cash from today's offering and buy food, with his blessing.

While the pastors prayed, Greta had an idea. She didn't wait and told her son to find Grandpa Arnold. When Pastor Craig and Connie arrived in the fellowship hall with money in hand, Joe Arnold had already placed a call to Mr. Gordon, who owned Gordon's Grocery. He was willing to meet Joe at his store and said he would work something out with the church after the crisis was over.

Joe and Carl took a few teenage boys from the Boys' Home with them in the church vans while the ladies began seeing what was available. That way they could relay the church needs after the men arrived at the store.

Opened Door of Provisions

Greta called Carl and told him not to worry about buying water. The Red Cross showed up with bottles of drinking water. When Mr. Gordon met the men, he offered them a large haul to pay for later on. They brought back all kinds of canned meats, peanut butter, pop tarts, sandwich spreads, milk, paper products, plastic cutlery, and toiletries. Mr. Gordon even donated fresh produce, several turkeys and hamburger meat that he would have to discard in a few days if not eaten. All he asked in return was a letter from the church saying the perishable goods were given as a charitable donation and give an estimation of what it was worth.

There was plenty of help in the kitchen. Everyone pitched in and was made to feel like family. They had turkeys roasting, vegetables being cooked and soups being made. Burgers had been patted out and were being grilled under the church awning. Instead of pacing and worrying, the people had fun during the chaos all around them. In the background, Abba and I heard Satan moan. Apparently, his imps couldn't free him from the bonds and he had to watch the happy gathering.

While the church basked in positive energy, Abba was also orchestrating blessings for the patrons who took people home with them. He blanketed the whole area with a simple command. "Do not be afraid of these people! I will help you assist them."

Doc and Mamie gathered the small boys from the Boys' Home and offered their home to an older couple who graciously accepted. Brent and Hope opened their home to Amber, her mom and Lacy, and another stranded family of three. Wade and Gina had the three teenage boys from the Boys' Home who had stayed with them the night before along with Gina's mom, Pam. Meshed families were being created and bonds were growing.

As soon as Gina and Wade returned home, Wade was called to the Veteran's Hospital for an emergency. Gina and her mom made sandwiches for the boys. It was during this time that Gina talked privately with her mother about God. I encouraged her to be polite with no condemnation.

She explained to her mother how it bothered her to see her so fearful instead of relying on God's love. When Pam asked for prayer Gina used the time to hug her mom tightly and share her gift. The flame of pure love surrounded them and Pam's fear vanished.

With little boys in tow, Mamie didn't waste any time when they got home from church. She excused herself and left Doc to entertain their guests while she changed the boys' clothes before lunch. In the living room, the two guests realized Mamie would also be staying with Doc. They assumed Mamie was his residential maid and were shocked to hear him say she was his wife. They didn't know how to act, they had been raised in the south, and couples their ages didn't mix races in marriage. The more Doc spoke to them, they could tell he was deeply in love with her and the disapproval subsided.

After everyone ate a late lunch, and Mamie had the boys down for their nap, the four adults spent the rest of the afternoon sharing their love stories. It was Abba's plan they meet. Another racist door closed forever.

When Brent and Hope returned home, Hope totally ignored her doctor's orders and immediately began moving their guests' belongings into her garage. Her willingness to help caused Insight stress. He paced around the room watching her like a hawk. Brent was upstairs in the house clearing out space for their guests to sleep when he heard the birds' weird squawk. When Insight squawked a second time, Brent stopped and ran frantically down the stairs to where Amber and her mom were preparing lunch and watching the kids. "Where is Hope?" He asked.

"She's outside with the Browns helping them move some of their things into the garage," Amber answered.

Brent's face turned white and he began praying as he swiftly walked away from the ladies to find Hope. Outside, Insight led him to Hope. She was bent over behind their cars vomiting.

"What's wrong?" Brent screamed.

Between gasps for air, Hope whispered, "A searing pain in my stomach has me sick. I can't bear the pain; can you help me get inside the house?"

Without saying anything, Brent scooped Hope up into his arms and ran skipping stair steps to get Hope in their bedroom. Amber followed him and asked if she could do anything and Brent told her to call Doc.

Doc arrived in less than ten minutes and was met at the door by Mrs. Simmons, who told him Brent and Hope were upstairs. Since Preservation wasn't acting crazy, he slowly climbed the stairs so he wouldn't be winded. After examining Hope, he told them, "Hope has strained the C-section site. She may have herniated herself. Rest will help, but she will need medical attention as soon as we can cross the bridge."

Brent asked, "What can we do to stop her pain? She can't take drugs because she is nursing the baby."

"Ice packs and Tylenol are all I can recommend. Other painkillers could cause her to bleed and with her low blood count taking them wouldn't be wise." Doc answered.

Doc's cell phone rang. It was Mamie worried about Hope and when he told her what happened she asked if she could talk with Brent. Doc handed his phone to Brent and told him Mamie wanted to speak with him. "What is it, Mamie?" Brent asked.

"You are Hope's husband and you have authority over her body. Speak to her pain and tell it to subside. Then tell her body to calm down and heal. Father God told me to begin speaking to our flesh when problems arise. He said to tell you, Zion would send positive energies Hope's way when she heard your words. Together they will keep Hope comfortable.

Brent did as Mamie suggested and it wasn't long before they heard Zion singing and her sweet song lulled Hope to sleep.

The Bathing's

The church patrons were tired. Some who had children had to find a place to rest. Others thought of ways to entertain and pacify the guests. Frank remembered the videos that Hope and Brent kept in the Fellowship Hall for the Young Adult movie nights. The Christian movies bathed and encouraged the guests with moving messages of love and redemption.

One movie seemed to open a door for questions about God and it allowed Pastor Reed to speak the truth. For a few hours, he had the pleasure of giving God glory and sharing His love. While they drank in the thought of a loving God, Abba took the opportunity to slip inside their hearts and calm their fears which would help when serious issues arose.

While everyone was trying to get some rest, or scrambling around in frenzy, Zion was taking her orders from Abba seriously. It was not her responsibility to judge or to choose what to wash if she found something Jesus marked that was her cue to scrub. She used her waters to run free and found pleasure using all her strength bathing buildings, cars, boats, animals, and people if they were marked.

Abba was watching evil being flushed out into the open for Jesus to handle while taking pleasure seeing Zion happy. It interested Him to see how she moved creating sinkholes and making new paths for the water to flow. She was making sure the rich and poor were treated fairly.

If she broke something in the process, He promised to replace them with something better. He felt it wouldn't have broken if it was strong instead of being sub-par. He wanted the new age to begin with new things, brought into existence because He was involved in their creation.

At Jackson and Jackson's office building, the Public Works Department were beginning to sandbag the area. Albert Jackson was being placated. He was happy with himself and made a conference call to the company's Vice Presidents to brag on how he got the city to do his bidding. After he finished the conversation, he sauntered down to the company's café to get a bite to eat out of the refrigerator before heading home. That is when he felt the building shake, and noticed the power going out.

He used the light on his cell phone and ran to the parking deck where he saw his car filling fast with water. Frightened out of his mind, Albert dropped the cell phone into the darkness to be swept away in the water. He turned around and groped his way along the corridors back to his office, and found the landline phone dead. He was trapped without a way to communicate.

The time he'd spent on the phone earlier plus eating wasted precious time for escaping. He looked out the window and saw that the city workers had left. Again, the building shook violently and that's when he noticed the road leading to the company collapsing and the river waters rushing over the barricade surrounding the warehouses. In that moment, Albert Jackson realized his dilemma and finally cried out to God for help. When Abba heard his pleas, angels were sent to guard and protect him from danger, but they could not fight for Albert's sanity, and his mind became his own worst enemy.

From the office windows, Albert watched power lines break and saw parts of his warehouse collapse from the rushing waters. Product worth millions of dollars, was being destroyed before his eyes. What Albert didn't see were the evils being flushed out into the open. Even while dying, they used their last breath to shame his tormented soul. They accused him of taking God's name in vain and made him remember the pride he had and what was said about the city leaders. Their wicked voices bathed him with condemnation and he completely lost his mind and slipped into a catatonic state.

Unwanted Guest

It was past dinner time and Gina hadn't heard anything from Wade. His absence caused her to call on me often. I comforted her as much as possible and told her to focus on her guests and assured her that Wade would return soon. She focused on making pallets for the boys. Then she went about changing sheets and laying out towels in the bathrooms. She was completely done with her tasks and talking with the boys when she saw headlights coming up the driveway.

Racing to the back door, Gina noticed that Wade was not alone. In the nightlight, she recognized the figure of a man. I whispered softly to her, "Gina, your guest is in need. Do not be afraid. Remember to treat him kindly and this will be a wonderful experience for all of you. Trust me and relax. Abba has a way of turning lives into miracles." I said.

"I'll try." Gina meekly replied.

When the light of the kitchen illuminated the man's face, Gina cried out in surprise, "Lyle!"

Lyle did the same, "Gina Grimes?"

Wade stood there stupefied, "Apparently, the two of you know each other. You can explain how while we eat some dinner. I'm starving."

Laughter coming from the kitchen filled Pam with curiosity. Wanting some good news, she left the boys and headed that way. When she saw Lyle Horne's face, she lost her composure and became indignant. "Get that rapist out of here! He's a lunatic and dangerous!"

Gina was embarrassed and went to Lyle's aid. "Mom stop! Lyle has become my friend, remember. We've made our amends. Apologize, please!"

Wade gently intervened, "Ladies, I have a say here. This man is homeless. Floodwaters swept his mobile home away and he has nothing left. He showed up at the VA hoping to find shelter, but the officials wouldn't allow him access to a room. He is a retired vet, for Christ's sake! He deserves a break!"

It took a few minutes but Pam found her manners, "Mr. Horne, I hope you can forgive me. I'm stressed and it is all I can do to trust the Lord's plan for my family. Wade is right. You deserve a break."

"I understand ma'am. It takes time for hurts to be forgiven. I hope I can earn your trust one day." Lyle said sweetly.

The atmosphere changed completely. Respect was overriding every evil emotion that had entered previously, helping Lyle to tell his story, "Two weeks ago, I was allowed out of jail on good behavior. My mental condition is stable and I can work. I had a job lined up before the flood came. I don't know what faces me now. The clothes on my back are all I have. My truck, my tools, and home are all gone."

Gina asked, "You weren't able to gather your things and leave before the water came?"

"No ma'am. The Guard fetched me off the roof of my trailer and once I was on dry ground they asked me where I wanted to go and I told them to take me to the VA. I was sure when I told someone at the VA that I didn't have my meds there wouldn't be a problem. I was sure they'd let me stay. When the nurse and an official told me I couldn't stay, I got scared and demanded my rights. They said the rooms were full and vagrants weren't allowed to sleep on the floors. Doc here, overheard the conversations and took pity on me. He believed I was a retired veteran and asked what my meds were. Then he prescribed what I needed, and had the pills bottled up from the hospital pharmacy. Before I walked out into the dark, he asked if I would stay at his house until the waters calmed. I couldn't refuse. I didn't have anywhere to go. My mom's place is on the other side of the river." Lyle explained.

"You are welcome here, Lyle," Gina said.

Then Lyle said, "I didn't know you married. You found a nice fellow. I'm happy for you."

Gina hugged the dirty man, "Lyle, when you are finished eating, go upstairs to the room on the left. That's the master bedroom. Take a shower while Wade and I find you some clean clothes. Then we'll get a room ready for you to rest and stay a while."

Wade remembered his father's clothes they'd boxed and stored in the garage after his mother moved to the apartment. They were going to donate them, but Lyle needed them more. He was almost the same size as Mr. Polk and they weren't ragged. When Lyle finished showering, he wrapped himself in a robe Gina provided for him and he came into the bedroom. Wade and Gina were waiting to shower him with nice things befitting a retired soldier needing a fresh start.

Corrupted

Abba called me to His side to update me on the situations. He said the VA and County Hospitals were the only corrupt places He would not have Zion wash with water. He had another plan for them. They had to be left untouched until the crisis was over. Too many innocent people were staying in them and having them tossed around would not be right; otherwise, they would be doubly scrubbed.

When Zion was ordered not to touch the facilities, her joy instantly changed to confusion. She wanted to scrub them raw. Abba confronted her and she told Him what she was thinking. Leaving them untouched felt like Satan had won because the hospitals harbored the most corruption. Abba began laughing and suggested she wash Satan instead. Her sadness changed to fury and she swam to the dirtiest one of all while Abba and I enjoyed the show. He even created two bags of popcorn and gave one to me while we lounged to watch our treat.

We noticed Satan was almost free from his binds when Zion faced him with a huge fist of water raised and ready to strike. She dared him to say a word. She circled him and taunted him with the threat of drowning. She was giving him a dose of his own methods. It was his turn to sweat and be forced to say something he didn't want to say. Abba and I both knew he couldn't keep his mouth shut for long. When she told him she would order the lava to grab him again, he broke and said, "Hit me with your best shot bitch!" She complied! After cold cocking him with her fist, she covered him completely with water she'd gathered from the sewers in town.

We watched him spit, sputter and gasp for air trying to stay above her waters. She beat him with all her strength using both hands, but his pride was ingrained and he would not ask for mercy. When she finished having her tantrum and scrubbing him raw with debris, instead of leaving him clean, there wasn't a place on his body or around him that wasn't covered in an inch of human feces.

Returning to Abba, Zion sat next to Him and cried.

He asked, "Do you feel better?"

"No! I don't want to be enraged. I want my heart to remain loving and pure like yours." She exclaimed.

"I'm not disappointed in you! I enjoyed seeing you defend your creation. Covering him with human feces was the greatest insult to him. Zion, I'm happy. Watching you humiliate Satan was very entertaining." He shared.

"I hate being mean - even to evil creatures," Zion replied.

"Zion, my world, my heaven, I understand why you lost your focus and plummeted Satan. I agree with what you did. He deserved everything you gave him, so please snap out of this depression." Abba said.

"I'm sad because I was corrupted with hate. I want you proud of me," she answered.

Abba emphasized, "Never think for one second that I disapprove of you! It takes tremendous force to restrain from killing something or someone who has tormented and disrespected you for so long. Flesh, no matter what form it is in, does not have a capacity for self-control without my influence.

Promise me, you will not dwell on this issue any longer. Calm your emotions. Allow your feelings to rest in my love for you, and begin returning the waters to their normal places." He said.

"I have another task?" Zion asked with curiosity.

"Got your attention, did I?" Abba joked with her.

Zion replied with a sniff, "Stop playing with me! I was certain you wouldn't want my help anymore after what I did."

"My dear, it never crossed my mind to exclude you. Breathe deeply from my soul, and then use our air to expel unpolluted oxygen from the atmosphere. Blow away every curse Satan forced you to think. Dry the soil and replant good things inside your heart and mind." Abba said sweetly.

I was jumping for joy because of what I overheard. For the next few minutes there wasn't a single word exchanged, but what I did hear was deep inhaling and exhaling between the two lovebirds. It made me smile. I knew real love was being exchanged.

— ◦❖◦ —

Satan screamed for Jesus. He refused to be humiliated by that slut, again. When Jesus arrived, he began a taunting rant, "Tell the whore you claim as 'God's kingdom' that she should have stayed away from me. Every doctor and nurse will be fighting a losing battle. Not only have I ordered more sickness, I've also ordered more death. We'll see who is stronger when the people begin doubting and complaining of a God who allows such destruction. Zion thought she had the upper hand against me, but when I get free of this rock I'll be the one who covers her face with crap."

It was Jesus' time to stand up to the beast, "We told her not to wash the hospitals and suggested she wash you. Try coming against her. For if you do, it will the last time you'll try for a very, very long time. I won't bind your arm and leg in this rock, but I'll throw all of you inside of it."

Acceptance and respect

During the middle of the night, church patrons agreed to take breaks so others could nap. The intervention was necessary to keep the offense at bay and to allow other people a chance to rest.

It wasn't because they feared their guest, it was to keep them from wandering the halls and searching for free electrical outlets to charge their cell phones, computers, etc. With guides, lights wouldn't be snapped on and off and the noise would be kept low.

When it was Frank Addison's turn to rest, he decided to snuggle down and sleep as his cell phone charged in his car. He hadn't talked with Cindy for over six hours and he was desperate to know how she was holding on. Twenty minutes into his rest, the cell phone began to chirp. It was Cindy, and she shared all the horrible details the media was reporting.

Frank allowed Cindy a chance to cry and he calmed her down with loving and kind words rather than belittling her for not guarding her heart against negativity. Most days she tried to stay positive, but the events she's faced recently had her emotionally distraught. He respected her for staying calm among her co-workers and not crying until she called him. Within ten minutes, Frank had Cindy laughing and comfortable enough to continue her work.

After talking with his wife, Frank noticed someone in an old truck parked beside his car. Even though it was a spring morning the air outside was very cold so he decided to encourage the man to go inside. The guy rolled down the truck window when Frank tapped on the glass and that's when Frank saw he was drinking whiskey to stay warm. "Why don't you come inside and get warm?" Frank asked the man.

"No one wants me in there, man. I've been drinking and ole ladies say I frighten little children with all my tattoos and piercings." The man replied.

"I know how you feel. People hate tax collectors too, but I don't let what they say keep me from seeking proper shelter when I need it. I bet you are hungry too. Stick with me and I'll make sure you are well taken care of. My name is Frank Addison. What's yours?"

"I'm Dillan Eubanks. Won't the people throw me out? I've been drinking." Dillan asked.

"I think you'll be surprised. You'll get stared at, but don't let that bother you. The way you want to present yourself is your business. The people in this congregation have been taught not to judge on sight and most of us follow that rule. We want people to feel welcome. Let me introduce you to some very sweet ladies and fine gentlemen who will feed you and treat you with respect." Frank shared.

Dillan followed Frank inside. Frank took notice of the snubs but he continued walking toward the kitchen where he knew he'd find Sue Joiner. Sue glanced up from washing dishes when she heard them approached, "Frank, who is your friend?"

"Mrs. Joiner, this is Dillan Eubanks. Is there any more soup? He needs something in his belly besides whiskey." Frank replied.

Sue wiped her hands dry and took Dillan by the arm, "There is plenty of food."

On the way to a table, Jim Joiner brought sandwiches to the table. He took one look at Dillan and said, "Son, you are a piece of art. My grandson would love to see your tattoos. Body art fascinates him. I bet you're the guy from who owns the tattoo parlor, aren't you?"

Dillan smiled, "Yes, sir! I've had my place for about a year. I hope the building survived the flood. I've spent every dime I had to get the space suitable and equipped for a safe business. I didn't want cheap equipment or underhanded methods in my shop."

————————⟡————————

A frantic knock on Pastor Reed's office door jolted him out of sleep, and when he beckoned the person inside, Connie burst in and said there was desperate situation going on in the Fellowship Hall. One of the guests who complained all night about being trapped with the lower class was having a seizure and was unresponsive to verbal questions. Many people were gathered around him trying to calm him and keep him comfortable.

Pastor Reed took control of the room by standing on a table, "Does this man have any family in this building? We want to know how to help him. This is not a time to be afraid or critical. Please come forward and talk to me."

A woman stepped forward and said she was the man's wife. She was also shaking. He jumped off the table and took the lady aside where they could talk privately. She remained quiet until he said he would have to call an ambulance if she couldn't say what the man was suffering from. She started crying and explained that she didn't want to embarrass her husband. He was an influential businessman who would lose his job if the company he worked for found out he was an alcoholic. That's when Pastor Reed realized they were both suffering from alcohol withdrawal and he feared she would seize alongside her husband if they both didn't receive attention soon.

Pastor Reed took this dilemma in stride and called Doc's cell phone and Mamie answered. When he explained the situation they faced at the church, she told him to get alcohol into their system, but to make sure they received small diluted doses. Any other time he would not have approved of drugs and alcohol in the church, but this was a dire circumstance and he had to make life more important than lifestyle habits. He climbed on a table again and shouted, "People, I need to make myself very clear! While we are in this building and on these grounds together, there cannot be any secrets between us. If you have an addictive issue, come clean now. I don't approve of drugs or alcohol use, but if there is a life dependency where you need them to live, I prefer you live instead of suffering. Right now, we need alcohol, so I'm asking, is there anyone at this church who has some they would be willing to share?"

A door slammed, and a few minutes later, Dillan Eubanks stepped forward and offered his bottle of whiskey to the pastor. The people who had snubbed Dillan at first were now staring at a generously and courageous tattooed man. One lady found him and expressed her gratitude and asked him to forgive her for being prejudice.

Abba and I watched everything. It warmed our hearts to see men and women talking without prejudices. Dillan was one of many that had his soul touched by love that day. Soon the love of God will have respect and acceptance forming a chain reaction of love that will flow from one to another.

Disturbing News

While Russ was taking a shower, Caylee was sitting in the middle of their honeymoon bed with her computer. As much as she tried, she could not find a stream of Pastor Reed's Easter sermon. She sensed something was strange so when Russ came in they turned on the television and saw the news. Russ got his cell phone and made several calls and Caylee began to pray, "Lord, not again! Our town went through a flood almost two years ago, and many people suffered. My heart broke for them then. Now they are facing more disaster. I can't imagine their fears or their panic."

I whispered, "Caylee, I'm here, talk with me."

"I'm scared for the people I love back home." Caylee cried.

"That's why I'm here. Tell me what else is disturbing you." I said.

"Russ is worried about his dad. He's been on the phone with the Office Manager for nearly thirty minutes. She told him, Mr. Jackson may be trapped in his office."

"Abba cares deeply Caylee, and Mr. Jackson will be fine. He'll survive the flood and manage to save the business. After the waters subside, they will rebuild. Things will be better for everyone." I told her.

"Should we go home?" Caylee asked.

"No! You and Russ stay here where it is safe. Cut back on so much spending and enjoy yourselves as much as possible. Walk the beach, cook in, stream videos and make love. The money you have with you needs to last. I don't want anything to tempt Russ into dipping into his father's money. We are teaching him a valuable lesson through all of this." I informed her.

"Why can't we go home and help." Caylee pleaded.

"The roads back home will be blocked and some even destroyed. Just wait here at the family's beach house until the waters recede. Don't focus on the news, call your friends. Talk with Hope, Gina

293

or Mamie, that way you'll know what is really going on with people you care about." I stated.

As soon as I finished answering Caylee's questions, Russ walked in the room with a worried frown on his face. He saw me standing next to Caylee and said, "Sir, I need to share something with you and Caylee. I am very upset with my dad. His Office Manager just told me what happened. He's threatened city leaders with lawsuits and various other legal actions if they didn't sandbag our properties.

A lot of people who work for us live in the low rent housing areas. He should be fighting for them. Why isn't he concerned about the people who make us money? Has he lost his mind?"

I answered, "Russ, your father is not the person you imagined. He loves you, but he has fallen more in love money and power. If you'll permit me, I will show you how it happened."

"How?" Russ asked.

"I can take you on a short spiritual journey through his past. I'll explain what happened along the way. Are you willing?" I asked.

"Can Caylee come with us?" Russ inquired.

"Yes! "Let's join hands before we go. Don't be afraid. Relax close your eyes and just breathe." I said.

We were off! When I determined the right time for us to set down, I asked them to open their eyes and watch the scene unfold like a movie. We were standing outside of the Jackson business looking through the window the day after Mrs. Jackson's burial.

Mr. Jackson sat at his desk, completely alone. He had no wife, was worried about his son, and had no other family or friends to count on for support. At first, he doted on Russ until he was forced to hire a sitter so he could work. He spent more time away from home. Prosperity came quickly and very abundant making him greedy for more things. He forgot his spiritual roots and allowed wealth and power to be his god. A few years later, he hired 'yes men' who were equally obsessed with money to work in the business with him and they made a living off low wage earners and underhanded practices.

We walked away from the scene so we could talk. I said, "Now you see why we asked you to live differently? It is better for you to learn the wisdom through God's covenant than become like your father. Your father is smart in worldly ways, but he doesn't understand which end is up anymore. It is far better for you to understand what it is like to come from rags into riches so you can rule with compassion. The day you succeed your father, there will be a battle with his 'yes men' over various negative procedures you wish to be corrected. By making working conditions right, you and Caylee will have a good future ahead of you. Trust us to see it through."

We joined hands again and were instantly transported back to the beach house. I said, "Do not be upset with your father. His heart will change and the two of you will be close. Enjoy yourselves. After all, it is your honeymoon. I'm never far away. Call me anytime. I don't think you want me to stay and watch." I said smirking.

The Criminal Escapes

The second day after the flood started, Satan escaped his bonds and he didn't waste any time killing, stealing, or destroying anything he could. Jesus had destroyed the tether Satan used to control peoples' minds so he had to find other ways to fling his fits. Most of his demons had fled or had been destroyed so he began breaking windows, setting properties on fire and just being bad.

He noticed the water had stopped rising and the people he once dominated were coming outside. The looters were coming out of the woodwork. Since he was no longer their puppet master, they were insane with their own beliefs that mostly stemmed from greed and envy. If they found homes or vehicles that had broken windows from the flood's debris, they took whatever they could find inside of them for themselves. They even stole from stores in broad daylight without a hint of moral values or concern for the economy. Police and the National Guard were forced to work around the clock to protect properties.

Jails were overflowing and temporary facilities were created to house troublemakers. Not only were thieves an issue, drug addicts were killing each other and mugging old people to buy drugs. Unprotected women were being brutally attacked or raped. Satan loved every one of their schemes.

After seeing what his fits caused, Satan began to think of other ways he could make offense rise and decided to go to his favorite haunt. Barricading himself in the County Hospital, he played with the hospital's rules and regulations, the payrolls, mixed medicine, and combined patient charts together. When he finished confusing protocol, he dove deeper into what ran the establishment and began placing fear into insurance practices and the policies supporting the insurance companies.

Satan loved being the head crook, and being the source of all the torment. He was having fun and liked playing havoc without demonic help. With knowledge of insurance policies and hospital protocol, he changed the prices for treatments and made sure people couldn't forward health care, and then created loopholes in their policies so insurance companies would refuse to pay claims. Creating offense was his primary focus. He wanted the people angry enough to blame Jesus. Accusing Him of not caring, and then started a war among the people. Once the atmosphere rang with mean and hateful practices, it wouldn't be long before more destructive conditions bred hate and from hate, war and war would create more war. He'd keep the negative cycle going with or without the help of imps, demons, giants, or the whore who thought she was better than him.

Three Days Later

Three days after the flood, Mamie had to call Brent and Hope for help. She and Doc had been called into work and had no choice but to drop the orphaned children off at their house until the Boys' Home was open again. Their older guests, Mr., and Mrs. Kelly, were incapable of handling smaller children by themselves and managed to find shelter with other friends.

Hope couldn't take care of more children. Shiloh was a handful, and she was ordered to stay in bed for a few days. Brent didn't have a choice but to inform Amber that more kids were coming and that, she and her mother were desperately needed. After speaking with them and making plans to feed extra mouths, he headed upstairs to change for work. He wasn't gone from their presence five minutes when a call came in from Social Services telling him they were unable to reach Greta.

Probing into why they needed his sister-in-law, they explained they needed her help placing four orphaned little girls in foster care since they'd lost their parents in the flood. When he asked if the children were local, the social worker said the children were the daughters of Louis and Gloria Harper. Brent knew the Harpers as they were friends who attended their church. It grieved him deeply so he volunteered to sponsor the children until other arrangements were made. With his head held low in sorrow, he returned to the kitchen where Amber and her mom were making breakfast, and told them they would have nine extra children in the house besides, Lacey, Greg, and Shiloh until things changed.

He hated to tell Hope about the Harpers, but when he returned to their bedroom to finish changing clothes he heard Hope talking on her phone with Frank. Cindy had called him earlier to tell him the bad news concerning Mr. Jackson. Frank knew Hope would have a way to reach Caylee and he wanted her or Brent to get the message to Russ. As soon as her conversation ended with Frank,

Brent told her about the Harper's death and the girls. Then they went to God in prayer. Desperate times called for desperate measures.

Russ was jolted from sleep by a call from Brent. Brent wanted to share the news about Russ' dad before his friend saw it on the news. The media was broadcasting that Mr. Jackson was assumed missing and possibly dead. After he spoke with Brent, Russ tried every phone number he knew with no avail, so he called the Office Manager who was his family's friend. Mrs. Wallace hadn't heard from Russ' dad either. Plus, she said the news reported him missing. Out of curiosity, she asked Russ if he was willing to take control of the company if his father wasn't found. He told her not to tell anyone who he was yet because he had to think things through.

Russ needed to call on me. He was completely wrapped in negative energy after talking with Mrs. Wallace and, his depression was making Romper moan loudly for him to regain a trust in me.

Caylee didn't hesitate to call on me. She knelt at their bed and quietly prayed for help. I presented myself and was ready to discuss the dilemma with her when Russ entered the room. Like a young child, he yelped loudly when he saw me and said, "I don't think I'll ever get used to you popping in on us!"

"I come when I'm called, Russ. Caylee was worried about you. Haven't you paid attention to her or Romper? Romper has been whimpering and pulling on his ears for hours while Caylee has been on her knees crying out to Jesus. You should have called me instead of facing all this alone."

Russ bowed his head and said, "Lord, Dad is missing, and I may be called into his position."

"I know. That is why we prepared you ahead of time. Your father is not dead, but he is in no condition to lead anymore. Until he recovers, we want you to play "undercover boss." Provide direction through telephone conversations with Mrs. Wallace until your Father can completely sign the business over to you. This way you'll learn who is honest within the company and who is not." I said.

"Do we need to rush home?" Russ asked.

"No. Stay here another day and then slowly work your way back into town. Within the next eight hours, your father will be in good care at a Mental Health Hospital and the roads will be more passable." I assured him.

"What's wrong with Dad?" Russ wanted to know.

"He has had a mental breakdown. He watched the company he worshiped be consumed with water, and what he feared most in life had now come upon him. People are hunting for him and he will be found very soon." I shared.

Caylee asked, "Will he be the same?"

"He will not be the hard man you know, Caylee. When he awakens, he will be a humbled man. He'll be the man Russ' mother married." I said cheerfully.

Before I left them, I took a moment to address the angels. I told Cherub to stay focused and watch after Caylee and then I looked at Romper and said, "Romper, next time Russ doesn't respond to your pleas and moans, you have my permission to kick his butt."

The angel looked at me puzzled and bellowed in worry. "No, lad, I actually want you to take your hoofed foot and poke Russ in his buttocks until you get his attention. That way he will know to call on me the next time problems arise. Understand?" The angel shook his large head and bowed in agreement.

Wade and Lyle were cooking pancakes for the boys when Pam came in the kitchen extremely upset. Ox and Thrasher were also bellowing loudly. She asked Wade, "Is Gina awake?"

"Yes, Ma'am. What's wrong?" Wade inquired.

She answered, "The police found Brady. He's being taken to the emergency room. They told me he has been hurt badly."

Wade told Lyle to watch the food while taking the stairs (two-at-a-time) to get Gina. When he entered their bedroom, she was completely engulfed in flames while talking to Mamie. He could tell Mamie had news about her father.

When the conversation ended, Gina looked at Wade but blurted out my name. "Whisperer! I need you!"

"I'm here Gina! Wade and I are with you." I calmly answered.

With tears streaming down her face, Gina asked, "Will he live?"

"This injury will not cause his death, Gina, but it will test his faith. You and Wade take a few minutes to calm your minds and trust in God's mercy. Then go to your mother." I assured her.

Gina quickly dressed and was ready to drive her mother to the hospital. Wade planned to meet them as soon as he had the boys and Lyle at church with Carl and Greta. Lyle wanted to stay and watch the young men, but Gina explained to him that it wouldn't be appropriate with his history and they didn't want to get everyone in trouble since the kids were under strict governmental rules.

On the way to the hospital, Gina explained to her mother that Wayne was called in to operate on her dad. Mamie was watching over him until Wayne arrived. At that moment, Pam asked Gina to pray with her and together they rested in God's loving care for Brady, and good to His word, Abba sent reinforcing angels to Brady's side to help Mamie and Healer until Wayne arrived.

Enemy Attack

While Gina and Pam were still in the car outside of the hospital, Ox began to loudly bark and growl. Gina's senses were heightened and fully aware Satan was near. To pacify Ox, she amped her protective shield of fire to include her mother as well as herself.

Gina checked in at the emergency room front desk and Mamie came out to usher them into Brady's room. Before they were allowed inside his room, Mamie asked them if they were prepared to see Brady in a bad condition. Gina assured Mamie they had prayed and asked God for help and were ready to face the consequences.

When Mamie opened the door, the black, blue, and bloody man lying on the bed didn't frighten them. Instead, seeing him alive gave them reasons to praise God. While Pam talked with her husband, Gina asked Mamie where Doc was, and Mamie told her he had to take the babies to Hope's but would be there shortly.

Wayne entered the room a few moments later and his facial expression was stern and all business. Gina had to pry answers out of him. He explained that his harsh disposition was due to his lack of help and Brady's condition. Brady needed immediate surgery and there wasn't another surgeon available to assist him.

Ox barked and Gina knew who was at the hospital. When she heard a loud scream and wail within the spirit realm there, she had no doubt who was coming in through the emergency entrance. Gina looked at Mamie and exclaimed, "Wade just entered the building! I hear screams? That means Thrasher is clearing the building of a demonic force."

Mamie laughed before saying, "Could be Doc. If Preservation thinks your baby is in danger, she may be on one of her rants."

Wayne overheard Gina speaking to Mamie and asked, "Wade is here?"

"I'm almost certain he is, why?" Gina questioned.

Wayne smiled and said, "Wade could help me operate on your dad! He would be the perfect assistant."

Satan hadn't expected to see Thrasher and Preservation at the same time. He knew he would have to face one of them someday, just not both together. The moment Preservation saw Satan, she pinned him to a wall and put her claws deeply into his ribs. Her mouth was opened wide showing her sharp teeth as she expressed herself with hot breath inches from his face. Thrasher drew his sword and held it under Satan's neck, ready to remove his head if necessary. He would stay with Preservation and make sure Wade and Doc had protection while they worked.

Ox and Healer joined the other two large angels in the emergency room lobby to make sure Satan was cornered on all four sides. Satan knew he was outdone so he growled low and stayed still until Abba walked in with Zion. The sight of her pushed him over the edge, and like a crazy person, he began spouting off insults and telling them what he'd done in the hospital.

Doc and Wade overheard everything Satan shouted and began asking Abba for advice. They were told not to worry or get offended. Jesus would set things right, while the angels Satan hated most had him in custody.

As Wayne and Wade operated on Brady, Abba comforted Gina and Pam while Zion answered Mamie's prayers. Mamie had prayed, laid hands on and spoken over Brady's body before anyone had arrived to see him. Now Zion was there exerting her energy into

Brady's flesh so he could respond correctly to treatment. While she worked on him, she reminisced and Abba and I read her thoughts. *Working with mankind again reminded her of the times she assisted Jesus before He went to the cross. She recalled the man born without eyes and how Jesus used some of her dirt mixed with His spit to give the man eyes to see. Lives were brought back from the brink of death and she brought fish to the fishermen. Smiling inwardly, Zion remembered Jesus telling His disciples to speak to the mountain and it would move for them. She wanted them to do what He asked, and she would have moved that mountain. It may have taken her many years to move enough for man to see, but she would have done so.*

She loved her job assisting the children of God when Abba was with her. But she was dreading the time when He would leave her again. The future caused her concern. Those days always seemed like a thousand years before He returned to her. She dreaded facing problems alone all over again.

It broke my heart knowing Zion was afraid of her future. Somehow, Abba would have to find a way to assure her she was never alone and to completely rely on Him. Jesus and I were always available to her just like we are available to Abba's children.

Out of Chaos There is Light

The days and weeks after the flood; life was hard. Many homes and businesses were destroyed or had to be torn down. Many people had to find housing with family members. Pastor Reed and Connie agreed to let two families who had nowhere to go stay in a room within the Fellowship Hall until FEMA brought in mobile homes. The circumstances weren't grand, but at least the people would have running water, toilet facilities and a roof over their heads.

News had gotten out to other churches about the way Pastor Reed operated his church. Gossip spread saying he'd lost his religion and was bending the Bible's rules ignoring ungodliness. Many people didn't agree with a non-exclusive church where anyone could attend, they believed in a wrathful God who punished sinners. As predicted, many patrons left his church, but the people he allowed inside the church during the flood and befriended began filling the empty spaces the others left behind as Abba intended.

On the upside, many homeowners needing home repairs would be financed through their insurance. Because of the flood two years prior, insurance companies forced mortgage holders and homeowners with fear tactics to buy flood insurance. At that time, the burden placed a financial hardship on the people. But now it turned to place the hardship on the companies who forced change.

The New Year had already begun to be hard, forced health insurance was being enforced on people nationwide before the flood even happened. Finances around the country were being strained. Now more than ever, people were being denied the care or medicine they needed, because of the type of insurance they could afford. Doc, Wayne, and Wade fought the government system as much as they could, but their words went unheard.

The injustice forced Doc to retire. He refused to turn sick people out of the emergency room. Instead, he kept his joy and positive energy by searching a place for Laughter House. Mamie stayed and continued to speak to human flesh but she planned to leave the hospital when Oxana was born.

Wayne, Wade, and a few other doctors opened a free clinic on Saturday's for people who had minor health needs. Some of the days they wouldn't get home until late in the evening. When it was Wade's time to work, Gina wanted to help, but he refused to let her. He worried the stress would make her overly tired and jeopardize the baby's health. Gina was not one to sit still. Instead, she went over to the Boys' Home on those Saturdays and helped Greta by entertaining the children while she worked on books until it was time to cook dinner for her and Wade.

Greta had taken the Boys' Home issues upon herself after hearing from the Elders. Since they weren't returning to work, she'd managed to gather the food from Gordon's Grocery, settle the boys in their rooms and found volunteers to care for the boys until she could make better decisions for the orphanage. Every Saturday she worked diligently at the home. The thought of leaving her governmental job to run the home by herself plagued her mind, until Carl came home one night several weeks after the flood and said he had a coaching job at the University.

The Harper children were still in Hope's and Brent's care, but Mrs. Simmons and Caylee assisted them when Hope had to have hernia surgery. Amber, on the other hand, started researching the necessary measures to begin a girls' orphanage. Somehow, caring for the girls during the flood had created a desire to solve a need in their community.

Amber hated her job at the Labor Department and wanted to be a CPA. So, with Greta's recommendations and Hope's financial aid, she found a place close to the Boys' Home where she could slowly start a girls' orphanage and have her own CPA practice.

Satan was still held captive in the hospital, just not by the angels who captured him to start with. Ox, Thrasher, Healer, and

Preservation were freed to assist their humans. Abba thought it only fair Satan be made to watch how they would overtake his stronghold. Before the angels left Satan, Abba gave them orders to bind him to a wall, place a gag in his mouth, and leave him with sword wielding angels to watch him on every side.

Who is Insane?

For two more months, Russ worked undercover making a few company decisions for his dad. He was the son of the owner and second in command during emergencies, but other issues the Vice-Presidents handled. He and Mrs. Wallace worked together well. She understood why he wanted to remain low-keyed for a while longer. When he was forced to address the two Vice-Presidents he did so by conference calls so they wouldn't know he was in the company spying.

Russ' main concern was the mass layoffs being made within the company. He knew the company was making money so whenever he didn't have a truck route to run, he would ask Mrs. Wallace to recommend him as a volunteer assistant to the secretaries of the Accounts Receivable Department and the Payroll Office so he could help with their filing. Seeing the paperwork that crossed their desks overwhelmed him, but he managed to keep the file bins emptied. Through the paperwork, he found dishonest practices and wondered if his father did business that way or was it kept secret from him. Russ was so disgusted by the way the money was handled, that he planned to report the discrepancies of Jackson and Jackson to Frank Addison, who worked at the Department of Labor ask him to audit the company records. When he told Mrs. Wallace to expect an audit letter soon from Frank, she asked him if he'd lost his mind.

───────────◇───────────

Everyday after Russ left for work, Caylee checked-in on Hope and the kids, and then drove over to the Mental Hospital where she could sit with her father-in-law. Mr. Jackson was slowly improving. He was eating, drinking, and independently performing bodily functions on his own, but he still was not speaking or acknowledging anyone's presence. His lack of attention didn't faze Caylee. She understood mental conditions since she worked at a State Mental Health Facility for several years. She read Forbes magazine and the newspaper to her in-law daily, in hopes something of interest would break through his mental barrier.

She was reading to Mr. Jackson, when Russ called her cell phone after he reported the company to the Labor Department. She talked to Russ about the business in front of Mr. Jackson and after their conversation, she laid her head down on the bed beside her in-law and prayed aloud. "Jesus, Russ needs you. He is trying to do things right, but he needs his dad's help. If Mr. Jackson doesn't wake up soon, he may bail on the company. There are so many issues with the business he hardly sleeps anymore. Many of his friends were laid off and he couldn't do anything about their circumstances and that is breaking his heart. Show us your plan, give us peace, or send someone Russ can trust to guide his mind and actions so he can find peace and rest in his decisions. This should be a happy time for us but it isn't."

Jesus had made sure Albert Jackson heard every word Caylee prayed. He wanted the man to hear her simple faith in God. The opening we created inside of Albert's psyche awakened him. Then Jesus gave Albert courage enough to ask for help, and Caylee's angel, Cherub, reached inside his skull and removed the demonic condemnation destroying the man's brain. Caylee's prayer was answered and Albert's mind was freed again. He reached out and patted Caylee's head while she was finishing her prayer.

"Hello, Dear," Albert said softly.

"Mr. Jackson?" Caylee sputtered.

Albert replied, "Jesus heard both of us. I need to talk with Russ. Will you please get him on the phone for me?"

When Russ heard his father's voice instead of telling him everything over the phone, he rushed to the Mental Hospital. Without any fear, Russ told his dad everything he'd done, saw, and eventually reported against the business. Mr. Jackson vowed that he was unaware of most of the payroll indifferences, but he had been an intolerant person with other issues. Russ asked his dad if he would assist him until he could return to work and Albert's reply was that he would guide Russ, but didn't want to work any longer, he wanted to spend the rest of his life loving the life God had given him and spending more time with family and friends. It was Russ' turn to be the boss.

———————◆———————

On July 15, 2015, Albert Jackson was released from the hospital. Prior to that day, legal papers had been signed making Russ President of the family business and "Jackson & Jackson" underwent an audit by the Labor Department's Unemployment Tax Division. After Frank disclosed his findings to Russ and Mr. Jackson, they decided it was time to have a meeting with the two Vice-Presidents who were responsible for the office payroll and shipping department.

Three days later, Vice-President Eric Jones and Vice-President Tyler Brown entered their office like any other day to see Albert Jackson in his office with another man. When they were called in the room, Eric recognized Russ instantly as one of the truckers from the shipping department, but he didn't know his name and wondered why an employee was in the boss' office.

Albert asked Tyler to close the door, motioned for the two men to find a chair, and then he placed a call to Mrs. Wallace asking her to hold all calls until they were finished. First thing on Albert's agenda was to inform the men of his retirement. Then he introduced Russ as his son and informed them he was the new President. After that, he issued each man an envelope with an unemployment notice inside. When they objected, Albert opened the Labor Department's findings and showed why they no longer had jobs. Not only was Jackson & Jackson in violation of State Employment Laws, the company owed the state $35,000.00 to cover payroll transgression and pay unemployment tax.

When Eric objected and started ranting like a crazy person, Russ took authority and sternly told him he could leave or go to jail, it was up to him. Tyler apologized but tried to pass the blame onto Eric. Russ also asked him to leave the room.

After the two men were escorted with their belongings out of the building by two security guards, Russ called Frank and asked if he knew of a good accountant willing to straighten out the company books. As Abba planned, Frank gave Russ Amber's cell phone number which would set her desires in motion.

Motherhood is Calling

Zion watched over the community as reconstruction and healing continued. Many times, we found her wandering away from Abba where she could nurture the people who were lost or homeless, and without knowledge of God's love. It broke her heart to watch some of them live off scraps, sleep under park benches or fight off attackers. She had to find ways to provide for them.

While meandering around town alone one evening, Zion came across Mr. Gordon. He was sad and she wanted me to find out why. We searched his heart and found the sadness was due to a new regulation passed onto the grocery business. He wasn't allowed to repackage old produce, still good enough to eat, but it had passed an expiration time. He had to throw the food away and take a loss for income tax purposes. I suggested to Zion, that she carry the issue to Abba.

Abba knew Zion was beginning to feel maternal again and He was happy she had started parenting even if it was without Him. He wanted nothing but her happiness. The attitude she had when she came to Him about the sad conditions of those homeless, and Mr. Gordon's procedure dilemma, proved she was not depressed any longer, restraining compassion or harboring love deep inside her heart any longer. She was willing to share His love without being told with the less fortunate.

That night in a dream, Abba had me give Mr. Gordon an idea. I showed him that he could still dispose of the produce so he could write off the cost, but to call homeless shelters and tell them the food was outside before it ruined so they could prepare meals for the needy. This made Zion very happy.

On Saturday, September 29, 2015, Oxana began making her entrance into the world. Because this was Gina's first pregnancy, she thought the ache in her back was from being so overweight. Wade went to work at the clinic and was halfway into the day when he heard Ox barking. It didn't occur to him that Gina was in labor until the large creature made an appearance and growled in his face.

Gina's water had broken and the contractions were growing strong. She had her phone in her hand to call Wade when he burst through the kitchen door. "Gina, he screamed!"

"I'm in the bathroom. My water just broke and hard contractions have begun," she hollered back.

Ox and Thrasher flew ahead of the Camaro, while Wade tried to drive the speed limit. Mamie, Hope, Caylee, and Pam were called and told the baby was coming. By 8:00 p.m., Oxana Polk, was born, and everything Abba had promised Gina was fulfilled just as she had seen the year earlier.

As predicted, the arrival of Oxana indicated Mamie's nursing days were over. She had purposely mentored another young nurse to take her place when that day arrived. On October 1st, 2015, Mamie turned in her retirement papers and left the old job behind and entered another mission alongside Doc.

Doc had been busy. Not only had he found a house, had it approved by the State and County as a proper place for a daycare, he also met with Russ and they worked out a plan where the ladies who had babies at Jackson & Jackson could leave children under three at Laughter House, while they worked at a reasonable weekly price. At present, there were six children happily enrolled in the daycare set to open October 15th.

Mamie loved her new mission. Every child had her heart wrapped around their little finger, but she and Doc couldn't watch them alone. They had to hire two other women to help them cope. When Gina asked if they could watch Oxana while she worked, Mamie felt her life had truly been blessed. She would be able to pamper little unity and watch her grow as if she were a grandchild.

———————

Albert Jackson had become a faithful churchgoer and had become a prominent figure within the church body. One Sunday, he took Russ and Caylee out for lunch because he had something he wanted to share with them.

The news Albert wanted to share was he was moving out of the big house, and into an apartment next to Martha Polk. He didn't like living in such a large place and felt it would be better used to have grandkids live in it instead of him. The apartment complex he purchased had people his own age who were active in church, golf and liked to watch NASCAR. He would be involved in fun activities and wouldn't have to worry about taking care of a large place.

Caylee was overwhelmed. She loved the Jackson mansion but didn't think Russ wanted anything to do with his parents' home. When he agreed to move them into the house, she almost fainted. Since Hope and Gina had children, she was eager to start a family of her own.

Zion's One Year of Freedom

On Christmas Eve, 2015, Jesus, Abba, Zion, and I went into heaven's banquet hall to celebrate. When we were at the table, Jesus stood and asked Abba and Zion, if they would allow His eight co-workers a chance to see how they felt about each other. It was a special night where Abba and Zion renewed their vows so Jesus wanted Brent, Hope, Mamie, Doc, Wade, Gina, Russ, and Caylee present while they professed their love to each other. Abba granted Jesus' request, and I was immediately sent to extend the heavenly invitation to our group. They were going to hear words straight from the mouths of Abba and Zion instead of reading them or having a pastor quote them.

When they arrived, places were arranged at the table for them to join the celebration and once they were seated, Abba took Zion's face in His hands and looked directly into her eyes before saying a word. Then He said, "You sit in my presence, and spend the night in my light. You should know without a doubt that I am your refuge. You can trust me to keep you safe!"

Zion whispered back to Abba, "I do! More than once, you've rescued me from hidden traps and shielded me from deadly hazards. Your huge outstretched arms protect me. I find comfort in them and feel perfectly safe. I know you will fend off all harm. In your arms, I fear nothing; not even Satan's voice in the dark times or when I must face him in the light of day. I don't worry when he orders punches to come against me because you will vindicate me. My heart is secure, knowing my body will be protected. No disease can prowl through the darkness or angry rages come against me at high noon. No evil will prosper.

Even if I must watch things succumb to evil all around me and drop like flies at my right and left, my heart rests knowing no harm will come to them or graze me. My heart remains fixed because you empowered me to stand, even when I had to watch your son's body of flesh turn into a corpse. You are God, my refuge, and I did not worry. I knew in my heart your son was not destroyed. You had His body safely tucked inside my heart until you had Him resurrected. Your angels guard me wherever my mind and body go. If I stumbled, they were ordered to catch me. Their job is to keep me on point.

Jesus, your promised child, stands as King over all my creation. In Him, other children will be able to walk with my Earthly body, unharmed among lions and snakes. They will be empowered to kick away anything that tries to rise above Him. Your promise to me belongs to them because Jesus took His manly shape from me, and became a human being. His example of love proved you will get them out of any trouble. Death has no power over them. Through your son, they will receive the best of care."

There wasn't a dry eye in the place when she finished speaking. Abba stood and declared, "It is a beautiful thing to give away these words in the presence of these children. The words we've spoken will sing anthems for as long as you believe in them. Agree with us and profess the same to each other.

Share these professions with others who have dulled and hardened hearts so they will take notice and receive and extend the blessing. I, your God, truly love my World and she shall be nurtured by all mankind. Just as Jesus explained, now I tell you. Ask, never take, and your lives will be richly rewarded. Give and you will be given in return. Love each other the way you wish to be loved. Guard your hearts against negative energies and focus on good things."

The Joys of Remembrance

After our meal, I escorted our Earthly group back home while Abba took Zion aside to have a private moment. He asked her, "What happened in there? When did you accept your position? Have all of your memories returned? When did you submit completely to me and put away all of your fears?"

...She said, "Once I stared into your beautiful eyes, my heart opened completely and trust took over me. Trusting completely in you, forced my body to relax, and I finally had an emotional breakthrough. When that happened, suddenly, I had revelation after revelation return to me, like the first time you said, 'let there be light'.

...All this time, my trust in you was faulty, I thought you left me alone to take care of business. Instead, it was me who left you and wandered off to care for creation. I apologize for thinking this way, I'm the untrustworthy one.

When I'm with you, I can act very confident in front of others. I thought it was because I thoroughly know about your covenant promises. I always try to focus on them so I can stay grounded, but it finally occurred to me I needed to trust in you, more than a promise made to me. I want you with me, as my mate in every way possible.

Then it dawned on me why you encouraged prophets to write down stories. All the stories were written so when a person talked about them, I wouldn't want to wander away and do things on my own, and they were written to woo me back and trust in you. Belief in your love and devotion should be enough for me, through any situation."

Abba confessed, "Oh, I would love hearing your interpretations of the stories the prophets wrote."

...Zion laughed, "Where do you want me to begin?"

"As far back as you want to go. I'm at your disposal." Abba answered.

Zion began, "The stories about creation were written to explain what you, Jesus, and the Holy Spirit accomplished. After you created my mind, and my heavenly body, the Holy Spirit mourned my constant emotional chaos until you commanded that I see the truth. Like I said, everything came together for me when you declared 'let there be light'. A few minutes ago, your offer of pure love calmed my chaotic emotions and my body and mind relaxed, and accepted peace and rest by submitting total trust in you.

"Do you remember the first time the chaos returned?" Abba asked.

"Yes! It was the sacrilege committed by Adam and Eve that broke my heart and caused anger to rise inside of me. They destroyed the spiritual seed you planted within my heart. I thought a spiritual seed would never prosper and reproduce from me because it didn't exist any longer. I was consumed with oppressive sadness. My thought my spirit was barren. I was not satisfied that my creative soil could reproduce. I wanted to provide spiritual babies to you." She said.

Abba asked, "Do you finally understand why I ran Adam and Eve out of our garden?"

"I do now. They were still spiritual beings that you gave a body. They were supposed to reinforce the spiritual blessing then wait for my soil to give them food. But, my emotions were very raw and I was angry with them. I realize now, I corrupted everything inside the garden with negative emotions that would have poisoned them." She confessed.

"Man, tried to restore peace. Did you ever see this?" Abba inquired.

Zion answered, "I knew they tried. Abel tried to restore my hope for a spiritual child. He offered up his first-born calf to you before it was even born. But he didn't kill a creature, there were no baby calves. Cain didn't understand why he planted, and then offered the fruit of his labor. When you redirected him, he became jealous and killed his brother, squashing whatever blessing that would have been created by faith.

I watched as corruption overtook humanity, but through Seth, you sent another man that would try and restore a spiritual balance. Noah and his family believed in the sanctity of life and they entered your Ark before the big flood, but by that time I was under Satan's thumb and couldn't understand your intervention. All I saw was death all around me.

It was Abram and Sari who changed the course of events for me. Their actions captured my attention. They lived out of sync with man's rules and views of the time. Even then, my ears and mouth were covered and I couldn't determine what was really happening but I knew you had to be involved." Zion shared.

"When did you break free?" Abba questioned.

"Testing me again?" Zion asked.

"Humor me!" Abba nudged.

"Abram and Sari faced many obstacles together. At times, she and I bonded, especially when she was captured by an Egyptian king who wanted her for her beauty. Her plight intrigued me and for once I wasn't focused on Satan's bondage over me. Then, I watched her grow old and give Hagar to Abram so her maid could be her surrogate. But after the baby was born, Hagar refused to give the baby to her. I knew Sari's pain. I provided Cain with fruit and vegetable seeds to place in my soil, but he never offered you a gift of faith before planting the seed in dirt like Abel did for you.

When the three angels appeared on the scene, Satan lost interest in me and I managed to remove the helmet he'd placed on my head. I overheard the angels call Abram Abraham and address Sari as 'Sarah.' Their new names confused me at first and I wasn't convinced you were involved until I heard one of them tell

Abraham the meaning of Sarah; 'princess', feminine royalty, equal to prince.

Sarah was then told to expect a baby. I was overjoyed. This ninety-year-old woman was going to have a child! *There was hope for me through her child*, so I thought. She didn't believe, and she laughed in the angel's face.

If Abraham hadn't taken Isaac to Mt. Moriah, the baby wouldn't have fulfilled your promise. Isaac willingly obeyed his father by giving his mind and emotions over to his father even if it meant he was going to die. When you saw Abraham's trust and Isaac's obedience you presented a scapegoat for man's sin and I was free.

You were the one who gave Isaac's spirit to me, not Abraham. Your loving gesture helped me share Isaac spirit with his biological parents." Zion told Him.

"Do you feel like telling me another story?" Abba asked her.

She asked, "Would you like another Biblical story about a woman or one concerning a man?"

"You choose. Hearing you tell my stories proves to me our parables do reach the lost and prove I have a loving nature towards them." He said.

The Woman Who Changed the World

Zion didn't have to think twice. She wanted to tell Mary's story the way she understood it happened. If it wasn't for Mary, the Word of God would not have existed on Earth as a man to become the blessing seed.

Zion said, "Satan managed to capture me many times after Abraham and Sarah, but the time I remember as being the worst entrapment ever was when he captured me during the Roman rule of Jerusalem. Night after night, he made me watch as the Jewish people were tortured, killed, robbed or imprisoned. It was the first time I experienced hate towards a supernatural being and I fed off the power it gave me. I hated Satan! I hated his giants, his demons, and his imps.

Little did I know, my rage and hate filled emotions totally took away any thoughts of You. I wanted vengeance! I didn't have a spark of love in me during those days. Isaac's children were trying to be my family and I couldn't do anything to save them because my chains had been severely restricted, and were holding me in one place, while I watched because my mouth and ears were covered once more." She said.

"Zion, I was with you, even then. I understood your pain. Seeing you unhappy and consumed by hate was why I sent Jesus. I knew everything on Earth would be affected by your emotions and anything coming from your body would be dangerous, if not deadly, for any form of life. I had to intervene before you self-destructed and took everything with you." Abba shared.

"Do you remember what got your attention then and gave you hope again?" He probed.

"Yes!" She answered.

"I remember watching a religious ceremony where a High Priest had to enter the Holy of Holies for all Jewish people. He came out without a voice and he was using his hands to confer messages to

321

the crowd. I understood his motions to mean, an angel spoke with him. He was smiling and explaining with his hands that he, and his wife Elizabeth were going to have a baby.

I noticed the laughter coming from the people around him but the priest walked away. The old priest's faith didn't falter. I focused on them instead of my anger and saw what he said manifested. The very next month his elderly wife announced she was pregnant. That day, Satan left my side and I knew it was my time to act. I needed the helmet removed from my head more than anything. I knew from experience I would be free and able to come to you again, and I didn't want to wait.

I threw my body on the ground and twisted my head around and around until I broke the latch that kept the helmet tightly in place. Even though it was still on my head the broken latch allowed voices and sounds to penetrate through to my ears.

Satan continued to focus on Zachariah and Elizabeth, so he wasn't constantly in front of my face. That's when I overheard another angel speaking to one of Elizabeth's relatives one night. Mary was her name. This young virgin girl changed the world. By faith, she accepted what you said and allowed the spiritual seed into her body. She became pregnant with Jesus even though she was not married. Being pregnant and without a husband, was frowned upon in those days and the women were shunned from their families. Their illegitimate babies were considered an abomination, but none of the negative consequences mattered to Mary.

She didn't understand her son's mission, but I did. He would become the savior of the world by becoming your Word made into flesh. Mary's body did something mine was not able to do. Your spoken Word was the way life was intended to flourish, not the consummation of man and woman. Without your blessed Word, man can do nothing correctly. That is why you used Mary instead of a man to fool Satan. You reversed the curse placed on women once and for all and proved to humanity a spiritual seed could never be destroyed. You proved you were the giver of seeds and could produce another through your Son and He would always find a way to break through hard hearts and evil influences.

It amazes me that people can't grasp Jesus' merciful act, and his wonderful blessing after He breathed power into mankind before returning to you." She shared.

The New Era

Abba said, "It is the flaw within humanity I've lived with, but I never stopped loving my children because they have psychological weaknesses. Like you said, we've lived through brothers fighting against each other starting with Cain and Abel, then through Esau and Jacob, right up until today. As you've witnessed, it takes a paradigm shift to open a door for me to show my loving nature. Someone must have a dramatic, mind-blowing event to make them question their life and lifestyle.

I want people to know me personally so we can reason with scriptures together. I know people have questions. The Bible of today leaves out too much truth. Due to fear, the men who wrote my stories left out important facts. With me, they can seek the truth instead of leaning on man's preconceived ideas and words.

I'm encouraging Pastor Reed to explain more of the Bible's history when he preaches. When people understand why King James had a Bible published, they will see how and why Hebrew Scriptures were manipulated.

This will create a hunger to know what Jesus said and accomplished. I want everyone to see that the key is to be like Him instead of relying on man's traditions for preservation."

Changing the subject, Abba said, "Are you ready to rake in a large harvest of spiritually-minded souls? I've declared my greatest desire to Pastor Reed. I want souls to prosper so flesh can. Without trust in me, souls cannot prosper. Calm emotions create healthy lives and lifestyles."

Zion's reply was, "I love you dearly, but I cannot promise I'll have calm emotions for long. You know I will not be complete until our sanctuary is full, and I have more children than any woman on Earth.

I want to wear maternity clothes when I'm out with you so I can live comfortably large! I need to hear sounds of joy and see dancing when the children receive new life.

Now that all my memories have returned, (and I remembered you did not leave me), I want to rest by your side and have faith in the process once again. Trusting in your words, protections and provisions, I think I can accept your loving gestures and feel pleasure from now on.

Please don't get upset with me if I have days I don't want to be bothered, remember I can't help that I'm drawn more to the lost and hurting, instead of a loving touch. I feel their emotional pain and it gets my attention quickly. Babies, especially have always been my downfall and Satan has used them to lure me away from you every time. Please forgive me if my demeanor can't stay fixed in a restful position when this happens.

I want to wait, remain calm, so I can follow your plan, but when I see innocents abused I step in and act alone."

"Don't you fret, my love! I will never be angry with you." Abba encouraged.

Zion asked Him, "How can I prevent history from repeating itself without staying locked away in our room?"

"You can't. From the beginning of time, you and I agreed your DNA chains would keep you in touch with every living thing and Jesus spoke that plan into existence before any cycles began. I know when a living thing hurts, and I know you'll be affected differently from me.

Understand that the DNA chains weren't created to shackle you in one place. They aren't a punishment. They were created to prove scientifically, that Earth's elements connect everything together as one system, one body.

When Satan attacks or threatens anything, try not to be offended. He will use your emotions to trap you. But if it happens you can rest assured, no matter how offended you were, Jesus has already redeemed and forgiven you.

He knows whenever you're offended because your feelings are manifested in the physical realm as Earthquakes, tornadoes, or hurricanes. Then He will signal us to intervene before you get so angry, guilt-ridden or fearful. Righteous anger is good when used to help others, but anger used to destroy anything, including Satan, is bad for you if done without me present in your mind.

The rights of retaliation only belong to One, and He makes sure justice is served correctly on Satan and his demonic followers instead of humanity. This is another issue people must understand before their beliefs can change. We do not wrestle against flesh and blood, but with powers and principalities within the world's many-dimensional systems. We give love, peace, and acceptance without exclusion to everyone because Jesus died for all."

"People will resist this," Zion said.

"I know. They want me to be a punishing God, who avenges unjust acts. I want love to change hearts, not revenge.

At first, people will think it odd when my pastors begin teaching that too much religion is a bad thing. Stories about wrath change nothing, but proving my love exists affects everything.

It will take time, and time on Earth moves slowly. You know words and actions concerning love should mesh together. Until this happens, angels will be constantly at work guarding mankind, and willing to assist you and me through every turn.

Eventually, slow moving time and heaven's rapid moving energies will collide and form a balance between heaven and Earth. I want the effect to be the same way it was for you when I screamed 'let there be light!'

So, even if you get trapped and forced away from home again, never forget I know where you are and will come for you. My love never dies."

Zion tearfully bowed her head and confessed, "I try to resist him, Lord. I promise I do! Why can't I remember how it feels to work beside you instead of wandering away and trying to accomplish things and relying on my own strength? When Satan has my chains pulled extremely tight and places that awful helmet on my head I forget everything."

Compassionate towards Zion's emotions, Abba softly said, "Zion, my sweet. Don't you understand that I know it's your emotions that pull your chains tightly? It makes me proud of you, not angry. Any good mother wants to be close to her child when they are hurting, troubled or threatened. Even most married women don't wait for their husbands and the single mothers have no choice.

…Satan's tool to deceive you is the helmet. All over the planet, many people pray and believe in me. But Satan wants to keep your eyes focused in small areas so he can abuse and mislead your thoughts. He does the same thing to Earthly mothers so they become controlled by emotions."

"Why was he able to keep me bound this last time?" Zion asked. "I grew fat, lazy and very depressed."

…Abba answered, "Our old enemy is not stupid. He suspected Jesus was fed-up with his schemes because He wasn't influencing men. He was choosing women to create new mindsets that included Him in their actions, even when they didn't have a mate.

Satan knew his time was short in the town where Mamie, Hope, Caylee, and Gina live. So, he placed the giant guard of idolatry to watch you, since this was the area he wanted to keep you focused.

Jesus ordered the giant to remove your helmet. Then He and Hope quickened your faith with their energetic light and voices so you could move. It took the Word who had been flesh and a woman of flesh operating in the spirit realm to set you free."

"I'm so glad they did," Zion said.

Abba says, "Enough of all this dreadful talk and pleas of forgiveness. I will not allow you to fall into depression when you're with me. It is time we enjoy the coming events. I'm looking forward to intimate and organic conversations with you and all of my people, instead of memorized prayers or desperate cries for help."

After their lengthy discussion, the two lovebirds re-entered the Grand Hall and Abba gathered the heavenly residents around them. Then He shared, "I gave out commission orders again this evening. Under my Son's supervision, underdogs will continue to get a fair break, and corruptive living will slow-down. It will be as if I threw mankind's disbelief in me in a sea of forgetfulness. Love must be proven, just like the day when I divided the waters for Moses and encouraged my children to cross over to a new kingdom. I will never stop showing love until every knee is bowed and every tongue confesses that I exist and care for them. I am a good father and I do not want my children to ever live in fear of anything.

It will be a glorious day when my people finally realize they can speak my blessings over their own lives by releasing their faith in my promises without losing hope. Heaven's time system works very fast but Earth's will eventually catch-up with it if patience is applied, and then there will be peace in heaven and on Earth together, forever." Abba finished.

Prologue

It was a glorious time in heaven, but on Earth, the promises were manifesting slowly. Many people lived in faith by God's spoken Word, but others hadn't developed a spiritual hunger for a relationship with Him. That does not matter.

As written, cycles go around and round, constantly repeating themselves.

God's love never fails and His redemption never ends. There are many stories to follow.

Bibliography

Specific scripture references were not given in this book. The author's interpretations of scripture were taken from the Message Bible's point of view.

About the Author

Raven H. Price, is a Christian fiction writer who uses romance mixed with fantasy and supernatural events to intrigue her readers. She also enjoys devoting her time inspiring and encouraging people to believe in themselves and trusting in a loving God.

She is happily married to her husband, Ralph W. Price, III, and they live in Leesburg, Georgia with a large dog and four cats. Since she is a cat lover, her Twitter handle is 'roaringpurr.' Her Facebook author page @Roaringpurr, is devoted not only to her books but as an outlet to encourage love, respect, and acceptance for all mankind.

Please consider leaving a review on Amazon by clicking on this, thank you.